HOT ICE

HOT
ICE

A Novel

CHERRY ADAIR

BALLANTINE BOOKS
NEW YORK

Copyright © 2005 by Cherry Adair

Published in the United States by Ballantine Books, an imprint of The Random House Publishing Group, a division of Random House, Inc., New York.

Ballantine and colophon are registered trademarks of Random House, Inc.

ISBN 0-345-47642-5

Printed in the United States of America on acid-free paper

www.ballantinebooks.com

2 4 6 8 9 7 5 3 1

First Edition

Book design by Susan Turner

To my dear friend Amber Kizer.
My right hand, and frequently my left brain.
I couldn't do what I do without you.

With much love,
C

Special thanks to

The wonderful folks at the South African Tourism Board (SATOUR) and Big Five Tours, Daniela and Alessia, I couldn't have done Zurich without you. To Gerry, Jane, and Susan, who understand the joys and challenges facing families affected by Down syndrome. Thank you for your commitment to education and willingness to share your experiences. Mary B at Circus to Circus, thank you for sharing your unique talents and expertise. "Mac," thanks for your help. But I repeat, no thank you, I would *not* like to accompany you next time! A *BIG* thank-you to Kelsey Roberts and Bonnie C for saving my sanity. And to all our men and women serving far from home—our hearts salute you. Thank you.

HOT ICE

One

DRESSED IN BLACK, SHROUDED BY THE NIGHT, T-FLAC OPERA-tive Huntington St. John melded with the darkness of the fetid alley behind the adobe jail. Night vision glasses made it possible to observe every inch of the inky interior of the cell through a narrow barred window high in the wall.

Empty.

Where in the *hell* was the prisoner?

It had taken six long, bloody months to discover this woman's identity. Six months, and the considerable resources of the counter-terrorist organization Hunt worked for. It hadn't been easy, by God, and he was not leaving without her.

He needed a thief. Someone resourceful, cunning, and unscrupu-lous. Someone at the top of his game. Hunt wanted the best. Nothing less would do.

Determined to find the right thief, T-FLAC's crack team had scru-tinized past burglary victims for the last five years. Limiting their search to individuals, or companies, with collections of fine gems who had *the* most sophisticated, advanced security systems. They'd compiled lists comprising thousands upon thousands of names. They'd cross-matched friends of the victims, relatives, staff, and lifestyle to find a common denominator.

Three hundred names had cross-matched, and 118 people appeared on more than six lists. A deep background check on those suspects turned up an interesting anomaly. Seventeen of the women had identical, or nearly identical, backgrounds. Or, rather, one woman had seventeen identities.

No one, other than himself and a few select T-FLAC operatives, even knew the thief was a woman. They'd finally connected the dots.

Hunt had his thief.

But where the hell was she?

An hour after ascertaining who she was, and with an educated guess, where she might be, he was wheels up and headed for South America. It was highly suspect that she just *happened* to be in the very city he needed her to be in. San Cristóbal.

In flight he'd knew she'd robbed José Morales followed by a quick arrest minutes before he touched down in San Cristóbal.

So, it was a *fait accompli.*

A quick, thorough search of her hotel room revealed nothing. Not a hint, not a clue. No surprise there. She never left clues. Ever. Which is why it had been so fucking hard to discover who she was in the first place.

This woman wasn't merely *extraordinarily* good at what she did, she was a *phenomenon.* And fearless.

She was the one he wanted. And by God, he'd have her. Even if, as he suspected, she'd been hired by someone else.

Despite intel to the contrary, her absence from the cell could be explained by one of three options: she'd been moved to another location, the other party had already extracted her, or she'd been killed.

Now *that* would be bloody inconvenient all around. He'd already invested enough time and energy. He wasn't about to start looking for someone else now.

Suddenly, footsteps echoed down a hallway. Clear, loud, deliberate.

Two pairs—heavy, booted. And the odd, incongruous sound of chains rattling, like something out of a bad horror film.

One of the guards kicked open the cell door. It slammed against the adobe wall and let in muted light from the hallway to illuminate the cramped cell. "*This* time, *bruja,*" the jailer threatened in Spanish, "you will *not* get free."

Hunt's mouth flattened into a thin line as he took in the tableau in the doorway.

Trussed up in chains, the woman couldn't brace herself as the guards flung her through the open door and onto the floor with a thud. Her head bounced on the cement and she let out a startled grunt of pain.

Hunt bit back a curse. This was precisely why he disliked women involved in missions. They were vulnerable and easily broken. He hated like hell seeing someone soft and delicate hurt.

The chains wrapped around her sounded almost musical as she rolled across the floor, until, stopped by the opposite wall, she lay still.

The two guards observed their prisoner for a few minutes from the doorway, speculating in rapid-fire Spanish as to whether the woman was a witch. Or worse. So, she'd attempted an escape, had she? He shook his head. Nice try, but no cigar, sweetheart. This prison built on the outskirts of town housed political prisoners, as well as the dregs of humanity. No one, including apparently a pro like her, had ever escaped.

Hunt was about to change that.

Listening to the conversation between the guards, Hunt shook his head. She'd given it her best shot *five* times. 5-0 wasn't a great track record, but it sure took guts. No wonder the men were pissed. No wonder they had a mile of bicycle chain wrapped around her body, and God only knew how many gleaming new padlocks fastened down her back. She'd be lucky to draw in an unrestricted breath, let alone stand.

The metal door clanged shut and the key ground harshly in the lock. *Sorry to disappoint, hombres, but she's mine.* He listened to the guards' footsteps retreat down the hallway toward the front of the jail.

The crunch of tires on gravel drifted between the buildings down the narrow alley where he waited. Headlights strobed over the single-story structures as cars and trucks pulled into the unseen parking lot of the seedy nightclub across the alley behind the jail.

Vehicle doors slammed. Glass clinked. Laughing voices rose. A band tuned up their instruments. The door of the dive opened and slammed. Opened and slammed. Opened, letting out the raucous sounds of the crowd warming up for the evening. All music to Hunt's ears.

He knew the bar would soon be packed to the rafters. The band would be loud enough to deafen anyone within a hundred yards, and the secondhand smoke would make a five-pack-a-day smoker look like a piker. This was almost *too* easy.

The night air felt thick and oppressive. Not even a glimmer of a star broke the blackness of the sky overhead. San Cristóbal in mid-summer was not for the fainthearted. He'd been here several years ago on another op. The sprawling city on the edge of the rain forest was too damn crowded for his liking. Known for its topless beaches and raunchy night life, it wasn't one of Hunt's favorite places.

The atmosphere was a South American version of spring break—noise, people, skin, and excessive drinking. The combination usually turned things ugly before midnight. It was a quarter till.

In the distance, a dog's barks turned to mournful howls. A car backfired. Lights continued strafing the roofline as more vehicles turned into the parking lot of the club. A steel guitar riffed in a jangle of bad chords, followed by the thump of sticks on the drum as the band continued its warm-up.

The chains wrapped around the woman chinked. Good. If she could move, she wasn't too badly hurt. As far as Hunt was concerned, as long as she could talk and think long enough to tell him what he wanted to know, that was sufficient.

In theory, he had no problem with her captivity.

She was where thieves belonged.

But not where he needed her to be for the moment.

Oblivious to the muggy heat causing his dark shirt to stick to his back, he gave a quick tug to the clamps he'd hooked to the bars earlier, making sure they were secure. A clever T-FLAC invention, the device, small enough to fit in his pocket, it consisted of a complex series of pulleys and thin metal cable, and needed very little pressure to act as a fulcrum.

The band segued into their first number. What the group lacked in talent they made up for in volume. The ruckus from the club would drown out all but an atomic bomb.

"Thanks," Hunt muttered dryly as he exerted the small hand movement necessary to activate the tool. Inside the cell the chinking of the chains abruptly stopped.

He stepped aside as window frame, bars, and chunks of plaster came out of the old adobe wall with a grinding *thunk*.

TWO

W HAT," THE ICY VOICE IN THERESA SMALLWOOD'S EAR
dripped fury, "do you mean *there was nothing there*? You
arranged for the arrest immediately when she got back to
her hotel, like I told you, didn't you?"

Sweat pooled in the small of Theresa's back as she pressed the receiver against her ear. The sound of the long-distance-distorted voice
crawled over her skin like the tiny feet of a dozen spiders. The
cramped phone booth stunk of pee, sweat, and fear. Theresa was responsible for two out of the three.

She shuddered, knuckles white as she clenched the receiver, and
forced herself to respond. Forced her voice to remain steady. Competent.

"No more than three seconds," she assured her boss. She prayed
she didn't sound as scared as she felt. They both knew how important
this assignment was.

How dare that fucking thief put *her* life in danger? Theresa
thought, still shaken with anger. She'd asked the girl to work for her.

She'd offered to pay her, and pay her well, to retrieve the contents of Morales's safe. Which, for Christ's sake, she was going to do *anyway*. The girl refused Theresa flat out.

"Smallwood?"

Theresa swallowed fear-thick spit. "She'd barely closed the door when the Federales grabbed her." She hadn't had a *chance* to hide anything. And Christ knew, she was too damn *slick* to have gone to all that trouble to hand it over to the police.

Theresa had waited a few minutes to make sure no one saw her, then tossed the hotel room. Politely. Professionally. No-one-would-suspect carefully. Nothing. Not a fucking thing. Nada. Zip.

"Then you have what I want," the voice said smoothly in her ear. Not a question. Never a question.

Theresa's armpits prickled with dread and her mouth went bone dry. She needed a drink, she needed one bad. "I'll meet with our Rio contact as planned. Tomorrow," she said with utmost conviction, the answer implicit.

The air seemed to vibrate menacingly around Theresa as the silence on the other end of the phone lengthened. When she heard a click instead of the ass-reaming she expected, she let the phone drop and slumped back against the bullet-riddled glass of the phone booth as though she were a puppet with her strings cut.

She'd find the bitch if it was the last thing she did.

She exited the phone booth, then strode across the gravel lot of the abandoned gas station to the rental car.

Oh, she'd find the girl all right. She'd find the girl, retrieve what she'd stolen, and *then* slice her skin from her skinny body in one long ribbon like peeling a fucking apple. Theresa hadn't gotten where she was by letting emotions get in the way of business. Business was brutal.

If she had to screw the brains out of every cop in this godforsaken city to find out where the woman was being held, she vowed she'd do it.

Theresa was proud of the small elegant black rose tattooed on the small of her back. One day soon she would have more petals added, and she'd be *the* Black Rose. Until then she'd do her job, and do it well. And when the time came, she'd carve that full-blown rose tattoo off the current Black Rose's skin.

She opened the car door, slid behind the wheel, and buckled up for safety as she pulled out of the dark lot. For more immediate gratification, she thought of the thief's big black eyes, that smooth, dusky skin, and decided she'd leave the girl's face for last.

Three

"HEAR ME NOW, DO YOU, SWEETHEART?" A MAN SAID SOFTLY IN the darkness.

Well, yeah. He'd just knocked down the wall and his shoes crunched in the grit on the floor as he walked toward her. Hard to miss. Taylor stayed where she was, the chains loosely covering her body, wondering if he could see she'd managed to free herself already? Nah. Too dark.

She twisted her body in the direction of his voice. Rancid air wafted through what she presumed was a hole in the wall. Stink had never smelled so good. "The cavalry, I presume?" she whispered.

"Something like that." His deep voice was rich and gravelly, his tone dry, and vaguely British.

She had no clue who he could be. Had the woman who'd approached her this morning sent him? It was the only logical explanation. She didn't know anyone in San Cristóbal. Or rather, she didn't know anyone who should know she was in jail. She didn't need or want a partner, and she'd repeat what she'd told Theresa Smallwood this morning, as soon as he got her the hell out of here.

He crouched down beside her before she realized he was that close. *Wow. Impressive.* He moved like a cat. A big, strong, powerful cat.

"Are you badly hurt?" he asked, hands moving over the chains. "Where's the start of this thing?"

"I'll live. They didn't have me quite as secure as they thought." Taylor shrugged the chains off her shoulders and staggered to her feet. He grabbed her upper arm as she swayed. The pounding in her head made her teeth ache, and she was grateful for the steadiness of the large hand holding her upright.

The cell was as dark as the black hole of Calcutta, but even though she couldn't see him, she could feel the heat of his large body beside her. She had an irrational urge to let her head drop to his chest. Only for a moment. The novelty of someone rescuing her shouldn't be wasted. Instead of succumbing, Taylor locked her knees. Air fanned across her face. He had, she guessed, waved a hand in front of her nose.

"Can you see me?" he whispered.

Lord he smelled good, she thought absently. For an instant her pulse accelerated with a purely female response. Then her survival instincts kicked back in. "Of course not," she whispered back. "It's pitch—" she tilted her head. "Can *you* see *me*?"

"Yeah. Even without the nvg's."

Night vision glass. Excellent. He was a regular Boy Scout. She stuck out her hand. "Let me try the glasses." He dropped the nvg's into her palm.

"It's possible your jailers won't have heard the wall of Jericho tumbling," he whispered sarcastically as Taylor fumbled to bring the glasses to her eyes. He reached out and turned them right side up in her hands without pausing. "It's possible they won't turn around and come right back and check on you again. It's also possible that some-one won't come back into the alley to take a leak. All of that's possi-ble. Like to stick around and tempt fate?"

She blinked a couple of times to clear her vision. Blinked again. No amount of blinking helped. She heard him through the thick buzz in her ears, vaguely computed what he was saying as her mouth went dry. She curled her fingers around the hard plastic of the nvg's, squeezed her eyes shut. Opened them.

And sucked in a horrified breath.

Black. Unrelieved black.

She couldn't *see*.

God help her. She. Could. Not. See.

They'd hit her, several times, and *hard,* the last time she'd managed to get away. Hit her with something heavy. The butt of a gun most likely. She'd lost consciousness for a few seconds and had a blinding headache as a memento. Taylor fingered the knob on the back of her head. Was the damage permanent? God. She couldn't go there. The ramifications terrified her.

"Well?" Despite the cacophony of noise from nearby, Taylor heard his soft words clearly.

She licked dry lips. "H-Houston, I think we have a problem. I can't see—anything."

There was a slight pause before he said quietly, "At all?"

"At all."

"Bloody hell."

She almost jumped out of her skin when she felt his hand on the back of her head.

"Your head bounced when you landed." He gently combed his fingers through her hair until he came to the tender spot she'd found a second ago. She winced when he brushed the area with a surprisingly gentle touch. "There's a nasty bump back here. Bleeding too."

There was no point mentioning that her jailers had rewarded her for each escape attempt by using her as a punching bag before they'd thrown her back in the cell. Growing up on the wrong side of the tracks in Reno, Nevada, she'd had plenty of experience with bullies' fists.

She'd had bruises before. They healed. It was her sight she was worried about.

He dropped his hand. "This complicates things."

Taylor almost snorted. "For me too, pal." It hurt to scowl. "Sorry to inconveni—"

He stuck a solid shoulder to her midriff and hoisted her over his shoulder in a smooth move. Taylor grabbed the back of his shirt for balance.

"Oh, God, please don't hang me upside down. I might puke." Which proved how badly her head hurt. Upside down was one of her specialties.

"Don't," he told her unsympathetically as he strode across the room.

She used both hands to clamp his impressively tight buns, to stabilize herself as he strode across the cell. Seconds later she felt and smelled—other air. It could hardly be termed fresh. It stank of unwashed bodies, fried food, and garbage. In this case, the smell of freedom.

His shoulder must have been made of solid steel. Her bruised stomach and ribs protested vehemently as he jogged. She had the mother of all headaches, her ribs felt like they were gouging her aching lungs, and nausea threatened to erupt into projectile vomiting any second. Taylor didn't utter a single word of complaint as he headed away from the loud music and sound of bottles breaking. Away from that cell.

She assured herself that the blindness was temporary. She just wished she knew how long temporary *was*. She'd also like to know *who* he was, and *why* he'd gone to all the trouble of rescuing her. But she could figure that out later. Right now she was simply grateful for his unexpected appearance.

His footsteps were surprisingly silent as he ran for what felt like an hour. Just when she was positive she was going to lose all of Maria Morales's delicious canapés, he swung her to the ground, then held her upright with a firm hand on the back of her neck. His fingers felt hot and hard on her clammy skin. A reminder of his strength and a heads-up that he could snap her neck like a twig. Out of the fire and into the frying pan?

The small fluttering wings of panic she'd been working hard to suppress for the past couple of hours unfurled a little more to beat an urgent tattoo in her stomach.

He wasn't breathing hard, and she was reluctantly impressed. He was big, strong, and physically fit.

But she was no lightweight. Five-foot-eight in her stocking feet, she might look deceptively fragile, but she was a solid 140 pounds. She worked out to keep her muscles tight and toned. In her business, every advantage counted.

Even though Taylor couldn't see anything, she closed her eyes to better concentrate. Trying to pinpoint where they were. She hadn't a clue. No traffic noise. No people talking. She could still hear the music from the club in the distance, muffled by buildings. There was no air movement, so they could be in another minuscule alley. Not being able to see him, or where they were, made her twitchy. She was used to relying completely on herself, and having to depend on a stranger for her safety and well-being made her extremely nervous. She tamped down the anxiety. It was counterproductive.

For the moment, he apparently gave a damn about her welfare. If and when that changed, she'd make sure she was ready.

A car door snicked open.

"In." He placed his palm on top of her head and shoved her inside. She'd barely dragged both feet into the car when the door was slammed shut. "Huntington St. John," he said as he climbed in behind the wheel and started the car.

"Annie Sullivan," Taylor said smoothly. "Thanks for the rescue."

He snorted. "Annie Sullivan? You're quick, aren't you?"

"Not quick enough to get away from the San Cristóbal police, apparently. Is it too soon to ask why you demolished a jail to get me out? Not that I'm complaining, mind you. Simply curious."

"You have something I want."

The tires crunched over gravel, and she had to lean into a sharp turn as he pulled the vehicle onto a paved road. "Really? And what would that be?"

"The contents of the safe you robbed earlier this evening."

Ah. So the woman *hadn't* taken no for an answer after all. "What safe?" she asked mildly, fumbling for a seat belt as the car sped through the single-lane streets of the city. There was no seat belt. Taylor waited to be catapulted through the windshield at any moment. The upside was, she wouldn't actually *see* Death coming for her. God had some sense of humor.

"Morales."

An unfamiliar ache squeezed her chest, and there didn't seem to be enough air in the car, which made her breathing erratic. She rubbed her fingers on the dull pain at her temple and tried to even out her breathing. "Never heard of him."

"See where we are?" he asked conversationally. It was a taunt if ever she'd heard one.

"No," Taylor told him coolly. "I don't."

"What did you do with the contents of the safe?" he repeated. No inflection, but she suspected he was annoyed. Too bad.

She could play the poor blind girl card—God only knew it was true. That might buy her time. Or flat out lie and keep insisting she had no idea what he was talking about. Or she could do what she did best. Shade the truth enough to weasel out of this as fast as possible.

"Okay," she said slowly, as if he'd dragged the truth out of her. "So I pulled off the Morales job. Unfortunately, the cops confiscated my take when they arrested me."

"Bullshit. They arrested you at your hotel."

"As I said—"

"There was nothing on you. Nothing in your room."

Of course not. Did this guy think she'd fallen off the turnip truck? She'd mailed the stuff on her way back to the hotel. "That's because the *police* have it." Taylor leaned her head against the headrest and closed her useless eyes. "Whether you believe me or not, those are the facts. Sue me. And since I don't have what you want, go ahead and drop me off at my hotel. I'll thank you nicely for the heroic rescue and say bye-bye."

"Don't get too ahead of yourself, sweetheart, you're not in any position to piss me off. I could always drop you off right here on a street corner," he told her with far too much relish for comfort. "Watch you stumble around for my own amusement."

If he wanted something badly enough to break her out of jail he wouldn't toss her out of the car onto the dangerous San Cristóbal streets, by herself, at night. Not until he had what he wanted. And that assumption wasn't based on the sexy, rough timbre of his voice or the heady fragrance of his soap. Both of which filled the car and her senses. "A hero and a charmer. My lucky day." She faked a yawn. "I'll consider myself kidnapped. Wake me when we get to wherever we're going, will you?"

"Don't you want to know our destination?"

She rolled her head in his direction without opening her eyes. "Would it make any difference if I said I didn't want to go there?"

"No."

Exactly. "Then let's keep it a surprise, shall we?"

Liberating her only to turn around and abandon her wouldn't have any payoff for him. And he'd want a payoff. He'd gone to considerable trouble to rescue her. So he wanted something that had been in the safe at the Morales estate, did he? What?

The Barter sapphires? No. She didn't think this guy would go to all this trouble for a necklace or two. Not the jewelry, despite its value. She'd netted at least five mil in jewels alone. A nice evening's work.

What *hadn't* been inside that safe were the Blue Star diamonds she'd hoped to find along with the sapphires. Like a dog chasing a car, she'd pursued the Blue Stars all over Europe and half the free world for the last five years. Once again Morales had moved them.

She'd been in an unaccustomed hurry with this job from the start. Usually, her heists were planned to a hair, and she didn't *have* to hurry. But she'd had a dammed persistent itch on the back of her neck all day. Taylor never ignored a sign. She'd speed-robbed the Moraleses. Instead of picking and choosing, she'd swept the contents into the thin black silk bag tied like a Colt .45 to her thigh, then split through the third-story window and down the side of the house via a conveniently placed trellis.

No sweat.

The self-addressed mailer, tucked down the leg of her jeans, had been stuffed and sealed as she darted between hedges and shrubs. She'd scaled the estate's wall, and avoided the Dobbies sleeping where she'd left them, courtesy of the doped treats she'd tossed them when she'd arrived.

No one had seen her. No one.

The mailbox had been on the way back to the hotel. The entire heist had taken barely an hour. Start to finish. Yet the local police knocked before she'd closed the door to her hotel room.

Taylor opened her eyes a slit to see if her vision had returned. It hadn't. Damn. She hurt all over. The least of her problems at the moment. Her heart, already beating a little too fast, sped up even more. She pushed the alarm back. *Don't panic,* she warned herself. *Do not panic.* She'd been in trouble before, and she'd always found a way out of it. Except she'd never been blind in a foreign country before. A hard knot of fear lodged in her throat.

She curled her fingers into her palms until the pain from her short nails digging into her skin centered her. *Concentrate.* Panic was wasted energy. Not having her vision put a large crimp in her plans, but nothing was impossible. She calculated the time close to midnight. Her flight left at ten A.M. All she had to do was make it through what was left of the night, grab a cab in the morning, and get on that plane.

Who'd tipped off the police? The woman who'd tried to hire her yesterday? Or—what was this guy's name? Oh, yeah. "Where'd you get a name like Huntington?"

"Call me Hunt."

"For short?" Taylor asked, almost amused. "But not for long?"

"You *are* quick."

The fact that after all these years of being invisible, two people had not only discovered *who* she was, but *where* she was, freaked her out. Where had she zigged instead of zagged? Taylor rubbed the warning prickle at the back of her neck. "Not quick enough apparently. How did you find me?"

"In that cell? Followed the police trail. In general? Thousands of man-hours."

Taylor's heart slammed into her ribs, knocking a loud and instant warning. She had to moisten her lips before she could speak. "*Thousands* of man-hours?"

"Yes."

How fast were they going? Lord, she couldn't believe she was ac-

tually contemplating jumping out of a fast-moving vehicle, God only knew where, when she couldn't see. "Care to explain?"

"No."

She'd never experienced claustrophobia before, but she did now. This entire situation, coupled with being unable to see, made her feel as though she were in a very small box without any air. Her stomach lurched with anticipation—*never call it fear*—as the vehicle slowed. She fumbled for the door handle. There wasn't one.

"Don't bother." The car stopped. "We're here."

Four

"LET'S GO," HUNT INSTRUCTED WHEN SHE SAT THERE UNMOVING, head tilted. Her eyes didn't track when he passed a hand in front of her nose. Hell. She still couldn't see. "Here, take my hand. Watch the curb."

Her fingers were slender and filthy dirty as she gripped his hand and let him pull her from the car. As she gracefully unfurled from the seat and stood beside him, Hunt realized she wasn't as petite as he'd first thought. Her head reached his shoulder, so she was at least five-eight.

He took a good look at her. She was dressed as he was, all in black. Jeans, loosely fitting long-sleeve black T-shirt, black running shoes. Body tall and slender. Skin: Mediterranean dark. Hair: shoulder length and a matted, dusty black.

Heavily lashed dark chocolate eyes focused a few inches to the left of his face. A fast-beating pulse leapt at the base of her throat, and a sheen of perspiration filmed her skin, but she sounded merely curious instead of frightened when she asked calmly, "Where are we?"

"Somewhere the authorities won't find you. For the moment. Come on."

There were no streetlights to speak of. The shops up and down the street were either abandoned or their owners just didn't give a damn. The T-FLAC safe house, Villa D'Este, looked like the dozens of other derelict hotels and businesses lining the city.

During the day and late into the night, *gamines* of all ages and sizes ran wild here, dodging vehicles and fists alike in search of a pocket to pick. The street kids were all bedded down somewhere for the night, so it was quiet at this hour. Come morning it would be a different story. The common denominators for the neighborhood were poverty and filth.

"Where the cops won't find me. Not a lot of information to go on," she told him dryly.

Was she really not able to see, or was she bullshitting? If it was bs, she was a damn good actress. "Fifteen steps to the front door, then one stair up."

As she walked beside him she blinked repeatedly as if trying to clear her vision. Hunt dragged his gaze away from the rapid pulse throbbing at the base of her sweat-dampened throat. Despite her bravado, she was scared. She had reason to be.

Her iron control over her emotions reluctantly impressed him, and he felt a mild twinge of sympathy. He dismissed the thought the moment it surfaced. She was nothing more than a means to an end, and, as good as she was, had already caused him months of delay. This was more than a recovery operation. She was a small—albeit vital—cog in the far more important wheel of the mission to come.

He hoped to hell this inconvenience wasn't an indication of things to come.

The open door of the hotel cut the darkness, spilling golden light onto the filthy street. Hunt kept her hand in his and angled his body to guide and stabilize her. Her fingers were clammy, her back rigid, as she walked beside him with a natural grace only slightly marred by her lack of sight. A fine shiver traveled down her body as she stumbled over a rough patch, and she clenched his hand in a death grip to keep her balance.

"Easy," he steadied her. "Step." Her hesitation as she took the step was infinitesimal. "This really discombobulates you, doesn't it?"

She stepped up carefully, allowing him to draw her into the dimly lit, grungy vestibule of the hotel before she turned her head to answer. "What? Being blind as a bat, led into a strange place, by a strange man, in a foreign city?" she said dryly. "Discombobulate isn't quite the word I'd use. But the situation certainly makes me uncomfortable, and cautious."

"Helpless."

She hesitated for a moment, as if considering the possibility. "Temporarily. *Very* temporarily." She stopped walking and pulled him to a stop.

Hunt looked down. She wasn't unattractive. He suspected that once cleaned up, her looks would improve.

"Just because I can't see you," she told him tightly, "doesn't mean I can't protect myself. You got me out of a bad situation, and I appreciate it. But if you've brought me here to something worse—think again."

He was close enough to see she wore contact lenses, and he wondered almost absently if she wore them to see better or to change the color of her eyes. "You're in no danger from me as long as you give me what I want."

"And you're in no danger from me," she shot back. "If what *you* want is what *I* want."

"I can be quite persuasive," Hunt told her, steering her across the lobby once more.

She turned her face up and gave him a sweet smile. "And *I* can be quite stubborn—What? A step?"

"No. Keep going." Her unexpected smile threw him for a loop and shot an unexpected jolt of desire straight to his groin. He reminded himself that he was past the age to be aroused by something as false as a woman's smile. His body vehemently disagreed.

Standing behind the reception desk, watching their slow approach, Gil hand-signed a question. Hunt pointed to his eyes. Gil nodded. The man had run the safe house autonomously for the past ten years or so, and he knew everything that went on in and around San Cristóbal.

In his weekly report to HQ, Gil had alerted T-FLAC to the arrival of the Morales family at their summer home. He'd also acquired a copy of the Moraleses' party guest list. He'd been the one who reported the theft.

Hunt didn't give a damn about the stolen diamonds. She could keep those. It was what was in the safe *with* the rocks that T-FLAC wanted. Their informant inside of Morales's organization had been vague on the details. The person had clearly been scared witless. All she knew was that the disk held data, possibly codes to access intel on yet another of *Mano del Dios*'s world domination threats. The information, however flimsy, from this particular source was enough to activate every available T-FLAC operative to discover what that disk held.

If things had gone according to plan, this woman would have stolen the disk for T-FLAC, and handed it over hours ago. What a bloody waste of time *this* was. By now the intel should be in the hands of people trained to put an end to Morales and his *Mano del Dios,* Hand of God, terrorist group. Instead, here he was, extracting and babysitting a blind woman.

"Do you require a doctor for the señorita?" Gil asked, handing over a key from the rack behind him.

Her head jerked toward the sound of Gil's voice and her fingers gripped his as she tried to orient herself. She'd thought they were alone.

"Need a doctor?" Hunt asked, taking the key with a frown. She'd become paler, her hand clammier.

She licked her lower lip. "Not here. If I need one, I'll wait till I get home."

He signed to Gil that he wanted the doctor there first thing in the morning. Gil nodded. "Sure?" he asked the woman.

"Yeah." She put a hand to her forehead. "I would like to lie down, though."

"One flight of stairs between you and a bed. This way." Gil had them on the first floor. "Twenty-two stairs and we're there." Hunt paused as she took a shuddering breath. "Want me to carry you again?"

A muscle jumped in her cheek as she gritted her teeth. "Pass."

Hunt set her hand on the metal rail on the left and walked on her other side still holding her hand. She was fading fast. Their footsteps echoed loudly on the wood floors as they emerged onto a landing. Peeling brown paint and the smell of cheap cigarettes were the high points in the decor. This was a safe house, not a luxe hotel. No one would confuse the two.

He unlocked a door halfway down the corridor and nudged her into the dark room. "It's clean." Hunt found the light switch. "Gil can send someone over to the cantina if you're hungry."

"I'm not. Describe the room for me, please."

"Fifteen by twenty. Bed straight ahead about six of your paces, bathroom to the left about ten. Two chairs at three o'clock."

He scanned her face, seeing that she was orienting herself. "Let's get you washed up so I can check the damage. I'm not so sure waiting until later for a doctor to examine you is such a smart idea. They worked you over pretty good."

"Believe me, I know," she said ironically. "I was there. Point me to the bathroom. I need a shower more than anything right now."

Christ, she was cool. If he wasn't looking right at her, he would never have known how nervous she was from her tone of voice. Hunt led her across the room and shoved open the door to the small bathroom. "Need help?"

She shot him a sightless glance that needed no interpretation. "Just show me the taps and a towel."

Hunt leaned over and turned on the water, then pulled the plunger to activate the showerhead. Water beat down in the clean but stained porcelain tub. "The room is only six feet wide. Get out of the tub, and the towel rack is right in front of you at twelve o'clock. Yell if you need me."

She swayed on her feet. "I won't."

The sweet smell of steam started filling the small room. "Right."

"I don't suppose there's a lock on this side of the door?"

" 'Fraid not."

She didn't move. "Close it on your way out."

The bathroom was intentionally windowless. She wasn't going anywhere. There was a nifty, completely hidden escape door in the wall behind the towel rack. But she didn't need that information.

"I'll be right outside." He'd be right here watching. As if he'd leave her alone even for a quick shower. He waited a beat, walked across the tiled floor, sidestepped into the shallow alcove in the wall beside the towel rack, then nudged the door with his foot, sealing them both inside. He needed to know how good an actress she was.

The second the door snicked shut, her shoulders slumped. "Shit. Shit. Shit," she whispered under her breath. "This is bad. Really, *really* bad."

She stumbled around the small room, brailling her way from tub to toilet to towel rack.

Hunt stayed absolutely still, barely breathing, allowing her to pass him by millimeters. He wasn't a voyeur. He simply had to be certain that she wouldn't die on his watch. At least not now, not while he needed information.

The contents of the safe were too important—hell, *critical.* She was the key. He wasn't letting her out of his sight for a millisecond until he had that disk in his hand *and* checked the data to verify it was what they expected.

Considering his body's unwelcome response to hers, he'd prefer waiting for her in the other room. He folded his arms and leaned against the wall as she started undressing. Her breasts were small and firm beneath a black sports bra, her skin blotchy with dirt and bruises. He scanned her slender body, noting the slew of old, faded scars; side, both knees, left shoulder. He was particularly interested in her more recent injuries. Nothing appeared broken and she wasn't bleeding.

She wasn't faking the blindness, however.

She toed off what looked more like black ballet slippers than sneakers, then dragged down the skintight black jeans apparently *not* painted on her long, slender legs, taking her panties with them.

Hunt's mouth went dry at the sight of those long, long, *long* legs, narrow waist, and tight ass. She winced as she shuffled her way to the tub, removing the confining bra on the way.

She turned, presenting him with the long elegant line of her back. He observed the brown streaks on her skin. Not only dirt and bruises, but the dusky Mediterranean complexion, which extended no farther down than her neck.

From her breasts down, Miss "Annie Sullivan," aka Serena Carstair, aka sixteen plus other, equally false names, was as white as the driven snow.

She banged a knee on the edge of the tub and swore soundlessly, then bit her lip as she spent several seconds trying to regain her bearings before stepping into the enclosure. Sliding her feet cautiously on the slick floor of the tub, she splayed her hand on the wall and backed under the spray, then, eyes closed, tipped her head back. The water immediately turned black as dye sluiced out of her hair.

Interesting.

What *else* was his brave little cat burglar hiding?

Five

THE ONLY SOUNDS TAYLOR HEARD WERE THE WATER POUNDING on the porcelain tub and her own heartbeat thundering in her ears. She didn't have time to freak out. Although her rapid breathing and even faster pulse warned that it might be imminent. She guessed she only had a few minutes of privacy to pull herself together and think this through before he started pounding on the door asking questions.

She pushed back the rush of panic that had been building since he'd liberated her, and felt along the wall for a soap dish. The "thousands of man-hours" worried her. It could be an exaggeration of course. But he didn't sound like an exaggerating kind of guy.

Her chest hurt. She drew in a ragged, shuddering breath, which didn't help. Where the hell was the soap? Her feet slid out from under her, and her heart leapt into her throat as she made a panicked grab for the slick wall. She caught herself, but her heart continued to race as frustration built.

The vise around her chest tightened painfully as hot water sluiced her head and face. Soap. Where was the damn soap? How hard could it be? The tub wasn't that damn big.

She took pride in knowing she was capable of extricating herself from tricky situations unscathed. She'd never met a lock she couldn't pick or a tight spot she couldn't wiggle out of. Be that actual or verbal. But she'd hit her first wall. And it scared the bejesus out of her how helpless she was right now.

Think it through. Concentrate, and think it through.

Over the years, she'd been in dozens of situations where she walked a fine line between success and capture. And she'd been *exhilarated, never* frightened.

This was different.

This was the first time she'd been caught. Imprisoned.

The fear had started as a dark flutter in her tummy when they'd tossed her into the jail cell. The flutter had beat a little harder each time she escaped and they'd caught her, bringing her back to that small room.

She liked to believe that she would have made it, even without help, on the sixth shot. Because Lord only knew, she wouldn't have stopped *trying*. The second they'd tossed her onto the floor and slammed the door shut that last time, she'd automatically started undoing the chains and locks the jailers had wrapped around her. And as she worked, she'd already started formulating a plan of action for her sixth and *successful* escape.

Now, the flutter became the frantic flapping of giant wings, and the fear built, twisting and turning in her stomach. She *had* to get the hell out of there. She wasn't back home in America where civil liberties and the threat of litigation would have guaranteed her physical safety while in custody. Nope, there was no review board. No human rights advocates.

Arrested meant you were at the mercy and whim of what passed for authority. There was no one in this country to say her jailers couldn't beat the crap out of her, chain her, then forget about her. And there was no extradition from San Cristóbal. She could've stayed in the cell for the rest of her natural life.

But what she'd felt in that jail was *nothing* compared to the moment she'd realized she couldn't see. Blind, there was no way to defend herself. No way to carry out even the simplest of escape plans, no possible way to survive—

Stop. She had to pull herself together. *Now.* The awful reality was that she might *never* see again. And if that were the case, she'd learn to live with it. Millions of other people did.

Oh God. She hated how fast her heart pounded, and the harsh sound of her own erratic breath. The vise around her chest tightened alarmingly. Was she about to have a heart attack?

"I'm okay, I'm okay, I'm okay," she assured herself out loud. Her voice sounded weak and scared to her own ears, which freaked her out even more.

Get a grip, she told herself with rising alarm as each breath became harder to drag into her lungs. *It isn't a heart attack. I'm as healthy as a horse. Find the damn soap, wash, dry, get out of the bathroom.* She'd be humiliated if what's-his-name had to come in here and drag her naked corpse out of the bathtub.

Shaky and getting dizzier by the second, she finally found the freaking soap and started to wash, but it was impossible to drag air into her lungs and she had to stop and hold on to the wall as her head spun. Scaring herself, she pressed a hand to her heaving chest.

Out of the blackness, hard hands gripped her arms above the elbow and gave her a little shake. "Take a breath for God's sake! You're having a panic attack."

It took her a second to replace a harsh breath with a strangled scream of surprise. She slipped and slid on the slick wet porcelain and grabbed at the only stable thing around—*him*—to keep from falling on her butt. "N-*Never* p-p-panic. Heart attack." Her fingers gripped his shirtfront like a lifeline.

"Ever had a heart attack before?"

"N-No."

"Then you're not having one now." He pressed a large hand to her midriff. "Take a breath."

"C-Can't."

"Inhale. *Now.*"

She sucked in a shaky breath.

"Hold it. Two. Three. Slowly breathe out with my count. One . . . two . . . Slowly . . . *slowly,* damn it. Again. Inhale. One. Two. Three. Exhale." He kept that up for several long, agonizing, embarrassing minutes until her breathing was more or less normal.

"Better?"

The water pounding her back was getting cool, but her skin was flushed all over. She felt a lot of conflicting emotions, but right now embarrassment was primary. How long had he been watching her? "S-Son of a bitch. What are y-you *doing* in h-here?"

"Preventing you from passing out and killing yourself, apparently."

Taylor drew in a shaky breath. His splayed hand on her tummy moved with the expansion of her ribs. The feel of his bare hand on her wet skin made her hot all over. Her breath caught with a purely female response to his touch coupled with the husky timbre of his voice. It was like being stroked by a cat's tongue. Sheet lightning shot from her nipples to her groin. She swayed. His hands shifted to grip her hips to hold her steady.

"I appreciate your c-concern," she said, trying to sound nonchalant in her naked state. "You can go now. I'm fine."

"Thought you were having a heart attack?"

No. She'd had an attack of the stupids. "Fortunately not."

"Sure?"

"Go."

"I'm staying. Inhale. Two. Three. Exhale. Three. Four. Don't want to be responsible for you dying on my watch. Here. Hand me that soap."

The large masculine hand splayed across her middle didn't feel the least little bit calming, the opposite in fact. Her body hummed with the contact of his warm fingers on her wet skin. It had been so long since she'd felt a man's touch, she'd forgotten how seductive human contact could be.

Everything inside her responded with a sharp, pleasurable buzz of desire that surprised her with its intensity. Lord, she couldn't be turned on. Not now. Not here. It was as unexpected as it was inappropriate. And wrong in more ways than she could count. She must've lost her mind as well as her sight. Unfortunately, trapped as she was in the darkness, her other senses seemed more acute.

He shifted against her, water splashed. Then he put an arm around her waist, plucked the soap out of her hand and started spreading soapy lather up her arm. A shiver traveled the length of her body as his slick fingers curled around the back of her neck.

Her breathing was still on the ragged side. "G-Get out."

"Here." He ignored her. "Hold on." He took her hand and maneuvered her fingers to his belt buckle. Oh, yeah. *That* made her feel steady and strengthened her resolve. Not. The back of her fingers were pressed against the hard muscles of his lower abs.

"Are you o-out of your *mind*?" Taylor shifted her hand to tightly grip the front of his already wet shirt. "You can't stay in here with—"

His warm breath fanned her forehead. "You have cuts and abrasions that need to be cleaned before they fester," he said roughly. "This is the most expedient way to get the job done." He paused as he slipped his large hand under her hair. "Don't worry. You won't fall. You're safe with me."

She wasn't worried about falling. In fact a good crack to the head might be exactly what she needed to regain some of her customary good sense. And safe wasn't the word she'd use right now. Her body burned.

He switched hands, then ran his palm up her left arm. Slowly. "It's a crime to stain such beautiful skin. Creamy, soft . . ." he murmured absently, leaving behind a trail of fizzy, popping soap bubbles and an ultra-awareness as he stroked. "What brought you to San Cristóbal, Annie?"

Lord, the man was methodical and diabolical. There wasn't an inch of arm unwashed as he slowly climbed from her wrist to her shoulder, spreading lather and little electrical shocks along the way.

"A tranquil, tropical setting?" she replied with a lightness she didn't feel. Her blood surged hot and fast through her veins in an increasingly rapid beat that was becoming impossible to ignore. This was crazy. Insane. She struggled to remind herself that her emotions had been on high alert all day. She shouldn't trust her body's sudden and absolutely irrational response to this total stranger.

His open hand glided from the ball of her shoulder to stroke across the base of her throat. Taylor's breath caught and held while her heart galloped. He kept his fingertips pressed lightly to the pulse there, feeling every erratic beat. "You know what I meant. What, specifically, were you looking for in Morales's safe?"

She struggled to clear the sensual fog from her brain long enough to answer as his open hand slicked down to spread across her breastbone. Her skin seemed to sizzle from the contact.

Lower. "Since you found me in a jail and managed to break me out of said jail, I'll assume we both know what the target was, right?" His fingers skimmed the top swell of her right breast. *Yes.* The breath she was already holding strangled in her throat.

"Twenty questions?" he asked.

"You first."

His breath fanned the side of her face. "Ladies first," Hunt whispered. "What do you think I want?"

"I know what I want." Taylor's breath hitched. She was one stroke away from forgetting her name and her occupation.

"How'd you know about them?"

"Didn't your thousands of man-hours manage to tell you what I am?"

"A woman. Yeah, I got that part."

"A thief. A jewel thief."

"That's not the only thing you steal, is it?" Why did he sound like he knew more than she did?

"Uh, no I guess not." Taylor played along. Knowledge was power, and knowing what he wanted would make keeping it away from him all the easier. Damn, she couldn't concentrate when he flicked his finger like that.

"The codes." Hunt murmured very close to her ear. "And *you* knew about them—how?" His thumb came close to her nipple, and piercing sweet need urged her body closer to his. Her hands tightened on his belt and she felt the brush of his erection on the tips of her fingers. She almost melted into a little puddle right then.

Mmmm. Over. Around. Brush. Stroke. Lost in sensation, she forgot to breathe. She leaned into him, lifting her face, wanting him to kiss her. What had he . . . "Wh-What?"

"How did you know about the codes?"

Taylor struggled to focus on what he said. "Codes? What codes?" She lifted her face, wanting him to kiss her. Dying for him to kiss her. The drift and glide of his fingertips across the swell of her breasts was driving her crazy.

"In Morales's safe. Those codes."

All her senses told her she was in danger and she'd better start *thinking* instead of reacting. But she couldn't think. "I don't know . . ." Her nipples were so hard and erect they hurt. She needed his mouth there, or at least his fingers. She swayed toward him. "I don't know anything about any codes. I was after the Blue Star diamonds. Are you ever going to—"

"You went after a necklace?" he interrupted.

She blinked, wishing she could see his face, read his expression, because she suddenly realized that there was nothing loverlike in his tone. "Of course." A chill crept across the heat of her skin, and she came up from the sensual fog of arousal like a deep sea diver surfacing. Her elemental defense system kicked in big-time. That he was equally attracted to her, there was no doubt. But unlike herself, he hadn't let that response cloud his mind in any way. He was all business.

Awareness morphed into righteous anger. Suddenly, she felt exposed and extremely vulnerable, standing in front of him stark naked like this. She dredged up the strength to release her death grip on his shirt, and resisted the strong urge to cover herself with her hands. Tilting her chin, Taylor stared in his general direction and pretended she was wearing her favorite red Valentino suit.

She drew a breath, exasperated. "I'm not playing this game," she told him flatly as she felt for the wall behind her and spread her hand on the cool surface for balance. She held out her other palm. "Hand over the soap and get out."

"Despite your platinum invitation, I'm not going to have sex with you," he told her flatly. "Nor do I have the time or inclination to wait while you fumble around trying to get clean on your own. It's more expedient for me to do i—"

"I beg your pardon?" Taylor's jaw locked. "What *platinum* invitation?"

"Your skin's flushed, your pretty nipples are hard, and I can smell your arousal."

Taylor's temper throbbed behind her eyeballs. The arrogant, egotistical—ass. She could feel his erection pressed against her stomach. She wasn't alone in this hormone haze. "Do you have a death wish?" she asked indignantly, fully prepared to give his demise her best shot.

"Lady, if you were capable of killing me, I'd rejoice. Right now you aren't even capable of bathing yourself." He pulled her toward him with a jerk, ignoring her shout of rage and the hand she was using to try and bat him away. "Close your eyes, I'm going to shampoo—Bloody hell!"

Her heart skittered. Oh, God. "Now what?"

"Your eyes are the most—I've never seen eyes quite that shade of blue."

Damn it. What else could happen? She'd obviously lost the brown contacts somewhere along the way. Her eyes were her most distinct feature. Pale blue and creepy-looking. And something she hid behind assorted colored lenses. *Always.* "Contacts."

"No, as stunning as your eyes are—no. Contacts couldn't produce that incredible shade of pure, brilliant blue. They're the real deal. My God, the color is incred— No, don't close them."

He lifted her chin with the tip of his finger. She could practically feel his gaze travel across her features. Since his touch, even one this light, sent shock waves directly to her very core, she gave him a glare from sightless eyes, then let a shudder of a sob slip through. It wasn't totally fake. Her emotions were on full overload. It had been a long, trying day, followed by a long, trying night. She was spent. Done. Exhausted. And at the frayed end of her emotional resources. She didn't have the energy right now for this verbal volley.

Apparently he felt the same way. "I'm letting go. Can you stand by yourself?"

Taylor nodded, then felt ridiculously bereft when he released her.

"Five more minutes. If you aren't out of here by then, I'm coming in to finish the job. Clear?"

"Crystal."

"I'll leave the door ajar. Call if you need me."

"I won't."

Six

TAYLOR WAITED UNTIL HIS FOOTSTEPS FADED BEFORE RUNNING a hand down her wet skin, checking as much to make sure the soap was rinsed off as to reconnect with her traitorous body. She'd never reacted that way to anyone. She'd been ready to throw herself at him.

Disgusted with herself, Taylor knocked her shin against the spigot. "Ow!" One more bruise. She fumbled around and finally managed to turn off the water, then stumbled out of the tub.

"You okay in there?" he called.

"Peachy, thanks for asking." Taylor grit her teeth. Hunt. What an appropriate name for him. The man had stalked her and played her like a lion in the savanna.

She grabbed the towel and buffed her skin with the cheap thread-bare cotton. Codes? What was he talking about?

She'd retrieved a *necklace.*

And why did she get the feeling he didn't work for Theresa Smallwood? That meant two people, or two organizations, wanted something Morales had.

If only she'd had time to really look at the items she'd shoved into the silk bag. Damn. She was playing blind. Literally and figuratively.

"Finished?" He stood in the doorway; she could smell him, and feel the heat radiating off him in waves.

"Yeah." Taylor felt him move behind her and propel her into the main room. "Could I have some clothes?" She'd felt around the bathroom and not come across the pile she'd dropped.

"Sure." He didn't move.

"Now?"

"No."

Fine, she could be naked. She loved naked. He wasn't using this situation against her. Taylor crossed her arms and hoped for a nonchalant pose.

"Give it up, Lady," Hunt growled.

"What?" Taylor kept her tone even. Even a few feet of space helped her equilibrium settle.

"You know what." She heard him sit down.

Back to the codes. What damn codes? Taylor cocked a hip. "Why should I give *you* anything?" she demanded.

"Because," he said softly, "you owe me."

She blinked. "Right. I owe you for the shower and trying to seduce me into submission." She snorted. "I'll write you a check."

"You owe me and you damn well know it."

"For *what*?" Taylor liked everything completely spelled out.

"For breaking you out of that San Cristóbal hellhole, for one thing . . ."

Hmm. Okay, he had something there. "Hey, I *said* thank you. I *did* appreciate it. But be honest. You didn't do it for altruistic reasons. You wanted those—codes, which you knew I had, and you thought the only way you'd get your hands on them was to spring me. So really you were doing yourself a fav—"

He kept going like she'd never interrupted him. ". . . for hauling your ass to a safe place—"

"A true gentleman. I especially liked the 'being treated like a sack of potatoes' thing."

"For not calling the authorities and having you arrested—again."

Shallow reason at best.

"A veritable prince," she said tartly. "Of course, if you *had* called them, you would have had to explain *your* part in breaking me out." She heard him move, the rustle of his clothes, the moment before his hands shackled her wrists.

What was he going to do? Rape her? Not likely this late in the game. Taylor opened her mouth to argue—

His fingers tightened a little more around her wrists. *Ow!* "Then who *are* you?" Taylor asked flatly. "Her muscle?"

His tone sounded at once intrigued and uncertain. "Her who?"

"You know her who," she snapped, then frowned because, really, they sounded ridiculous. "I appreciated her offer, and you be sure to tell her that. But like I told her, I work alone. Always have. Hey, even in grade school I got detention for not working and playing well with others."

She felt the subtle tension in his muscles. All the way down her body. It felt good, but she was sure it didn't bode well. Clearly, this information was news to him. And not good news.

The calluses on his hands did amazing things to the inside of her wrists. She wished she could see him.

"Imagine my surprise," he murmured, shifting his weight. "Who was this woman, and what—specifically—did she want you to do?" He had a way of speaking ordinary words that made them sound ominous and threatening. He pushed her down onto the bed and draped himself across her. He seemed deceptively relaxed.

Space. She needed space. "We didn't become best friends." Taylor's brain spun as she tried to figure out exactly where this man fit into the picture. If he *wasn't* in with the woman who'd tried to hire her to do the Morales job, then who *was* he? When the hell had she become so popular? Geez, couldn't a jewel thief get *any* privacy anymore?

"I'm assuming other people wanted a piece of my action. And you know what?" She arched her hips in an attempt to shove him off her body. She couldn't even raise her hips a millimeter off the mattress.

She drew in another calming breath. They couldn't stay glued together forever. Sometime in the next—however long—this man was
going to *have* to move. Dear God make that sooner rather than later.
Already she could feel the heat pooling in her groin. It was only a
matter of time before he accused her of overtures. She didn't want
him. Dammit.

"Stop trying to get a rise out of me," he snapped. "And finish the
bloody thought!"

She relaxed, as best she could, meeting his gaze head-on, at least
where she hoped his gaze was. Ho, boy. Never let them see you sweat.
Or pant. She'd be damned if she'd be the only one turned on around
here. If he could stand it, then so could she.

Glaring up in his direction, she said flatly, "I don't know what she
wanted, and I didn't give her a chance to ask. I told *her* no, and news
flash, bubba—I'm telling *you* no too. If you're not working with
what's-her-name, then tell whoever you *do* work for that I work a *single* act. I don't do partners, and I don't pay off muscle."

As she said that, his arm flexed. Too bad. "So if that's it, let's let bygones be bygones, and you can trot off to wherever you came from,
and tell your friend, boss, mistress, gun moll, whoever—that I'm *still*
not interested in taking on a partner. And by the way, I don't like
being fol—"

Hunt covered her mouth with his hand. He needed to think. Did
the woman ever shut up?

He wanted Morales. He was *this* close to having him. And by God,
nothing, *nothing,* would stand in his way. Especially not this woman.

Morales's *Mano del Dios* had been around for more than twenty
years. They targeted their interpretation of sin, whether that was people or places. The *Mano del Dios* ranked number two on America's
Most Wanted List. *Mano* had a religious agenda. Something T-FLAC
followed closely 24/7. Morales's group adhered to an extremist interpretation of Christianity that justified violence against civilian targets
to achieve political ends.

Morales planned to take over the United States and then the
world. His combination of religious righteousness and his ambition
were a toxic and dangerous mix. Over time, the *Mano del Dios* had

emphasized the imminence of the end of the world and stated that they would initiate Armageddon by starting World War III unless transgressions were stopped and people started leading righteous lives. The man was a religious zealot with an agenda. A bad combination.

Under Morales's leadership, the terrorist group had assassinated religious leaders worldwide, bombed nightclubs, theaters, movie houses, liquor stores, pharmacies, and abortion clinics. The group had raised its operational profile in 2000 with two attacks against international targets. It had been involved in clashes in Northern Ireland in December 2004, and carried out a rocket-propelled grenade attack on the Russian Embassy in Beirut in January 2005.

She was trying to gnaw his hand.

She didn't have the market on frustration. Jesus. The woman had a potent effect on his dormant libido. Ten seconds after seeing her naked, he'd wanted to be inside her. A heartbeat after touching her soft skin, and it was all he could do not to crush her beneath him right there in the fucking bathtub and push himself deep inside her until they were both begging for mercy.

Hunt looked down at her. Her brilliant eyes were narrow with anger and frustration as she glared at him over his palm. She *was* a witch. *Bruja*— "Bloody hell!" He rolled off her and cradled his hand. "You bit me."

"You put your hand in my mouth." Hell, she sounded reasonable except for the heaving chest and wild eyes.

"I wanted you to shut up."

"Well, I wanted your hand off my mouth."

Her face was pink and shiny from the heat of the shower and he suspected, temper.

Hunt shook his hand. He'd asked to be bitten, which pissed him off. Hell, he'd bite too. He leaned over the bed and grabbed her neatly folded pile of clothes.

He tossed them at her. "I checked. Nothing in them."

She fumbled for her clothes like a drowning woman grabbing a life ring. "No kidding. I don't keep anything of value on me, Hugh."

"Hunt." It needled him that she didn't remember his name.

"Hugh. As in Grant. As in bumbling guy with a British accent."

Hunt hadn't a clue who the hell she was talking about. She redressed in her own clothes and combed her wet hair back from her face with her fingers.

"Feel better?"

"Dandy."

He almost smiled at the edge in her words. "There's a chair to your right three paces."

She found it and sat down like a queen about to give an audience. The lamp beside her illuminated her milk white skin, making it look like porcelain. "No bright lights or bamboo shoots?"

"Not my style." Neither was intimidation by caress, but it had almost worked. And he felt almost ashamed at how much he'd enjoyed it. Fortunately, his legendary control had kicked in to prevent him from making an ass of himself. "You cleaned out a state-of-the-art safe."

She smiled, and Hunt glanced away for a second from the potency of those pale, incredible eyes, alight with pleasure. "The unbreachable Faulkner KS796? I certainly did," she said with unassailable pride.

"There were other things in that safe. Keep everything?"

She shrugged. "If they were in there. Maybe. I had a bad feeling all night. I just wanted to go in and get the hell out. So yes, I took everything."

"What did you do with the take after you left Morales's house?"

"I told you!"

Her bravado was impressive, but downright dangerous right now. Those codes were an integral part of an act of terror *Mano del Dios* had scheduled for October 13. Just two months from now. They had barely sixty days to get their hands on the launch codes and then locate the missile.

Sixty days to unravel a crisis and avert disaster. Hunt hoped it was long enough, but he was tired of playing guessing games with Annie Sullivan.

T-FLAC had averted *Mano's last* attack—a nerve agent scheduled for release during Mardi Gras in New Orleans last February. There had been nothing overt from the group since. But Morales, religious zealot that he was, hadn't been idle.

He gave her a cool look. "It's no sweat for me to deliver you back to those goons exactly as you are right now. Blind and exhausted. Try again, sweetheart." If T-FLAC could have done this without her, they would have. God knew, they'd tried.

"I have a partner. *He* took everything."

She was lying through her pearly white teeth. "And this convenient *partner* of yours didn't give a damn that you were caught and tossed in that hellhole of a jail?" Hunt walked closer to her.

She shrugged. "Apparently not."

Hunt had an urge to put his fingers around her throat and squeeze. Except he did not want to touch her. Because he realized with dawning fury that he couldn't touch this woman in anger. One brief contact would turn into a caress. The caress into hard, fast sex. Sex into—

Hell. She'd drive any poor, stupid bastard crazy with that innocent tone and a look from those big beautiful eyes. "And you're meeting up where?" he demanded, at the edge of his temper.

He never lost his temper. Not ever. It was all a matter of control. He considered himself a master of control. Yet his jaw ached from clenching his teeth.

"Rio."

"When?"

"Thursday."

"What's this person's name?"

She hesitated. Thought about it. He could almost see her roll through a list of names and pick one. "Toby."

A muscle jumped in his jaw. God, she was a piece of work. "Toby—?"

"Now why would I tell you? Okay, fine. For God's sake. I'm exhausted, and I've answered your questions. Toby *Blackman*."

He didn't believe her for a second. Yet he'd never met anyone, male or female, who lied with such panache. It was not a trait he admired. "Lover?"

She crossed one long jean-clad leg over the other and leaned back in the chair. "Uncle."

Her hair was starting to dry about her shoulders. It was slightly curly, and a silky chocolate brown. Touchable. Striking, with those ice-blue eyes and cream complexion. He rubbed the flat of his hand on the rough texture of the blanket beneath him. "So this is a family affair?"

"You bet." She paused and said lightly, "You don't really think simply because you ask, that I'm going to hand my diamonds over to you, do you?"

He didn't give a continental fuck about the diamonds. "How much?" Fine. He'd pay. He had the resources.

"How much what?"

His jaw was about to shatter from gritting his teeth so hard. "How much do you want for the contents of Morales's safe?"

She didn't even blink. "Forty million dollars."

"Greedy girl." God. He had to put an end to this before he did something incredibly stupid. "Street value's approximately four point eight mil."

She shook her head. "Five point two to be exact."

"I'll give you four mil. Cash. U.S. currency. For everything you took from Morales's safe." Hunt would pay her in kittens if that's what it took.

"I'll think about it." She looked at him, her expression as guileless as a baby's, and yawned. He'd never seen anything as sexy in his life. He almost groaned out loud.

"Can we discuss this in the morning?" she asked, sounding frail and weak. It was a nice touch, but he didn't believe it for a second. She looked wide-awake and revitalized. And she wasn't the frail, weak type. She was cunning and clever and heartbreakingly beautiful and trying to play him like a violin.

She was as dangerous as hell. "What's your real name?"

She tilted her head, chin up. "I told you—"

"Cut the crap, lady. Give me a name. The one on your birth certificate will do." He'd touched that milk pale skin. Skimmed his fingers over that gentle swell of her breast. Could almost taste that flush riding her high cheekbones. A fire of lust burned in Hunt's belly as he watched her. He was rock hard, and destined to stay that way, it appeared, for the duration.

"I'm hurt, I really am." There was a smile in her voice that she was smart enough not to show him. "After all this, you still don't trust me?" She sounded like the victim in this mess.

"No."

"Life's full of little disappointments. I'll live."

"Come to bed." Hunt tugged her toward the oversized mattress, feeling feral.

Her eyes widened. "Are you out of your mind? I am not sleeping with you." Her feet planted on the floor by the chair.

Ten minutes ago she would have done any damn thing he'd wanted her to do. His dick leapt and reached out for her as if it had a mind of its own. Hunt ignored the clambering of his body, exerting his iron will. "It's three A.M., and there's only one bed."

"I'll get another room."

"Got money?" He smiled.

"I'll sleep in this chair."

"Doesn't look comfortable, but suit yourself. We'll talk more in the morning. Give you time to rethink some of those answers."

Seven

TAYLOR WAS HANGING ON BY A HAIR. *He* MIGHT'VE FORGOTTEN what had happened in the still steamy bathroom not ten minutes ago. But she hadn't. She had pulse points in places she hadn't realized she had pulse points. A good night's sleep would hopefully return some of her missing brain cells, giving her a good dose of smarts. A few hours without being under the gun would, please God, resolve the blindness problem.

God, she still couldn't see. Pitch-black. No shadows. No light. No movement. Just pure colorless night.

She hated being this vulnerable. And she *loathed* being vulnerable with this man in particular. She knew he was playing with her like a very large cat with a very small mouse.

She didn't hear him move, but between one breath and the next he'd crossed the room and plucked her out of the chair.

He carried her away from his body, and upright so her feet dangled above the floor. Like something he didn't really want to contaminate his hands with. The man was not only a manipulative son of a bitch, but he was incredibly strong. Taylor took note.

"This is more expedient than waiting for you to be sensible." Three strides and he dropped her onto the bed with a bounce.

She scrambled to get her bearings. "And where will you sleep?"

"Right here."

Taylor rolled over and felt around for a pillow. She stuffed it under her cheek, turned her head and closed her eyes.

The mattress dipped as he sat down beside her. She ignored him, even as her body temperature zoomed up feverishly at the thought of having his hands on her again. His mouth— *Stop it!* she warned herself. This guy knew what the hell he was doing. *He's playing you as expertly as you're trying to play him. Get a grip here and concentrate.*

A drawer opened. Closed. A rubber? Her teeth ground together. She'd kill him with her bare hands. His arm brushed hers as he leaned over her. Lightning fast, he took her hand and wrapped her fingers around one of the metal bars on the headboard over her head. She heard a *chink*.

"Hey!" The cold bracelet of a handcuff snapped shut around her wrist. She inwardly sighed. "How could you?" She put a hurt quiver in her voice, though she didn't blame him. She would have done the same thing in his position. It didn't make her hate him any less. She was tired of trying to sound innocent and victimized.

"Who hired you?" he asked. Again.

"Nobody."

Look helpless, she told herself. Pitiful. Sincere. "Nobody. I swear. I'll give you Tony's phone number. Call him and negotiate a—"

"No partner named either Toby or Tony." Hunt shifted to wrap his large hand lightly around her throat. "Who has the contents of the safe?"

He squeezed gently.

She tried to pry his fingers away from her throat. "I tol—"

His hand tightened. "Think I won't kill you?" he asked silkily, his breath fanning her face as he leaned over her. "Think again."

She believed him. "I—ha—I can't breathe."

His fingers didn't so much as loosen by a hair. "You can breathe just fine."

Bullying bastard. "*I* have e-everything, damn y-you." When he still didn't release her, Taylor dug her nails into his fingers trying to pry them loose. "Tr-uth."

He let go, shifting away from her. "Address."

She rubbed her hand over her sore throat. "In a time-lock safe at *Banco Central de San Cristóbal,*" she lied smoothly. "The *Costa del Sol* branch." A town three hours away. "It opens at seven A.M. I'll give you the combination."

"It'll open now," Hunt told her flatly. "Number?"

"Left twenty, Right sixty-two, Left forty-one, Right ninety-five."

She heard him pick up the phone, wait a few seconds, then repeat what she'd told him. By car it would take three hours to reach the bank. By chopper, perhaps forty-five minutes total. She figured she had less than forty minutes to get away.

"Get some sleep," he told her when he'd completed his call. "Knowing I'll be right here beside you. Keeping you safe."

"Watching me, you mean." Taylor lay her head back on the pillow and shut her eyes as if mortally wounded by his betrayal. The cuffs felt like Stark 923s. Old-fashioned. Quaint, actually.

"Sleep," he ordered, settling down beside her.

"My arm hurts," Taylor complained, and felt not even a mild twinge of guilt when he bunched a pillow to support her forearm and wrist.

"Better?" His voice sounded strained. Irritated.

Too bad. She wasn't feeling particularly happy with him either. "Much," she told him sweetly, hoping the erection she'd felt earlier would get hard enough to cause his penis to fall off altogether. A girl could wish.

"Will you sleep?" He shifted a few inches away. No longer touching, but close enough for her to feel the heat of his skin.

"Yes." She managed a nice big yawn. "I'm exhausted." Wired. Sexually frustrated. Confused. "Is there a cover? I'm a little cool." Taylor didn't want him looking at her when she couldn't glare back at him.

The sheet was light and scratchy as he impersonally dropped it over her. "You've had a busy night. Get some rest. We'll talk again in the morning." He almost sounded paternal.

"Sure." *Only if you have long distance service from San Cristóbal to the States.* Right this second she didn't have a clue how she'd pull off a speedy escape. But she sure as hell wouldn't be here when this guy woke up. Taylor rolled over as best she could and whimpered because he deserved it. " 'Night."

"You're safe here," he said quietly into the darkness.

She was annoyed to feel the prick of tears behind her lids. "Thanks," she said, meaning it. She couldn't remember when, in twenty-seven years, anyone had ever said those words to her. It would be stupid to believe him of course, but just for that moment in time, the saying of the words made her *feel* safe.

She waited an eternity for his breathing to regulate and even longer before she felt the mattress give as his large body relaxed in sleep.

The headache had faded to a dull memory. Taylor turned onto her back in the surprisingly comfortable bed. She opened her eyes and stared at the orange drapes as she considered how long she should wait before she snuck o–

Blinked. Looked again.

Yes! Oh, God. Yes! She could actually *see* the limp fabric illuminated by the lamp on the table across the room. Her vision was a little fuzzy around the edges, but she could see. *Thank you, Jesus.*

She took a lightning-fast inventory of the room. Two doors. Bathroom. Exit door. One window.

They lay on a queen-sized bed with tangled white sheets and a brightly colored cotton cover. A couple of bedside tables, a cane-backed chair, two mismatched lamps, and a hideous hanging lamp near a table by the open bathroom door. Drapes hung over a narrow window in the far wall. The wooden floor, while bare of rugs, was spotlessly clean and polished to a dull sheen.

If she ever visited San Cristóbal again, she'd stay here, she thought with amusement as, noting escape routes and possible weapons, she turned her head to look at the sleeping man beside her.

Oh. What a fascinating face. She'd brailled the uncompromising jaw, rough with stubble. Seeing his features with her fingers, but now she could see him. Slightly hazy, but who was complaining? A strong Roman nose rose proudly from a face far too austere to be considered handsome. Deep-set eyes weren't in any way softened by the brush of those short, straight black lashes. *Man, oh man.* This was one serious-looking guy. She couldn't picture a smile breaking across those firm straight lips.

Taylor's gaze lingered on his mouth before she tried to roll over. She was pulled up short by the cuff on her wrist.

She gave a small huff of amusement. As if— And freed her right wrist with barely a sound. Very carefully she held on to the cuff, still linked to the headboard, so it didn't clatter. His hand was conveniently flung over his head. It would be a bit of a stretch, but she could snap the free bracelet onto his wrist in a heartbeat. She considered the necessary choreography for a few seconds. No. Her gut told her he'd be wide-awake and on her like white on rice if she so much as made a move in his direction.

Of course, there were moves and there were moves . . . Carefully, she rested the cuff against the headboard, then shifted to run her fingers lightly up Hunt's chest, enjoying the crisp silkiness of his hairy torso. Yum. He didn't stir. She leaned over and open-mouth-kissed his rock-hard six-pack, when she really wanted to take a big, painful bite out of him.

He hummed low in his throat, confirming her gut's warning. His large hand came up to cup the back of her head. She nibbled her way *up* his chest to the steady throb of his pulse at the base of his throat, sliding her body over his like a blanket. She lay her cheek over his heart, listening to the slight elevation in his breathing.

His skin felt scalding hot beneath hers.

His penis rose to meet her.

She rubbed her chest against his, enjoying the friction against her nipples. His lashes fluttered and a tweak at the corners of his lips could've been the start of a smile.

Taylor did *not* want him smiling at her.

She kept one arm extended as though she was still cuffed to the headboard, and put her palm across his eyes. "Keep 'em closed," she purred.

"Yes, ma'am." His voice was thick with desire as he shifted his hips beneath hers. His willpower wasn't quite as rock solid when he was half asleep. She sat up slowly to straddle his narrow hips with her knees.

You are going to be so sorry you messed with me, Taylor thought, touching his face as she shifted up his body to sit lightly on his chest. She slid her knees into position over his biceps. His jaw was prickly with stubble. She wanted to run her mouth— *Damn it. Concentrate!* Every second counted.

Still stroking his face, she snatched up the lamp on the bedside table, at the same time pressing her weight onto his chest and pinning his upper arms with her knees. He froze beneath her, alerted to the movement.

Damn. With a hard swing, Taylor brought the heavy lamp down at the same time he jerked upright. Assisted by his own momentum, the heavy base of the lamp struck his temple with a dull thud.

The sound of ceramic on skull made her sick to her stomach, and she jumped off his limp body as if jet-propelled. She hoped to hell he'd been completely knocked out, because if he wasn't, she feared for her life.

He wasn't moving, and the blow to his temple had already formed a darkening knot, and bled sluggishly.

Heart in her throat, and feeling the urgency to get the hell out of there before he opened those pitiless eyes and looked at her, Taylor felt for a pulse under his jaw. Still steady. Still vibrant. He'd live.

Taylor swiftly handcuffed Mr. Huntington St. John to the bed, yanked the phone cord from the wall, and carried the lamp across the room to the table. She paused on her way out, then returned to the bed to look down at him.

He appeared no less menacing unconscious.

She brushed a finger across his straight lower lip. "Bastard," she said softly.

Eight

JOSÉ MORALES ENSCONCED HIMSELF IN HIS ORNATE LONDON OF-
fice. It was less than a day after the burglary, and his wife, Maria,
was not happy she'd been left alone to deal with the *policía*.
She reported they'd claimed to have captured a woman they believed to be part of the gang who had robbed him. But when José had
demanded to interrogate the woman himself, they'd informed him
that she had escaped. *Tontos estúpidos!* The bumbling idiots hadn't
caught *anyone*. They'd made the claim to save face.

José opened the bottom drawer of his desk, took out a bottle of
prescription antacids, and shook four into his palm. He tossed them
into his mouth all at the same time and swallowed them down with
vitamin-enriched springwater. He twisted the crystal glass between
his fingers, watching the light play on the precise leaded cuts.

When he'd discovered the empty, open safe in the upstairs den the
night of the party, he'd excused himself and gone into his bathroom
to vomit.

He'd been guaranteed, unequivocally, by both the safe's inventor and the manufacturer, that the new safe was impossible to crack. It was *everything*-proof. Fire. Chemicals. Mechanical devices. The only way to open the thing was with an intricate combination of both numerals and letters.

He'd never have trusted something as invaluable as the codes to the safe in San Cristóbal if he'd had a second's thought about the veracity of the men who had designed and built it.

They had sworn on their lives—and those of their families—that what they said was true. Only he had the combination, and he hadn't opened the safe.

Somebody had helped the thief get into the safe.

Worse, somebody he trusted implicitly must have told the thief to take the disks, which had the codes on them. And there were only a handful of people who knew of the codes' existence.

This thief had not only eluded his top security people patrolling the walled grounds of his estate, but that same thief had breached the inside security and violated his home. Then, with a house full of party guests, had opened an impenetrable safe and absconded with the contents, undetected. Impossible. But fact.

" 'But know this,' " José quoted out loud, " 'that if the goodman of the house had known in what watch the thief would come, he would have watched, and would not have suffered his house to be broken up.' "

He hadn't stopped begging God for answers since the theft. He was doing His work. Surely God wouldn't allow some criminal, no matter how clever, to steal his life's work?

God had come to him in a vision when he was twelve years old. He had told him of a rise in religious belief. Prophets and saints would appear and lead the faithful to safety. God had decreed that his debt was to cleanse the Earth of the unworthy and wicked. In this way he could avoid Purgatory.

God had chosen Friday, October 13th, as the day. His day. Throat dry, José picked up the glass and drained the last few inches of water. If not punishment, a test, then. God was asking him to prove himself.

José knew. In fifty-nine days, five years of careful, meticulous planning would change the world for the better.

"Matthew 24:35-36." José quoted by rote: " *'Heaven and earth will pass away, but My words shall not pass away. But of that day and hour no one knows, not even the angels of heaven, nor the Son, but the Father alone."* But God had shared the day and hour with José. José was to act as God's hands.

On Friday, October 13th, he was going to rip the evil out of this world. The antichrist was alive and living in Las Vegas. And God had instructed him to kill the antichrist and all his followers.

The plan was assiduously thought out to the last minute detail. But to perform this mission, he had to have what was buried impossibly deep in the earth. And to access it, he needed the codes.

The codes on the disks that had been stolen.

The elaborate codes, on five tiny minidisks, held the means to fulfill his promise to God.

And God helped those who helped themselves.

Waiting for José on the other side of the ten-foot-high carved mahogany doors were his top six lieutenants, called in from their posts all over the world. It was dangerous to have them all here together in London. Dangerous, but the most expedient way to handle the situation.

He stabbed the intercom button with a well-manicured finger. "Send them in."

His people trooped in. Men who, to a causal observer, would appear to be nothing more than prosperous businessmen in their expensive hand-tailored suits and custom shirts and shoes.

They didn't know why they were here, and they all looked slightly discomforted, but hid it well. He trusted these six men as much as he trusted anyone. But nobody was *completely* trustworthy. Everyone had a price.

He nodded to each man as they seated themselves in the waiting semicircle of chairs before his desk. "The safe in my San Cristóbal home was robbed last night," he told them baldly. "In it were the codes to gain access to the . . . items housed in South Africa. Without the proper codes, the multilevel security system will prevent us from retrieving the merchandise. Any attempts to circumvent the system without the codes will result in immediate detonation of the facility and the contents."

He waited a beat for the ramifications of this information to sink in. He was the only one with knowledge and access to the complex codes. He'd been to the location many, many times. But even with his brilliant mind, he couldn't remember all those numbers and formulas. And his darling Maria, the love of his life, and one of his greatest rewards, could not be expected to memorize such things.

All his lieutenants knew was that the location was somewhere in southern Africa. Anyone and everyone who had ever worked on the ten-year construction project was dead. It was enough.

None of the men before him had been with him to the secret location. All they knew was that within the next two months all members of *Mano del Dios* must be ready for their largest display of God's powers. Faith. They knew and lived it.

His hard gaze paused on each face. "I want this man found, my codes retrieved, and him killed. *Slowly,* and *publicly.* As a warning to any other would-be thieves."

"The theft took place while you slept, or during the party?" Harold Sark asked, his eyes black and intent on Morales's face.

"During the party. And before you ask," José said flatly, "it was *not* one of our guests. It was a small, intimate affair, and we had only our closest friends and family in attendance. People I have done extensive background checks on."

"The same friends and family who attended your wife's birthday event on the yacht two years ago?" Sark asked in a calm, flat tone.

He'd had a similar robbery on board his yacht then. "A member of the catering staff was caught red-handed. A simple theft." He'd claimed. To save face. But it had been no member of the wait staff who had robbed him. Someone had broken into the safe. But it had been a relatively simple safe. One any common thief could crack. The thief had gotten away with the czar's Imperial Fabergé egg José had given his wife for her birthday. The same egg had mysteriously reappeared a month later, back on its stand in a private collection in England. The original theft had not been reported, and its return had gone unremarked upon.

Nobody but himself and Maria knew it was on board and how it had come to be there.

"Yet immediately thereafter," Jacques Montrose said quietly, tenacious as a dog with a bone, "you ordered the elimination of the entire staff of two security firms, fifty-four members of various catering companies, and replaced your ship's captain. Twice, I believe."

"One can never be too cautious." José had lost track of the number of household staff eliminated, in all of their homes around the world, over the years. Perhaps Maria might know, but he doubted she cared either.

"Open channels and find this thief," he told them flatly. "Do deeper background checks on every single member of my family, every staff member, every friend and associate, everyone who has attended any event I might have been present at over the past year. I want every available resource utilized until we find this man."

"Do you think that it was directed at you specifically, or was this a regular run-of-the-mill thief who could just as easily have robbed any one of us in this room?" Sark asked after a moment.

"There was nothing *simple* about it." Again he looked at each man in turn. "The San Cristóbal safe was *invincible*. And the only people who knew the portions of the combination are sitting here with me in this room," Morales told him coldly. "The thieves, or thief, were clever and resourceful. Or . . ." His pause was enough to make the men shift uncomfortably in the seats. ". . . or the thief sits here among us."

The men glanced at one another, then back to Morales. If in fact it was true, he didn't know which of them it was, and he couldn't afford to kill them all. Not now.

"Do you think this is personal, José?" Andreas Constantine, his oldest and most trusted lieutenant, asked.

José raised a brow. Of course it was personal. Wasn't everything?

"I mean," the Greek said quickly, "do you believe the thief was specifically targeting the codes? It *is* possible that the theft was random. Wealthy families suffer such things frequently."

It felt personal. But then, everything did. Personal or random act.

The codes were gone. That was all that mattered. "Find out," he instructed.

"I will," Constantine assured him. "It's possible that he was not aware of exactly what it was he stole. It's likely that he was after Maria's well-publicized jewelry collection, nothing more."

José steepled his fingers. "It is possible." The thought had occurred to him. *Afterward.* He'd forgotten that Maria's diamonds had already been in the upstairs library safe, instead of in the bedroom, as they normally were. It was possible the thief had come for her jewelry.

It was, of course, impossible to memorize all the information contained on the disks. That was the point. Making access to the mine complex, and perhaps impossible, without them.

If the thief had specifically stolen the disks, knowing what was on them, it would be that much harder to find them. Either the man was affiliated with another terrorist organization that would utilize the information for their own purposes, or the thief would sell the information to the highest bidder.

But if the thief had accidentally taken them when he'd stolen Maria's jewelry, then José knew he was still screwed. Because not knowing their value might cause him to discard the disks as worthless.

The hot hand of God fisted in his stomach.

The contents of the disks held the key to his legacy—the tool necessary for leaving his mark on the world—something for his children and their children and their children after them. Future generations would speak the name José Morales with reverence.

He let his eyes speak for him about retribution if the job was not done. The men surrounding him knew the expression. At one time or another all of them had witnessed firsthand what happened to anyone who crossed purposes with him. He depended on that. Traded on it. And he intended to make an example of this thief.

It would be graphic.

No. Epic.

"Find him. Find him now."

Nine

S HE MOVED WITH STEALTH AND SURETY. CLEARLY, SHE'D RECOV-
ered her sight. Good, Hunt thought savagely. He wanted her to
see his face when he caught her. Looked forward to those unforgettable blue eyes widening as she realized that *this* time, God help
her, she wasn't going to get away from him.

He watched her on his small wrist monitor as she drifted like
black smoke through the midnight-dark halls of the Houston museum. "Damn, she's good." If he hadn't been here specifically to find
her, if he wasn't scanning every inch of the wide hallways, he wouldn't
have even known she was there.

Liquid motion, footsteps silent, she moved swiftly toward the gem
exhibit at the end of the south corridor.

Where he patiently waited.

It had taken him—and the extensive resources of T-FLAC—
almost a month to find her. Again. Once more they'd had to pull people off other assignments to locate this woman.

One bloody woman had eluded the best trackers in the world.

He'd thought he'd had her in Chicago three weeks ago. *Knew,* damn it, that he had her. But when he'd stormed into her hotel room, she was gone. And for the next fortnight her tracks had gone cold. Ice cold. It was as though she'd vanished into thin air.

Hunt enjoyed a challenge. But not this one. Time was running out. He not only despised wasting time, he didn't have any more to spare. And he hated like hell acknowledging that this woman had managed to best him.

Even thinking about what she'd done to him in San Cristóbal irked him. As he'd suspected at the time, there'd been no time-locked safe at the *Banco Central de San Cristóbal.* And he had to live down being handcuffed to the bed. Jesus.

Now, he observed her as she moved about the exhibit hall in this small, obscure museum in Houston, Texas. *Got you now.* As she appeared, framed by the wide doors opposite his hiding place, Hunt pulled down his nvg's. Her face was covered by a dark mask, but he didn't need to see her face to ID her. He'd recognize that sinuous body anywhere.

He was surprised—and more than a little annoyed—to find his heart rate elevated with her this close. Anticipation. Annoyance. And, damn it, *arousal.* He hadn't felt any of the three in months, and experiencing *any* of them *now* seriously pissed him off.

She'd had a busy, and highly profitable, month. Heists in Paris, Edinburgh, Madrid. She'd pocketed several mil in gems.

Hunt had followed her trail like a damn bloodhound, made a few guesses, followed his gut, and finally caught up with her here in Houston. Out of five possible jobs she could have pulled that week, Mick the Greek's collection of jewelry, on loan to the Houston Museum, was one. Hell, it had been a long shot. But a long shot was better than no shot at all.

It had paid off.

He was going to keep his eyes fixed on her for the duration. She wasn't going to be slipping by him. *Not this time, sweetheart.*

She played a dangerous game, targeting only those with questionable backgrounds. She didn't rob the Trumps or the glitterati of the entertainment industry, heads of state, or financial titans. She robbed people who had something to hide. People who didn't want a bright light shone under their rocks.

In fact, some of the very individuals Homeland Security, and T-FLAC themselves, targeted. Coincidental? Not bloody likely.

Very clever.

The gems and jewelry in this exhibit were on loan from one Michael B. Corda. Corda, or Mick the Greek, a midlevel mob boss who'd done very well for himself in arms sales to the Middle East. Mick was smooth and sophisticated, and very, very wealthy. This display of his wife's jewels was a taunt to the authorities who hadn't managed to catch him. *Yet.*

Precisely the kind of setup his girl liked, Hunt thought, watching her uncanny stillness through narrowed eyes. No, damn it, not *his* girl. He frowned. But *not* precisely the overpriced, oversecured venues she usually robbed. The Houston museum's security systems were basic, and no frills. Typical of most tightly budgeted small museums. Even with the few high-tech additions installed for this exhibit, hardly a challenge to someone with her skill and talent. And it was more than likely she didn't know that anything had been added.

Hunt leaned a shoulder against the wall and settled in to be entertained. *"Okay, sweetheart. Let's see you do your thing."* But he knew this time she'd bitten off more than she could chew. The traveling gem and jewelry exhibit was valued upward of $25 million. Most of the gems were big and flashy—like Mick. Obviously, the guy believed size mattered.

Infrared was passive, not the clearly visible red lines portrayed by the movie industry, and therefore invisible to even the most sensitive equipment. Hunt had an addition to his nvg's to see the lines surrounding the display cases quite clearly.

The grid was basic. But basic or complex, since *she* couldn't see it, she was about to set off the silent alarms. And he was quite content to hang back and wait. "Let *her* feel handcuffs for a change." And a fat lot of good that would do, he thought wryly, since apparently she could quite easily slip out of them.

He had to think like her. So, to see just how hard it would be to stay in the museum after closing, he'd paid his six bucks and entered with the rest of the crowds. He could've, of course, gone the official route. But she wouldn't have had that advantage.

Blending with the crowds, he kept an eye out for a slender woman with brilliant blue eyes. Yeah, right. As if she wouldn't hide such a distinctive feature. Still, he'd looked at everyone. Twice. Hell, it was like looking for a needle in a stack of needles. Just before closing, he found an excellent hiding place in the exhibit hall and settled in to wait. It was now 8:00 P.M.

No alarms had gone off, which meant she hadn't breached the perimeter security system to enter the building. He deduced she too had paid admission, then hidden until the guards had slipped out for dinner and the cleaning people were done and gone.

She'd go for the sapphires, he knew instinctively. There were seven cases containing the entire sapphire collection. They weren't the biggest or flashiest gems in the exhibit, but they wouldn't draw unwanted scrutiny once they were recut, and they'd turn her a very nice profit on the secondary market. Somewhere around the two-million mark if she got them all.

Her task was impossible. Hunt knew it. She had apparently failed to notice. First of all, because the cases were intentionally spread the full length of the exhibit hall. The logistics alone would prohibit her from successfully breaking into seven secured display cases set fifty feet apart.

Second, in addition to the extra security of alarms, sensors, and infrared, there were pressure-sensitive pads surrounding each polycarbon column containing the jewelry and loose stones. If the polycarbon was touched, an alarm went off. If the stones or jewelry were lifted from their own pressure-sensitive pads deep inside one of the clear poly tubes, the alarms would sound.

No, she wasn't going to be able to pull this one off. But it would be interesting to watch her try.

And then he'd have her.

He couldn't fault her on her timing. He glanced off to the left. The security guards inside the vast room were as far from her now as they were going to get. She had a grand total of five minutes fourteen seconds to get in and get out.

Wasn't going to happen.

He turned his gaze back to the doorway.

She was gone.

TAYLOR DREW IN A CLEANSING BREATH AS SHE RAPIDLY WALKED toward exhibit number seventeen, hugging the wall. It was always so much more interesting when the guards' routine wasn't carefully timed. The good thing about these two was that they were pals, and one had recently returned from his two-week vacation. They had a lot to talk about. And they walked slowly. The hum of their low voices was a nice counterpoint to the steady beat of her heart.

She'd given herself four minutes to get the necklace and earrings and be gone. The gems had been reset but, fortunately, not recut. And the collection she wanted was conveniently all in the same display case. Number seventeen.

Taylor had retrieved their original exquisite and very distinctive platinum setting from the fence in Holland a year ago, before it could be melted or sold.

By tomorrow the sapphires, in their original setting, would be reunited, and back where they belonged.

Her slippered feet moved soundlessly as she started running lightly across the marble floor. She'd counted the steps from the wall to the pedestal as she'd polished the floor earlier.

She'd also managed to stick a piece of chewing gum directly over the eye of the motion detector on the pedestal holding her target. She couldn't see the invisible infrared grid, but she knew where it was *supposed* to be from the rough drawing she'd lifted from the guard's station two days ago.

Warm air from the un-air-conditioned room fanned her face as she ran, picking up speed. The slick black bodysuit hugged her every curve, covering her from head to toe. Only her eyes were exposed.

The marble floor had an intricate geometric design of alternating squares of black and cream, with a wide black band bordering the room. Inside that black band, and bisecting the three-foot-tall, black marble bases of the eight-foot-high, clear polycarbon tubes, was the infrared grid. All she had to do was go up and over it. *Up* three feet, *over* twelve.

When Taylor's toes touched the inner edge of that border she exhaled, then launched herself high in the air, like a trapeze artist, without the trapeze. A double tuck midair and she landed as light as thistledown on the outer edge of the square base supporting the number-seventeen polycarbon display tube. Three minutes eleven seconds to go, she counted off mentally. Plenty of time.

She did a deep knee bend, sliding her torso down the outside circumference of the tube. There was a button under the lip of the base . . . *Ah. There.* She turned off the microwave detector she hadn't had time to deactivate earlier, then paused before standing upright. Alert to the smallest sound, she held her breath and listened.

Nothing but the indistinct voices at the other end of the hall. Still, an icy shiver raced up her back like a premonition.

A couple of weeks ago in Chicago she'd sensed someone following her. She hadn't seen anyone, and it had been for only a few hours, but she'd crisscrossed the city. Backward and forward. Changing her appearance at every stop until she was positive she'd shaken the tail.

She'd trusted the feeling enough to go straight to the airport from the house party, instead of returning to her hotel.

Tonight that feeling of being watched was back in spades. She never ignored her instincts, and right now every nerve and muscle in her body warned of impending danger. If she was fanciful—which she frequently was—she imagined a jungle cat, sleek and black, watching her from the darkness. Waiting to pounce. Her heart hammered.

She forced herself to crouch there, absolutely still for a few more valuable seconds as she listened carefully for the slightest out-of-place sound, a movement, a change in the air around her.

Nothing.

Nothing.

Another precious few seconds passed as she waited. Still nothing. If danger lurked in the darkness, it wasn't going to disappear while she hung around waiting for it. Time to get moving. Taylor suddenly had a quick, visual memory of the man in San Cristóbal—

No, damn it. Concentrate. No sudden jarring moves. Keep it smooth. Steady.

She couldn't afford to use a light, but in her mind's eye she visualized the necklace on its cream velvet bed shooting blue fire. *Come to mama.*

The clear poly tube was eighteen inches in diameter and eight feet tall. The exhibits had been carefully placed on motion-sensitive pads, then the open-ended tubes lowered over the top to fit snuggly into magnetic rims on each base.

Other than removing the tube—impossible without large equipment—the only way in to the gems was to lower herself down inside the tube.

Standing on her toes, Taylor jumped up, gripping the outer edge of the display tube between her tightly gloved hands, and without missing a beat, lifted herself up over the rim. She went down headfirst into the cylinder, her feet hooked over the rim to hold her in place. It was a tight fit.

Two minutes forty seconds. Piece of cake.

Blood rushed to her head with the sound of the ocean roaring as she unhooked a weight from her belt while feeling carefully with her other hand for the cool silver links of the necklace at the bottom of the case.

Velvet . . . velvet . . .

Bingo.

She skillfully exchanged the weight for the necklace, another for the earrings, then stuffed both into her leg pack and inched herself backward out of the tube.

Barely out of breath, sitting balanced on the thick rim, legs dangling inside the display case, Taylor gave herself a few seconds to readjust her equilibrium.

She couldn't shake the sensation of being watched. But she could see the guards wending their way back—still hundreds of yards away. And the red eyes of the cameras were dark. She'd clipped a few wires and looped the security feed earlier. No one was watching her, of course, but the hairs on the back of her neck said otherwise.

To hell with it.

Pushing off the rim with her palms, she withdrew her legs from inside the tube, then crouched on the outer edge, like a frog about to hop. She grinned. Damn, this was fun. Slowly, she rose to straddle the opening, arms extended for balance to stand eleven feet above the floor.

The victory smile slipped from her face as she heard a sound to her right. She froze. No, not a sound, more a feeling of that dark presence. Someone else *was* out there watching her.

The hair on the back of her neck prickled, and her heart leapt into her throat.

Her imagination.

No. God, no. She *felt* someone there.

Where? She looked around again, careful not to topple off her perch, trying to discern who, *where,* in the inky blackness.

Nothing but the thick darkness, and the approaching twin beams of the guards' flashlights looming ever closer.

Time to get the hell out of Dodge.

Flexing her knees, arms raised above her head, palms held high and flat, she jumped. Her left palm struck the air-conditioning grid above her head with a soft click while she grabbed the edge of the exposed opening with her right hand and swung, not quite balanced, for precious seconds like a chimpanzee at the zoo. She managed to haul herself into the opening, slither her body into the duct, and press the grate back in place.

Not a moment too soon.

All hell broke loose. The alarm shrieked, the noise deafening in the confined metal shaft. "Shit!" Someone had activated the alarms. She wasn't worried. They weren't going to find her. But she was cutting it close, having them start to look for her when she was still on the premises. It had never been *this* close before.

Shouts. Running feet. Brilliant lights. The metallic crash of security doors slamming shut over the regular doors, and the shrill scream of the alarms reverberating throughout the building. All amplified in the narrow confines of the metal ducts.

Scrambling on all fours, Taylor almost went deaf from the sound of the alarms and sirens bouncing and echoing through the shaft. The black silk pouch secured to her thigh was a solid, happy weight despite the drama going on below.

Even with the clarion sound of the alarms reverberating in her ears and vibrating through her palms and knees, it never occurred to her that she could be caught red-handed. But the adrenaline rush of the close call made her blood sing and her heart thump arrhythmically as she crawled faster than she'd ever crawled in her life.

"Move, Taylor, *move.*" It would take nine minutes to traverse the labyrinth of ducts and emerge through an exterior side wall vent four stories above the ground. And every second, every *nanosecond,* she felt . . . it—*him,* breathing down her neck. Like a living Sword of Damocles. She crawled faster.

T e n

F EELING CONSIDERABLY CALMER SEVERAL HOURS LATER, TAYLOR strolled across the lobby of the Four Seasons Hotel in the wee hours of the morning. It was almost 2:00 A.M., but she wasn't tired; she was invigorated by a job well done. She barely noticed the admiring glances of several men leaving the lobby bar as they passed her.

The red silk Betsey Johnson slip dress exposed a lot of skin. It was designed, and worn, to attract attention. Taylor wanted people to remember the blonde in the sexy red dress, both leaving and returning to the hotel.

She picked up speed, heading toward the elevator bank in a flash of bare leg and shimmering silk. She pushed aside the frilly cuff of the lace glove on her left wrist to check her watch. For the past five hours she'd been looking forward to a long shower, a glass of champagne, and a good piece of chocolate. She'd spent the rest of her evening mentally recapping the heist. She knew she almost made a false step earlier when she'd imagined a Boogeyman watching her as she worked. But it was no Boogeyman who had sounded the alarm. *She* hadn't set it off. So who *had*?

"Work it out. Move on," she murmured. In the morning after a good night's sleep, she'd go over each step of tonight's heist to analyze how anyone could possibly have known the museum was being robbed on that particular night. At that precise time.

The elevator doors pinged as they opened, and Taylor stepped inside just as a man dashing across the lobby yelled, "Hold it!"

She automatically put her hand out to keep the doors from closing. The guy, tousled haired and dressed in a dark suit, was tall and interesting-looking, with a lean, hunter's face and penetrating eyes. He gave her short red dress and blond hair a glance of approval as he jogged the last few yards to the elevator bank. The corners of his eyes crinkled attractively as he stepped into the elevator and shot her a smile. "Thanks."

He reminded Taylor a little of that guy from San Cristóbal. The memory of that night made her pulse leap. And not necessarily in a good way. She had no trouble remembering his name. *Huntington St. John.* She just didn't want to jinx herself by thinking it.

The man turned around to face the door, glanced at the control panel, but didn't make a selection. They must be on the same floor. Her floor.

Coincidence?

Oh, for— She shook her head at her paranoia. *Get a grip.* Taylor smiled back absently, then opened her small clutch for her key card.

"Good party?" he asked politely.

She glanced up and said wryly, "It had its moments."

They stood side by side, watching the numbers above the door. Every one of Taylor's senses was on red alert. She remembered the sensation of being watched, and tried to get a good look at the guy beside her from the corner of her eye.

After all, you weren't paranoid if they really *were* after you.

The doors pinged open on the ninth floor and they both stepped out. "Good night," the man said politely, turning left.

" 'Night." Taylor turned right, only realizing when she turned to see where he was going how tense she'd been. He opened a door way at the other end of the corridor and disappeared inside. The breath she hadn't realized she'd been holding released in a sigh.

She shook her head. "Okay, paranoia's one thing. Psychotic is a whole other thing." Lord. She needed a vacation.

She'd settle for sleeping in, and having the massage she'd booked for later that afternoon. In two days she was leaving for Hawaii, and the Yashitos' annual beach party. And the fabulous tanzanite and diamond collection Yoko's husband had "acquired" for her from Mrs. Jonathan Ling in New York.

A working holiday, then, she thought with a smile, as she pushed open the door to her room. She put a hand out for the light switch on the wall as she snapped the door closed, locking it automatically behind her.

Before her fingers found the main switch, the light beside the bed blazed on, illuminating both the room and the man sprawled on her bed, hands behind his head, looking at her with the feral eyes of a predator. Maybe not an animal. He was too . . . elegant for that. But certainly not a mortal either.

Oh, damn! Think of the devil . . .

Seeing Huntington St. John again, especially since she'd thought his name not two minutes ago, and therefore jinxed herself, made dread lurch in the pit of Taylor's stomach. She'd underestimated his determination. And that mistake had come back to bite her in the ass. She knew without a shadow of a doubt that she was in big trouble. Ignoring the shiver that slithered up her spine, she opened her eyes wide.

Woman alone. Strange man in her room. She would be both startled and afraid. Neither was hard to fake. She sure as hell was startled to see him. And one look at the tundra in his eyes and she knew she had cause to be scared.

He gave her a look of undisguised hostility from pale, chilly eyes. His lean, muscled body looked poised for . . . attack? Poised to block her? Poised for—something. He had a dangerous stillness about him, lethal power ruthlessly harnessed. Despite his relaxed pose, she strongly suspected he was pissed off and ready to detonate.

She hadn't been able to get a good look at him back in South America. But her vision was 20/20 now, and for a second Taylor's pulse accelerated with a purely feminine response. He *looked* even better than he'd felt. And that was saying something. He wasn't so much good-looking as he was arresting. His dark hair, combed straight back off his face, had grown a little too long out of an expensive cut, but still looked immaculate. His tanned face was lean, almost severe, with slashes of black brows over glittering storm-colored eyes. His tall, powerful body was clothed in dark pants and an open-necked, crisply ironed, pale blue dress shirt. He had the look of wealth; suave and elegant. He also had the look of a guy with a very long, very slow fuse. She had a sinking feeling she was about to see it blow.

He sure as hell is persistent, she thought as her elemental awareness of him gave way to anger mingled with a large dose of fear. *What does he really want from me? Surely he's not still after those stupid computer disks?*

She'd considered returning to Switzerland to look in the box and see what the fuss was about. But she'd had better things to do. Now she was sorry she hadn't taken the time. She was really curious. Curious, but getting more nervous by the second.

Any normal person would jump to fill in the thick silence. *She* didn't dare until she knew just what his game was, and *he* didn't seem to be bothered by it at all. He'd make a good chess player. Or an excellent cat waiting at a mouse hole.

What he was, she thought with an inward shiver, was a predator.

After what seemed like several days, his sensual mouth curved into a small smile. It was a benign smile, but the hair on the back of her nape rose. "Hello, darling," he said with soft menace, the upper-crust British accent a little more pronounced than she remembered it. "Have a profitable evening?"

Wary, every sense alert, she felt behind her for the door handle. It refused to turn. Fine. She'd bullshit her way out of this. Play the affronted hotel guest. Lord. How had he found her again? Until two months ago, *nobody* had *ever* caught her. First that woman had come to her hotel in San Cristóbal. Then he'd shown up. And he'd done it twice. She pushed back panic and concentrated on righteous annoyance.

"Who the hell are you, and what are you doing in my room?" she demanded, keeping her attention on him while her mind raced with options.

The door behind her clearly wasn't going to open. He'd disabled the locking mechanism. She dropped her hand to her side. Given a few uninterrupted seconds, she could easily undo whatever he'd done to the lock. Unfortunately, she didn't have that luxury.

The sliding door on the far wall opened no more than nine inches and led out to a narrow faux balcony. She already knew slipping through that opening was possible. Knowing she had a way out was reassuring.

"No. Never mind introducing yourself. Just get out," she said furiously. It wasn't acting. She *was* the indignant woman returning from a fun party to find a strange, threatening male in her room. She couldn't explain it—she simply *became* someone else when she needed to *be* someone else.

She could huff and puff as much as she liked, apparently; he wasn't going anywhere. The man looked like he'd taken root.

His mouth twitched as he followed her line of sight to the drape-covered doors and back again. He gave her a benign look from steel-gray eyes. Taylor wasn't used to a man looking at her with such complete dispassion. And being the perverse creature that she was, she found herself intrigued. She shoved the ridiculous notion out of her head as he said gently, "The slider's been disabled as well."

She opened her eyes wide. "Good Lord. Surely you don't think I'd climb out of a window nine stories above the street?" She'd rehearsed doing exactly that, three times, yesterday. She knew, to the second, how long it took.

Despite being on the ragged end of furious with her, Hunt could still admire her *cojones* for putting on such a bloody good show. "If it would save your ass, yes, I do," he told her.

Her expression and tone would have done a Broadway actress proud. It was only the telltale hammering of her pulse at the base of her pale throat that gave her away.

She kept her back to the door, but he saw every taut muscle in her body ready to spring into action any second.

"What do you want?" Not a flicker of recognition in her eyes. Green contacts tonight, he noticed. The lady was one cool customer. There was a faint, almost imperceptible tightening at the corners of her eyes, but her expression showed only annoyance mixed with curiosity. She gave no indication that coming back to her hotel room in the early hours of the morning—alone—to find a large, pissed-off male sprawled on her bed was anything more than a mild annoyance.

Well, he'd give her *annoyance.*

Hunt took in the short, spiky, silvery blonde hair and clingy red dress—what there was of it—and hunger flickered dangerously to life in his body. With all that bare skin, the short black lace gloves covering her hands shot his lust level higher.

"You're late," he told her, not moving from his prone position as he did a lazy inspection of a body that he remembered only too well. The lady was built for speed, with sleek lines and elegant curves. She had a little more cleavage than he remembered, but he hadn't forgotten her pale pink nipples, or the feel of her creamy skin beneath his hand.

They locked gazes, and the flicker inside him became a flame. Hunt tamped it down with ruthless control. She was everything he fancied. Sophisticated, sexy, available.

And God only knew, everything he bloody well despised. A liar. A thief. An outstanding con woman. She should have been completely forgettable. So why the hell, when he hadn't had anything that passed for a relationship in the last—however many years—had he thought about this particular woman for two months and three days, 24/7?

Because she had something he wanted. That was why. She'd stalled an important op, leaving them precious little time. He'd forget about her the second she handed over those codes.

He dragged his mind firmly back to business.

The sapphires weren't in that tiny purse she held, and she sure as hell didn't have them anywhere on her. The red silk fit her body like a good paint job. "That was quite a chase you led us on tonight," he observed. "I must say, I'm impressed by your ingenuity."

She frowned, as though he were speaking Farsi.

"Scaling the outside wall of the museum like Spider-Man—no,

that would be Spider-*woman*—impressive. Running behind that industrial park and emerging dressed in jeans, tennis shoes, and a sweatshirt . . . You're a regular little Girl Guide, aren't you?

"Let's see—next you took a cab across town to the Hyatt. Another change of clothes there. That was the brown business suit and mouse brown hair, right? The cab ride to the airport led us by the nose for a good ninety minutes. Yet another change of clothes, *this* change of clothes, and another cab ride back into town to the party on Franklin. Enjoyed the party, did you? You hung around for two hours, eight minutes, called yet another cab, and here you are."

She'd led his people on a merry chase. He grudgingly admired her ingenuity and thoroughness. She'd almost lost them several times. And that was a hell of a thing to have to admit.

She stalked across the room, picked up the phone on the dresser, then punched a long red nail at the zero. "That's a fascinating story." She kept an eye on him as she waited for the hotel operator to come on the line. "But you clearly have me confused with someone who gives a damn."

Hunt heard the dial tone from the bed. She glared at him, then glared at the phone. Punched Operator again. Same dial tone.

"Disabled," he told her.

She put the phone down with admirable restraint, considering that her heart was beating fast enough for him to see the throb of it at the base of her long slender throat. Fear or anger? She tapped her fingernail on the back of the receiver, the delicate *click, click, click* sounding out in the room like another heartbeat.

She gave him a hot glare. "I'm too damn tired to play games." Her hands curled into fists at her sides as she stood her ground. "Get out of my room before I do something violent."

"Like what?" Hunt asked politely. "Hit me over the head with a table lamp and handcuff me to the bed?"

"Some woman beat you up?" she asked, amused. "Poor baby. Did you forget to eat your Wheaties that morning?"

He swung his feet over the side of the mattress and stood. He gave her points. She didn't back up. "Think you're going to get another shot at me?" he asked, threading menace through the silk.

Big green eyes widened. "Who, me? Beat *you* up? Are you kidding? I'd break a nail."

Oh, well done, he thought furiously. The angle of her head, the widened eyes, the mocking tone all indicated a woman not smart enough to fear him. She should be bloody terrified at this point. He was ready to—Bloody hell. "No violence." Hunt let his tone convey that *that* card wasn't completely off the table. "Give me the disks and no one will get hurt."

"If you've been in here for more than five seconds," she said, cool as a cucumber, "you know I don't have a computer, let alone disks. I have nothing worth stealing."

Her expression didn't waver. She kept those expressive eyes fixed on his face as she surreptitiously opened the small clutch purse at her side with two fingers of her right hand. He remembered the feel of those dexterous fingers, and gritted his teeth with annoyance. Hunt grabbed her arm.

Her wrist felt slender and fragile in his grip as he jerked it up and plucked the small beaded job out of her nerveless fingers. "What have you got in here?" he demanded with lethal softness. "A gun?"

She shot him an incredulous look. "A *lipstick* you— Hey!"

He kept a firm lock on her wrist as he dumped the contents of her bag onto the rumpled spread. Several hundred dollars in tens and twenties unfurled, a credit card, driver's license . . . "And what's this?" He tsked. "Mace?"

She shrugged creamy shoulders. "A girl can't be too careful."

Hunt realized that she'd done something to the bones in her wrist. Compressed them, contorted them or something, because her entire arm felt thinner, less substantial. He tightened his fingers until she stopped whatever the hell it was she'd been doing. "We can make this easy," he told her. "Or we can make it hard. I only want one thing from you. Hand it over and you can go back to your life of crime unimpeded."

He was close enough to see the faint rim of the contact lenses she wore covering her blue eyes. Close enough to smell her sultry perfume drifting up from the deep expanse of her velvety cleavage. Close enough to see a suggestion of nerves in her expression.

Good. I want you scared. This isn't a game.

She met his gaze straight on, then muttered, *"Debil."* Moron in Polish. "You obviously have me confused with someone else."

"You think?" He leaned over and picked up the driver's license from the bed. He shot her an amused glance. "Sharron Stone? The extra R's a nice touch, but it doesn't sound Polish to me."

"I'm only a quarter Polish," she informed him icily. "I *told* you I wasn't who you think I am."

Her current appearance matched the license. He scrutinized her face as though he was starting to doubt himself. "Her hair was dark of course." He put a hand to her crown and whipped off the blonde wig. Shiny black-coffee-colored hair tumbled to her shoulders. He reached out and touched a strand. It clung to his fingers. He quickly untangled the filaments as though he'd been burned. "Dark hair suits you better."

Her jaw clenched. "There's no law against a woman wearing a wig."

"Hmm, true. The woman I'm looking for was less . . . well endowed than you are . . ." He ran his gaze down her décolletage. Creamy white breasts plumped over the low-cut neckline. "I'd say she was more a B than a D."

Hunt slid his hand between the thin red silk of her barely there dress and the smooth silkiness of her breast.

Taylor's outrage was so great words failed her, a fact that didn't bother her visitor one iota.

"Very nice, he murmured, and she yelped in shock as he pulled out first one, then the other, silicone pad supporting her naked breasts. "But totally unnecessary. You have perfectly lovely breasts that need no padding." Her Anna Nicole bustline immediately went down to a respectable B cup.

The sensation of his callused fingers against her naked breast shocked Taylor into action. She swung up her left hand to slap him. He grabbed her wrist and blocked her lightning-fast knee to his groin, then held her away from him.

His English accent was far more pronounced now as he bit out, "You are *the* most provoking woman."

"And *you* are *the* most insufferable man." Heart racing, she matched him glare for glare.

One of the ways she'd used to deal with the instability of her life when she was a kid was to accept any challenge, any dare that came her way. Wasn't every job she'd ever taken as an adult merely a continuation of that dare? As a kid she quickly learned which walls were scalable and which fences were barbed. She still had the scars where she'd ripped her side open on a fence after accepting the dare to feed the Anderson's rottweiler. Rowdy had wanted to eat nine-year-old Taylor for lunch.

There was a lot of rottweiler in this guy.

She let her eyes shift to the door as she leaned slightly in that direction, as if ready to make a break to the right. His grip tightened on her left arm. *Oh, please, as if—*

With a quick jerky movement she broke free and dashed left. Straight for the slider.

"Bloody hell, woman."

Two seconds, and the door slid open the full nine inches. She slipped through as quickly as a greased eel and onto the foot-deep false balcony. Safety was seconds away. He couldn't possibly fit through the slider to come after her. Triumphant, heart pounding with exhilaration, Taylor threw a leg over the wrought-iron railing—

Only to be unceremoniously jerked backward. Hard fingers gripped her upper arm and yanked her back through the opening. He couldn't squeeze his large body after her, but he had long arms. The whole thing had taken all of five seconds!

Damn.

"Jesus Christ, woman. Do you have a death wish?" He hauled her into the center of the room, not releasing his merciless grip on her arm. Taylor's fingers went numb. He jerked her around to face him. They were close enough for her to see the unadulterated fury in his steel gray eyes. Yeah? Well that made two of them.

"Why? Because I tried to jump?" she demanded, heart still doing the adrenaline gallop. "Or because you think I should be scared of *you?*" The slider was still open. The drape dancing in the breeze. She'd make it the next time.

The shackle of his fingers slid down her arm to her wrist. "You should be a damn sight more afraid of *me* than of taking a header down nine stories."

"Is that so?" She struggled in his grasp, all pretense at serenity gone in a flash of red-hot temper. "Well, I'm not scared of either you *or* heights. I'm freaking *pissed off.* Who the *hell* do you think you are breaking in here and manhandling me like this?"

Eleven

H UNT WASN'T FEELING SANGUINE HIMSELF. ANGER, AROUSAL, and admiration all vied for supremacy. Anger was the most appropriate. "I'm the guy who caught your ass. Again."

He tightened his fingers around her wrists until her hands went pale and bloodless. Satisfied that she'd stay put, he wrapped his hands around her slender, white neck, thumbs feeling the unsteady jump of her pulse at the base of her throat. If he so desired, he could snap her neck like a twig.

She gave the ceiling a look, before staring right back at him. "What are you going to do? Kill me?"

"I'm quite aggravated enough to do so, so don't push it." His voice hardened and became deadly. "No more games. I told you we could do this easy or do it hard. Either way suits me— Jesus fucking Christ! Are you *crying*?" He used his thumbs to tilt up her chin.

Accusatory green eyes sparkled with welling tears. One spilled over, trickling down her cheek as she looked up at him pleadingly.

"Y-You're hurting me. Please. Let me go. I'm n-not who you think I am. I'm really n-not."

For a split second Hunt felt a sharp stab of guilt, but that was gone in a heartbeat. All it took was remembering that this woman was the one who'd left him unconscious and handcuffed to a bed. He slid his hands from her throat, over her smooth shoulders, and down her arms in a caress, seeing the subtle triumph in her shimmering eyes before she lowered those long silky lashes to hide from him. *Oh, no you don't, darling.*

He gripped her fragile wrists in the hard vise of his fingers and, using them as a fulcrum, twisted her onto the bed. She gave a startled cry as he followed her down, covering her slender body with the weight of his own.

A few more crystalline tears dribbled down her temples, her lower lip trembled, but she lay passively beneath him. Hunt transferred her left wrist to his other hand, then used his thumb to wipe away a tear. "You're a real piece of work, you know that, lady?"

The tears were still coming, but behind those fake, tear-filled green eyes was a mind going a mile a minute. If he hadn't been looking at her so closely he might have missed the shift from pitiful victim to seductress.

Her tongue came out briefly to wet her bottom lip. Darker lip liner inside her natural lip line made her lush lips look thinner, but they were the same lying lips he'd felt against his skin in South America.

"P-Please." Her voice held a plaintive wobble. "Please don't hurt me. I'll do anything you want. Just don't h—"

Hunt had two choices. Listen to the latest script she was constructing—or create his own diversionary tactic.

No contest.

He dropped his head down to crush his mouth over hers.

Oh, for . . . An aching warmth spread through Taylor's body as his hardness pressed her into the mattress. It was pretty damn hard to think when she had a ton of rock-solid male on top of her. It was even harder to concentrate when said male kissed her in a blatantly aggressive move that shut off her brain for those critical few seconds she might've used to escape.

She prided herself on thinking on her feet. The fact that she was usually mentally several steps ahead of anyone trying to catch her had saved her butt a time or three. But she wasn't on her feet at the moment.

What was with this guy and beds?

Instead, she lay there being tasted as if she were Huntington St. John's last meal. This was no tentative exploration. No getting to know the shape and feel of lips and tongues. No slow buildup, no leisurely investigation.

This was deep, hard-core French kissing. Raw. Carnal. Possessive. They hadn't kissed in San Cristóbal, yet the taste and texture of his mouth was shockingly . . . familiar.

Helplessly, she clutched his shoulders as lightninglike bolts of pure, white heat zipped from her lips directly down to the juncture of her thighs. The sensation vibrated there like the hum of a tuning fork. She wanted to curl her legs around his hips, but she couldn't move. Her world narrowed until she became pure sensation.

His lips. His teeth—God—his *tongue*. His agile, clever, *devilishly* clever tongue. When he slid it over hers, Taylor swirled her own in response. The flavor of him made her breath come faster, and echoed in her ears with the rapid pounding of her heart. She wanted to touch him, but he controlled both her wrists over her head with one hand.

Every thought, every *bit* of sense in her brain, dissipated like mist on a bright, sunny day. *Well, hell* . . . Her last intelligent thought before she sank beneath the deep sensual waters of the kiss was *escape* . . . later.

He cupped her cheek, his hand cool on her hot skin as he turned her face a little, slanting that clever mouth down her throat. Taylor sucked in a shaky draft of air as he found the spot behind her ear guaranteed to have her arch beneath him.

He murmured against the delicate skin there as her hips moved restlessly, and the echoes of his sexy murmurs sent more shock waves through her. He pressed his hips hard against her, and she thought, *God, yes. More. Harder.*

He took small bites along the tendons in her neck, then laved her sizzling skin with a slick, damp tongue. Taylor about shot off the bed as every nerve, every tendon, every muscle, every cell in her body did the happy dance.

She tried again to free her hands. He wasn't holding her that tightly, but she couldn't break free. She was double-jointed. She could squeeze free of anything. Usually. But no matter what she tried, she couldn't get free of him. Damn him. She attempted to rub her aching nipples against the hard plane of his chest. But he was too heavy to allow even that small movement.

His lips brushed her ear. Taylor's fingers curled and her nails dug into her palms. She *had* to touch him—

"Where are the disks, Taylor?" he asked through a trail of sweet-hot kisses. Faint stubble from his beard scraped against her throat as he lazily nuzzled and nibbled his way up to her ear.

If he'd only release her hands . . . She frowned, then opened her eyes. He'd called her by name. Her *real* name. Oh. My. Lord. He knew her name! *How?* "Wh-What?"

"Disks?" he repeated shortly, not sounding in the least bit loverlike despite the weight of his body pressing intimately in the cradle of her thighs, and his breath whispered across her ear making her shudder. "What. Did. You. Do. With. The. Disks?"

Taylor struggled to bring the room and the man back into focus. His question made her feel like hot tea being poured over ice. The chill was sudden and effective. She scrambled to regroup mentally, while her body parts wept in disappointment.

She blinked up at him while her heart thudded and galloped in her chest and their breath mingled intimately. She could read ab-solutely nothing in his enigmatic face. He might have been made of stone as he looked down at her, apparently unmoved. He was intently, wholly, focused on her. And not in a good way. She felt uncomfort-ably as though he could read her mind.

"You seem awfully damn determined to butt into my business," she said, breath unsteady. She struggled to sound as emotionless as he, while battling equally hard to ignore her body's still clamoring re-sponse to his close proximity. Damn and double damn.

Unlike herself, more fool her, he clearly hadn't been engaged in this activity one iota. She had to hand it to him. It was pretty damn effective. He'd actually conned her into believing he'd been caught up in the passion as intensely as she'd been. She could take lessons from this guy.

She'd been outconned.

He lifted his head to look down at her. His body, his long, lean, *heavy* body, stayed put. His eyes frosted from storm gray to sleet. "I want everything. Papers—documents of any kind. And those disks. Keep the jewelry."

"Keep . . . ? Good of you to allow that."

"Damn good of me. Considering."

"Considering what?"

"Considering that you lied to me about the location of the disks, knocked me unconscious, and left me handcuffed to a bed."

Oh, yeah. She could see that indignity stung. Poor baby. "Okay, I give you those. I can see how they must've looked to your friends. I felt really, really bad about that," Taylor assured him sincerely.

How much did he weigh, for God's sake? A ton? She couldn't *move. Don't freak,* she told herself, trying for a few deep cleansing breaths. Unfortunately all *that* did was press her nipples against his chest and revive her awareness.

Uneasy under such close scrutiny, Taylor shifted. The slight friction between her dress and his shirt against her breasts was enough to cause her nipples to tingle. The hard ridge of his impressive erection, exactly where she wanted it, proved he wasn't as immune as he appeared.

Good Lord. The man was, to her, like Kryptonite to Superman! He made her itch from the inside out.

Her confused emotions—fear, sexual awareness, and intrigue— were dangerous. All three emotions gave her a rush. And God only knew, in her line of work she thrived on that adrenaline rush like a junkie. But it had never manifested itself like this. And the sexual awareness. *That* was a new sensation. She'd never desired any man quite so intensely. And the fact that he intrigued and fascinated her clanged all of her self-preservation alarms.

She had to get out of his force field PDQ. "Look," she said reasonably. "Let's get up, maybe call room service for a snack, and talk about it. I'm sure we can make some sort of equitable deal."

He didn't move. "I don't trust you."

Well, ditto, pal. "Excuse me? *You're* the one who broke into *my* room. I get to be the one not trusting."

If he'd get off her, give her the five seconds it would take to get to the slider and another four seconds to scale the balcony—she'd be gone like the wind. Everything next door was ready for a lightning-fast getaway. A minute and a half—tops—and she'd be a memory.

"I can understand your annoyance," Taylor assured him with utmost sincerity. "Nobody likes to be put in a compromising position. But quite frankly, your request is unreasonable. And might I point out—it's downright *lazy* of you to think you can simply *ask,* and I'll hand over my take just because I did something you couldn't do, and it's *easier* for you."

"Has it occurred to you," he asked dangerously, "that I might be a *good* guy?"

The look he was giving her right now, from *very* close range, was that of a man contemplating dismemberment, and the stuffing of a body—*her body*—into a convenient viaduct. "Not really. No."

Taylor turned to look at the door as a loud knock sounded. "Who—" In trooped four men in dark suits. Hunt didn't seem surprised to see them. Well, *she* was. And not in a good way.

"This is how you interrogate the prisoner?" the man from the elevator asked dryly. He waited until the others were inside, then closed the door and leaned against it, hands in his pockets. So much for thinking he looked like a nice guy earlier, Taylor thought as her heart picked up speed and her brain riffled through escape possibilities.

Jesus, she was a piece of work. Hunt could practically hear the cogs turning in that quick brain of hers. "Kept her from running," he told his men. "Draw your weapons before I release her."

Her fake green eyes widened, and a little color leached out of her cheeks as all four men reached beneath their jackets for their guns. Her eyes came back to Hunt's. "Isn't this overkill?" she said.

"I didn't tell them to shoot you," he told her flatly, as if that order was an option at any time. Still holding her wrists, he levered himself off her, pulling her to her feet with him as he stood.

"Anything?" Aries asked, bending to pick up the wig and silicone pads from the floor. He shot Hunt an amused glance as he tossed them onto the rumpled bed. "You have an interesting interrogation technique."

"Expediency is my middle name." Hunt nudged Taylor Lindsay Kincaid toward a straight-backed chair and reluctantly let go of her wrists. She rubbed her skin with her fingertips, and he winced inwardly as he saw the red marks he'd left on her fair skin. He got over that little ping of guilt in a hurry by reminding himself exactly how slippery she was.

"Sit," he told her firmly. She was like a coiled spring. He didn't see how she could even imagine she was going to make a break for it with five armed men in the room. But he was damned sure she was trying to come up with a way. This time he wasn't taking any chances.

Bishop, Aries, Hallowell, and Tate spread themselves about the room. Hunt took the chair across the small table from her.

She gave him a stony glare. "What's next?" she asked tightly. "Rubber hoses? Water torture?"

"You do have an overactive imagination, don't you?"

"I'm not imagining *this*." She looked around. Her gaze resting briefly on each gun before coming back to Hunt. "Who are your friends? Feds?"

"We work for a counterterrorist organization called T-FLAC."

"Never heard of it."

"If you were a terrorist, you would have."

"Really?" She glanced at each man in turn, up and down, tie to shoes, and back again. "Geez, the government must be paying *really* well these days. Three-thousand-dollar suits and six-hundred-dollar shoes?" She shook her head. "I don't think so." She wiggled her fingers. "Let's see some ID, guys."

"Not government. No ID. Terrorist Force Logistical Command is a privately funded, freelance antiterrorist organization."

She shot him a skeptical look. "And I'm supposed to believe this on faith? Exactly who do you 'freelance' *for?*"

"Anyone with a terrorist problem."

She raised a dark brow. "America?"

"Frequently."

"In other words you work for the highest bidder. You guys are mercenaries."

"You could say that."

"I did. Who decides who the bad guys are?"

Hunt couldn't help but reluctantly admire her nerves of steel. Annoying as hell. A liar, and a thief. But she had brass.

"We do." She was full of questions, and opened her mouth with another one. "Conversation over," Hunt told her flatly.

It pissed him off royally that he could still feel the imprint of her body, supple and yielding against his. Still feel and, God help him, *taste* her on his lips. Still feel reluctant desire thrum through him as keenly now as it had earlier when they'd been alone. As if he still had her pinned to the bed.

She clasped her hands and rested them in her lap, not leaning against the seat back. Ready, Hunt thought sardonically, to make a run for it. He was almost curious enough to allow it, just to see what she'd do. Almost.

"Say I believe you—On *faith,* mind you. Since you expect me to trust you guys without a shred of proof that you are who you *say* you are. *I'm* not a terrorist."

"But you stole something from José Morales, who *is,*" Hunt told her.

"Cut to the chase. Where the fuck are the disks, lady?" Bishop demanded.

Like the rest of the team, Hunt knew Neal Bishop wasn't appreciative of the wild chase she'd led his team on for the last several months. Chasing her had wasted a hell of a lot of time. And everyone on the team was keenly aware of that.

She turned to give Bishop a hard look. "Two things. One, watch your language. Two, don't talk to me in that tone of voice. I don't give a damn who you guys are, I won't be treated with disrespect because you think you can get away with it. I'm listening, but play nicely."

Hunt's lips twitched. "How well do you know José and Maria Morales?" The woman had more balls than good sense.

With her pale skin and wild mane of dark hair, and wearing that red scrap of a dress, she looked like some half-wild wood sprite. Without the bravado, she looked softer, more vulnerable than Hunt had ever seen her. Not weaker, by any stretch of the imagination, but less brittle, less on the defensive. "I've been to several of their parties."

"How did you meet?" Hunt asked her.

"The Konstantinopouloses' yacht party a few years ago."

"Neo Konstantinopoulos?" Bishop asked.

She nodded.

Max's and Hunt's eyes met before Hunt said flatly, "Also a known terrorist."

"Also?" she asked carefully. She was surrounded, but she didn't fidget or even look nervous. Because, Hunt suddenly realized, she had a plan to get away from them before the going got rough. At least, she *thought* she did. She was in for a rude awakening.

"Are you telling us," Hunt raised a brow, "that you *aren't* aware that José Morales is a terrorist?"

"It's not something that has ever come up over cocktails, so the answer is no, of course not." She examined her manicure before glancing up. "All I know is they're an interesting couple, and they give fun parties."

"And you enjoy stealing from your friends?"

"Acquaintances."

Hunt nodded acquiescence. "Your *acquaintance,* Morales, had papers, one or more disks, and possibly a small handheld device in that safe. You removed said items. We want them."

She gave them a considering look. "I don't know about the other things. But there was nothing heavy enough to be a handheld anything. And before you feel obliged to repeat yourself, your friend here already asked. I'll give you the same answer I gave him. *Not going to happen.* I don't take the kind of risks I take to hand everything over to a second party. Besides, *if* I took them—and that's a big *if,* boys—I wouldn't admit it and incriminate myself."

"You stole items critical to national security," Hunt told her, cutting to the chase.

She turned her head to look from Max back to Hunt. If he didn't know better, Hunt might've been fooled by her fragility too. But he did know better. He had a small, months-old scar over his left eyebrow to prove it.

"Why do you guys always hide under the umbrella of 'national security'? If this stuff you're looking for was so damn important, why didn't *you* steal it yourselves?"

Hunt ground his back teeth together and ignored her little jab. She'd done what Fisk, T-FLAC's best sticky-fingers operative, *couldn't.* Opened the bloody safe. Frank Fisk, on hearing that she'd not only opened the Morales safe, but gotten away with the contents, had been bowled over and impressed by her skill. It took a hell of a lot to impress the taciturn Fisk.

Hunt, however was merely annoyed. "Are you under the erroneous impression that our questions are multiple choice?" he asked. "If you don't hand over those items, you'll go to jail for treason." He waited a beat for another thin layer of her confidence to erode.

"Treason is a capital offense. Execution isn't out of the question. Cooperate and we might be able to convince the U.S. Attorney to take the death penalty off the table."

He saw the stark reality sink in. She gave him a level look. "I mailed everything."

She wasn't stupid. Good. That saved time. "To whom?" Hunt asked.

"Myself."

He raised a brow. She'd been arrested in her San Cristóbal hotel room within minutes of arriving back from the party. "Really? And when exactly did you have time to do that?"

She inhaled sharply, let her gaze wander around the room as if considering whether to tell him. When she finally looked to him again, Hunt knew she'd made her choice. "On the way from the party back to my hotel. I carried an addressed, prepaid mailer with me."

"What's the address?" When she hesitated, he gave her a hard look. "The truth."

"I want a lawyer." She folded her arms across her chest, crossed her legs as if she were a debutante at a tea party, and gave him a look that said she was through talking for a while.

Twelve

H UNT ACCESSED SOMETHING ON THE LAPTOP, THEN TURNED the monitor so Taylor could see it. "Sure you can lawyer-up. No problem," he told her. "And we'll send him a copy of *this* so he can start working on your defense."

After a brief hesitation, she glanced down at the monitor. Her real passport photograph was at the top of the page, followed by smaller pictures from each of her alias passports. The text blurred, and her fingers shook as she scrolled down, giving every appearance that she was randomly scrolling, when in fact she was looking for a specific name.

"It's all there," Hunt informed her. "From Reno, where you were born, to the heist this evening at the Houston museum. And everything in between."

She dragged her attention from a grainy photograph of the apartment building she'd lived in as a child to Hunt's face. "How?"

"You weren't thinking about fingerprints in the safe house in San Cristóbal."

Taylor's heart stopped beating for a few horrified seconds. Oh God. She *always* wore thin latex gloves for *work*. And she always pulled on a second pair as she left the scene, a third pair at the first clothing exchange, a fourth on her way back to wherever she was staying. Right now she wore thin latex gloves beneath the frilly black lace. She felt sick to her stomach.

She'd thought of *none* of her usual safety precautions that night when he'd engineered her escape from jail.

Dread filled her. She put a hand up to her forehead, horrified to notice her fingers shook. *Think. Concentrate and think.* Men responded better to a faint than a woman throwing up on their shoes. And although she'd once *done* it to get out of a sticky situation, it was really, really hard to throw up on command. Not that she wasn't perfectly prepared to do it now if it became necessary.

"I—I feel faint," she said weakly to no one in particular. She didn't need to see any more. It was all there. "Can I lie down for a few minutes?"

Hunt turned off the computer and shut it with a loud *snap.* "No." Tundra gray eyes met Taylor's. Her breath shuddered in her lungs, then stopped altogether at Hunt's expression.

"Now that you know that *we* know you aren't really Ginger Grant who is registered in room 902, or Mary Ann Wells—the name you used for this room—maybe you'll wise up and cut the crap."

"If I give you what you want, *I* keep the jewelry. That's the deal." She spoke only to Huntington St. John. As far as Taylor was concerned, there was no one else in the room.

The woman had cojones, Hunt thought with irritated admiration even as he raised a brow at her audacity. "You're in no position to make deals, sweetheart."

"Actually," she countered, "I'm in a *great* position. You want what I've got. Who do you think has the power here?"

"Not the one who's surrounded."

"All in the way you look at things," she said. "And what's wrong with giving me an incentive to share?"

Hunt figured she was buying time. Probably not a good idea to let that incredible mind of hers work unchecked for very long. "How about not going to jail for the rest of your life? How's that for incentive?"

"Please. If I was worried about jail would I be a jewel thief?" She shrugged, then quickly added, "That's *alleged* jewel thief."

"Oh, for fuck sake—" Bishop snarled.

Hunt put up his hand to stop Neal's blustering and kept his attention on Taylor. "Now that you're aware that Morales is a terrorist," he said, giving her the benefit of the doubt, "do you for a moment believe that he too isn't looking for you to get back what you stole from him?"

"*He* can't possibly know who I am."

"Why not? We do. And what about the woman who approached you in San Cristóbal before the robbery?" Hunt pushed harder. "The one who wanted you to steal the contents of the safe for *her*? Who do you think *she* was? A nun looking for a donation to the church? We believe she was a member of the Black Rose."

"The Black Rose?"

"Another deadly terrorist group known for their senseless torture of informants, enemies—hell, pretty much anyone. By design or default—and we don't really give a damn which it is—you've not only compromised national security, you've made some powerful and lethal enemies."

As if dealing with one terrorist organization wasn't enough. Jesus bloody Christ.

Hunt continued, "You're caught between Scylla and Charybdis."

"And *you*."

"And me," Hunt agreed. "*We* found you. The Black Rose found you in San Cristóbal. How long do you think it'll take them, or Morales's *Mano del Dios,* to track you down again?"

She bit her lip, the only sign that they were getting through to her. When she realized what she was doing, she stopped. Her chin came up.

"Uncomfortable having so many people breathing down your neck when you're trying to do such a good job keeping that low profile of yours, isn't it?"

Hell, yes, Taylor thought, she was more than *uncomfortable* knowing that so many people had discovered her identity. Up to and including her real name.

She could see the suave Mr. Huntington St. John out of the corner of her eye. He moved with the sinuous tread of a big cat. No wasted motion, no abrupt movements. It was unnerving. As though he were waiting for his prey to bolt from the tall grass and make a run for it before he streaked after her, all determination and ripping white teeth.

Her wild imagination was going to trip her up if she wasn't very, very careful. *Get a grip,* Taylor warned herself. *Just get a grip.* No matter *who* he was, or *what* he threatened, he was only a man. She reminded herself that she interacted with wealthy, sophisticated men every day of the week.

The other guys didn't bother her nearly as much as he did. "I want to make a phone call."

"No."

No matter who these guys *said* they were, good guys or bad, she'd die before she led them, or anyone else, to Switzerland and her sister. She hadn't seen Amanda's name in their document. But that didn't mean they didn't know about her. Did they? She had no reason to believe, as thorough as they'd been, that they'd miss Mandy. She could only pray that *somehow* they had.

If she went to jail, if she *died,* Mandy would be well taken care of for the rest of her life. Taylor had promised herself that no matter how horrible it might be for herself, she'd do whatever it took to protect her sister. *Whatever* it took.

All eyes were focused on her, but Hunt's were the only pair that unnerved her. She paused several beats as she considered her options. "All right," she told him flatly. "Give me forty-eight hours to retrieve what you're asking for." She'd fly to Switzerland, see what she had, and go from there. If she deemed the take to truly be of importance to national security, she'd courier it back to them. If not, seeing as how it was so damn important, she'd *sell* it to them. For a pretty penny for the inconvenience.

"Let you out of my sight?" Hunt said blandly. "Not going to happen."

How much should I give them to back off? Everything, she realized. Hunt would settle for nothing less. "It's in a secure safety-deposit box in Switzerland. I'll have it couriered to wherever you like."

"Contact the airport," Hunt told the elevator man flatly. "And what?" Hunt turned to ask her. "I'm supposed to ask you for the location and a password again?"

"The password isn't the problem." Oh, God. She hated this. Hated giving up this much information. Hate, hated, *hated,* letting anyone get this close to Amanda. But she was short on options. At least for now. "It requires a retinal scan."

"Look around you, sweetheart. Do we seem like amateurs to you?"

She swallowed and shook her head.

"High-powered plasma lasers are a *problem.* Retinal scans are child's play."

"So, I give you the password and you handle it from there?" she asked, feeling a tad relieved knowing this ordeal was almost over. "Great. I'm glad we could reach a mutually satisfying agreement. I'll jot down the password and be on my merry way."

His expression lingered somewhere between a scowl and what she was sure, for him, passed as a smile. That look made the hair on the back of her neck lift.

"That's one option," he agreed.

Too easy, she thought.

"But that would mean I'd have to remove one of your eyes in order to get past the retinal scan."

She should have known. Taylor felt and tasted revulsion and pulled a face.

"Didn't think you'd be too keen on that option." His fingertip reached out and gently grazed the side of her face. "And I didn't have any desire to disfigure you for life. So we'll go with the less . . . invasive option."

"Which is?"

"We're all going to Switzerland."

Thirteen

I HAVE ASCERTAINED NOTHING ABOUT THIS MAN," ANDREAS CONstantine told Morales over the scrambled private line in José's London office. "This thief has never been caught, never so much as been *seen*. He is a ghost. A chimera."

"Unacceptable." José Morales sat down heavily in his chair. His empire was crumbling, and no one was helping him shore it up. "*Someone* must know the name of this offal who has robbed the *Mano del Dios* of their future." The San Cristóbal *policía* originally claimed to have captured a female member of the gang. But that information had proven erroneous.

God showed his impatience by sending an excruciating pain through José's belly. He clenched his teeth and rode out the pain, refusing to take his medication in front of his people. No sign of weakness was permitted. "One million American dollars to whoever delivers the person stupid enough to steal from me, José Morales. The man will first pay with his fear, then with his life."

"The word is out there. Everyone is trying to find out who he is.

We'll find him soon, I assure you." Constantine said flatly. "But we have another serious problem, José. There is speculation that T-FLAC is involved."

"*Madre de Dios,* Andreas. *T-FLAC?*" José crossed himself. "T-FLAC is aware of the theft? Now? So close—?" His mind raced with the ramifications of this new piece of information.

If the counterterrorist organization was responsible for the robbery, then they had access to the mine. He prayed that this was not so. "*They* sent this person to rob me?"

Constantine paused. "Either T-FLAC or Black Rose."

"*I will call upon God, and the Lord shall save me.*" Morales crossed himself, and shut his eyes. "*Evenings and mornings and at noon I will pray and cry aloud and He shall hear my voice.*" The men bowed their heads until he finished speaking, then said in unison, "Amen."

Fourteen

TAYLOR DIDN'T SAY A WORD, SARCASTIC OR OTHERWISE, ON THE drive from the downtown hotel to the airport. But Hunt read something in her eyes. Fear? Apprehension? Nope, mutiny most likely. Knowing Taylor, she was probably already plotting her next great escape. He wasn't about to let that happen. Again.

His men accompanied them, and all waited, much to her obvious amusement, while she retrieved a suitcase from a locker in the busy concourse at George Bush Intercontinental.

She'd escaped him once, and if it entertained her knowing it took seven men to watch her every move in a crowded public airport, so be it. Hunt curtly refused her request to go into the restroom to change out of the outrageous red dress. Time enough for that once they were in flight.

Then, if she wanted to get away, her only option would be a free fall at thirty thousand feet. She was a lot of things, but he didn't think stupid or suicidal were among them.

"How many suitcases are waiting at how many airport terminals, do you think?" Max Aries asked Hunt as they watched her wrestle the small case from the locker. The two men stood slightly apart from the others.

"With this woman? Probably at least one complete disguise in every airport in the world," Hunt answered flatly. They'd emptied the second hotel room of her personal effects before she'd returned and found another disguise. Wig, brown contacts, a change of clothing, and another passport.

Frowning, Hunt watched Austin, a younger agent, help her with the recalcitrant case, and dissolve under Taylor's smiling thanks. He'd have to caution Austin about the dangers of smiling women— especially *this smiling* woman—at the first opportunity.

Annoyed, and not quite sure why, Hunt motioned the others to get the lead out. They had a plane to catch. No matter that it was a private T-FLAC jet, fueled and waiting for him and his team. The point was, they had a schedule to keep, and by damn, he was through letting the little jewel thief screw with his plans. She was both an aggravation and a lure.

Hunt fell behind with Max as the group finally moved, *en masse,* down the concourse, Bishop now carrying the small case. "Whoever the hell's making her passports is a genius," Hunt said. "With her ability to completely change her appearance, coupled with brilliantly forged documents, no wonder she can disappear into thin air. She's good. But without those perfect papers, she'd have been easier to catch. Never seen anything like them. You?"

Max shook his head. "Work like that doesn't come cheap."

"She can afford it." And more. She must have enough money to buy a medium-sized country, for God's sake.

What could she possibly be talking to Bishop and Austin about? And why in the hell did he give a continental damn? Still, he'd lengthened his stride, to close the gap, when Max put a hand on his arm. "Maybe you should let someone else head up this portion of the mission," his friend said.

That stopped him. He snapped Max a dark look. "Who'd you have in mind? You?"

Max shrugged. "It's a little too tame for me, but my head is on my shoulders, not between my legs."

"When I need your damn advice on when to get laid, I'll let you know."

Max lifted both hands and shook his head. "I'm just saying—"

"I know what you're saying and my pants are firmly zipped. Not that it's any of your damn business." He'd said it mildly enough, but wanted to punch out his friend for being *that* good at reading him. "Hell, it's tame for both of us. But not for long. The second we have those codes, we'll mobilize, and you'll have all the excitement you need."

"Promises, promises."

Max Aries was an adrenaline junkie, a trait Hunt was fairly sure he had in common with Taylor Kincaid. If her performance at the gallery was any indication, she did her best work under pressure. Impressive, Hunt thought, too bad she'd chosen to use her powers for bad instead of good. Criminal deeds instead of something in a more legal arena.

She was attracting a lot of attention. At this ungodly hour of the morning most people were bleary-eyed and looked as though they'd dressed in the dark. Barely five A.M., and Taylor was still wearing the painted-on, short, tight, screaming-red cocktail dress. Maybe his curt dismissal of her request to change had been a minor tactical error on his part. Taylor looked as out of place strolling through the airport as a hooker at a church picnic.

And poor helpless morons were swallowing their tongues and walking into walls while taking in the low-cut dress parenthesizing her breasts. The breast men's eyes stayed on the pale twin globes. Glazed and greedy. The leg men let their attention skim her body down to her creamy pale, mile-long legs encased in high-heeled sandals. One poor idiot walked into a pillar. Another tripped over a trash barrel.

An irritated glance showed Hunt the ass men, turning around when they passed, or even walking backward to keep her in their sights. Jesus.

He almost wished that Interpol and the State Department had been called in to interrogate and remove her.

Hunt stepped between her and Bishop like a guy cutting another man out on a dance floor. He glanced at her profile as they walked side by side. Apparently oblivious to the attention she was garnering, she stared straight ahead. But if he knew women, which he did, and this one in particular, which he did, her brain was going a mile a minute. As stupid as it would be for her to try, he was braced for her to make a run for it at any moment.

She glanced at him, a glint of humor in her eyes as she lifted one perfectly shaped brow. "Do I have something on my face?" Now he could see that she was indeed aware of the reaction she had on the men around her. She'd dressed to impress.

He picked up the pace. Her long legs kept up easily. He imagined her smooth, creamy thighs—the fractional area not revealed by the short dress—as she walked, and found his jaw aching from grinding his teeth. "No," he finally replied.

"Then stop staring at me," she told him crisply.

Hunt was doing his best to ignore her considerable sex appeal. It was an uphill battle. He'd never had a weakness for milk white skin, but he was rapidly developing one. God only knew. She was exposing most of hers in that barely there scrap she was wearing.

She not only looked like a walking centerfold, she exuded an "I'm available for the taking" signal that was unmistakable. The depth of his annoyance came as a surprise. Why did he give a flying fuck *how* many men wanted her? Or how many passersby stared avariciously at her long, pale legs and velvety décolletage? "A cat can look at a king," he told her sharply, irritated at himself.

She frowned. "What does that mean?"

"It means," he snarled, "if you want to go unnoticed, don't wear a dress that shouts *Hey, buddy, check me out!*"

"That's very caveman of you."

"You asked."

"And believe me, I'm regretting it." She glanced up at him. "Besides, it's not my fault. I *wanted* to change clothes, remember? *You're* the one who said no."

"And believe me," Hunt told her grimly, "I'm regretting it."

"Whatever," Taylor muttered, her cheeks flushing with—must be anger, no woman dressing this way could possibly have an embarrassed bone in her body.

Hunt picked up the pace again, forcing her, and the whole team to catch up in a hurry. She shouldn't really be pretty, for God's sake. Average nose. Average chin. Dark hair. Good body. Great legs. No big deal. But somehow, it was. *She* was.

A tired-looking businessman glanced up, saw Taylor strolling toward him, and did a classic double take. Then he walked into a row of seats and did a pratfall.

Jesus. She was a lethal weapon.

And unlike him, these strangers hadn't seen her most spectacular feature—her incredible blue eyes. And it wasn't as though they'd touched that skin and *knew* it felt like velvet.

One incredibly amazing *almost* sexual encounter shouldn't give him this possessive feeling of ownership. It never had before. They hadn't even gotten to the good stuff. His annoyance needle zinged completely off the meter. Hell, all he'd done was kiss her . . . touch her . . . bloody hell.

Bishop held the door open for her, and she passed through to the secure area flanked by his team. If she so much as looked as though she was going to—what? Hunt asked himself. What the hell did he expect her to do? Anything. Everything.

He didn't *know.* He just knew she'd do *something.* And soon. She'd make her play before boarding the plane. No way was she going to meekly go along with this. It wasn't in her nature.

They passed through the TSA checkpoints unfettered. He drew everyone to a halt at a conveniently placed table through the doors onto the runway. "Hand me that," he told the younger man. Austin passed him her case.

"Hold on to her," he told Bishop. "And, all of you. Watch her like hawks. Don't even blink."

He wanted to remind them that the woman was ostensibly their prisoner, not a prom date, for sweet Christ's sake. But if he gave *them* that lecture, he'd have to listen to it himself, and he wasn't in the freaking mood.

"Shoot her if she moves more than half an inch." He tossed the not surprisingly heavy suitcase onto the flat surface and sprang the latches. "Not in the head though. Go for the leg. Or a gut wound. We'll need her eyes."

Taylor shook her head as if he were nuts. "I'm behaving," she reminded him, irritated. "Which is more than I can say for you."

"Lady," Hunt growled, "trust me when I say if I wasn't on my best damn behavior, you'd be bound and gagged and tossed into the cargo hold. So don't fucking push me."

Both of her eyebrows lifted. "I'm guessing there weren't any charm schools in your background."

"You'd be guessing wrong." Although charm school wasn't what the schools he'd gone to were called. "Don't get any ideas." Hunt flipped the lid, then systematically went through the suitcase, looking for any concealed weapons or anything else she might have stashed in case of emergency. Hell, it wouldn't surprise him if she had a parachute packed away—just in case.

This woman didn't leave anything to chance, so neither would he.

She stood by, unmoved, watching him sift through silky panties and see-through bras. He removed two passports, one in her own name, Swiss, and another in the name of Gloria LeRue, from the Netherlands, and tucked them into his back pocket. Satisfied by his inspection, and hating the fact he'd been turned on by the feel of her sheer lingerie, he slammed the lid and closed the case.

Aries and Bishop preceded them across the tarmac and boarded the jet. The others would leave the airport after takeoff, awaiting further orders. Hunt indicated the rolling stairs beside the plane to Taylor. "Move it."

She laid her hand on her chest and heaved a dramatic sigh. "Since you ask so nicely . . ." She gripped the handrail and started up the metal stairs, giving him a spectacular view of her taut butt beneath the clingy red silk, and a close-up view of her truly spectacular bare legs as she climbed ahead of him in those sexy high-heeled sandals.

His own observation, and his reaction to her, continued to piss him off. He didn't *want* to find this woman sexy. She was merely a means to an end. But it was impossible to forget the feel of her supple body beneath his, or the taste of her mouth.

She disappeared through the door, and since he'd lagged behind to ogle her, he had to sprint up the rest of the stairs to catch up. He was male, she was certainly all woman. A man would have to be dead, buried, and nailed into his coffin *not* to react to such overt sensuality.

Fine. His body could crave all it wanted. His dick wasn't in charge. His brain was.

But damn it to hell. It was worse than a sexual attraction. He found Taylor Kincaid . . . *fascinating.*

In less than twenty-four hours, Miss Taylor Kincaid would be someone else's problem. Twenty-two hours, thirty minutes, ten seconds . . . not that he was counting.

Fifteen

As Taylor walked several paces ahead of Hunt, her hips swaying gently beneath the silk, he was disconcerted to realize just how much he admired her. Because, God only knew, he *distrusted* her. In spades. Still, he couldn't deny he admired her moxie. It was frankly disconcerting to find himself more emotionally in tune with someone—male or female—than he'd been in *years,* despite the fact that he disapproved of her lifestyle.

He fervently hoped that there would be enough intel on the disks to make her further presence completely redundant.

Although the Bombardier Challenger could easily carry fourteen, for this twelve-hour flight to Zurich there were only the six of them aboard: Aries, Bishop, the pilot, co-pilot, Hunt, and his unwilling travel companion.

"I'll put in the call," Max paused to tell Hunt, as he followed Bishop down the aisle between two rows of wide leather seats.

"I'll join you in a minute," Hunt replied. The two other men strode to the back of the plane, then went inside the aft cabin and closed the door.

"Everyone on board?" Hunt turned to acknowledge the co-pilot, Paul Roberts, as he came out to secure the cabin doors. "We're cleared for takeoff whenever you're ready."

"Ready," Hunt said, turning back to keep an eye on Taylor as she walked ahead of him.

"Tailwinds most of the way," Roberts told him, heading back to the cockpit. "We'll make good time."

As far as Hunt was concerned, every second shaved off the time he was around Taylor Kincaid would be greatly appreciated. It was a test of his own self-control to keep her isolated and insulated from his team, but he'd overcome worse. He couldn't risk her seducing one of his men to escape. The thought of her with another man had Hunt seeing red.

He put out his hand to touch her shoulder to get her attention. Bad idea. He didn't want to touch her, and jerked his hand to the side to grip a seat back instead.

"Is piloting a plane one of your talents?" he demanded more harshly than he'd intended.

She glanced at him over her shoulder, a small smile tweaking the corners of her lush mouth. "Scared I'll stage a hijacking?"

He did his best to remain unmoved by her smile and the glint of rueful humor in her eyes. He was almost sorry now that he'd let her remove the fake green contacts before leaving the hotel. Every time he looked into those pale, crystal blue eyes, his body felt as though it were under attack, or in the grips of a fever. Fanciful nonsense, he warned himself.

"Can you pilot a plane?" he repeated. He wouldn't put that skill past her. Not that he was concerned. This was a T-FLAC aircraft, and as such, had more fail-safes than an average plane.

She chose one of the comfortable leather seats in the center of the craft and sat down, then buckled herself in as he intentionally loomed over her. "I don't know how to fly a plane," she assured him with utmost sincerity as she took her sweet time crossing her legs. "I don't

know how to parachute either. You already know I don't have a gun."
She held her arms away from her body. "You can see I don't have any
concealed weapons on my person."

Oh yes you do, he thought, not jumping to the bait.

Her eyes sparkled as she taunted him with a small smile. "You can
relax and feel completely at ease knowing I'm absolutely defenseless.
Satisfied?"

He felt a lot of things, but satisfied wasn't among them. Nor at
ease. Far from it. *And* she'd be defenseless only around a blind man. A
blind man with no sense of smell, Hunt thought with annoyance,
acutely aware of the subtle floral fragrance of her pale skin.

"I'll let you know." He tossed a handful of magazines into her lap
as the plane started taxiing down the runway. "Amuse yourself. I have
calls to make."

She frowned. "Wh—"

"Business," he told her flatly. "Stay put until further notice."

"I'm starving. When will you be back with food and complimen-
tary beverages?"

"This isn't British Airways, sweetheart. If you're very well be-
haved, I'll let you get up and go to the galley after we're in the air. It's
self-serve, so you can get anything you want."

"A sharp knife?" she asked sweetly as he passed her.

"Not bloody likely. I wouldn't trust you with a dull spoon." He met
and held her gaze. "Stop treating this like some game for your personal
amusement. You're in my world. My rules. Don't underestimate me."

"Or what? You'll kill me? Only after you have what you want, of
course," she pointed out with a dangerous glow in her eyes.

Jesus. Did the woman have a death wish? "Consider your quality
of life between now and then," Hunt warned through clenched teeth.
"I'll be watching you."

Without waiting for a smart-assed reply, Hunt strode off to join his
men.

The custom jet featured a private aft cabin containing a compact
but extremely efficient high-tech office and second bathroom. Wall
units discreetly housed either a small conference table or a couple of
fairly decent beds.

The conference table was in the center of the room. The other two men were on the speakerphone. Hunt indicated they all use headsets. He left the door ajar so he could see her. After buckling himself into a chair, he slipped on his headset.

As the plane roared down the runway then gathered itself for the leap into the sky, Hunt watched her. Her fingers tightened briefly on the arms of her seat, but her features were placid, relaxed, *beautiful*.

She wasn't reading any of the magazines. Instead she stared through the porthole at the scudding clouds. What was going on in that agile mind of hers? he wondered, before being forced back to his conversation with their Control.

There was no need for Michael Wright, who was the Control on this op, to rehash Black Rose's involvement. Nothing new had come up. However, Black Rose's interest in Morales's codes was cause for grave concern. The group seemed to be all over the place as far as terror attacks went.

T-FLAC hadn't been able to ascertain who Black Rose's leader was, nor any of its members. They didn't know where they met, or how they communicated. The only lead they had was that each member of the group had a black rose tattooed on the small of their backs. Not much to go on.

Black Rose wasn't the issue at the moment, Wright said. Morales and the *Mano del Dios were*.

"We have confirmation of the Antwerp/South America connection," he told them. "Belgian police arrested Hans Ausberg two days ago on charges of diamond smuggling and illegal weapons sales. When they analyzed bank records and other data on his computer, they made the connection to Morales. Didn't know what to do with the intel, contacted Interpol, who in turn contacted T-FLAC."

Hunt's men looked at one another. They should have known this would get more complicated.

"Blood diamonds via *Mano del Dios*?" Austin asked.

"Blood diamonds" were stones mined and sold by warring factions in Africa. From Angola to the Congo and Sierra Leone.

"More than likely," Hunt agreed.

Despite the UN-mandated embargo on stones mined in Sierra

Leone and Liberia, the gems were currently openly smuggled into Antwerp, Belgium, and other diamond centers, where they melted into the anonymous diamond chain worldwide. Diamonds were an integral part of the finances of terrorists precisely because they were the one commodity that knew no boundaries and no allegiance to any government. A diamond sold in Amsterdam based on carat weight, not country of origin.

They were the perfect currency for criminals of all sorts and terrorists specifically. They were easy to smuggle, transport, and sell. And terrorists understood better than most legitimate brokers how to take advantage of the deregulation that had come with globalization, where international financial transfers were instantaneous and almost impossible to trace. In exchange for the diamonds, Morales would be paid—handsomely, Hunt assumed—in cash and weapons. Then the whole cycle began again.

"So *Mano del Dios* is laundering diamonds through Antwerp to purchase arms. Not a revelation." Damn it. They needed something solid. Something concrete to go on. Right now they didn't even know which bloody continent they should be looking at. Hunt leaned back in his chair and looked out to make sure Taylor was sitting quietly.

"Correspondence indicates Morales was looking to buy sophisticated surface-to-air missile systems and powerful rockets from half a world away," Max reported. "The order from Morales went to Antwerp, then was relayed to Central America. Mejía Luis Godoy in the Nicaraguan army, with the aid of a South African arms dealer based in Panama and a Russian based in Guatemala, filled the orders."

"Despite increases in diamond mining activity in Africa," Wright added, "export figures show the numbers plummeting for the last six months. Our analysts have been keeping a close eye on it."

"And?" Hunt asked. There had to be more.

"We don't know where the hell the diamonds are going," Wright told them flatly.

"Let me know when we figure it out," Hunt told him.

"Will do." The line went dead.

"So that's it," Hunt said to the others. "Conjecture is, the diamonds are going to Antwerp in exchange for the weapons."

"A drop in the bucket, according to Wright," Bishop pointed out. "We're not sure that it *is* Morales taking those diamonds." The frustration level rose.

"Let's say we *are* sure," Hunt offered, "and take it from there." He walked over to the maps and flipped them to access a map of the world.

Bishop tapped a pen on the table. "Then he's stockpiling them to purchase more ordnance."

"Or stockpiling them to drive up the price." Hunt placed colored pins on the map where they currently had intel or men on the ground. "Either way, where would he stash them?"

"Africa? Sierra Leone perhaps?" Max Aries answered, staring at the map.

Hunt wasn't so sure. "Too volatile. Someplace easily bought, easily manipulated."

"I agree with Neal," Max said. "Africa. Sierra Leone is part of al Qaeda's financial architecture. Morales would ship them out of the region. Fast. Before bin Laden's people know they're missing." Max wrote notes on a tablet in front of him.

Bishop jumped in. "Wright sent this information via encryption." He scanned it, then read out loud. " 'We intercepted an encrypted e-mail from Morales to his representative in Hong Kong about an order.' " He then paraphrased the message, which noted the usual rifles and ammo, fifty SA-8 missiles, a thousand rockets for BM-21 multirocket launchers, several thousand Dragunov sniper rifles, and untold smaller, portable munitions. "And an end-user certificate," Bishop concluded. "The order was made sixty days ago and the ongoing discussion is about payment for the order. Or lack thereof."

Hunt didn't like the sound of that. "The asking price must be pretty bloody steep if Morales is stalling."

Bishop cleared his throat.

Hunt sharpened his gaze. "What is it?"

"The payment? One point seven *billion*." Bishop coughed out the last word.

The oxygen was all but sucked out of the room. Billion. Morales wasn't playing.

"Jesus," Hunt said.

Max took a long drink of soda. "What's the bet that's from the blood diamonds he's been stockpiling?"

Bishop frowned. "But why hasn't he retrieved them and paid up out of the thirty billion we estimate they have stashed?"

"He's spent, or spending, the money on something else," Hunt offered.

Bishop and Max clearly had no answer. If T-FLAC knew, they'd all be flying on a mission to retrieve or disassemble the weaponry.

Morales wasn't simply collecting traditional munitions. No, he'd spent the last year acquiring chemicals and biological components as well. In massive quantities.

"Confirmation on the chemicals?" Hunt asked, still watching Taylor through the partially open door as he got up to grab a sandwich; old chicken salad, his favorite.

"Yeah. He's got 'em up the yazoo now," Max said, his tone grim as Hunt resumed his seat at the table. "The Pakistani shipped the nerve agents and paralytics three days ago. Japan's EBINA supplied him with military-grade liquid explosives."

He knew the EBINA didn't mess around. They dealt in high-tech stuff. An epoxylike combination of agents that could be transported safely in separate containers, but mix them, and bang! Serious blow-up power.

"Holy crap," Aries said, getting up to go to the small hidden fridge. "Merely having all that shit in the same place is enough to turn my hair white." He returned to the conference table with several cans and set the sodas in the middle. They'd need caffeine, sugar, and sustenance before this briefing was over.

Their headsets buzzed—never good when Control called twice in the same thirty minutes. They hadn't even finished reading the intel he'd sent.

"We're listening," Hunt said, giving the go-ahead.

"He's done amassing." Wright's voice was grim. "We've deciphered the dummy shipping manifests. Everything's been shipped, very quietly and efficiently to southern Africa via Mozambique."

"What does he want in Africa?" Max said. "Doesn't make sense.

Sierra Leone I get, South Africa? What's the attraction?" Max demanded.

The pieces began to fall into place. "They have AIDS in Africa," he pointed out. "But he's already bombed several clinics there in the last five years. Not that he wouldn't keep destroying them as long as they have patients." AIDS was a hot button to Morales because of its sexual connotation. "He's going to kill them to save them. Makes sense in his fucked-up brain."

"Yeah," Wright agreed. "It does. But we haven't tracked any unusual activity on that continent since he did the South African Embassy sarin gas episode in The Hague, in 2004."

"Who's inside?" Hunt asked.

Wright answered, "Coetzee's been on red alert in Jo'burg for the past three months. He's got a rock-solid contact on the inside of *Mano,* but there hasn't been a whisper there about any impending activity in that region."

"How in the bloody hell is he keeping something *this* big, *this* quiet?" Hunt frowned. Friday the thirteenth. New York? They'd checked, double-checked, and triple-checked. Nothing significant was scheduled for that date.

"We have a time," Wright told the team. "Confirmed. Friday, October thirteenth. Eleven thirty-three GMT."

"Eleven *thirty-three*? That's pretty goddamned precise." Hunt rubbed his jaw. "Is this from a reliable source?"

Wright's chuckle was a bit rusty. "In our line of business? We've been contacted by our female informant on the inside. Who the hell knows what ax she has to grind, but it's all we've got, so let's go with it until we learn different."

The mystery woman had been tipping them off for several months. Never *enough,* however. She was always extremely vague. And extremely frightened. They speculated that she worked in the Morales household in a trusted position.

"She didn't give us a location?"

"Negative."

"Then let's hope to hell she contacts us again. Soon. In the meantime, let's say *not* East Coast time," Hunt suggested. "Central? Mountain? I doubt it, but check, would you? Pacific Time . . . that would make it 3:33. We've already looked at San Francisco. But look again. But if I were a betting man—"

"And a religious zealot," Max added.

"Las Vegas," Hunt finished, coming to the same conclusion at the same time as Wright and Max.

"I'm on it as we speak." Through his headset, Hunt heard the computer keys clicking from Michael Wright's end.

"My gut tells me Vegas is *Mano's* Friday the thirteenth target," Hunt repeated. He *knew* he was right. And so did the other members on the team. Las Vegas was exactly Morales's twisted cup of tea. A large city filled with sinners. Perfect. Perfectly twisted. Hunt felt a familiar sensation in his gut.

He didn't know *how* he was this sure, but God help them all, he was positive. "He's going to do a long-range, soft-target launch from somewhere in southern Africa."

"Christ." Wright was typing furiously in the background, sending the intel to relevant operatives to confirm or deny. "Inputting the data . . . sounds far-fetched as hell. But my educated guess is, you're right . . . Sending it to . . ." He spoke away from his mic. "Yeah. Okay. Done. We're on it." Then, back with the team, he continued, "I've put in to take inventory of guidance chips and hardware."

Mano del Dios had a long-launch guidance missile hidden, and hidden bloody well. *Somewhere* in Africa.

"Bloody hell," Hunt said, more to himself than the others. "The son of a bitch is just crazy enough to try it. But a seven-thousand-nautical mile air strike? Who has the necessary tech knowledge to make that happen?"

"We'll find out," Wright told him, not a shred of doubt in his voice.

Sixteen

HUNT WATCHED TAYLOR THROUGH THE PARTIALLY OPEN DOOR, not distracted at all by the length of her pale, smooth legs as she propped her crossed ankles on the seat opposite and stared out of the large porthole.

"We're ready to move at a moment's notice," he told Wright as she lay her head back and closed her eyes. "Have the rest of my team deployed to Zurich. As soon as we have the disks, we'll transmit."

"Forty-eight hours," Wright reminded them unnecessarily. "Aries, I need you in Poland ASAP. Let me know when you're clear."

Max gave Hunt a shrug. "Will do."

"What are you going to do with the woman once you have the disks?" Bishop wanted to know.

"Hand her over to Interpol when I—we're done with her," Hunt told him flatly. "Or whoever else wants her. I'm sure the list is a mile long."

"And on that list," Max reminded him without inflection, "are

Mano del Dios and possibly Black Rose. She'd better hope Interpol gets to her first."

"Interpol," Bishop inserted as he rose. "At least she'd have a fighting chance with them." He walked into the head and closed the door.

"*If* that tango connection has been cleaned up," Hunt remembered, feeling a distinct chill. Another T-FLAC group was following leads on an Interpol/terrorist connection. Releasing her would be certain death—but he doubted she'd want their "protection" anyway. Too damned independent for her own good, Taylor Kincaid wouldn't thank anyone for trying to save her.

Not his bloody problem, Hunt cautioned himself. But the thought of her in the hands of either the Black Rose or *Mano del Dios* bothered him a great deal. "We could send her to Montana, I suppose," he said reluctantly, annoyed that what happened to her—one way or the other—impinged on him at all. By suggesting she be sent to HQ in Montana, he was taking tacit responsibility for her safety. Hell. When had he started to feel responsible?

"I'll start the ball rolling," Wright offered. "Control out."

"She's going to be trouble," Max told Hunt blandly, removing his earpiece. Trouble, Max's eyes told him, for both him *and* T-FLAC.

"*Going* to be?" Hunt said dryly, tossing his headset onto the table as he stood. "She's a pain in the ass now."

"Remember *the Curse*," Max said quietly.

Right, Hunt thought grimly. *The fucking, always there, not to be bucked, Curse. Let's never forget* that. "Not applicable," he assured Max.

"*Always* applicable," Max shot back.

Hunt shook his head. Max was way off. "Are you nuts? I've known the woman for all of five seconds. Love isn't even close to the emotions I feel when I'm around her. Pissed, frustrated, hell—*homicidal*—would all be more appropriate."

"Horny." Max smirked.

Hunt wouldn't deny the obvious. He wasn't a monk. "That too. And perfectly controllable."

"It's a lot easier to control a hard-on than it is your emotions."

"Is that a fact?" Hunt responded, forcing a lightness into his tone he didn't feel. For the last several months "easy" wasn't what he'd call his control over his irrational lust for Taylor Kincaid. Since the moment he'd met her he'd wanted her.

He had only eight more hours of this sheer physical torture to endure, and then she'd be gone. He could do it. He *would* do it. Lust was eminently controllable. He knew he was very good at compartmentalizing his emotions.

Lust was controllable. *Love* wasn't.

Which he'd learned the hard way, and to his eternal detriment.

Twenty-nine-year-old Sylvie had been tall, blonde, sophisticated, and five years older than Hunt when they'd met at a boring fundraiser in D.C. He'd just obtained his law degree from the University of London and returned home to D.C. to visit his father. He'd had a month's vacation due before reporting to T-FLAC headquarters in Montana for briefing.

It hadn't taken the entire month for Hunt to fall in love with the beautiful young law clerk. He'd been crazy in love with her halfway through their first week together. He and Sylvie had been inseparable—

"You've already tried bucking *the Curse,*" Max reminded him, reading his mind as only a good friend could. "It almost killed you."

"*Almost* being the operative word," he replied. "The experience inoculated me. I've been completely immune ever since. Besides, in a few hours the situation will resolve itself." The plane would land in Zurich, *she'd* hand off the disks, and he'd never see her again.

Max gave him a steady look. "Only fools and the terminally arrogant think they can beat it."

"Those words are permanently engraved in my DNA," Hunt assured him.

"What curse?" Bishop asked, coming out of the head.

"The L-O-V-E Curse," Max spelled out for the younger man, still looking at Hunt. "The most deadly curse of all. One of the reasons we do our frikking job so well is because we're all alike. We have a need to control our environment. And we *do* that with the work we do. Until we—"

"Until we're fool enough to bring a woman into the equation," Hunt inserted. "Then we're screwed. There's not a bloody thing a man can control about love. It's messy, painful, traitorous, and unstable."

"Love is the Curse," Max said. "It's a no-win situation, and the sooner you wrap your brain around *that* one, kid, the better off you'll be."

Bishop frowned, glancing from Hunt to Max and back again. "There *are* exceptions . . ."

They both shook their head at his näiveté. "Famous last words," Hunt said. "Famous bloody last words. *We* said and believed them ourselves—once." Hunt mock-saluted Max and strode out of the aft cabin.

He had eight hours to kill.

Taylor was curled up, fast asleep in her seat. Obviously she hadn't been the least bit bothered by his scrutiny during the briefing. Skirting a low table, Hunt swiveled the chair opposite so it faced hers, then sat down.

He stretched out his long legs and rested his clasped hands on his flat belly, allowing himself a few quiet uninterrupted moments to study her when she didn't have all her defenses up.

One could learn a surprising amount from observing someone as they slept. A person who had nothing to hide, who felt safe, might sleep spread out. Open. Vulnerable.

She lay curled like a child, a hand beneath her cheek, the red dress hiked high on her hip, exposing miles of creamy leg. She looked innocent lying there. The girl next door. Only better. More like the centerfold next door.

Why the bloody hell did he have to keep reminding himself that she wasn't the innocent? When she was captured—as she most assuredly *would* be one day—she'd be thrown into jail for a good twenty or thirty years.

Innocent she wasn't.

Why would a woman like this—an exquisite sophisticate, who must have men slavering at her feet like whipped dogs, men who would give her anything she could possibly want or need—*steal?*

What drove her? What motivated her? He guessed the answer lay in Zurich. His gut told him she was still hiding something.

The steady drone of the engines relaxed him. In a while he'd get up and read through her file again. In the meantime he could look his fill. She was a dangerous woman, Taylor Kincaid. He'd do well to remember *that*, instead of . . . other things.

Seventeen

W HAT DID YOU SAY YOUR NAME WAS?" JOSÉ MORALES ASKED the woman who'd shown up unannounced at his office an hour ago.

She gave him a cool look from black eyes. "May I sit down?"

He waved an open palm toward the too-soft, too-low, leather chair opposite his desk.

The woman sat, ankles crossed, hands in her lap. She looked to be a well-preserved forty, with dyke-short black hair and an understated, man-tailored navy business suit. "My name, Mr. Morales, is Theresa Smallwood. I believe I have some information that could prove to be of value to you."

José doubted it. He didn't know what she was up to, but a man as busy as he had little time to waste playing games.

"Cut to the chase, Miss Smallwood. You managed to talk your way into my office by claiming you have information about a certain robbery?"

"The safe in your San Cristóbal villa was robbed just over two months ago. I know the woman who took the contents."

Morale's pulse leapt. A *woman*. No wonder the people investigating the robbery hadn't come up with anything. They'd been looking for a *man*. But then, who would have guessed a thief as able as the one who'd stolen from him would be a *woman*?

He wanted the bitch. She'd managed to bypass laser alarms and integrated systems that were wired into explosives, along with trip wires designed to stun or kill an intruder. Yet she'd left the safe unharmed. How? How had a *female* managed to do the job?

"This woman? Was it you?"

"No."

One dark eyebrow lifted and his hands itched to slap the supercilious smirk from her face. She obviously had *cojones* to come into his office and face him down. In fact, she had far more guts than brains.

"And I'm supposed to take your word for that?"

She smiled. "Why not? If I were the thief, I certainly wouldn't come to you in this way and incriminate myself."

"Then you're here to trade information for money. Fine. We understand each other." A blackmailer was nothing but a bug to be squashed. With the touch of one finger to a button beneath his desk, he could have the woman killed the moment she left his office. "How much do you want?"

She laughed. An unattractive sound that grated on José's nerves. For some reason the foolish woman was obviously convinced that *she* was in charge here. Had she really no idea who she was dealing with? She was a minnow swimming with sharks. Forward. Stupid.

"I don't want money from you, Mr. Morales," she said. "What I want is a position in your organization."

His eyes narrowed on her. Suspicion rattled bells inside his brain. Was she a plant? Sent by his enemies? A not-so-friendly outside government? He'd had her searched before seeing her. But not *strip*-searched. "This is an export-import firm, Miss Smallwood," he said tightly. "What kind of position would you consider yourself qualified for? And why would I give you—a stranger—a job?"

"We both know you head *Mano del Dios.*"

The oceans shall shrink, he told himself, recalling the prophecy while hearing the woman's voice as though through a veil. *Deserts shall expand. Crops shall fail; there shall be massive starvation. Widespread emotional and mental collapse; increase in crime and violence. Changing weather patterns; basic laws of nature shall be disrupted.*

Satanic demons shall appear in broad daylight. War, pestilence, and world-wide plague. Good people who repented of their sins would be saved, while cruel tyrants would be cast into the burning fires of Hell.

Mankind would disappear if José Morales did not do something to make them change.

Morales fisted one hand atop the desk as she kept talking, unaware or uncaring of his inattention.

"So let me, as you say, cut to the chase," she said unctuously. "I am no longer content in my current position."

He wasn't going to hire her. All he wanted was the information—then he wanted her out of his sight.

"I am a lieutenant in the Black Rose."

José's eyes narrowed. A trick. It must be. Black Rose was developing a reputation, and now, cutting into his interests. It had begun as a small, irritating enterprise and had grown in both power and accomplishment in an amazingly short time. The Black Rose had become a true thorn in his side. "Why would I believe you?"

"Why would I lie?" she countered silkily.

"Prove it."

She shrugged as she stood, then turned her back. Unbuttoning her jacket, she removed it and laid it, carefully folded, over the high back of her chair. Then pulled the hem of her white shirt out of the waistband of her skirt, lifting it up and away from her body.

The smoothness of her flesh was marred by old, crisscrossing scars from repeated whippings. He had similar marks. He ignored both her body and the proof of her suffering—neither of which interested him in the slightest. What *did* interest him, though, was the small, neat tattoo on the small of her back.

A black rose.

A tattoo his people had discovered on the backs of every Black Rose member.

He suppressed a smile. This could be worth his while after all.

She looked at him over her shoulder. "I'm not moving up the ranks in the Black Rose as fast as I would like . . . May I?" She indicated the shirt.

José nodded, still stunned. A Black Rose operative. Here. He couldn't believe his good fortune. *And for this purpose also I labor, striving according to His power, which mightily works within me. Colossians 1:29*

After tucking in the shirt, she donned her jacket and resumed her seat. "Black Rose wanted the disks in your safe. In fact, I was sent to hire the thief to get them for us. At first, she feigned interest in a partnership. Then she double-crossed me."

"And how," José asked her dangerously, "did you come to know of the existence of such disks?"

"Black Rose has someone inside your organization, Mr. Morales."

A pit opened beneath his feet. A traitor. He'd known, of course. This information was too sensitive. Held too closely to his vest— "Who is this person?"

"I do not know. I swear to you. I do not know. I'm only aware that such a leak exists. I can of course try to find the information for you."

José had no sympathy for this stupid *puta*. Now he understood why she was not climbing the ranks in her organization. She was weak. Foolish. And worst of all—*disloyal*. Loyalty was paramount. Any commander knew his power was only as good as the loyalty he invoked.

"She robbed *me*," José reminded her, congratulating himself on the iron control keeping him from slapping her to the floor. "How did she double-cross you, Miss Smallwood?"

She slid one nylon-clad leg across the other. A move calculated to bring a man to his knees—yet it was wasted on Morales, a staunch Catholic and a good family man. Anyone who knew him, even if marginally, knew how devoted he was to his Maria. She was second only to his love of God.

"Your security is the best in the world, Mr. Morales. Completely proven one hundred percent reliable and trustworthy. Not so?"

"Your point?" The words were ground out from between gritted teeth. He had thought his security impenetrable. Until the thief had stolen from him. Of course, his new security "expert" had paid for that insult. And that was one body that would never be found.

"Your San Cristóbal safe," the woman mused, "as with all your security systems, is top of the line. Invincible. Impenetrable. Impossible to crack."

When would she get to the point?

"This is true." Nothing short of a nuclear bomb should have been able to open the San Cristóbal safe. A safe so foolproof, so impossible to open, that the company had sent out the man who invented it to show him how to operate it.

He'd been a pleasant young man, clever, useful. Quite brilliant, really. Not, as it turned out, brilliant *enough*. But the next security man he was sent would be better at his job. José had made certain his employees would have the proper incentive by having them witness the brilliant young man's execution.

"*I* gave this woman the last piece of the combination," Smallwood said smoothly. "The piece that only three people knew."

José interrupted. "Am I to believe that *you* knew what no one else did? You waste my time. Anyone could come here and foolishly claim this information."

Her red-painted mouth frowned. "The unique feature of the safe required the operator to enter the combination twice in uninterrupted succession, followed by another unbreakable code of a combination of six numerals and three letters . . . Should I go on?"

He nodded.

"The thief was confident she could open the safe. Until *I* told her that even with her expertise, there was a key element she couldn't possibly know."

So. This *puta* had a hand in robbing him. *Idiota.*

"Had it not been for my information, she would surely have been caught in the act."

God save him from women who thought they were as intelligent as a man. "So I have *you* to thank for the insult of that robbery?" Was she really so stupid to think he wouldn't kill her for this? Even though she lied.

The information she claimed had been the final key necessary for the thief to open the safe was incorrect.

"Black Rose wants whatever information is contained on what the thief stole. With the information . . ." She shrugged.

She wanted the information. But she, and therefore Black Rose, had no idea just how much power they would have if they knew what was hidden in the subterranean cavern in South Africa.

Dark eyes glittered. "I would have given what was stolen *back* to you. Ah. I see you doubt me, and wonder why I would do such a thing." She smiled. She had teeth like a rodent. "To show my loyalty. To *you*. I have a proposition for you, Mr. Morales . . ."

Loyalty. What did this bitch know of loyalty? She was here turning on her employer. He should trust her to be loyal to *him*?

"First," he said, "tell me who gave you the combination." Half the secret combination *had* been correct. He knew who must have given it to her. It hurt his heart. But of course he knew.

Only one person could have betrayed him.

She didn't hesitate. "Samuel Larson."

The man he'd put in charge of his San Cristóbal operation. The man he'd trusted like a son. José felt the sharp stab of betrayal and then the cold sweep of reason.

Samuel's entire family would have to be killed, of course. That pretty young wife. The three children. The mother-in-law who lived with them. And naturally, Samuel himself, once he'd been forced to watch all he loved die. Then he would have to find someone else to take Samuel's place.

Inconvenient to find someone to move up at such short notice. "Go on."

"I will tell you what you need to know to find, and retrieve, what was stolen from you. And in exchange, you place me in a prominent position in your organization." She looked smug.

Morales opened his lap drawer and removed what looked like a tooled silver pencil box. "You know the thief's name?" he asked as he carefully lined up the container in the center of his desk with the index finger and thumb of both hands before looking up at her.

She met his gaze dead on. "I can give you a full physical description. She is about my height. Five-foot-six. She has extremely dark brown eyes and shoulder-length black hair. She is between twenty-five and thirty. Medium build, Mediterranean in ancestry. Dark-skinned." She bubbled enthusiasm as if she thought she'd won.

"That is it?" Disappointment crushed his chest. *Madre de Dios.* He'd thought—he'd hoped . . . "You come here," he said with cold fury, "claiming to have information. And all you give me is a description that could be one of twenty million women? You're wasting my time. Good day, Miss Smallwood." He rose.

She stayed seated and looked up at him. "I might not have her identity, Mr. Morales. But I do know who she is *with,* and I know where they are *going.*"

Eighteen

TAYLOR DRIFTED UPWARD THROUGH LAYERS OF SLEEP LIKE A deep-sea diver breaking the surface. Two things struck her simultaneously. One, she still had a tight knot of foreboding in her stomach. And two, she was being watched.

Without moving, she slitted her eyes open. Just enough to see him through the screen of her lashes.

He was lounging in the seat opposite, silent and watchful as a large, sleek panther. He'd changed into black slacks and a crisply ironed shirt the color of his eyes, and looked as though he'd stepped from the pages of *GQ*. His dark hair, which was combed straight back, did nothing to soften his face.

Taylor recognized the strategy of seating himself with his back to the only light in the cabin. His face was shadowed like Phantom of the Opera. She, of course, was bathed in golden light from a wall lamp directly behind him.

Words rushed to her brain grouped in related pairs—hard and uncompromising. Humorless and ruthless.

Oh yeah.

Sexy and hot.

Lucky her.

Taylor scrutinized him the same way he dissected her with his eyes. Her sense of foreboding didn't dissipate, and now an equally disconcerting attraction had been added. No, more than that. Attraction was too mild a word for the way he made her insides feel. Call it what it was: lust. She didn't have to guess how that broad chest would feel beneath her hand, her cheek, or her *mouth*. She remembered. Vividly.

She didn't need to speculate about how it would feel if he slid his body over hers either. She remembered that vividly too.

She didn't need to wonder about the taste and texture of his mouth. Now she knew. God, did she know. Just looking at him made all her juices flow and her temperature rise. She'd never had such a visceral reaction to a man before.

But she enjoyed sex, and sometimes an appliance just didn't do the trick. She needed warm skin, and the physical contact of another human being. Closeness—

But here? Now? With *him*?

Why not? Here. Now. She was faced with a man who was turning her blood into steam—and he already *knew* her secrets. Well, most of them. Why shouldn't she enjoy a little *distraction*?

Love had never been in the cards for her. Not that she hadn't thought about it now and then over the years. She'd considered what she might be missing; the intimacy, the pleasure of lying in a man's arms with no need to have sex because you knew you'd be together tomorrow, next month, and next year.

But love required trust. And trust was a luxury Taylor couldn't afford. She didn't anguish over it. Why worry about things you can't control?

She dated occasionally. But her selection pool was somewhat limited to friends and acquaintances of the crooks she had to deal with. In her line of work, it didn't pay to get too close to anyone. Although she'd had several marriage proposals over the years, and plenty of indecent proposals as well.

She'd had only two lovers. Daniel Turner, another ex-pat in

Switzerland, when she'd been a scared nineteen-year-old living in a foreign country. And Jörn Peterson, whom she'd met at a party on board Neo and Julia Konstantinopoulos's yacht three years ago. The same party where she'd been introduced to José and Maria Morales.

She'd cared deeply for both men in turn, and the sex had been pleasant, sometimes even incredible. But she'd had no expectations from either relationship. In both instances, the fire had eventually fizzled and they'd parted ways. Jörn amicably. Daniel with a small tug of heartache on both sides.

And yes, once in a while she missed the physical closeness. Although the longer she lived without it, the less she seemed to miss it. Then Huntington St. John stepped into her life to disprove *that* theory. *He* knew what she did and who she was. The thought excited her, and she felt the same sensation in her stomach now as she did when poised beside a safe. Or running across a rooftop. Half fear. Half excitement. All . . . *alive.*

Lids at half mast, she watched Hunt from behind her lashes. Lord, he *fascinated* her. He scared her too. His cat-watching-a-mouse-hole stillness was unnerving. He had a way of scrutinizing her with those smoky gray eyes that made her feel as though he could read her mind.

But he *couldn't* read her mind. And he didn't know any of the deep, dark secrets of her soul that she had trusted to no one. Things that wouldn't be revealed in any of those files he had on her. He was no threat to her if she kept this quick and gave him what he wanted. She had to remember that.

Unfortunately, she had to admit—if only to herself—how drawn she was to this man. His quiet strength intrigued her. His tenacity. His *aloneness* called to something deep inside her soul. She was fascinated by his intelligence and discipline. She wanted to know what made him tick.

Thank God their association was going to be short-lived. The second they landed in Zurich, she'd take him directly to the bank and her safety-deposit box. Ten miles. About twenty minutes. Half an hour tops in traffic. Then hand over whatever it was he wanted and wave bye-bye.

"What are you scheming in that agile brain of yours?" His voice was low and a little more gravelly than normal. The effect of that rough tone on her was almost physical. Little pulse points all over her body sprang to life. The delicious sensation was like happy champagne bubbles popping and dancing inside her veins.

She stopped pretending she wasn't watching him and blinked her eyes into focus. "My brain was filled with sheep jumping hurdles wearing little numbers pinned to their fleece," she said lightly as she straightened, dropping her bare feet to the floor. "How long was I asleep?" As she ran both hands through her hair, Taylor took a quick glance down to make sure everything was where it was supposed to be.

The silk of her halter dress kept everything confined but not actually covered. Nope, her erect nipples were easily outlined by the thin fabric. Great timing, she groaned inwardly. She might as well be wearing a sign around her neck with marquee lighting that proclaimed she wanted him. *Now.* She gave a mental shrug. She couldn't control her body's reaction to him.

He didn't glance at his fancy-dancy wristwatch for the time, but his short black lashes fluttered down as he too looked at her breasts. She felt the heat of his gaze on her body, and it raised her own body temperature by several sizzling degrees. Then his lashes lifted as he met her eyes without expression. *Okay, I get it. You're immune.*

"You slept two hours." He answered the question she'd almost forgotten she'd asked. Which was a good reminder, Taylor thought, to keep sharp around this guy. He never seemed to lose track or have a problem with focusing on his objective.

Great. At least another seven or eight hours cooped up in the air with him. What she wouldn't give for a parachute. "Got any cards?"

"I do. Yes."

She waited for the punch line. After a long, looong pause, she looked at him expectantly. "And?"

He raised a brow. "You asked if I had cards. I answered."

Taylor shook her head, then started looking around for her shoes. "Do you study being a pain in the ass, or is it a gift?" she asked in German.

"It's a gift," he answered fluently in the same language. "Is that where you make your home? Germany?"

"I'm a quarter German." Which of course didn't answer his question, nor was it true. Languages came easily to her, and Taylor wanted to know how much he'd understand when they reached Zurich. Now she knew. "German-Austrian, actually," she finished in English.

"Thanks for the genealogy update, but I'm more interested in what you're hiding."

Bent over, one shoe in her hand, she glanced up. "Hiding? You searched me before we boarded." And it had been an exciting if rather impersonal experience. At least for her. Because the second he'd put his hands on her, her body remembered a shadowy room in San Cristóbal.

"Hiding in Switzerland," he prodded.

Taylor blinked. She was starting to get twitchy about those damn eyes of his. The thundercloud gray seemed to probe directly into her brain. She didn't like the idea that he could read her mind one bit. Here was a man not in the least distracted by her breasts, or her smart mouth, or any of the other smoke-and-mirror tactics she usually used to hide in plain sight.

He *saw* her.

Oh, please. Get a grip. No, he didn't. It was her overactive imagination working at full throttle. Ah. *There* was her other shoe. She slipped it on, then leaned back in her seat and slid one smooth leg over the other. She noticed a small muscle clench in his jaw. "We've already had this conversation. Remember?"

"What's in Zurich besides your lockbox?" He wasn't going to give it up.

Neither was she going to be easy to crack. My sister, my home, safety. "Clocks? The Alps? Cheese? Watches? Unbelievable chocolate? Take your pick."

"Lax banking regulations and no extradition treaty." That slight trace of British accent clipped the words as neatly as a privet hedge.

Taylor rubbed the goose bumps on her arms and shrugged. "Well now, if you *know* that, I'm not hiding anything, am I?"

"There's more here you're not telling me."

"Well, in the vernacular, *duh.*" She glanced around the room. "Where are the other two stooges?"

"Kipping in the back."

Taylor widened her eyes. "Lord, I hope that isn't as nasty as it sounds."

"Sleeping." The gray of his eyes seemed to swirl and settle as he watched her, expressionless, from hooded eyes. "What caused you to become a thief?" he asked evenly.

Daniel's Uncle Ralph had hired her to work in his Zurich company, Consolidated Underwriters. She'd been seventeen, scared, hungry, and willing to do just about anything. He started her in the mail room, and moved her up the ladder quickly. She'd had what Ralph Turner believed to be a God-given talent. She could save the company billions of dollars a year in claims by retrieving, and returning, stolen property.

"My mother is very sick," she told Hunt. The lie came easily. *Just a small quiver. Don't overdo it.*

"Still?"

"It's been protracted," she answered soberly, smoothing the thin silk over her knees and making her eyes look sad. "Yes. A very long time. Her medication is so expensive. Surgery would help, but we have no insurance." She quickly considered; *Brain tumor? A new heart? Restore her sight? What lasted a long time and was expensive?*

"Remarkable woman," he said.

Huntington St. John was the . . . *stillest* man she'd ever seen. He didn't fidget, or shift in his seat. He didn't cross his legs or tap his fingers. He just sat there watching her.

She forced herself to be just as still, giving him a guileless look.

"She must have amazing fortitude to hold on and suffer so . . . this long after her death," he said dryly. "She passed away when you were, what? Seventeen?"

Shit. Had her mother really died when she was seventeen? She had no idea. She and Amanda had been in Zurich by then. For all she knew, he was making it up. But just in case he knew something she didn't, she said, "I was talking about my *step* mother." Who didn't exist. Taylor couldn't tell by his *Hmm* if he believed her or was giving her enough rope to hang herself. "I—It's too hard to talk about."

"I'm sure it is. You're very . . . athletic. Let's talk about that instead." He changed topics with ease, as if they were conversing over coffee at the park on a Sunday afternoon.

Gymnastics, ballet, and a natural ability. "My daddy trained me as an acrobat," Taylor said, suddenly feeling Southern, and adding a little lilt before she thought about it. "He was in the circus."

"Of course he was." His lips twitched. Or she thought they did. But when she looked again, his mouth was a thin, grim line. Good. She didn't want to amuse him. She wanted to snow him.

"I loved it," Taylor told him, just warming up. "Of course, I was only allowed to visit him in the summers—my parents were divorced by then—but I adored the animals, and the smell of the greasepaint—"

"Called?"

"Max Factor?"

"The name of the circus," he said patiently.

"It was small. Family owned, so it wasn't very well known . . ." She needed a name—quick. "Coretti. The *Coretti* Family Circus. They traveled around from town to town. Drew pretty good audiences. They had three magnificent white tigers, four African elephants, and of course the lions. Pumbaa, Mufasa, and Scar."

Oh, that was a nice touch. It was always good to keep things simple, not *too* much detail, but just enough to give verisimilitude.

"And clearly the owner of the circus liked Disney," he inserted, voice Sahara dry.

Damn, he was quick. She could not imagine this man sitting through *The Lion King,* but she'd do well to remember not to underestimate him. "Oh, the circus was around long before Disney stole our lions' names. Actually," she leaned toward him as if spilling a state secret, "I think Pop Coretti is getting together a lawsuit. He figures if Disney wanted to steal his lions' names, then they should have paid for it. I don't think he has a shot, but Pop is a hard man." Was he buying this? She couldn't tell. She held his gaze, her own steady as a rock. No blinking.

One heartbeat. Two. Ten.

A small muscle leapt at the corner of his mouth. "Pop sounds like a stubborn man." He was sounding more British by the minute. What did that mean? He was relaxing? Believing her? Or just the opposite?

"Oh, you have no idea. I was practically adopted by the trapeze artists," Taylor informed him. "My father was always so busy, you know? So I learned as the Coretti children learned. Being an only child, I loved being among them. Eleven kids. Meals at Mama Coretti's caravan were insane, noisy, and filled with laughter." *Lord. She could almost see it. Taste it.* "It was a wonderful life. I hated going back home in September."

His lips twitched. "I'm sure if one word of that fairy tale were true, that would've been the case."

"Damn." Taylor smiled at him as she curled her legs under her. Lord. How could she resist a man who *got* her? "What gave me away? It was the lions, wasn't it?"

"I'm sure," he said quietly, "that if you truly wanted me to believe that story, I *would* have believed it. You're too damn good to slip up."

"I'm not sure if that's a good thing or a bad thing." She was intrigued by the way his eyes crinkled at the corners when he was amused, yet he refused to crack a smile. She cocked her head. "Do you ever laugh?"

"If something is amusing."

There was . . . what? A lessening of tension around his eyes? A warming of the familiar permafrost? "When was the last time you found something amusing?"

A glint flickered in his winter-gray eyes. Intrigued, she suspected he was secretly amused, yet his expression remained grave. "Your story was pretty damn funny."

Taylor leaned back, her smile widening. "I certainly enjoyed it."

"If I ask you something, will you tell me the truth?"

Her smile slipped a little. "Completely?" When had she last told the truth to anyone other than a member of Consolidated's Super Hush-Hush Recovery committee? A long, long time ago. She was far more adept at fabrication than truth. "In my line of work the truth doesn't come up that often."

This was the first time in over ten years that Taylor had been tempted to spill every secret she had. *Tempted.* But she wasn't foolish.

"Now would be an excellent time to start," Hunt said, not moving. "And yes. Completely."

"How about *mostly*?"

He inclined his head slightly, dark hair glossy in the muted light. "*Why* do you steal?" *The accent was back. He was back to being annoyed.* "Surely to God you must have more than enough bloody money for fifty lifetimes by now."

Taylor met his gaze with a level look of her own. "I make five percent of what I retrieve."

"Retrieve . . ." His eyes glittered. "*Insurance.* Jesus bloody Christ. You work for an *insurance* company? You might have *mentioned*—"

"Underwriters. A group of European gentlemen," she told him, "who prefer to remain anonymous. And the job title on my business card reads 'International Real Estate Broker.' "

"How long?"

Taylor shrugged. "Close to ten years now."

He sat up straighter. "And where the bloody hell was this group of '*European gentlemen*' when you were being beaten senseless in a San Cristóbal jail?"

"They aren't responsible for my well-being," she told him, puzzled by his anger. "I was the one who got caught."

She saw a muscle clench in his lean jaw. "You could have *died* in that hellhole."

"Thanks to you," she said lightly, "I *didn't*."

"Do you know how much fu—how much frigging *time* you could have saved by just telling me who you were and what you were doing in Morales's safe?" he asked with lethal fury.

"I didn't know who *you* were," she pointed out reasonably. "I had absolutely no reason to trust you, and plenty of reason not to."

"Do you trust *anyone*?" he asked flatly. "Anyone at all?"

Taylor frowned. "I don't understand you. Why are you so livid? We played the game. I forfeited. You won."

"Answer the question."

"No," she told him, baffled by the question, and his anger. "There's no one I trust." His expression was back to being inscrutable. "About the same amount of people *you* trust," she added lightly. "Right?"

He rose to tower over her, blocking out the light. Taylor's heart leapt into her throat as she looked up at him.

Hunt wanted to strike something. *Hard.* "There might only be a handful," he told her. "But there *are* people I trust."

Jesus bloody Christ. There was *no one* she trusted? No one she could depend on? No one guarding her back when she risked life and limb for some lifeless cold pieces of metal and stone?

Worse. She clearly didn't *expect* it to be any *other* way. She was bloody *fine* with it. With remarkable restraint, Hunt reached down, slid his hand under her silky hair, and curled his fingers around her nape. Her eyes widened as he pulled her to her feet, his gentleness in inverse proportion to what he was feeling. Which was wild. Primitive. Feral.

Anticipation, not fear, showed on her face as she rose on her toes so they were almost eye-to-eye. Air locked in his lungs as he looked his fill. He wanted to put his mouth against the rapid pulse beating at the base of her throat. He wanted to take her down on the floor and fill his hands with her soft pale flesh.

"Isn't it supposed to be the other way around?" she asked, un- aware, or uncaring of his mood. Her pretty mouth curved into a smile as she stood on her toes, sliding her palms up his arms for balance. "After *I* tell *you* everything, *I'd* have to kill y— *Mmmph!*"

He took her mouth in a slow, soft, drugging kiss. The kiss was in- evitable. Predestined. She let him in, her breath soft on his face. He kissed her lightly. A brush of lips. An exchange of air. He threaded his fingers through her hair, cupping the back of her head to draw her closer. She felt fragile beneath his hands. Slender bones and creamy skin. Agile, well-toned muscles and a quick-thinking mind. None of which would help her if, no, *when* she was finally bloody well *captured.*

He studied her for a long moment.

"That's a pretty ferocious frown, Mr. St. John," she murmured in a husky contralto, sliding her arms about his neck. "Are you contem- plating kissing me properly, or killing me?" She pressed her soft feminine roundness against him, and he struggled to restrain his elemental response to her touch.

"Kissing you . . . *im*properly." A shudder of need clawed through him, but he did his best to keep his cravings banked as he wrapped an arm about her waist and bent his head, keeping his exploration of her mouth tender. His tongue dueled with hers. God, she tasted sweet. Fiercely, hungrily, he feasted on her mouth, feeling as though he'd never kissed a woman before.

While one hand tangled in her hair, the other spanned the small of her back, his thumb caressed her smooth skin through tissue-thin silk. He was starving to touch bare skin, but kept his hands where they were. Silky hair and the promise of satiny skin. He had to be satisfied with those. For now.

His lips trailed a path across her cheekbone, then he traced a pattern with his tongue around the shell of her ear. She trembled. Her skin heated and warmed as he moved to her closed eyes and pressed a kiss to each lid. Her lashes fluttered against his skin, and the scent of her skin made his head swim.

Hunger, insatiable and not even close to satisfied, made him take her mouth again. A little deeper this time. Slow and deep until she shifted restlessly against him, pale eyes hazy and unfocused . . .

Nineteen

TAYLOR HAD NEVER EXPERIENCED ANYTHING AS PROFOUNDLY exciting as Hunt's kiss. A sharp, sweet spear of sensation pierced through her entire body as his mouth continued to move over hers.

The lights in the cabin were dim, and the unobtrusive hum of the aircraft surrounded them in a quiet, protective blanket. She loved the heat and taste of his mouth, loved the texture of his tongue playing with hers. The pleasure of touching him, of him touching her, made her shiver with heat. Taylor tightened her arms around him.

Every part of her participated. Lord. It was like drowning. Or being reborn.

In a move so coordinated it could have been choreographed, Hunt started maneuvering her backward without breaking the kiss. *As long as he holds me in his arms, and I stay on my toes,* Taylor thought fuzzily, *I won't fall.*

A door opened behind her. She lifted heavy lids, then blinked to bring her surroundings into focus. A bathroom. A quick flash of bronzed mirror-covered walls, plush carpeting, and soft, golden light. Like the rest of the plane, it was sinfully luxurious despite its small size.

Hunt freed the hand he'd used to cup her skull and reached out to push the door shut, closing them inside. The absolute control he used to close the door *that* quietly was so obvious she almost expected to feel the vibration and hear the sound of it slamming. Instead it closed with a quiet *snick*.

Her heart raced. Knife-edge anticipation. She had a quick flash of all those old black-and-white movies where they lit just the villain's eyes. She shivered, but was too mesmerized to be scared. Although some small, sane part of her brain warned her that she should be. Sizzling mutual awareness rushed in to fill the air between them with heat.

Taylor reached out to touch the pulse beating in his lean, unshaven jaw. He trapped her gaze. She wondered how she had ever thought his gray eyes cold.

"This is what you want." It wasn't a question.

Her "Yes" was soundless. Was there any doubt? She couldn't breathe as electricity arced between them. Want unfurled in her belly, and her pulse throbbed unevenly all over her body.

His mouth caught hers again in a kiss so carnal, so devastating, she went blind and deaf as he ruthlessly used his skill to arouse her to fever pitch. He stroked his tongue into her mouth, slow and deep, until she reciprocated.

They broke apart, breath ragged. His eyes, glittering like fancy black diamonds, pinned her in place as he settled large hands on her hips. Bunching the thin silk of her dress in his fists, he backed her against the counter. Then slowly drew the fabric—inch by maddening inch—up her thighs.

She said his name in a hot, restless, urgent whisper as she clutched his arms for support. The tile was cool against her hips, but Hunt's body was scalding hot as he crowded her. The ridge of his erection pressing against the cleft of her thighs made her dizzy. Fire danced in her veins as his hands skimmed across her bare skin, pulling the bit of red silk over her head and tossing it aside, forgotten. It floated to the floor.

She stood before him wearing two small scraps of sheer red lace and felt a flush of pleasure suffuse her skin at the hot look he gave her.

"God," he said reverently, tracing the upper swells of her pale breasts with the back of his fingers. "I've never seen anything this perfect." His deft, elegant hand moved lower, fingers skimming, *too* gently, as if learning every curvy inch of her.

Taylor's head dropped back as his fingers glided down the damp valley between her breasts, then stroked the blue-veined skin beneath the edge of the demicup bra.

Her nipples, drawn tight and hard by his touch, ached. She fumbled to reach for the clasp.

"Porcelain—" His English accent was back in the ragged, hoarse tone.

"About to shatter," Taylor said brokenly as he took his sweet time undoing the front clasp of her bra, then slowly drew the straps down her arms. It too landed somewhere on the floor. He cupped one breast, moving his thumb cleverly back and forth across the hard distended peak of that nipple until she had to bite her lip not to cry out.

His large, tanned hand looked shockingly male against the milky paleness of her skin. Hands trembling with urgency, she started unbuttoning his shirt, peeling the fabric away from the furnace of his skin.

He hooked his thumbs in the narrow ribbons on her hips and yanked the lacy thong down her legs. She kicked it off, hands going to the crisp dark hair on his chest, leaned forward and pressed an open-mouthed kiss to the center of his chest.

She looked down at the heavy erection tenting his neatly pressed black slacks, then up, her lips curved in a smile. A cat-with-cream kind of smile, she knew. He reached down and unzipped his pants. Dropped them, kicked them aside.

She didn't move as his gaze traveled her naked body with the impact of a physical touch. There seemed to be a direct line from his eyes to whatever body part he was looking at. Little flairs of electricity danced across her skin. Air seemed to be in short supply as she struggled to fill her lungs. But breathing was a two-edged sword as the scent of him made her head swim. "You seem to have a thing about bathrooms."

"I seem to have a thing about you," he corrected thickly. Using both hands, he wrapped them gently around her throat, thumbs at the heavy pulse pounding at the base, fingers cupping her skull beneath her hair. Instead of squeezing the life out of her, his thumbs moved up and down her throat in a caress that made Taylor's nipples harden painfully and her breath hitch.

She licked her lips. "I'm not buying that one. Your body's telling me it's not killing me you've got in mind."

His large hands, callused and strong, moved down her shoulders, brushing the sides of her breasts as they skimmed down her arms. "You have a smart mouth, you know that?"

A tremor rippled across her skin at his touch, excitement leapt in her chest at the heated look in those fire-and-brimstone eyes. She tilted her chin up. "Why don't you put it to good use, then."

He bent his head, his mouth hot as he skimmed his lips across her cheek in a caress of barely restrained greed. His fingers hurt as he tightened his grip on her elbows. "I don't want to want you."

Taylor slid her hands up his chest, paused to feel the heavy *thump-thump-thump* of his heart beneath her fingertips, then wrapped her arms about his neck. She turned her mouth up to his. "Door's . . . there. Go."

She waited to see if he'd do it. Slam the door. Leave her in here alone. His pupils contracted to pinpoints, his mouth thinned in a hard straight line as he looked down at her with the eyes of a predator about to feast. Her mouth went dry as lust surged and intensified to the brink of pain.

Anticipation traveled along her nerve endings at the speed of light. Bright and white. She imagined him, a sleek animal lying in wait in the tall grass, every muscle taut with awareness, eyes and ears tuned to his prey.

She smelled the starch in his shirt, felt the crisp scratch of it against her naked breasts as time stretched. The edge of the counter behind her pressed into her bare butt, cool and hard. Hunt pressed against her front. Hot and hard.

The hum of the plane's engines took up a counter rhythm in Taylor's body. She felt like a ripe juicy peach about to burst as she waited, pulses pounding in interesting places. She refused to look away as their gazes locked, battled, and challenged. Tossed a silent gauntlet she wasted no time accepting.

"Does this heat scare you?" Hunt's voice was thick, ragged. His tight grip cut off her circulation in her arms, but she didn't give a damn.

"No. Only your self-control," she said thickly, smelling her own arousal and feeling the heaviness and moisture between her legs. *Insane. Crazy . . . Hurry.*

After what seemed a torturous eternity, he took her in an open-mouthed kiss that rocked her off her feet. No. He'd lifted her onto the cool countertop, she realized as her tongue met his in a bid for supremacy.

They both won.

The kiss went on and on. Hot and wet. Erotic enough to steam up the mirrors. Tongues, slick and in constant motion, slid and slithered in a motion mimicking penetration. Taylor's breath hitched and caught.

He slid one hand up her leg, drawing her toward him. She wrapped her legs around him, shoving his shirttails up in back with one foot so she could feel the rock-hard muscles of his behind. She crossed her ankles and pulled, using muscles she'd used only to scale balconies and air-conditioning ducts.

This was better—oh, God, so much better.

He stood between her legs, huge, dark, and powerful. He slid both hands up her thighs and thrust inside her wet, ready heat with barely restrained ferocity. She made a sound in the back of her throat and shuddered with the beginning of a hard, fast climax.

"Not yet," he muttered thickly, withdrawing a little and dragging in a harsh, ragged breath, hard fingers gripping her ass cheeks. "Not . . ." He rammed home again, Taylor's back arched, as she shot another three feet up the lust ladder. "... yet." He pulled out, slick and hard. Hot and greedy.

He brought her to the very edge. Again and again. Prolonging the climax in a dance that had her clawing his back as violent ripples wracked her body, making her pant and sweat and moan his name.

Soaking with sweat, shaking with mindless need, she tried to tighten her grip on his hips. He was trying to control her. Show her who was boss. Silly, silly man.

"Bastard," she choked out, ripping her mouth from beneath his to take a much needed breath as he withdrew yet again. Each time he did, it made the buildup more intense, more exquisite than the last.

"Hellcat," he ground out, crushing his mouth back down on hers as he thrust back inside her as if determined to come through the other side. Strong and relentless, he controlled the speed and intensity of his thrusts as if he could read her body's every action and reaction.

Harder and harder, closer and closer together, until she couldn't tell where he began and she ended.

Staked. His. Lost.

Blood thundered in her ears, roaring through her veins in a sweet blaze that left her shaking. This time she didn't let him pull out. She held him with every well-toned muscle. Inside and out.

He plunged into her like a hard-driven weapon. She didn't give a damn what he was trying to prove. And she didn't think he did either. Not anymore. Now, hunger was its own reward and carried its own demand.

Taylor buried her face against his shoulder to muffle her scream as they climaxed together. Hard and fast.

Twenty

LISA MAKI WAS A STUNNINGLY ATTRACTIVE, STATUESQUE BLONDE with the face of a Botticelli angel. In her mid-thirties, she looked twenty-five, and easily passed as a student. Which she frequently did. She and her small group were responsible for the student uprising at the University of Madrid earlier in the year, resulting in many new, if unsuspecting, supporters and hefty donations for Black Rose's coffers.

She'd successfully hijacked an American airline flight from Paris, and had been responsible for two embassy bombings. One in Valencia, and one in Rome. She was proud of the work she did. The Black Rose cell in Spain was small, only seven members, but she made sure their numbers counted.

When her phone rang, she answered it eagerly, ready for her next directive.

"T-FLAC has the woman en route to Zurich. Be there," her leader informed her without greeting. Lisa's heart pounded with anticipation. *At last! Madre de Dios! At last!*

This was the Black Rose's most ambitious act of terror; over-throwing the *Mano del Dios* was no small task. Taking down another terrorist organization was a bold move. Particularly one of *Mano*'s strength and worldwide control. Participation was a guaranteed star maker.

Lisa would be the Black Rose's star player, if she had any control over the situation. She'd do everything in her power to make her move count. But stuck here in Spain, she knew there was little chance of her seeing any of the action. Until now.

"ETA Kloten, six hours, fourteen minutes." Her boss proceeded to give her the exact flight particulars and the call numbers of the T-FLAC private jet. Lisa committed the information to memory. She already had photographs of the T-FLAC operatives involved, as well as a quarter-profile photograph of the woman they held. It was enough.

"Take your team, intercept them inside the terminal. Do not make contact. Do not let them out of your sight. Do not let them see you."

Lisa didn't take notes on the call. She didn't need to.

"They will wait until the last minute to hire a car and driver. Do *not* underestimate these men. St. John is both determined and tenacious. He won't let the woman out of his sight until he has the disks in his hands *and* is assured that it holds the information he needs. The information *we* need. Keep in mind, he trusts no one and has eyes in the back of his head.

"Let him do our job for us. When he is satisfied, *I* will be satisfied. Follow them, confirm delivery, then eliminate them. *All.* No mistakes. I will expect to receive the disk—from you, in person—first thing to-morrow morning in your office. Understood?" The line went dead.

Lisa understood perfectly. She couldn't wait.

Twenty-one

Y OU SHOULD TRY TO SLEEP," HUNT TOLD TAYLOR QUIETLY AS she came out of the head. She'd changed into softly pleated gray slacks and a cream-colored, long-sleeve shirt that crossed her breasts with no apparent means of fastening. He preferred her naked.

Narrow-eyed, he watched her lithe walk with unconscious intensity. He'd been with her not ten minutes ago, yet seeing her now, hair wet, pale, slender feet bare, made his lungs feel constricted. He'd never seen anything so sexy in his life.

They'd made love again in the small shower stall while hot water pelted them and the plane went through fifteen minutes of turbulence. For Hunt, it had been an unforgettable experience.

The cabin was quiet, the lighting muted, and the drone of the plane's engines soporific. Yet he was wired. He'd had her twice, and wanted her again. The feel of her skin, the smell of her hair—all of it. Soon. Now. For the first time in forever, his focus felt blurred. He should've been thinking strategies and terrorists, and instead was drifting back to her.

Taylor tossed the matching jacket she carried over a chair back, then ran her fingers through her wet hair. She resumed the seat she'd had earlier. This time Hunt had chosen the plush chair beside instead of opposite her. As soon as she sat down, he handed her a glass of wine, noting how transparent the cloth of her blouse over her right breast had become where her wet hair soaked the fabric. She wore no bra. His pants immediately became as constricted as his breathing.

"Mmm, thanks," she murmured, accepting the glass by the stem. "I'll have plenty of time to sleep." She took a sip. "This is wonderful. I'm going to take a few weeks off."

The fragrance of her skin made his mouth water. She drew her feet up on the seat, then rested her chin on her bent knees and turned her head to look at him as he asked, "In Zurich?"

She took another sip of her drink. "I'm not sure. Maybe the South of France. It's nice there this time of year."

Not the South of France, he knew instinctively, and probably no vacation either. Not surprised she lied, he wondered why she'd bother. He leaned back, holding his own glass. "How many jobs do you average a year?"

The diffuse lighting made her skin look luminescent. He knew how soft it was to the touch. He knew how sweet it tasted. He resisted the powerful need to touch her. The strength of that urge, and the fact that he still *felt* that urge, annoyed him as much as it intrigued him.

She twisted the stem of her glass between her fingers, her attention on the light reflecting off the surface. "Sometimes one, sometimes, like this year, three or four."

"And you've never been caught?" He wished to hell the thought of Taylor incarcerated didn't bother him so much. Law of averages would catch up with her eventually.

"Once was enough," she said dryly. "Were you born in England? It's hard to tell, your accent is so faint most of the time."

"Born in Boston, moved to Essex when I was nine, moved back to the States, D.C, when I was fifteen, went to school in London when I was seventeen." He'd been recruited by T-FLAC while in college, and it was at their suggestion that he'd entered law school. He'd never regretted either choice.

"That's a lot of moving around."

"Father's a career diplomat."

"What about your mom?"

"She died. Cancer. I was seventeen. My father adored her—hell, everyone did. He never remarried." Hunt didn't add that his father had rarely smiled since. Genetic thing, since, come to think of it, he didn't smile much either. Until recently. Until her.

"Tough losing your mom at that age," Taylor murmured sympathetically.

"Yes, it was. She was an amazing woman. Funny as hell." He half smiled at the memories. "Brave—Jesus, toward the end . . . I consider myself fortunate to have had her for as long as I did."

"How long was she sick before she died?"

"Four and a half years." They'd made the most of those years too, the three of them. Hunt felt his mouth curve at the memories. "She had a . . . *thing* for *National Geographic* and the Discovery Channel, and was an enthusiastic armchair traveler . . ."

Taylor leaned her elbow on the armrest between them. Her damp hair smelled of the fragranceless stuff all the operatives used. On her it smelled of flowers. "Don't stop." She brushed her hand over his.

"When she was diagnosed, she decided she wanted to see all those places for herself." He rubbed his thumb back and forth over the silky skin on the back of her hand. "We took her to Spain. She said it was to see the flamenco dancers, but we figured she wanted to check out the matadors. We pretended to be appalled." God, how she'd laughed at their teasing. "We went to Italy." He and his father had sat, pretending not to be comatose, through an opera at La Scala in Milan. "And another trip to Loch Ness, so she could look for Nessy." He shook his head at the memory. "Just as boring—and with dreary weather. Another time we packed up and went off to Easter Island to see the Moai monoliths along its coastline. And the last year . . . we returned to Boston. To wait.

"I gained an appreciation for orange Popsicles and 7-Up," Hunt said, remembering the rock in his chest as he watched his mother fade a little more each day. Watched his father die with her. "Both of which she'd always given to me when I was ill as a kid. They helped her with the nausea. She died in my father's arms."

"You really loved each other a lot. I envy you that." Taylor's voice was wistful.

"Yeah. I was lucky. Enough about me. Tell me about Taylor Kincaid, the child."

She smiled. "You have that big fat file on me. Didn't you read it?"

"From cover to cover. Several dozen times," he told her dryly. Her dark hair had started to curl a little around her shoulder. Her eyes, crystal blue, were clear as she watched him with a small smile curving her mouth. Looking at her made his heart twist strangely.

"Then you know my father was in prison."

"High Desert State Prison, Nevada." His voice was cool, nonjudgmental. "Armed robbery."

"Yes." Her eyes clouded. "It makes my heart hurt to think about him—"

"Jesus, Taylor," Hunt said roughly, reaching out a hand to brush his fingers lightly over her damp hair. "How can you be such a tough cookie and talk like that?"

She gave him a puzzled look. "I loved him."

"Where was your mother?"

"Worked days, partied nights." She shrugged, as if with that one motion she could slide away old memories. "She left when I was twelve. She didn't much like being a mother. It put a crimp in her social life big-time. We were better off without her."

She narrowed her eyes. "Did you make that up earlier when you told me my mother was dead?"

"No. Didn't you know? She died when you were in your early teens. A single-vehicle car accident in the desert just outside Las Vegas."

She shook her head, then looked down at her toes, but not before he noticed a sheen of tears. "I had no idea. I—We thought she'd just . . . gone. But I somehow always imagined she was out there—somewhere."

He should get up and walk away. *Now.* He didn't want to feel compassion for her. He didn't want his own fucking "heart to hurt" because she'd had a bloody lousy childhood. He picked up his glass, shifted to rise, then sat back. Because he couldn't leave her. In a few minutes. But not right now. "I'm sorry."

"No. Don't be. It's just . . . strange. I don't know how I feel really. Relieved. Angry. Sad, maybe."

"What about your father?"

"He was around. Pretty bewildered with raising dau—raising a daughter alone." The slip was infinitesimal. But there. "It wasn't easy for him. He was a building super in one of the big apartment complexes in Reno, so he could spend quite a bit of time with me. But, oh, Lord. His job bored him to tears. Still, he was pretty good at it." Her smile pierced his heart. Hunt was glad she at least had a few good memories.

"He liked fixing things," she continued, nodding when he held up the wine bottle to refill her glass. He poured, and she immediately took a large gulp. "Machinery that broke down, cars, air conditioners—he couldn't have cared less if old Mrs. Solomon's linoleum was coming up or if Mr. Engel's door hinge had a squeak. But, boy, give him a broken engine, or anything with moving parts, and he was a virtuoso. I loved following him around."

Light played against her cheekbones, making him itch to stroke them; it took a concerted effort to keep his hands to himself. "Is that how you got started? Watching your father?" God, he loved watching *her*. Expressions flitted across her freshly scrubbed face like clouds across the sky, and her eyes sparkled like moonlight on fresh snow.

And he was becoming dangerously poetic.

Hell with it. He gave himself the duration of the flight to indulge his fancy. After that it was business as usual.

"Him and his buddies. God . . ." Taylor smiled, looking poignantly young as she did so. "When I couldn't sleep, I'd go down to Uncle Hank's apartment, where Dad and his cronies were playing cards. I learned to play poker at seven, and started winning at nine."

"The early start of those nimble fingers of yours." His lips twitched. "Why aren't you a card shark?"

"No money in it. Not the way I played, anyway. Uncle Hank worked as a security guard at one of the big casinos. As a lark, he taught Pop to open the safe at his cousin's gas station. Not stealing anything—the cousin was there, just as a gag. Of course if my dad did it, I had to try too. It became a game for the three of us."

"Interesting game to teach a kid," Hunt murmured.

"Hey, some kids play with dolls, I played safecracker. Another friend of Pop's was an illusionist, close up. Sleight of hand, card tricks mostly. I was a willing pupil, and they loved teaching me more and more complicated tricks. Then they'd bet on me. See how fast I could open a safe, or get some poor rube to bet on spotting the mechanics of an illusion. I was a kid, and cute." She laughed. "And I was *good*. Man, I was good. Pop made a mint on me. I was dexterous and quick, and got a percentage of my father's take. I loved it."

She shook her head. "He was caught robbing the local 7-Eleven when I was fifteen. He took Hank's safecracking lessons seriously. Unfortunately," she added on a sigh, "he wasn't as gifted as I was. And I have no idea where the hell he got that gun. He was shivved then strangled in prison a few weeks after he got there."

"What happened to you? Social Services?"

"Are you kidding me? I wasn't going to wait for them to show up. I pulled my first job the day after Pop was arraigned. Some small-time hood had put the squeeze on Uncle Hank for payback on a racing bet—"

"Jesus bloody Christ. You robbed a *bookie*?" Admiration warred with pity that warred with the urge to protect. Damned if he didn't want to travel back in time and look out for her. Although, he admitted, a teenage Taylor would have fought his urge to help every bit as much as she fought him now.

"You bet. He was a lousy bookie, and a nasty piece of garbage. Had twenty grand in used bills in a child's play easy-to-open safe in his basement. I was in and out in six minutes."

Hunt shook his head. "Then what?"

"I went to a Goodwill store, bought a wig and a suitcase, asked Hank to get me a fake driver's license because I was still underage."

"You were only *fifteen,* for Christ's sake."

She shrugged. "I could look considerably older, believe me. From there, I went to Sacramento, applied for a passport, stayed at a motel for a couple of weeks, and when the passports came, left on the next flight for Europe."

Hunt wondered who she was protecting. "Who was the second passport for?" he asked easily, watching her eyes.

She looked at him blankly. "What do you mean?"

His jaw clenched, then he said easily, "You went to Europe alone? At barely fifteen?"

"Me and—" She yawned. "And twenty thousand American dollars."

No, darling, Hunt thought savagely. *Not you alone. You and somebody important.* Who? A boyfriend? A lover? "Then what?"

"I bummed around Europe for a while, then ended up in Zurich and went to work for Consolidated Underwriters. The rest—" She yawned again. "Is history."

He rose, placing his half-full glass on the pull-down table beside him with care. Lust mixed with anger was a lethal combination. "Try to sleep," he told her flatly. "I'll wake you before we land."

She straightened, gave him a puzzled look. "What did I miss? What just happened?"

Hunt ignored her as he walked away.

He gritted his teeth as he moved rapidly to the rear of the aircraft. He'd fucked away the last remnants of his intelligence. Why the bloody *hell* had he permitted the intense, insatiable, unquenchable fever in his blood to win?

Why her? Why now?

It was a madness. As if he'd somehow cease to exist if he didn't have her. Right then. Right there.

His training, his life, his work—everything he did, he did with unrelenting control over his emotions. His choices were driven by logic, his actions carefully calculated. He never made a move without being certain he considered the possibilities and was satisfied with the projected outcome.

He'd *never* allowed himself to be swept away on a tidal wave of

emotion. Until now. He raked his fingers through his still–damp hair. Jesus Christ. He'd lost his fucking mind.

He slammed open the door to the aft cabin with more force than necessary. The room was dark. He brutally flipped on the lights.

"A simple knock would've done it," Max bitched, opening his eyes. He'd been sleeping in the desk chair. Bishop, obviously immune to loud noises, snored in the narrow bunk across the small room. A second bunk was tucked up against the bulkhead, but Max hadn't bothered to lower it.

He narrowed his gaze on Hunt as he came over to lean against the desk. "My God. You're *smiling*." He rubbed his eyes and pretended to get up. "Alert the media. Huntington St. John cracked a smile."

Hunt raked his fingers through his hair, scraping it back away from his face with both hands. Much as Taylor had done a few moments ago, he realized. "Wiseass. I smile." Although the smile now felt more like a grimace to him.

Max leaned back in the chair and looked up at his friend. "I've been keeping track. Not a damn thing has amused you in the last decade."

"As I recall," Hunt said wryly, "I laughed uproariously last year when that snake latched onto your ass—and wouldn't let go."

"No, you didn't," Max reminded him. "That snakebite was potentially serious, and as *I* remember it, you refused to suck the poison out. Said twenty years of friendship didn't warrant you kissing my butt."

"It was hardly more than a scratch, and here it is a bloody year later and you're still whining?" Hunt mocked. "Poor big bad T-FLAC operative. Hell, the snake probably died. Maybe I should've got Catherine to come and kiss it better?"

"God, no." Max contorted his face, making Hunt smile genuinely. "That taught me to learn from my friends' mistakes."

Hunt rose, not wanting his mind to wander down the Catherine path. Old news. Lessons learned. For both of them. "I tried to lead by example." Restless, he paced the small cabin.

"Problem with our guest?" Max asked, watching him pace.

"A few," Hunt admitted. "She presses my buttons."

"Pulls your handle too, I gather."

"Unfortunately. Damn hard to concentrate with a permanent cockstand. Tomorrow can't come soon enough for me," he said grimly. This insane lust had to stop. "What do we hear on Morales?"

Twenty-two

W HAT'S IN THE PARCEL?" THE HEAD OF BLACK ROSE HER-
self motioned to Clive Urbach.

"As you see, I have not opened—"

"Fetch it." Didn't he understand he was paid—and paid well—to inspect packages? She stayed exactly where she was.

He rose, walked across the room. Returning, he offered her the package, and she wondered if she should take it. The address label was typed.

ROSE AND SON
Purveyors of Fine Linens
London

And the Black Rose's address. Nothing more.

She waved a hand at Urbach. "Open it." It was too light to be a bomb. And too tightly wrapped to contain a live insect, poisonous or otherwise. But there were hundreds of topical poisons that could kill

instantly on contact. She stepped back to be on the safe side. Urbach was eminently replaceable.

He shrugged, removed a small sharp knife from his breast pocket, and cut the brown string. He laid the box on the coffee table between them and used the tip of the knife to open the wrapping. Inside there was a small, plain white confectioner's box.

Still using the knife, he tipped off the lid. She recognized the smell.

He frowned. "What is it?"

On the knife's point, he speared the four-inch-square lump of raw meat from the bloodstained, white tissue-paper-lined box.

It stank of putrefied flesh, and she covered her nose. The knife glittered in the lamplight as he turned it so she could better see what he'd speared like a shrimp on a skewer.

The gruesome offering captured her full attention.

Beautiful in its own way, the graying skin with its ragged, blood-crusted edges indicated the warning had been cut purposefully and premortem.

The message was clear.

In the center of the filleted flesh was a tattoo.

The tattoo of a Black Rose.

They were missing only one member.

"I'd wondered," she mused out loud.

Who would send her such a gift? She tapped a bloodred nail against her chin.

So this is what became of Theresa Smallwood.

Twenty-three

A BLACK LINCOLN TOWN CAR WAITED FOR THEM BESIDE THE private arrivals terminal at Zurich's Kloten International Airport.

"Tell the man where we want to go," Hunt instructed Taylor as he stepped into the car after her, neatly sandwiching her between his large body and Max's.

In brisk Swiss-German she gave the driver the name and address of the bank, then instructed him to take the N3 directly to the financial district. Hunt reached up and slid the privacy window closed, although she was pretty sure they wouldn't discuss anything classified on the trip anyway. She turned her head, her attention on choppy Lake Zurich as they drove parallel to it into the city proper.

Even when she wasn't looking at Hunt she was aware of everything about him. He'd changed into a beautifully tailored dark suit before they landed. With it he wore one of the light grayish blue shirts he favored, and a subtle print tie. He smelled delectable. Not cologne or soap. His skin.

She frowned as she looked out of the window. How odd. If they stuck her in a dark room with a hundred men, she would be able to pick Huntington St. John out by the scent of his skin. A useless talent she'd never have to utilize.

She didn't need his kind of complications. She had her work, and Mandy . . . and that was plenty. In an hour or so he'd be gone, and she'd resume her normal life.

Good. Fine. Great.

Exactly what she wanted. Sex wasn't hard to come by. She was reasonably attractive. If she wanted straightforward, unencumbered sex, she knew where to find it.

"Which hotel?" Hunt asked.

Taylor turned her head to look at him. She didn't need a hotel. Home was a four-thousand-square-foot condo overlooking the lake. She let out a breath she hadn't realized she was holding since leaving Houston. At least he wasn't going back on his assurance they'd let her go once she handed over the goods.

"I haven't decided yet," she told him sweetly. "Why? Thinking of staying over a few days and enjoying the sights?"

"No."

She shook her head at the typically monosyllabic response. "Anyone ever tell you that you talk too much?" she said mockingly.

Hunt stared her down.

"It's very annoying."

She turned back to the passing view.

Whatever. It wasn't her job to civilize him. Apparently, he was one of those men she'd read about who got surly after sex. He'd barely said a word to her in the past six hours.

So much for their bonding moment.

Get a grip, she told herself firmly. They'd had sex. *Superlative* sex. But it was only sex. And this wasn't a holiday fling. The man was *working.*

Though there was a feeling of *And now what?* that she couldn't quite shake. Taylor stared out of the rain-spattered window and asked herself what she'd expected.

Answer: *nothing.*

What did she have to show for their incredible bout of lovemaking?

Answer: a membership in the Mile High Club? Which amounted to—nothing. Her lips twitched.

"Whatever you're planning, forget it," Hunt said point-blank as their eyes met.

Sparkles, like effervescent champagne bubbles, darted through Taylor's bloodstream, as bright and happy as Hunt looked somber and cranky. She *liked* the annoying man. Go figure.

"I'm thinking about a hot bath," she told him serenely. "Which, as far as I know, isn't against the law in Switzerland."

Max Aries's lips twitched.

"Don't even *think* about attempting anything slippery." Hunt gave her a stony look. "I'm not in the mood to chase you all over hell and back. *Again*. The easier you make this for us, the easier it'll be for you."

"Yes, sir," she said deferentially, earning herself a hostile glare. She smiled at him. Really, she couldn't help it. The man was such a stuffed shirt, it was impossible *not* to be amused by him. She turned back to look out of the window. It was still raining.

She'd never met anyone like Hunt St. John, and she guessed she never would again. He was one of a kind. She'd miss him, Taylor decided, a little surprised. Miss him. Think about him, and once in a while, pull out the memory of him and wonder what it would've been like to make love all night in a big warm bed. To wake up with him, bathed in late morning sunlight, and read the Sunday paper together.

And maybe, Taylor gave herself a mental shake and a reality check, *maybe she could have a frontal lobotomy so she didn't remember him at all.*

She was relieved at the distraction when they pulled up in front of the bank ten minutes later. Max opened the door and stepped out into the drizzle. She swung her legs out and glanced at Hunt over her shoulder. "If you'd like to wait—"

"We wouldn't," he assured her, indicating, impatiently, that she should keep moving. "Stay with the car," he instructed Bishop.

She hadn't thought they'd wait for her in the car. But it had been worth a shot. She got out and, without a backward glance, went through the imposing wrought-iron doors of the two-hundred-year-old bank. She strode across the cool marble lobby, greeted the receptionist in fluent Swiss-German, and waited for the bank officer to accompany her to the vault.

One area was reserved for the thousands of secure mailboxes. Another for safety-deposit boxes. And of course she also had her bank accounts here. But today all she was interested in was her mail.

Taylor punched in her code outside the high-security area and waited for the light to blink green. The bank officer then did the same. A screen lit up, and she kept her eyes open for the retinal scan. She thanked the gentleman, who'd wait outside, then preceded her entourage into the large silent room.

It took a matter of minutes to slide the large metal box from the wall and return to the table in the center of the room where Hunt and his men stood waiting.

"Might as well take a load off," Taylor told them, sitting down herself after lowering the heavy box to the table. She unlocked it and flipped the lid.

The last envelope she'd mailed to herself was on top. She removed the padded envelope and set it aside.

"A little something splashy?" Hunt asked wryly.

"The Elliott emeralds."

He shot her an unfathomable look. Taylor wondered how he'd react if she closed the foot of space between them to kiss him.

"Jesus," he said roughly. "That smile scares me."

She patted his thigh. "Anything unfamiliar is always frightening. Don't worry, I'm harmless." She felt the flex and play of his muscles beneath her hand and wanted to fan herself. She'd always loved the adrenaline rush of danger. And Huntington St. John personified it.

The legs of his chair scraped across the carpet as he shoved it back out of range and stood. "Insidious, you mean."

Max laughed.

Taylor shrugged, then removed the package she'd mailed from San Cristóbal.

Hunt and Max came up on either side of her.

"Back off," she told them firmly. "I'm here. You're here. The envelope is here. Breathing down my neck isn't going to make me open it any faster."

"Open the damn thing and let's get on with it."

She picked up the small knife she kept inside the box to slit the envelope.

Hunt's hand shot out and gripped her wrist. "No knife."

He wasn't holding her tightly, but there was no way she could break free. The knife fell from her numb fingers with a small clatter. A fabulous trick, and one she'd love to learn.

"Geez." She looked up at him. "What do you think I can do to you with this little thing?"

"We're not going to find out. Here, I'll open it."

"*I'll* hold the envelope. You cut." She didn't want them to know the weight of the contents. They could have the disks. But whatever else was in the envelope was none of their business.

"Fine." He slit the top of the large padded envelope. "Pour everything out on the table."

She could see the Barter diamonds from Morales's safe coiled like a glittering snake at the bottom of the heavy padded bag. Her heart did a little excited lurch at their fiery beauty. She would have them couriered to the office in the morning, along with the emeralds.

She stuck her arm into the envelope and pulled out a stack of papers, envelopes, interspersed with what looked like mini-DVDs in plastic cases. There were two left deep inside the bag, tangled with Maria Morales's necklaces.

"Here." She handed the unwieldy bundle to Hunt with her left hand, while palming the other two small disks with her right.

Insurance.

She had absolutely no proof, other than Huntington St. John's word, that they *were* the good guys. And although she believed it 99.9 percent, there was always the possibility of a double cross. It never hurt to watch your own back because, basically, people never did what you thought they were going to do. They were all out for number one.

Well, so was she. She had to be. As long as she took care of herself, Mandy was taken care of. And that was all that mattered.

"Thanks, Taylor." Max smiled. He had a nice smile, easy, relaxed, friendly. It might not reach all the way to his eyes, but it was there nevertheless.

She smiled back at him. Max Aries was a lot easier to get along with than Hunt. Too bad she wanted the guy with no sense of humor. Go figure.

"You're welcome. Now, no offense, but—nice knowing you. Good-bye." She quickly got to her feet, slamming the lid down.

Hunt grabbed her wrist. "Not so bloody fast. Empty the envelope onto the table. Now."

She looked down at his dark hand circling her pale wrist, trying to figure out how such light pressure could hurt so badly and how his grip could be unbreakable. Damn. He was full of neat tricks. She gave him a hurt look from under her lashes. "You're hurting my wrist. *Again.*"

"It's not broken. Yet. Don't push me. Dump it."

Taylor flipped the lid of the metal box open with a thump, then took out the envelope and jabbed it into his rock-hard stomach. "Here. Open it yourself. And don't even think about taking my diamonds, they're my paycheck."

Hunt released her wrist and took the bag from her, tossing the contents onto the mahogany tabletop. The diamonds looked even better piled all together on the dark wood. Taylor rubbed her wrist. Clearly there was nothing else in the envelope but jewelry. "Satisfied?"

"You have no idea. Let's go. We'll give you a lift to a hotel on our way back to the airport."

"How lovely for me." Taylor secured the box, returning it to its position in the wall, and walked ahead of them out of the room. She went through the exit security measures by rote.

Fifteen minutes from start to finish and they were back in the waiting limo. The rain had stopped and the early morning air smelled clean and fresh.

"Where to?" Hunt asked. He didn't seem to care. Which was just fine and dandy with her.

"The Hotel *Baur au Lac,*" she told the driver. It was a quick train ride from home.

The car pulled away from the curb. They passed a flower seller packing up for the day. There was a stall near home. She'd stop there on her way out of town and buy a bunch of colorful flowers to take Mandy. Her sister loved color. And the simple amazement of scents. Not like the interior of the car. It smelled . . . wrong.

Rain made the view through the windows waver. Odd. She thought the rain had stopped. Taylor frowned, suddenly feeling sick to her stomach. She swallowed bile. There was a carafe of water and several glasses in a little bar near Hunt, but she was afraid if she moved, she'd throw up. She never got sick. Never. It was one of the few things she counted on when working all over the world.

"Carsick?" Hunt asked, his image large and menacing in the dusky light inside the car. His eyes seemed to glow in the semidarkness as he loomed over her.

Black dots swirled in her vision. "Nope," her voice slurred. "Don' get ca—"

Everything went black.

Twenty-four

HUNT CAUGHT TAYLOR AS HER EYES ROLLED AND SHE STARTED to slide off the seat to the floor. "What the bloody hell . . . ?" He hefted her gently onto his lap, fingers going to the pulse at her throat. Normal. Her face was pale, but cool to the touch. No fever.

"Stress?" Max asked.

"She *induces* it," he told Max absently, tilting her face up and feeling for a pulse beneath her ear. Even she couldn't fake this. Her pulse was too slow and even, her eyelids didn't flutter, and her body lay limp and boneless against him.

He cupped her cheek in his palm. He'd never seen her face this unanimated, and seeing it this way now gave him a strange hollow feeling in the pit of his stomach. She wasn't the type of woman to swoon under duress.

"Taylor? Wake up, love." He reached back to slide aside the privacy window, but it was stuck. Bloody hell. He rapped on it to get the driver's attention. "Get us to the hospital. *Now.*"

His head jerked around at a loud, hollow *thump*. Beside him, Bishop was slumped against the door. Unconscious.

"Fuck." Hunt realized too late that something was seriously wrong. He fumbled beneath his jacket for his H&K in the shoulder holster. The grip seemed to slip through his fingers. Bloody hell. He'd never been this butterfingered in his life. He tried again and finally managed to withdraw the weapon. It felt as though it weighed twenty pounds.

"Hold your breath," he yelled at Max, who was also scrabbling for his own gun. "Open the goddamned windows." Hunt saw his friend's glassy eyes roll. Max jerked himself upright, felt for the window control. Cracked it an inch. Shook his head. Tried again.

Still holding the last breath he'd taken, Hunt shifted Taylor's limp body to the seat between himself and Bishop and reached for the automatic window button on his side. It was as though he were moving through treacle.

Too late.

His fingers touched the small square button, but it felt soft instead of hard. His head spun.

Get . . . everyone . . . out of . . . ah . . . what? Car. Out . . . Car.

Trees and buildings whizzed by in hyperdrive. The windows appeared to buckle as he tried to force his fingers, eyes, and brain to cooperate.

Max slid in slo-mo across the seat toward the window closest to him. "Ga—" He didn't make it. He slumped, then slid into an ungainly heap to the floor at Hunt's feet.

Gas. Yes. Hunt knew. His vision grayed out, then returned, dim and useless. He felt himself slipping under and gritted his teeth trying to hold on.

Window. Door. Out.

Throw Taylor from the speeding vehicle? She'd be safe. Dead, but safe. The car had to slow for something. Traffic. Lights. Pedestrians. *He must be rea—* Hunt shook his head trying to clear the thick fog. *Must be ready.*

Using every muscle and tendon, he attempted to straighten his sagging body, but nothing worked. His automatic dug into his rib cage as his body and brain melted and dissolved.

Weapon. Must. Tay—

HUNT OPENED HIS EYES, HEAD BRACED AGAINST THE WINDOW TO HIS left. Red danced and wavered in his vision. He blinked several times to bring the surreal, Salvador Daliesque world into focus. The car was parked in a field of brilliant scarlet poppies spotlit by a white half-moon.

He straightened, removed the H&K from the seat beside him, and checked his inside pocket with the other.

The three disks were gone.

Fucking bloody hell.

He turned to check on Taylor. She was exactly as he'd left her—he glanced at his watch—Jesus! *Three hours ago.* He felt for her pulse while doing a lightning-fast scan of the interior of the vehicle. Bishop was gone. Max was still unconscious on the floor.

Powerful shit to have them out this long.

And why, he asked himself, *would someone go to the trouble of gassing them only to leave them alive and still armed?*

Without a doubt it was because whoever had utilized the tranq gas had believed it would *kill* them all. Sloppy. Extremely sloppy not to positively confirm the hit. He couldn't imagine Morales being this careless.

Bishop? Hunt wondered, furious with himself for letting down his guard for a moment. Had the operative turned rogue and betrayed them? Tranqed them, stolen the disks, and even now headed to sell the intel to the highest bidder?

Hunt sprung the latch and pushed open the car door. Cool damp air rushed in. It felt good on his face. He bent to feel Max's pulse. Alive, at least. He nudged him with his foot. "Rise and shine, old son."

Max raised his head, groggy but, Hunt knew, immediately aware. Max pulled himself back on the seat across from Hunt and rubbed his jaw, eyes still glassy. "Jesus. What hit us?"

"*Who?*" Hunt said grimly. "They got the disks." He reached for

Taylor, then thought better of it and stepped out into the high, damp grass alone to reconnoiter, leaving the door open to the chilly, late-night air. She couldn't have had anything to do with this, could she? His gut told him she was nothing more than a not-so-innocent by-stander.

"Ah, crap." Max got out of the car as well, weapon in hand. Who-ever'd hit them was long gone. "Just fucking perfect."

Other than a centuries-old oak tree in front of the vehicle, there wasn't a damn thing to see for miles around. They were in the middle of bloody nowhere. Not even the city lights were visible.

"Bishop's split," Hunt told Max grimly. "I'll check the driver." He walked around the back of the car. "Tire tracks. We had an escort." He paused to inspect the deep ruts in the wet grass. "Following in be-hind us. Truck, it looks like. Two sets of footprints here—men. One five-eight, five-ten, hundred and sixty. The other taller, about two hun-dred pounds. But check this out. Another vehicle . . ." He crouched down to get a better look. "Four-door sedan. Five, six people. Lighter weight. Small guys." He rose, followed the crisscrossing steps.

"Scuffle here by the rear door. Did what they had to do, then got back in their vehicle—truck, by the look of the tread—and peeled out fast. These guys were in a hurry . . . The sedan took off behind them. Look at the tracks going off over there. They were burning rubber following the truck."

"Working together?" Max asked.

"If they were, they fought about it," Hunt said dryly, looking at spatters of black-looking blood on the grass and the side of their limo. There was a great deal of it. Either someone had bled out and they'd taken the body with them, or several people were seriously in-jured. It was impossible to tell.

He opened the driver's-side door. The sour-sweet smell of blood hung thick in the damp air. "Christ. Driver's gone. But I found Bishop. He's up here, tucked nicely and neatly in his place." He had a momentary twinge of guilt for believing that Neal Bishop had turned on them, but was over it in an instant.

Bishop had been buckled into the driver's seat and was slumped over the steering wheel. Hunt reached in, feeling for a pulse beneath the younger man's ear. Slow but steady. His forehead bled sluggishly, like lava, from the Mount Vesuvius of a bump in the middle of the poor bastard's forehead. That was going to hurt. But he'd live.

The windshield was shattered. A spider's web radiating from where Bishop's head was supposed to have hit it. Crumpling the front end of the limo was the huge oak tree. A neat "accident," cleverly constructed.

Bloody, bloody hell.

"He'll be all right." Hunt straightened, looking over the roof of the car. "Helluva headache, I suspect."

"Ah. The master of understatement," Max said laconically, breathing fast enough for Hunt to know he was fighting nausea. His own stomach didn't feel too hot either. "*Mano del Dios,* Black Rose, or another tango we haven't connected yet?"

"Even odds," Hunt responded, scanning the vast field they were in. "The real question is, how in the bloody hell did they know we were in Zurich?"

"Flight plan." Max rubbed his face. "Man, that was some powerful stuff."

Hunt shot him a pointed look. "Flight plan?" T-FLAC rarely filed a correct flight plan. It was yet another way to stay a step ahead of the tangos. "No, I suspect they were keeping close tabs on Taylor."

"Maybe. But there's no way in hell they could've landed in Zurich before us," Max pointed out. "Absolutely no way."

"Satellite tracking of the plane." Hunt dipped his head to see how Taylor was doing on the backseat. Still out. He straightened, leaning an elbow on the car's roof.

"The news about her Houston museum heist was in the paper by the time we reached the airport. If you're looking for a thief, you follow jewel thefts. They had her in Houston."

"Or the Mediterranean, or wherever else someone pulled a jewelry heist in the past two months," Max pointed out, his color returning. "She's spectacularly good, but she's hardly the only jewel thief in the world."

"They'd do what we did. Follow up on *every* lead. No matter how small. Like us, they'd eventually figure out the who and the why. Then they'd have the where."

Though their pilots would have filed a false flight plan on takeoff, even T-FLAC couldn't go over international airspace without talking to traffic control to let them know exactly where they were. *Bingo.* "One call with the correct destination, and they had someone waiting to follow us from the airport. And talking about calls . . ." He felt in his breast pocket for his cell phone, frankly not expecting to find it.

"Look at this." He held it up for Max to see. A bad feeling swirled in the pit of his stomach, and it had nothing to do with gas. "They left us with not only our weapons, but also a way to contact help. The bastards were confident their knockout potion would kill us."

"*Very* inefficient," Max agreed.

"Indeed. Come and get Bishop."

"How come *I* don't get to rescue the pretty girl?" Max demanded, walking around the back of the limo to join him on the driver's side. He tugged at Bishop's sleeve, then grunted as Neal Bishop fell into him.

"Because you're too ugly. You'd scare her the moment she comes around. We need her thinking clearly, not reeling." Hunt shrugged out of his jacket and spread it on the ground, then reached in for Taylor.

She felt light and deceptively unsubstantial in his arms. Odd, when her personality was so much larger than life. Kneeling, he gently settled her onto the meager covering. Wet grass beat the god-awful stink of death hands down.

"Bishop's coming out of it," Max reported. *"Ah, man!"*

Hunt chuckled as he heard the unmistakable sound of vomiting. He rose and reached into the car for the carafe of water for Taylor, then thought better of it. Who knew if the gas they'd inhaled was also water soluble? Or if the person who gassed them had taken the extra precaution of spiking any open container in the limo? He grabbed a can of soda instead. The carbonation would help her nausea.

It was another fifteen minutes before she opened her eyes and groaned. By which time Max had called in and requested backup,

Bishop had ordered the pilots to stand down, and Hunt had walked behind the vehicle tracks looking for clues, *anything* to indicate who had hit them and where the hell they'd gone.

"Nothing?" Bishop asked, looking a little green about the gills as he leaned against the side of the vehicle.

Hunt crouched beside Taylor. "Nothing."

She opened dazed eyes when he touched her clammy cheek. Blinking, she swallowed several times. "What—" She licked her lips and stared up at him with pain-stricken blue eyes. He could see her brain trying to function. Trying to process. Trying to assimilate what had happened.

"What did you do to me?" she demanded.

How like her to assume he was the culprit. One corner of his mouth quirked. "Sorry, darling, but it wasn't us. And it wasn't done only to you. We're minutes out of it ourselves. Someone pumped the vehicle with some sort of nerve gas."

"*Someone?*" She frowned. "Why'm I the only one lying down?"

"Smaller frame, lighter body weight." Her dark hair, misted by raindrops, curled around her stark white face. Her cheek felt hot and clammy in his palm. "How do you feel?"

"L-Like sh—" Her throat convulsed. He quickly moved his hand to support her forehead and rolled her over. In the nick of time.

When she was finished, Hunt handed her a neatly folded handkerchief. "Done?" He watched her carefully as she pressed it to her mouth.

She squeezed her eyes shut and whispered fervently, "Please God."

"Ready to sit up?"

"I feel kinda pukey," she admitted, throat moving as she swallowed repeatedly to keep from throwing up again. He did what he could to check her pupils by moonlight. A bit dilated.

"That's to be expected. Here, let me help you." He assisted her, holding her as she fought back the nausea. He handed her the open can. "Sip slowly on this until it passes."

She managed to gulp down a good portion of the cold drink, and a little color came back into her face. "Is everyone else all right?" She pressed the can to her cheek.

"All present and accounted for."

"Oh, God." She rested her head against his chest. Her body felt warm against his, her silky hair brushed his chin, smelling of wet violets. "Why would anyone—" Her head shot up and she stared at him. "Oh my God. The disks! It was those damn stupid *disks* they wanted. Wasn't it?"

"Yes."

"That gas was meant to *kill* us." She dropped her head into her hands. "I would've been responsible for killing— Oh, my God."

"Water over that bridge," Hunt said unsympathetically. Although he certainly felt a smidge as she peeked up at him over her hands with such a look of horrified contrition that he wanted to gather her in arms and— *Jesus fucking Christ.* "None of us died." *Not today.*

"The authorities are on their way," he said. "You're going to the hospital as soon as they get here." He held his weapon ready as several pairs of headlights broke the night. The rain began again in a soft, barely felt mist. He wanted her out of the weather and in a warm bed. Preferably with him wrapped around her. Jesus, what a bloody mess. Literally and figuratively.

Twenty-five

THE NEXT FEW HOURS PASSED IN A BLUR FOR TAYLOR. HUNT refused to let the authorities interrogate her until she'd been checked out. The nausea subsided by the time they reached *Universitäts Spital,* but by then she was too exhausted to protest when he remained with her for the entire examination. A clean bill of health and a nasty lecture to get good rest were all the hospital offered.

Max and Neal waited for them outside the hospital, beside what was presumably a rental car. She looked around in surprise to see that the rain had cleared and it was already well after dawn. The air smelled clean and fresh; the light glowed a hazy, pale yellow of a canary diamond. Pretty.

"Okay?" Max asked, scanning her face as she and Hunt approached.

She gave him what felt like a wan smile. "I'm going to have to postpone that tractor pull I was so looking forward to."

"Disappointing," he said gravely. "Why not take a nap instead?"

"God, don't toy with me."

"The authorities contacted HQ," Max told Hunt when all the doors were closed. "We answered what we could, no need for either of you to be interrogated. We're free to go." He opened the back door for Taylor. "In you get, beautiful."

She looked at the car warily, then glanced up at Max. "Are we completely sure about this one? No more poison?"

"Checked it out myself, princess," Max assured her with a wink.

She climbed into the backseat. So tired, so wrung-out, she would've accompanied them to Interpol if they'd offered her a bed in a dark room to decompress. Right now it took all her energy just to breathe in and out.

Hunt walked around and got in on the other side. Cozy. She would've liked to crawl into his lap and take a nap with her head snuggled on his broad, manly chest. She gripped the armrest and looked out of the window instead.

She thought of kidnap victims who fell in love with their captors; Stockholm syndrome, they called it. She had suppressed the little girl who'd once lived inside her. The kid who'd yearned for someone to stand between her and the world, someone to keep her safe.

She'd buried that child at fifteen when she learned, and accepted, that the only person she could depend on to protect her and Mandy was herself.

"Team'll be here at 1900," Bishop told Hunt as they pulled out into early morning commuter traffic. Max drove like a NASCAR race was in progress.

When Bishop turned sideways, she saw the huge black-and-blue knot right in the middle of his forehead. She felt his pain.

"You have me for another few hours before I have to bail," Max told him. "Damn. I hate to miss all the fun."

Taylor rested her head against the seat and closed her eyes. How long had it been since she'd grabbed those few hours of sleep on the plane? And how long before that? Too long. Her body was an eighth of an inch away from complete shutdown.

"Where to?" Max asked beside her.

She rolled her head in his general direction and cracked her eyes open to see where they were. "Take the next right at the gas station, go six blocks and turn right again at the blue house with yellow shutters and the barking dog. I'll tell you when."

She knew she should have directed them to a hotel. But she just wanted to be home. Wanted the familiar surroundings of her condo. Her own bathroom, her own bed. But before she could do that, she had to call the school. Fortunately, they never told Mandy she was coming until she was actually on the school grounds. To her sister, each second she had to wait for her was an eternity.

"Weren't you going to a hotel?" Hunt asked.

She opened one eye to glare at him. It didn't have much impact. But it was the best she could manage. "Don't push me, big boy. I'm having a bad day here."

Throwing up while her new lover was holding her sweaty head ranked up there with Life's Most Embarrassing Moments.

"It isn't over yet. Don't fall asleep. You need to tell us where to go."

She managed a smile. "I've told you *that* a dozen times at least. You never listen." She leaned over to touch Max on the shoulder. "It's the gray building on the corner with white trim."

The condo complex had high security and a doorman 24/7. Taylor had owned two condos in this complex for the past nine years. The one on the third floor was in her own name, and the smaller one, on the second floor, as Beth Tudor. Never hurt to have a backup hole to crawl into.

"Doesn't look like a hotel," Hunt said as Max pulled the car into the curved driveway under the portico.

"Condos." She really didn't have the mental fortitude to bs at the moment.

Her door opened and she looked at it stupidly. Actually, she looked directly at Hunt's groin. It was a very nice groin, but she was too damn exhausted to get properly excited about it right now.

"You live here?"

"Uh-huh." She closed her eyes for a second. Really. Who cared that he knew where she lived? He'd traveled halfway around the world to find her, against all odds, in Houston. If he wanted to, he could find her again.

"Something you might have mentioned earlier," he said flatly. "You can't sleep in the car. Hop out."

"There will be no hopping this early in the morning, pal." She could barely move. She opened her eyes again and swung her legs from the car. Her lovely silk pants were filthy and grass-stained.

Hunt leaned over her and snapped the seat-belt buckle to release her. Okay. *That* made it easier to get out of the car. His arm brushed her breasts coming and going. Nice, but right now, no cigar.

He extended his hand to help her out. "Sir Huntington, are you?" she managed to ask, smiling up at him. "Very gentlemanly. Thanks." Taylor took his hand. It felt strong, warm, and safe wrapped around hers.

A little electrical shock traveled up her arm at his touch. Not sharp or brilliant white, but a little zing of warmth. She let him pull her forward and stepped onto the sidewalk, wobbly on her feet.

"What if those people followed us?" she asked suddenly, stopping in her tracks. It was daylight, and they'd left the hospital in full view of anybody and everybody. The nausea she hadn't experienced in several hours churned once again in her stomach.

"I hope to hell they *have* followed us," Hunt told her, eyes glittering with fury. "We look forward to meeting them formally. Although, unfortunately, it isn't likely since they believe us to be quite dead. Still, we can live in hope. Come on, you have to lead the way."

"What happens now?"

He steadied her by curving his arm about her shoulders. Taylor used up her last reserves by resisting resting her head against the solid plane of his chest.

"Now we escort you inside, and everyone gets some shut-eye."

That had a reviving effect. "*Everyone? Stay here?*"

"Here." He walked her into the lobby, his arm about her shoulders. Max stayed close to her left side, and Bishop brought up the rear, almost treading on her heels. Max handed the concierge the car keys, who in turn passed them discreetly to a waiting valet.

"What floor?" Hunt asked.

She wanted to tell him he could *not* stay with her. Because, damn it, he was supposed to be a one-night stand. Okay, a *two*-night stand.

And this whole thing was supposed to be *over* by now. He should be riding off into the sunset, not crowding her in the elevator of her own damn building.

This was her sacred ground. No one crossed the threshold of her condo, not ever. "What floor?" Max asked.

"Four," Taylor told him. She looked at Neal Bishop. "That has to hurt." He had a big, extremely painful-looking black-and-blue knot in the middle of his forehead. It reminded her that they could all have woken up stone dead, instead of pukey and hungover. There were several extremely bad guys out there who'd already tried to kill them once.

Maybe it wasn't a bad thing to have the good guys hang around a little longer.

Bishop gave her a stony look. "I'll live."

The door pinged discreetly on the fourth floor. The moment the doors parted, Taylor strode down the wide, elegantly wallpapered hallway to her door at the far end, not looking back to see if the three men followed.

Nobody said anything. She prayed old Mrs. Hildebrandt next door wouldn't come charging out of her place on her walker, hair in rollers, to find out what was going on. Taylor couldn't muster the energy to be interrogated at the moment.

She practically tiptoed past her neighbor's door.

"Which one?" Hunt asked. He spoke so softly, Taylor was amazed she heard him at all. She pointed to her door. He took her purse from her with the ease of a gardener plucking a newly sprouted weed. Without a word, he opened her lovely smoke gray, snakeskin Prada clutch and pulled out her keys.

Hunt inserted a key. The right key the first time, no less.

"Wait out here," he ordered very softly. The hand signal activating the others was immediately followed by a lightning-fast series of clicks as each man chambered a bullet. Then, with guns at the ready, Hunt and Max slipped inside her condo like oil over water.

"Let's go," Bishop told her shortly, taking her elbow in a no-nonsense grip. She didn't protest as he shoved her down the hallway ahead of him. Not because his gun was a nasty-looking thing. Which it was. But because she wasn't stupid.

Clearly these men knew their way around guns and violence. She didn't. She was all for scaling rooftops and crawling through air-conditioning ducts with rent-a-cops after her. She loved the adrenaline rush. But if there was going to be shooting—at close range, no less—she was out of there.

The thought that somebody—*anybody*—was in her home without her knowledge gave her the heebie-jeebies. The thought that it was the *same* people who'd already tried to kill them gave her the *über*-heebie-jeebies.

Bishop pulled her with him into the doorway to the stairwell, beyond the elevator bank, then released her arm and stepped aside. He didn't look happy.

"Guess you drew the short straw, huh?" Taylor whispered.

His answer was to shove her behind him. He held the gun up as if fully expecting to blow away the first person coming around the corner.

Lord, this was insane. The closest encounter she'd had with a gun before meeting Hunt was that time in Paris a few years ago, when the guard had chased her across a rooftop. He'd been a lousy shot, and more scared than she was. She had no way of knowing for sure, but she'd bet he was as relieved as she'd been when she got away.

With that flame tattoo curling up his right forearm and a wicked scar on his left, Neal Bishop looked more like a biker than a reliable protector. "What happens if—"

"Quiet," he hissed, not looking at her. "Not another word out of you. I'm listening."

"For what?" Taylor whispered back.

"Gunshots."

Shit.

Twenty-six

ZURICH

LISA MAKI SAT IN THE ONLY CHAIR IN THE ROOM AND CROSSED her legs. She lit a French cigarette, inhaled deeply, then let the acrid smoke curl from her nostrils. She picked a piece of tobacco off her tongue with short, unpainted nails before she spoke. "Which of you?" she asked, her voice thick with fury, and, *Madre de Dios,* fear, though she would never let them see it.

"*Which* of you," she repeated to the three people standing before her, "will be fearless enough to tell her we have failed? That despite our brilliant and careful plan, *Mano del Dios* moved faster, intercepted us, and from beneath our very noses took our prize?"

Somehow, the *Mano del Dios* operatives had arrived in Zurich almost simultaneously with Lisa. How this was possible Lisa did not know. She hadn't even seen that they were being followed from the airport until the big black truck overtook them and swooped in to take the prize.

Her man, driving the limo, had been killed first.

Marcos and Felicity were dead. Their bodies, stripped of identity, were still in the rental car parked behind the motel. Gregory was bleeding on the cheap hotel rug. Without proper medical care, he too would be dead come morning.

The only thing that had gone *right* was the three T-FLAC operatives' deaths, as well as that of the woman. The XC11 gas she'd used was quick and lethal. The supplier had guaranteed his product with his life.

Half her job was done. But her brilliantly executed plan had, unfortunately, assisted *Mano del Dios* in retrieving the disks as easily as a mother plucked a teat from a baby's mouth.

The ramifications of her failure made Lisa feel numb. She looked at her remaining three members through a veil of terror. "Well?"

Their silence was punctuated by the sound of rain hitting the windowpane.

"I will do it," Stefan said when the quiet stretched unbearably. He had the body of a man and the mind of an adolescent. His accuracy with a pistol was nothing short of miraculous. His stamina in bed impressive.

"No." Lisa stood. "It is I who bears the responsibility." Taking her cell phone from her pocket, she nodded to Stefan as she flipped it open. Stefan removed a Ruger from the pack he carried. Before Christina or Gregory knew what he was about, the boy shot them. One shot each to the temple.

Pop. Pop. They hit the floor almost simultaneously and lay still. Dead still.

"Good boy." Lisa smiled at him as she hit the speed-dial number for her own office in Barcelona. As the phone rang on the other end, she walked over and gently removed the gun from Stefan's hand. "Good with a gun, but *not* a good driver, I'm afraid. Five minutes faster and we could've retrieved the disks and completed our task." She raised his pistol. His innocent eyes widened and his mouth contorted with terror. Without hesitation she pulled the trigger.

Stefan stared at her blankly for a moment. His mouth moved. She wasn't sure she'd hit him. But from such close range . . . Still looking at her from sightless eyes, his knees gave way and he crumpled atop Gregory's body and lay still.

The ringing phone was picked up. Bile rose in Lisa's throat as a cool voice spoke in her ear. "You have my disks?"

Twenty-seven

N O GUNSHOTS.

"All clear," Neal told Taylor after several long, *tense* minutes of silence.

She could have told him that. Most of the residents in the building worked, and mornings on the fourth floor were usually pretty quiet. If there'd been any untoward noises, Mrs. Hildebrandt, with her bat ears and her walker, would be in the thick of things.

Thank God there'd been no shots fired. Shooting meant the police. Possibly a dead body. Which all sounded exhausting and more than she wanted to deal with at the moment.

She stumbled after Neal, who'd started down the corridor. He continued to hold the big, menacing-looking gun. Taylor walked directly behind him, using his tall body as a shield.

Hunt waited for them at her front door. He too still held his gun. "After you," he said, gesturing her inside as if she were a guest.

"No Uzi-wielding bad guys lying in wait?" Taylor asked as she walked past him, kicked off her heels to clatter on the marble floor, and kept right on going. Marta, her bimonthly char, used lavender furniture polish on all the wood pieces, and the entry hall welcomed her home with open arms.

Neal followed her inside, then Hunt closed and locked the door. "Place is clear," he said, following her. "Nobody's been here for a while."

She looked at the vacuum marks on the plush, cream wool carpet. Marta had her own machine, and she vacuumed her way out of the front door every other week. Except for a few sets of large, wide depressions, presumably Hunt's and Max's, the carpet was Marta-pristine.

"Not since last Tuesday anyway," Taylor agreed as she continued through the spacious, gold and black living room without stopping. A jungle of plants, saturated by early morning sunshine pouring through the windows overlooking the lake, had grown inches in the month since she'd last been home.

"There's a shower in the guest room," Taylor told the three men. "Gym is third door on the right, if you have the urge to punch something. And if you're hungry, check the kitchen."

Marta usually stocked up for her every couple of weeks, in the hopes she'd be home more often. "Coffee's in the freezer, and there's always frozen or canned stuff. Help yourselves."

Taylor yawned, beyond ready for a quick shower and a long nap. Without waiting for their response, she started down the long hallway.

The glide of a drawer being opened stopped her in her tracks, and she retraced her steps to see what they were up to.

Hunt stood beside her Chinese credenza with the top drawer open. The piece had been a gift from the House of Chu six years ago, in thanks for the return of a six-hundred-year-old jade chess set made of rare and expensive purple jade. It was a lovely and generous gesture, but her commission alone had paid the deposit for her second condo, down on the third floor.

"Can I help you find something?" she asked a little too politely, too damn tired to be fully irritated, but knowing that she was. "I don't own a gun. And if you guys are searching for something to eat, the kitchen is that way."

"Feel free to do whatever it is you'd do if we weren't here," Hunt said absently, riffling through her *Rapallo* lace tablecloths.

Annoying man. If *he* wasn't here, *she* wouldn't be here. She was *supposed* to be in London at the Hardings' house party. Retrieving a gorgeous choker of perfectly matched Burmese rubies. Stolen a month ago and already reset.

"Now *there's* a dangerous weapon," she said dryly. "Why don't you check the freezer in the kitchen? I keep the weapons-grade pluto-nium in the ice trays."

Hunt looked up. "Got any electrical tape?"

"No." Maybe he wanted to *shut* her up, or he wanted to *tie* her up. Taylor wasn't in the mood for either. "Keep the noise down in here. And don't worry about the front door when you leave, it'll lock be-hind you automatically."

She went back down the long, wide hallway leading to the master suite, firmly closed both doors, then locked them.

Taylor drew in a ragged breath as she picked up the control from the bedside table and closed the electronically operated drapes, shut-ting out the spectacular lake view and the bright morning sunlight with full-length, blackout-lined, rose velvet drapes. The room imme-diately went dark.

Removing her jacket, she tossed it in the general direction of the wide, king-sized bed. It slid to the floor as she stalked into the opu-lent bathroom and turned on the gold faucets adorning her sumptu-ous shower stall.

"There's nothing that says I have to cooperate with them for the rest of my natural life, is there?" she demanded as she stripped. "No," she answered herself as steam filled the room. "There sure as hell isn't." She bent down to retrieve the two small pieces of insurance she'd hidden in a specially constructed and totally concealed pocket sewn into the waistband of her ruined slacks. Only then did she walk naked to the gilt mirror disguising the medicine chest.

"I accompanied them halfway around the world." She opened the mirrored door, took out a jar of face cream and twisted off the lid. "I took them to the bank." She removed a few good pieces from the jar—earrings, and a diamond-encrusted watch—and tossed them into a crystal hair-clip bowl by the sink.

"I *gave* them what they asked for—no, *demanded.*" Taylor inserted the two disks from the bank into the empty container, then reached back into the medicine cabinet and removed a large box of body powder. "I was asphyxiated, almost killed. It should not be this impossible to get rid of a man."

She sprinkled a goodly amount of loose powder from the second jar into the first, then tapped it on the counter to settle around her contraband. She tightened the lid, placed the jar back inside the cabinet, and snapped the door closed.

"Now, damn it." She jerked open the shower door and stepped into a stream of temperature-controlled water with a sigh. "*Now* I have squatters with guns in my sanctuary. This is just wrong in so many ways."

And then, because clearly the poison gas had addled what little was left of any intelligent brain cells, she wished Hunt would come into her room and join her in the shower.

Twenty-eight

I HAVE RETRIEVED THE DISKS," ANDREAS CONSTANTINE TOLD
Morales over the phone. He was a good man, Andreas. A loyal fol-
lower and an excellent leader to his men. He would be richly rewarded.

A sense of monumental relief swamped José at the news. God
answered his prayers as He always did.

Vengeance is mine, saith the Lord.

Each small disk held hundreds of bits of complex information.
They also stipulated in what order each set of highly detailed instructions should be used. Not even a mathematician could comprehend
or calculate the variables necessary to gain access to the underground
vault through the various booby traps without those disks.

"You have done well, my friend—"

But Constantine was still talking. "Not only from T-FLAC's very
hands," he said smugly, "but from those of *another* group equally eager
to have them."

The interruption in and of itself was annoying, but— "*Another* group? *What* other group?"

"Black Rose?"

Morales twisted his water glass between his fingers. Faster and faster. God clenched a tight fist in his belly. "Are you *asking* me," he demanded, pulses of light burning behind his eyes, "or *telling* me?"

There was a pregnant pause. "One was seriously injured. But we killed two. Each had the Black Rose tattoo."

Morales closed his eyes. Black Rose.

They were too small a group to wrest world dominance away from him, no matter how much they wanted to try. Still, they were an irritating burr beneath his skin. Them, he would deal with at another time. He drew in a calming breath. At least he had the disks. "You have all five disks safely in your possession, *sí?*" he confirmed.

The plan would proceed as planned. God was pleased.

He listened to the silence on the other end of the phone. "Constantine?"

"*Gamw'to!*" Andreas Constantine whispered. "There were *five* such disks?"

Twenty-nine

WITH BARELY THE ENERGY TO DRY OFF, TAYLOR PADDED back into the cool, darkened bedroom. Home sweet—

Beneath the rose and cream quilted velvet spread, now haphazardly tugged free, she saw a large lump right in the middle of her bed. Her pulse did a little hop, skip, and jump.

Carefully, so as not to wake him, she pulled the covers back. *Mmm.* Sliding into her own bed after a month's absence felt like sheer heaven. Discovering Hunt waiting for her was a bonus. She smiled, moving across the cool silky sheets until her bare, damp body came flush against his warm back.

His wet hair smelled of Mandy's never-used shampoo, but the fragrance of his freshly soaped skin was pure male and as familiar to her as her own heartbeat. Taylor's breath caught as sleep and arousal commingled, drifting through her body like the gentle eddy of steam.

He didn't stir. He really was sleeping.

Disappointed, Taylor let out the breath she held. It was probably for the best. As far as she knew, he hadn't slept at all since leaving the

States. And she doubted he'd wasted much time sleeping while searching for her all over God's creation either. Even a powerful warrior like Huntington St. John required sleep once in a while.

She was surprised to realize that meeting Hunt had profoundly changed her life in an elemental way. She was more than physically attracted to him, which intrigued her. This was more complex than anything she'd felt for either of her previous lovers, although she'd liked them both. *Like* wasn't the way she'd describe her feelings for Huntington St. John, however.

She wasn't quite sure how to describe it. This felt . . . *richer.* More textured. More layered.

She wished she had more time to think about and explore it. But their time together was finite. And there were still too many secrets between them, too many concealing layers between them, with no time to peel them away.

She'd have liked him to stay, she thought sleepily, rubbing her cheek lightly over his shoulder. Just for a little while. Long enough to have the opportunity to get to know him. To find out if the face he presented to the world was the real Huntington St. John. She suspected that Hunt, like herself, had to be a chameleon to blend in with his surroundings.

Was there anyone in his life that he could be his authentic self with? Was he ever lonely?

Eyes closed, Taylor ran her hand lightly over the smooth skin and hard bone of his hip, then draped an arm over the dip in his waist. She hadn't given her loneliness much thought over the years. It just . . . was. A by-product of what she did, and who she did it to. Each of her personas had acquaintances. But no one could ever know who she *really* was.

And that wasn't a bad thing. There were times she didn't know who she was either. But she wasn't unhappy. She had no complaints about her life or her lifestyle. After all, she had chosen the path, known the pitfalls. She loved the couturier clothes, the beautiful custom-made shoes, the exquisite bling her job afforded her. And most of all she adored the excitement, the danger, the never knowing what was around the next stairwell.

She was an adrenaline junkie. Nothing wrong with that.

Taylor ran her fingers lightly up his biceps. His skin felt satin smooth, and hot beneath her touch. She suddenly realized how seldom she was touched. Even her sister, whom she adored, didn't like any type of physical contact. She understood babies could die from lack of physical contact, and wondered how she'd done without it, so *blithely,* for so long. She brushed her lips lightly over his shoulder, inhaling the fragrance of man, of Hunt, then sank into sleep.

She woke several hours—or maybe it was minutes—later, to find herself on her back, a large hard body nestled between her legs. Pleasure unfolded inside her like a butterfly opening its wings. Palm-to-palm, fingers linked with hers, Hunt held her hands shackled above her head.

She'd never felt anything as piercingly sweet as the warm, wet suction of his mouth, that clever, clever mouth, on her left nipple. Desire drifted through her like slowly rising steam. Soft and poignantly gentle. *"Mmmm,"* she murmured, not opening her eyes.

He lifted his head, leaving a cool place on her skin. "Awake?"

"Nuh-uh."

Warm lips skimmed her breast, trailing to the curve between shoulder and neck, then swept a sensitive spot with his tongue. The feel of his damp mouth on her skin shot through her body like brilliant sunlight reflecting on water. She arched her throat, curling her fingers tightly between his as sensation shimmered and danced through her.

He lifted his head, reached over and turned on the bedside lamp. "I want to look at you," he said softly.

Her body was poised, ready for him to resume where he'd left off, and the bright reading light made Taylor blink. His broad shoulders, limned by golden light, filled her view. His dark hair, still wet, hung loose, dripped droplets of cool water on her cheek.

She wanted to touch his face. She tugged a hand free. "Come back to me."

He turned his head, and the intensity of his smoky gaze as he looked down at her made her breath catch in her lungs and her heartbeat accelerate. The hunger in that look was as potent as a physical caress. At that instant Hunt was one hundred percent focused on her, as if she was the only person in the universe.

"It's a little unnerving having you look at me like that," she told him honestly, curving her palm against the strength of his jaw because she wanted every part of her to be touching him. He'd shaved, and his skin was smooth and warm beneath her fingers.

"Are you afraid of me?" he asked, voice thick. His breath caressed her mouth. He'd been drinking coffee, and she wanted to taste it on him.

She shook her head and smiled. "Exhilarated."

A low sound of pleasure hummed in her throat as Hunt settled on top of her. The crisp hair on his chest pleasurably abraded her sensitive nipples as he slid his torso over hers.

He brushed a strand of her hair out of her eyes, but all Taylor felt was the satin-hard length of him pressed intimately against her. She shifted beneath him, her blood hammering so turbulently she could barely breathe.

"You are so unbelievably sexy," he murmured against her throat. "So pretty right here." His tongue stroked her nipple into a hard, tight bud. "I've never seen skin this pale, and when I touch you like this . . ." He swirled his slick tongue around the hard bud. ". . . you get rosy pink all over, and these sweet little nipples get raspberry pink and beg me to suck them."

Her nipples tightened at his words, but when he drew one deep into the hot, wet cavern of his mouth, she whimpered. He trailed kisses between her breasts, bringing a hand up to caress the one his mouth wasn't paying attention to.

She arched under the straining leash of sensation, her legs moving restlessly beneath sheets without feeling them. How had she ever imagined that four-hundred-thread-count sheets and cashmere blankets could compete with the sensation of Hunt's hands and mouth on her body? He nibbled his way up her arched throat to her mouth. Then bracketed both wrists above her head, while the fingers of the other hand played with her nipple until she arched her back and moaned low in her throat. "So soft. So sweet."

He teased his thumb lightly over the hard bud of her nipple. She lifted her face. Their mouths met. She felt the urgency in his body, and expected him to take her mouth in a rush of hunger. Instead he brushed his firm mouth back and forth over hers languidly, his lips warm and smooth. She caught a hint of soap on his skin as his tongue flirted with the corner of her mouth.

"I can taste your smile, you know," he told her, his gravelly voice made huskier by his hunger.

"Mmm." She threaded her fingers through his drying hair. It felt thick and silky to the touch, and long enough when it was loose like this to frame his face. "How does a smile taste?"

"Like sunshine. Like hope. Like truth."

His words flowed through her, a caress of their own. "All that? Let me taste." Her tongue glided delicately across his lower lip, then traced the seam before moving to his upper lip. "Not sunshine," she whispered against his parted lips. "Fire. Heat. Refuge." She parted her lips against his, inviting him in.

His tongue glided inside, tasting hot, familiar, dangerous. In a heartbeat the kiss went from languorous to nuclear. A claiming. Their needy groans blended as he went in deeper, tongues teasing and twisting together.

He was an exceptional kisser. Not only kissing her mouth, but making love to it as though the kiss culminated the act. His tongue was nimble and inventive, his flavor heady, and dangerously seductive.

It was the unrestrained wildness of the kiss that excited her, the hint of his shredding control that fired her own base needs. He made her own desire a clawing, untamable *necessity.*

Her breath came swift and uneven when he let her up for air. Only to lavish kisses on her eyelids, her cheek, the curve of a brow. She shuddered as his body slid a little higher between her legs so she felt the hard ridge of his erection where she needed it most. She could count his heartbeats as he pulsed against her heat.

A hard shudder of pleasure ripped through her, and she shifted her hips, feeling him strain against that invisible leash he kept on himself as he purposefully held that part of himself tantalizingly out of reach.

Annoying, annoying man.

Tearing his mouth from hers, he lifted his head. After a nano-second of inactivity, Taylor opened her eyes. He was frowning down at her, so close she could see a rim of charcoal around the hot gray of his pupils. "I don't want to want you this badly."

"I can tell," Taylor said gravely, running an open hand down the hard plane of his belly to the jut of his very impressive erection. "It's a good thing you're not trying very hard to kick the habit." Her fingers closed around the hot satin length of him. "Your willpower sucks."

"Even when you annoy the hell out of me—*Jesus. Yes!*" His voice went guttural as she caressed him with her thumb, a leisurely arc over the tip. "I want you."

Delighted, she smiled. "Then you must want me all the time."

"Why in the bloody hell can't I get enough of you?" he demanded hoarsely, hips arching toward her. Her thumb did a slide, a light stroke that had his breath hissing through his teeth.

"Because I have your joystick in my hand?" She wrapped her fingers around him firmly, drawing them up, then down again.

"Now," he shuddered. "Not always."

"I don't know. But I'm not complaining."

Without answering, he brought his mouth down on hers again in a kiss so incendiary it made her toes curl and her heartbeat quadruple in a flash fire of response.

She drew both hands up his sides, using her nails to lightly score his skin. His back arched and he clenched his teeth as she wiggled her fingers between the burning heat where their bodies were flush.

His pelvis pressed down, trying to keep her away. Taylor tsked. "Now that is *such* a waste . . . of . . . energy. I can pretty much . . . get . . . my hands into any space. Ah."

When she closed her fingers around the satiny smooth length of him again, his penis jumped in response. She stroked up and down his pulsing heat, feeling her own damp heat on the back of her hand. In response, he shifted his hips. As impatient as Taylor was to have him inside her, the free access to his body parts was too good an opportunity to miss. She tightened her fist, using his own moisture to glide her hand up and down his length. Velvet over steel.

"Bloody Christ, woman." He spoke through clenched teeth, his voice guttural as he buried his face against her neck and took a love bite that made her entire body jerk, then shimmy with pleasure. "Are you trying to kill me?"

His fingers wrapped around hers, showing her how he liked it. She was a quick study; she could tell by his groan of pleasure. Taking away his hand, he left her to it. Taylor felt the strain of his incredible control as she touched him to her heart's content. His every muscle and tendon quivered as she fondled him, but otherwise he didn't move.

She cupped him gently. He was well proportioned, everything matching his height and breadth. Her own breath came in unsteady gasps as she took her sweet time memorizing his body.

Finally his incredible control snapped and he wrapped his long fingers around her wrist and moved her hand away. "Enough."

Before she could protest, he brought his mouth to her breast, tasting her skin with warm strokes of his tongue. She shuddered as his teeth grazed her nipple. His other hand stroked a heated path down her rib cage, caressed her belly, then moved down to her mound.

While he tasted her breasts, he rubbed his palm against her, until Taylor shuddered at the duel assault.

"Hunt." Her voice was barely recognizable, even to her own ears. "I can't—breathe. If you don't— *Ahh.*"

His answer was to close his teeth gently on her nipple as he slid two fingers between her intimate folds. The ball of his thumb continued rubbing a maddening circle on the small bud nestled there. The sensation built until it was too sharp, too intense, and it was her turn to grip his wrist in fingers that shook.

Taylor's laugh was choked as she shifted, drawing her legs up alongside his narrow flanks and tilting her pelvis to receive him.

He yanked a pillow from the head of the bed and stuffed it beneath her hips. "I feel like a kid," he said roughly, resting his forehead against hers and trying to grab a stray breath from a room where Taylor already knew there was no oxygen.

"No." She ran her hands over the solid breadth of his shoulders. "You feel like a man. Come to me." She wrapped her legs high around his waist.

He ran the flat of his hand up her calf as he sank slowly into her, his muscled thighs spreading her wide for his entry. Her body was more than ready, and the sensation of him inside her was so sharp, so pure and perfect, Taylor didn't want to move.

He retreated, a long, slow glide, then returned, deeper, harder, better. The sumptuous whip of need unfurled through her body like the petals of a flower.

He eased in deeper, impossibly deeper. Taylor walked her heels up his back, feeling the flex and play of his muscles as he moved in a rhythm as old as time.

"More," she demanded, tightening her legs about him, wrapping her arms about his neck as she sought his mouth.

"I'll hurt you."

"No way." She bit his lower lip. Hard. "Double . . . jointed."

"Double—" He huffed out a laugh. "My fantasy woman."

Taylor tightened her strong legs around his lean flanks, drew him inexorably deeper. She took all of him. Reveled in the full sensation, the slick heat of his powerful thrusts that made her head toss and her heart careen out of control. "Yes. Like. That. Just. Like—"

He pushed and retreated, pushed and retreated, until their bodies were slick with sweat and their muscles quivered. Sound and light obliterated for pure sensation.

"Tell me—"

"Perfect. Again—*yes.*" Her pleasure pulsed and burned, climbing impossibly higher and higher until she was incapable of drawing a breath. She dragged her mouth from beneath his and gasped for air, her teeth against his sweaty throat. She took a bite of salty male flesh and felt the answering contraction deep inside her.

With a fractured groan he plunged deep inside her, setting a new, more intense rhythm. Harder. Faster. Deeper. Inner spasms converged into a spiral, and she writhed against him as her body demanded release. The pleasure built, coiling tighter and impossibly tighter, until his name was wrung from her, a plea. A demand.

His hips hammered hers until he could go no deeper. Then he withdrew. Then thrust again. "Come for me, love," he crooned, his voice thick with passion.

"Yes. Oh, God, yes." It was a desperate plea as her body kept gathering tighter and tighter. The pleasure was so sharp, so intense, tears started in her eyes. Mindlessly, she walked her heels farther up his back, opening herself to him even more, then dug her fingers into his sweat-dampened hair.

"That's it, sweetheart, let go for me." He drove into her hard and fast, pushing the tightening spirals inside to an unbearable intensity until her cries became whimpers.

He plunged impossibly deeper for the final, mindless strokes until, with a final violent thrust, she arched. Shaking uncontrollably, her climax came at her in a blinding rush of pure white light and sensation too sharp to name.

Hunt's face twisted in a grimace of sublime pleasure as his muscles tightened and his large body vibrated with his own powerful orgasm. Taylor, feeling the intimate pulses of his release deep inside her, convulsed again.

He took her with him as he rolled to his side, taking his weight off her. Which was a good thing. She couldn't catch her breath. After what seemed like an eternity, she spoke, her voice thick and slurred. "Pretty dangerous stuff."

She was grateful to hear that he wasn't breathing too well yet either. "Sex?"

"Making love with you." She rolled up on her elbow to look down at him, then couldn't resist running her fingers through the mat of hair on his chest. His skin was filmed with perspiration, his hair tangled about his face as he watched her.

"I have no defenses against a man like you," she told him, her chest tightening with the truth of it. "I've never had to. I've never met anyone like you."

"Jesus, Taylor—"

Her hair brushed her back as she shook her head. "No, let me finish. I know I give the impression of being sophisticated and terribly experienced. But I—it's mostly for show so I can blend with the people my job requires me to mix with. I'm twenty-seven years old, Hunt, and I've had two lovers. And even fewer relationships. This— *you* mean something to me."

She lay down, settling her cheek in the curve of his shoulder, her hand over the steady beat of his heart. She yawned, then gave his chest a light, secret kiss, breathing in the scent of his skin. "I just thought you should know that before you leave."

Thirty

I T WAS FULLY DARK NOW, AND WINDBLOWN RAIN BEAT A RESTLESS tattoo on the black windows as Hunt walked through the darkened living room toward the kitchen and the sound of voices.

He'd never had sex like that in his life, never known a woman who could meet him stroke for stroke. Could meet and match him physically in every way. Her soft cry seemed to be lodged in his brain. The sensation of her silky skin gliding across his own much rougher hide seemed to have somehow become a part of him.

She had no defenses against *him*? He raked his hair back with his fingers. How could—*why would*—a woman leave herself that open and vulnerable to a man?

Especially *this* woman, who had a defense for every situation. "I just thought you should know that before you leave," he repeated through gritted teeth. "Bloody hell."

Hunt suspected that Taylor lived for her job, had few close friends and few, if any, outside interests. Which could account for the statement. It meant nothing, he assured himself, just something said in the aftermath of the heat of the moment. A "Thanks, you were great" kind of thing.

Shaking his head, feeling vaguely disquieted by her announcement, he didn't need to glance at his watch: forty-eight hours to the thirteenth at 3:33 deadline. Jesus, they were cutting it close.

Pleased that he was mentally back on track, he walked into the brightly lit, crowded kitchen. More of his team had arrived. The four newcomers sat at the bar counter. Bishop and Aries sat at a small bistro table. Remains of pizza and empty soda cans indicated they'd finished eating.

A space had been cleared on the black granite countertop, and the small computer was up and operational. The screen blank at the moment.

"Wright's about to transmit," Max told him.

"Good," Hunt said in masterful understatement. And not a bloody moment too soon. "Austin . . . Escobar . . . Savage . . . Fisk," he said, greeting them, pouring himself a cup of coffee and leaning against the counter to wait.

"Have a nice kip?" Catherine Seymour, aka Savage, asked, her voice suggestive and husky, with a slight Liverpool undertone, as she implied his nap was anything but.

The slow, catlike smile she gave him had at one time heated his blood. Now it left him cold. "Not nearly long enough," he answered smoothly. He'd slept for less than an hour. It was enough. He felt refreshed, invigorated, and ready to roll. His phone rang. "St. John . . . Right. Excellent. Audio or live stream?" He clicked Wright onto speaker, then put the phone down beside the computer.

"Wheels up in one hour, gentlemen," Michael Wright instructed, his voice as clear as if he stood in the room with them. The computer screen blinked to life. "Destination: South Africa. Morales owns a mine. Depth 4,581 meters. The missile is there, people. Coordinates and satellite imagery uploading."

The computer screen filled with fast-moving images being downloaded to the hard drive.

"We believe this facility will have characteristics of Morales's beliefs," Wright told them. "Think biblical. Apocalyptic. Our analysts are working on this as we speak. We should have an educated idea of what you can expect ASAP. I don't have to be there to see all of you looking at your watches. We're as aware of this ticking clock as you are." Wright's voice was tight and controlled.

"Entry to the mine is said to be impenetrable without the information held on those disks," he added. "Rumor has it, without them, not even Morales can get in."

"He'll get in just fine if he was the one who took the damn disks from us," Bishop pointed out grimly.

"Maybe the *Black Rose* has them." Savage picked up Bishop's Coke can and drank.

"Makes no difference *who* has them," Hunt told them. "We'll be waiting at the front and back doors to greet all arrivals. Navarro and Daklin?" The best T-FLAC had in missile and toxic chemicals.

"Already dispatched," Wright confirmed as Taylor walked into the kitchen. "They'll be waiting on board. Their teams dispatched to Jo'burg airport with the—"

"Hold a minute," Hunt told Wright. "You can't be in here right now, Taylor."

"I've been listening for the past ten minutes," she kept coming, rounding the counter toward him, her expression serious and determined. "I have—"

"We'll be out of your hair in a few minutes," he told her impatiently. Didn't matter what the hell she wanted. She didn't belong here. "Wait in your bedroom till we're through."

"T minus forty-eight hours to get in and deactivate the missile, people," Wright's disembodied voice reminded them unnecessarily.

Two feet from Hunt, Taylor took her hand out of the front pocket of her jeans. Between her slender, agile, *thieving* fingers were two flat powder-dusted minidisks. She extended them to Hunt. "I believe these will help."

Thirty-one

CHRIST ALMIGHTY." HUNT PLUCKED THE SMALL DISKS FROM TAYlor's fingers. "She lifted two disks right from under our noses yesterday," he told Wright.

"And thank God she's even better than we gave her credit for," Wright said dryly over the speaker. "Transmit. Let's see what we have."

Not looking at him, Savage offered her handheld unit to Hunt. "Here, use mine."

Hunt already had his own specially modified PDA, out on the counter, and one of the minidisks inserted. He hit the transmit button. Encrypted. No surprise.

"Transmit the second one," Wright ordered. "Then stand down, I'll get back to you ASAP." The phone went dead.

Taylor, leaning against the counter sipping his coffee, looked quite pleased with herself. "Am I good. Or am I good?"

"You are, without a doubt, incredible," Hunt said tightly. "It would have been nice to have a heads-up before this, however."

"If Taylor hadn't taken them, we'd be screwed." Max pointed out the obvious as Hunt plucked his cup—his *empty* cup—from her fingers.

"Exactly," Taylor said. "Thank you, Max. You should all be thanking me. Turns out you're lucky I *did* take those disks." She tilted her head to look up at Hunt. The piercing pure blue of her eyes was almost unnerving in their intensity. "He's right and you know it. Without those disks you'd be—as Max so eloquently pointed out—screwed. The least you could do is—"

Stepping away from the subtle lavender fragrance of her, Hunt cut her off to address his team. "Two out of five doesn't necessarily mean we're any less screwed," he reminded them grimly. He ran a glass under the faucet, then drank the cold water as he marshaled his annoyance. Two steps forward, one step back.

God only knew, he *was* grateful she'd palmed the bloody disks. But he was also furious that she'd managed to nip them right under his nose. And, he thought, ire rising, that she'd felt the *need* to steal them back *at all*. He brought himself up short, lifted the glass to his mouth and drank again, letting the cold water soothe his tight throat.

He knew the two irritants were nothing more than his bruised ego talking. She'd outsmarted him, and she didn't trust him. His ego would survive. The fact that they *had* two of the disks was all that counted. He gave her a hard look. "Well done."

She beamed. "You are quite welcome."

The phone vibrated on the granite countertop. Hunt snatched it up. "St. John." He listened for several minutes, his blood slowly turning to ice. Everything in him went rigid as Michael Wright talked. This wasn't going on the speaker. The others watched him in silence. He turned his back on Taylor and his team and walked out of the kitchen.

"The answer to *that*," he said flatly, crossing the darkened living room, "is an unequivocal *no*."

Wright kept talking as Hunt strode down the hallway, pushed open the door to Taylor's bedroom, and slammed it shut after him. The room smelled of her. Lavender and sex. Promises and lies.

Hunt trusted Michael Wright with his life. But in this case the man was wrong. Dead wrong. He interrupted Wright's monologue again, this time to say through clenched teeth, "Yes, it was. And my prerogative to change it. Which I have. I said no bloody way. I won't do it."

After Wright responded, he said, "Because my feelings about women in the field are well document— Yes," he bit out. "I'm aware of that."

He didn't give a continental damn about what happened to *Savage*. "She's a specially trained operative and knows the risks . . . Yes, damn it. A.J. too. But not—"

Hunt's jaw ached because his teeth were clenched so tightly. "Yes," he said, and sat down on the edge of the bed. "I realize this was the original . . . Maybe not. *Fisk* is here, he's—"

The door opened and Max walked in.

Hunt shook his head.

His friend plucked a broken drinking glass from Hunt's hand, then pressed a cloth into his palm, forcibly closing Hunt's fingers around it. Hunt gave his bleeding hand a mildly surprised glance, not realizing he'd broken the glass in his agitation. "That's absolutely bullshit, Wright. *Bullshit*. Are you telling me, in the entire T-FLAC organization, we don't have *one* fucking person skilled enough to get us through those seven levels? Not a one?"

After listening a moment, he interrupted again. "Why in the bloody hell do we *need* to *finesse* our way in?" he said, hanging on to his temper by a fragile thread as he got up to pace. Max stepped out of his way but stayed in the room.

"It would be more expedient to blast our way through those seven fucking levels than take the time to unravel all the gyrations built in to keep us out."

"Possible nuclear warhead?" Max mentioned dryly as Hunt passed him for the fifth time.

Hunt stopped, looked at his friend, then closed his eyes. "Yeah," he said flatly as Wright repeated the words. "Max just reminded me."

Thirty-two

FILLED WITH NERVOUS ENERGY, TAYLOR HADN'T BEEN ABLE TO stand still and had busied herself making a fresh pot of coffee, and disposing of the take-out pizza paraphernalia.

He'd been furious that she'd lifted the disks, and she understood why he was annoyed. But she wasn't obligated to tell him that she hadn't known at the time whether she could trust him. And if he'd been annoyed before, he was absolutely *furious* during the phone call. She didn't know if that was a good thing or a bad thing.

Neal Bishop introduced her to the others. Apparently, none of them had first names. Taylor did a lightning-fast assessment of Hunt's group. These were the people who would be with Hunt when he did whatever it was he was going to do.

She knew instinctively that Hunt would put his life on the line for them. Would they do the same for him?

She studied each of them carefully as they were introduced.

Austin: surfer type, sun-streaked hair, dangerous eyes, lazy smile.
Escobar: cold black eyes, twitchy, filled with nervous energy, pacing as

they waited. Savage: the only woman, strikingly beautiful, green-eyed redhead, controlled. Fisk: black guy, shorter by a good foot than the other men, slight, good hands, easy smile.

If she imagined really hard, she could believe they were here for a party. As friends. *Um, no. She wasn't that good at self-delusion.*

She started another pot by the time Hunt, followed by Max, returned to the kitchen. Hunt's expression was grim, his hand wrapped in a bloodstained towel. She wondered how that happened.

"This is what we have," he said, standing in the doorway. He was back to being the chilly man from Houston and the antagonist from San Cristóbal. He was also all business.

He walked into the room and stood beside the flashy redhead. "HQ broke the encryptions," he told them, his tone grim. "Morales appears to have replicated Dante's seven levels of hell inside the abandoned mine. The missile, according to Satcom and infrared photos, is at the base."

Nobody said a word. Nobody moved.

"Thanks to Taylor's sticky fingers," he went on, not looking at her as he spoke, "we are now in possession of the access codes for levels three and five. But even *with* these codes—and remember, it's only two out of seven levels—it won't be easy. Morales has had years to think this through. *And* the best, most creative minds in the world to help him.

"Our analysis department and our think tank guys will work on variables and possible scenarios while we're in transit. So far we know that scientists, mechanical engineers, and—God only knows what the hell *this* means—the movie industry, were involved in the ten-plus years it took to construct this place."

Hunt looked from one member of his team to the next, his eyes skimmed over Taylor without pausing. "According to our intel, sixteen hundred men gave their lives for this project. *I* believe that everything José Morales has worked and strived for since the inception of *Mano del Dios* is hidden inside that mine. Destroy what he has hidden, and we destroy *Mano del Dios.*"

"Is that before or after we deactivate what could possibly be a nuclear warhead?" Daklin asked, grabbing his jacket as he slid off a bar stool.

"After," Hunt told him, ignoring Daklin's sarcasm. "The plane's engine is running. Wheels up, twenty minutes."

He hadn't glanced at her once, and Taylor realized that he had no intention of taking her with them. "Why did you take 'thousands of manpower hours' to find me in San Cristóbal, Hunt?" she demanded as everyone hustled and bustled around them, preparing to leave.

They stopped what they were doing. Silence fell on the room like a shroud.

"Wasn't it so that I could help you break into whatever facility it was that those codes were for?" she asked quietly. Her heart beat too fast and her palms were slick with nervous perspiration.

He gave her the tundra look that made icicles form in Taylor's veins. Gone was the lover. Here was the T-FLAC operative with a mission.

"I only needed you to get into the safe," he told her dismissively. "You'd already done that by the time I got to San Cristóbal. If you'd given me the disks at that time, we wouldn't be here arguing right now. "

Unfortunately, very true. Still, the idea of getting through a major terrorist's version of Dante's seven levels of hell intrigued her, and actually gave her all those lovely preheist anticipatory palpitations. "Your boss wanted me to go with you," Taylor pushed. "Didn't he?"

"Michael Wright is not my boss," he told her.

He wasn't saying no. "Didn't he?" She hadn't had a really exciting challenge in months. This would certainly be that. And probably more. Not to mention she'd have a valid reason for spending a little more time with Hunt.

Hunt glanced around at his team, who weren't even pretending not to be intrigued by the byplay between them. "Ready?" he asked them.

"I'll go. On one condition."

"Wrong answer," Hunt told Taylor, his eyes so dark a charcoal they looked demonic as he glared at her. "And in case you're not as smart as you look, the answer is *no*. Listen to yourself—it didn't take you five seconds to come up with a damn *condition*."

"It's important—"

He walked over and grabbed her by the upper arm. "Come with me."

"What is this? You Tarzan, me Jane?" Taylor asked as he strong-armed her through the living room and down the hallway, and opened the first door he came to, her office.

He pushed her inside and kicked the door shut with his foot, still holding her arm. He flicked on the overhead light and spun her around so they were face-to-face. "Morales is an insane son of a bitch and a dangerous psychopath. I'm smart. I'm wily, I'm experienced, and I'm determined, and it's taken me six years to get this close to him.

"The man believes that the antichrist is alive and well and living in Las Vegas, for Christ's sake! The coordinates on one of the disks indicate the missile is pointing in that direction. He's stockpiled God only knows *how* much sarin gas and other biohazards and chemicals down there. He's been collecting weapons and arms like baseball cards for years. Saving them for October thirteenth at 3:33. *Precisely.* That's less than forty-eight hours."

She gave him a steady look. "I can get you in faster."

"Jesus, Taylor. How can you ask me to put you—a *civilian*—into *that* kind of danger?"

"You didn't ask. I'm offering."

"I don't want *you* within a thousand miles of him. You heard what we said out there. He has a *missile* in that mine. Possibly a nuclear weapon."

"I know, I—"

"He's planning on blowing up an entire city of over a million people in two days. Do you think for a moment that a man who would go to *such* lengths as to duplicate Dante's levels of hell to protect what's his won't have a fucking *army* there to protect it as well?"

"No, but—"

"Have you ever fired a gun?" She shook her head. "Ever *held* a bloody gun?" Taylor shook her head again. "Know what it feels like to be shot? It feels as though an animal is ripping open your flesh with its teeth and claws, and then someone pours acid over the open wound. *That's* what it feels like! You bleed. Real arterial blood. You could *die!*"

Hunt closed his eyes, then opened them again, his face stark. "Jesus bloody Christ, Taylor, don't ask me to—"

She put two fingers over his mouth. "I'm not saying I'm not scared. I'd be a fool if I wasn't. This situation is terrifying. And to be honest, I know I'll be a lot *more* terrified once we get there. But I *have* to go with you. If there's anything resembling a safe, or a combination lock, or a keypad, *anything*—I'm the only one who's skilled and experienced enough to get you through those levels. And with only two of the five disks, I'm guessing you'd need what I can do."

He raked his fingers through his hair. "It won't work."

"Of course it will. Stop being stupid and stubborn. You know damn well I'm the very best there is," Taylor snapped. She wasn't bragging. She *was* the best. And they both knew it. It had taken T-FLAC, with all of their considerable resources, working around the clock, to find her in San Cristóbal. And that was because Hunt had wanted the best of the best.

"You're too bloody independent."

She smiled a little. "You say that like it's a bad thing."

He looked at his watch, his expression grim. "How good are you at taking orders?"

"Usually, not very," she told him honestly. "But in this instance, I'll do whatever you tell me to do."

"No hesitation? No explanations?"

"Yes."

"You better be bloody sure, because once we're there, there won't be time to negotiate or give explanations. I'll be your commander just as I am for my team. I give the orders. You obey them. Immediately. No question."

"I can live with that."

"See that you do. Your complete compliance could very well mean your—or a member of my team's—life or death. Now, what's your one condition?"

Thirty-three

JOSÉ MORALES KEPT HIS HEAD BOWED AND HIS BLOODY BACK straight as he knelt on the cement floor of the small stone chapel behind his home outside Johannesburg. Everything had been in readiness when he had arrived in South Africa two days ago. While Constantine finalized the last few details to Morales's satisfaction, small matters only, José had gone directly to the chapel. He had knelt before the shrine for hours.

God was pleased. Filling him with power and strength.

José's anticipation level was high, and his euphoria rose with each passing hour. He felt God's presence more powerfully when he was here.

He had not eaten in three days. Had not slept in two. Rhythmically, he scourged his own back again with the short-handled leather whip. *"Solamente Dios. Solamente Dios. Solamente Dios. Solamente Dios."*

Only God.

His voice was hoarse as he repeated the chant over and over for hours on end. The rough hemp of his robe bit like fire ants into his knees. *"Solamente Dios."*

When God granted him another vision, he could rise.

It would be time.

"Solamente Dios." José didn't flinch when the sharp teeth of the metal-studded leather whip bit the flesh of his back, wet and raw, exposed from the repeated lashings. *"S-Solamente Dios."*

Even with only three of the required five disks to guide him, José Morales knew that his God could again lead him through each level of the mine. His God, after all, had given him the skills and contacts to execute the design. His God would help him again—disks or no disks. All he needed was his God. His light. To show him his true path. *"Solamente Dios. Solamente Dios. Solamente Dios."*

He had seen the seven levels in a vision. As clearly as if he'd been right there. In his vision, God had led him to South Africa and shown him the mine. *"Solamente Dios."*

Building it had been an act of devotion, a labor of love, as well as a necessity. In his line of work, he trusted no person. Only God. The devious complexity of the mine provided him with a foolproof place to store the spoils of his labors. Over the years, many lives had been sacrificed so that God's prophecy of his, José Morales's, greatness could come to fruition.

"Solamente Dios."

The whip cracked in the stillness.

Tiny bits of metal gouged the torn flesh of his back.

And every pain was offered as penance.

As sacrifice.

"Again," he muttered as the whip slowed. Instantly, agony erupted within. *"Sola—Solamente Dios."* Again. And again. *"Solamente Dios. Solamente Dios."*

His God would never fail him.

As his vision dimmed, he begged for guidance.

Thirty-four

THE CONDITION TAYLOR HAD STIPULATED WAS THAT HER SISTER Amanda be protected and kept safe while she was gone.

That Taylor *had* a sister was news to Hunt.

In the dossier T-FLAC had compiled on her, there were several minor references to a baby in the Reno, Nevada, apartment. But they hadn't been *looking* for information on an infant. And since her mother was gone and Taylor had been about ten at the time, no one had thought anything about it. It was her *adult* life they'd shone the spotlight on.

And Taylor, being Taylor, had purposely omitted Amanda from her life story.

Hunt didn't blame her for wanting to protect the girl. Seventeen-year-old Amanda Kincaid had Down syndrome and lived in a private-care facility just outside Zurich.

Much to Taylor's relief and gratitude, Max, after being given the information, immediately arranged to have the girl and her attendant transported to the T-FLAC training facility in the French Polynesian Marquesas Islands. Paradise Island was unspoiled, and beautiful; Mandy would have a wonderful vacation. And the entire island was run by and crawling with T-FLAC operatives. There was nowhere in the world safer.

After Taylor called the school and spoke to Kim Butler, her sister's attendant, Max had gone to pick up Mandy himself. He'd personally deliver her and Kim into the hands of four T-FLAC operatives waiting for them in Germany. They'd leave first thing in the morning.

Once her sister's safety had been confirmed, and *reconfirmed,* Taylor spent several minutes talking to Amanda on the phone to prepare her for her fun "vacation." Then, satisfied that Mandy was safe and well, Taylor was all business. She added a few things to one of several prepacked bags she kept at the ready and within minutes was accompanying the team to Kloten Airport.

And Hunt would've given his left nut to have her on the flight to Paradise Island with her sister instead.

As soon as they were airborne, everyone gathered in the aft cabin to discuss strategy. Since Morales favored everything from arcane Machiavellian puzzles to high-tech wizardry, his seven levels of hell could consist of just about anything. Via computer, they were sent twenty-year-old schematics of the mine, the only ones HQ had been able to find, and more satellite photographs and topographical maps of the area.

A deep, narrow river snaked between the gently rolling hills. No roads. No airport. Thermal imaging showed approximately a hundred people in a small village nearby.

They'd fly into Jo'burg, an eleven-hour trip, and should be able to make their way to the location of the mine by late afternoon the following day. Leaving just hours to locate the missile and deactivate it.

"Analyze what you have. When we get more on this end, we'll shoot it over to you," Wright told them, then signed off.

Taylor rose from the table as the screen went dark. "Is that it?"

Hunt stood too. "For now. Why don't we all try and get some sleep?" He glanced at his watch. "We'll reconvene in three hours, rehash what we have then. Taylor can sleep in here." Her skin looked translucent, her eyes paler blue surrounded by the smudges of fatigue.

"No thanks. I want to study some of this stuff. Can you print it for me?"

Hunt didn't argue, figuring she was already at her emotional limit. "Sure." He nodded to Fisk to activate the printer. "I'll bring it through when it's done."

Daklin leaned back in his seat and waited until Taylor left the room. "Can she do it, do you think?" he asked.

Fisk didn't wait for Hunt to answer. "I'd like her to teach a few classes to the rest of us. Shit, man, she's tops. She has moves I've never even heard about."

Hunt was ambivalent about it. He was glad to hear Fisk say she was good. But he also wanted to hear that Fisk was as good as Taylor, so he could send her back home. "And you know this how?" he asked T-FLAC's best chance without Taylor.

"Went snooping in her office back at the condo while you were . . . elsewhere." Fisk grinned. "She has every safe manufacturer's codes, schematics, and blueprints—thousands of them, all marked up with notes. Smiley faces on the ones she's breached. And just looking at the jobs she's pulled in the last few years?" Fisk whistled. "She's scary good."

"Better than you are?" Hunt demanded, knowing the answer, and hoping for a different response anyway.

"Think toddler and marathon runner."

"Precisely what I was hoping, and exactly what I was afraid of," Hunt said, taking the sheaf of papers Fisk handed him from the printer. As much as he loathed having Taylor involved in T-FLAC business, he knew she'd be an integral part of the operation. And a huge asset. But now, for the first time, he wasn't only thinking about a successful op. He was also concerned about Taylor.

It had been a hellishly long couple of days. The members of his team were trained to subsist on very little sleep. Taylor, however, was not. At least not by T-FLAC standards. Since she was here, despite his objections, she needed to be in top form in order to do her job.

"She's not going to be capable of anything if she doesn't get some sleep," he told Fisk, and started for the door. "Let me know if HQ makes contact."

She looked up as he settled into the wide leather seat beside her. It didn't take a mind reader to hear Taylor's thoughts loud and clear. He answered before she could voice them.

"You spoke to her not an hour ago. Didn't she say she'd just eaten the biggest banana split in the 'whole wide world' and was happily watching TV with Kim?"

Taylor had spoken to her sister twice since they'd been in flight. And to Kim Butler three times. The girl was having the time of her life in the hotel in Germany. She was safe, secure, and happy.

"I know. Thank you." Taylor closed her eyes for a second—a quick prayer, Hunt thought—then she looked down at the papers in her lap. "As long as I know Mandy's safe, I'm good to go.

"It's strange that we've both been after Morales for all these years," she mused, rotating the stiff muscles in her neck. "He has this interesting habit of giving—" Hunt slid his fingers beneath her hair and started massaging the stiff cords in her neck.

"Oh, Lord, that feels wonderful . . . Giving Maria things he 'acquires' from museums. How do you think he reconciles that with his hellfire-and-brimstone philosophy?"

Hunt's body tightened when she moaned as he dug his thumb into a particularly tight tendon.

"I've retrieved a couple of things from him." She flipped a page, but he could tell her eyes weren't scanning. "A lovely Fabergé egg. And, of course, the Barter sapphires in San Cristóbal. But what I *really* want, my Holy Grail, are the Blue Star diamonds Morales 'acquired' six years ago from the Romanov Collection in St. Petersburg."

"And what will you do when you have them?" Hunt asked, still massaging her slender nape. He enjoyed watching the play of light on her hair as his wrist shifted the strands.

She turned to look at him, her sleepy eyes so clear and blue they took his breath away. She smiled. "I'll win," she said simply, and flipped a page.

"He's one *sick* puppy," she went on. "It doesn't take a shrink to figure out why this guy thinks like he does. Look at this. He was stuck in Abadia de Solo Dios abbey at the age of nine by his prostitute mother. Weird how such a bad guy can be so obsessed with religion and yet still do such incredibly vile things, isn't it?"

Every tango Hunt had ever dealt with had justifications for their acts. "Not so weird, really," he said. "More damage has been done to humanity in the name of God than for any other reason. Besides," he added, "villains don't consider themselves villains. Sure, he had a hard life. But I know plenty of other people who were abused as kids, and they turned into upstanding members of society."

Many of them worked for T-FLAC. "Morales was already a sociopath at nine. What were you doing at that age? Playing dress-up?"

"Taking care of Mandy. Our mother left when she was less than a month old."

"You were responsible for an infant, *alone,* at nine?"

"Tenish. I grew up fast."

"And at—what was it? Fifteen? You had twenty grand in your pocket, and the responsibility of a handicapped five-year-old? Why Europe? Why not a school in the States?"

"I saw a picture in a magazine while I was in the doctor's office one day. Special-needs kids like Mandy sitting out on a lawn, surrounded by caring people, sunshine and flowers. It seemed like heaven to me, to have Mandy somewhere safe. I tore the page out and kept it folded in my wallet for a couple of years.

"Of course, it never occurred to me that the people in the ad were paid models, or that the place could look like something else entirely. *That* was what I wanted for my sister. I'd settle for nothing less. Fortunately, the ad was the real deal, and *Sans Souci* turned out to be as amazing as I'd prayed it would be.

"Mandy's happy there, and they not only take excellent care of her, they *love* her." She leaned her head back and closed her eyes. Hunt kept his hand on the back of her neck, gently stroking the baby-soft skin of her nape with his thumb.

"Okay, enough about me. Why a spy?" Her voice was soft and drowsy.

Hunt did the math. Three hours into the eleven-hour flight to Johannesburg. If she crashed now, she could get in a solid eight hours. He let the silence stretch before answering.

"A recruiter from T-FLAC found me while I was in college." He watched her chest rise and fall. Her body began to relax, and he kept his voice low. "Suggested I get a law degree. Joining T-FLAC was the best—"

He stopped talking. She was out like a light. Removing the stack of papers from her limp fingers, he set them on the nearby table. Other than the steady drone of the engines, the cabin was quiet, the lights dimmed.

He rose, and activated Taylor's seat to a fully reclined position, then found a light blanket and draped it over her. She shifted to a more comfortable position on her side, but didn't wake up as he sank into the wide seat beside her and closed his eyes.

It might be quiet, but it was like a bloody railway station as his team moved about the aircraft. He kept his eyes closed, recognizing by their footfalls who was passing.

Hunt would have liked Max's company on the plane, but he was grateful that a man he trusted as much as he trusted Max Aries was responsible for Amanda Kincaid's safety and well-being.

Fisk and Bishop had grabbed the beds in the aft cabin, and Savage was up in the cockpit with the pilot and co-pilot, the door closed. Navarro was sitting near the galley, close to food and, as usual, doing whatever it was he did on his laptop. Daklin was in the head taking a shower.

Hunt knew he should sleep, God only knew he bloody needed it. Instead, he rolled his head, opening gritty eyes to watch Taylor as she slept. Reaching out, he tenderly stroked the back of one finger down her cheek. Warm. Smooth. Flawless. Her lips were slightly parted, allowing a soft little sound to escape.

He felt a clench of fear in his gut. The mission was always more important than the players. This one even more so. But, oh God—he did *not* want Taylor within a thousand miles of Morales and his madness.

If he hadn't been positive, *without a doubt,* abso-bloody-fuckinglutely—*positive,* that they couldn't make it all the way through Morales's seven levels without her extraordinary skills, she'd be on that plane to Paradise Island right now.

No ands, ifs, or buts.

God, he didn't want her with them.

Their job once they reached the mine would be phenomenally dangerous, even before they managed to get to the lower level and Morales's *pièce de résistance:* the missile.

As of yet, they had no idea whether they'd find the bloody thing loaded with a nuke, or some sort of toxic biochemical. Hard target or soft target? They had no freaking idea! Jesus.

He knew he had to be wholly focused every second of every minute of every hour, until the job was done. He raked his fingers through his hair, then brought his hand down and held it out level. Jesus. His hands were shaking.

Thirty-five

THE ONLY GOOD THING ABOUT FELLATIO WAS THAT IT GAVE A woman ultimate power over a man. When a man had his dick in a woman's mouth, he was defenseless. But in some instances, Lisa Maki thought, resting her palms on the table behind her, that control had to be seasoned with necessity. A man with his head buried between your legs was almost as defenseless.

She had Morales's man exactly where she wanted him. She let him do his thing while she stared out of the dusty window. Waiting.

She wasn't good at waiting.

The Black Rose had given her a second chance. A nod to her sterling reputation. But a second chance was all she'd get. How Black Rose had so much inside information, Lisa had no idea. Maybe when she completed this mission, the Black Rose would take her into her confidence. And maybe not.

Lisa squeezed her thighs closed, trapping the man's head close and holding him there. He made a muffled protest and used his palms to try to pry her knees apart so he could draw a breath. It didn't work.

"I repeat. When will your boss be here in Blikiesfontein?" she asked, checking her manicure, bored out of her mind.

He made another muffled protest, tried to lift his head, or at least get up off his knees. She contracted her strong thigh muscles even harder. He subsided. Like a monkey with its hand in the jar, the idiot wouldn't just close his mouth and release his prize to free himself. Jesus, men were like children.

"Let's try something else," she told him, giving him a moment to lift his mouth off his target to gasp for air as she pulled her tote bag closer and started looking for an emery board.

Like a starving man at a banquet, he forgot the momentary danger and went back down for more. Paradise was right under his greedy mouth, and he was too busy satisfying his greed to concentrate fully.

"Members of the Black Rose," she told him in a sultry voice, as she filed the rough edge off her thumbnail, "have killed your five friends." They had, of course, killed considerably more than Morales's five incompetents. There'd been a dozen people in the small burg who hadn't wanted to give up their chicken-scrabble homes to her or her people.

Honest to God. Sometimes it was so much easier to kill than to argue endlessly. No challenge, of course. No creativity needed. It'd been like shooting fish in a bowl.

She inspected the rest of her nails then, satisfied, tossed the file back in her bag and glanced down at the dark head bobbing between her thighs. "José, I'm sure, is en route from London. When should I expect the pleasure of his company?"

Her people, *new* people, were in place. A small select team. The Black Rose had sent her twenty-three men and women for this all-important job. It made her a little nervous that none of them had ever worked together before arriving in South Africa yesterday. It made her nervous not knowing the strength and weaknesses of her group.

Unlike Morales, who enjoyed wielding his sick power with might, *she* used her smarts to make her point.

Black Rose would be *the* most powerful, the most respected, the most feared terrorist group in the world. And she, Lisa Maki, would be right there near the top.

Couldn't be easier. It was like fucking taking candy from a baby. She stared out of the window. Where the fuck were they anyway? She'd been here for hours already, and she was bored, bored, bored.

No point getting any closer until T-FLAC brought the girl and she'd done her thing. Now *that* thought gave her heart an excited kick start. She crossed her booted ankles across his back, digging in the sharp, black, five-inch heels. "One more chance, dickhead. When will José be here?" She knew damn well José would want to park his zealotous butt in this little no-nothing dust bunny of a town as he waited for *someone else* to get him in to his treasure.

Soon to be the Black Rose's treasure.

What a fucking *moron,* to actually allow this to happen in the first place! The time for *Mano del Dios* time was over. Morales was too crazy, being afraid of God's wrath, to be fully effective. *She* had no such problem.

God didn't bother her and she didn't bother Him. A good arrangement, all in all.

She almost laughed. Except this was no longer amusing, just annoying and time-consuming.

Using her muscles like a vise, she started squeezing, effectively clamping his head and holding him inches away from what he craved. His hot, struggling breath rushed at her damp heat. "Last chance. When's he coming?"

"Fucking hell, honey, gimme a minute to come first, 'kay?"

"One." She tightened her ankles. Oops, her heel tore through the cloth of his shirt leaving a bloody gash down his back. He bucked at the pain. "Two—"

"Okay, okay, fuck. *Okay!* He'll be here first thing tomorrow. Please, baby, let me—"

She tightened her knees, gripping harder, giving an expert twist, up and around from her powerful leg muscles. She loved the sound of a breaking neck. Almost like a chicken bone—but better.

Thirty-six

TAYLOR HAD NEVER IMAGINED SPRING IN AFRICA.

If anything, she'd pictured a blazing sun above parched, seared-brown vegetation. Or maybe green, junglelike foliage teeming with creepy crawlies and wild animals. Neither image fit with the reality she saw stretched on either side of the two-lane road they traveled several hours north of the cosmopolitan city of Johannesburg.

Impressed in spite of herself, she'd observed the military precision of Hunt's team as they mobilized for the trip. They were met at a private airport and driven to an industrial park on the outskirts of the city, where a dozen more members of the T-FLAC team waited with five fully equipped all-terrain vehicles. Within fifteen minutes the jeeps were loaded, everyone had their last-minute instructions from Hunt, and they were off.

Now, several hours into the journey, the late afternoon sun beat down on their Land Rover and they hadn't seen a house or a human for miles. She sat in the back with Hunt, who stayed in contact with the others through a lip mic.

The driver—Piet Coetzee—was as tough-looking as a piece of jerky, and quite friendly. Of course, to these spy types she'd been meeting, quite friendly was a relative term, she thought with an inward smile. He'd actually greeted her and almost smiled when they were introduced. Coetzee was probably in his late forties, but with his tanned-leather skin, and with more salt than pepper in his military-short hair, he looked about sixty.

Daan Viljoen, sitting up front in the passenger seat, was, Taylor was discovering, the usual manly man T-FLAC operative. Monosyllabic and focused. Short and wiry, with reddish-brown hair. Both men wore khaki . . . everything. Pants, shirts, hats. Very *Out of Africa*-ish.

Other than their own convoy, there wasn't another car in sight. On either side of the road, as far as the eye could see, spring-green grass gently waved in the breeze. It was dotted with thornbushes and the occasional gnarled and ancient-looking baobab tree. "Will we see any animals?" Taylor asked as they zoomed along the road.

"*Vasbyt.* In about an hour," Coetzee told her. "When the sun starts going down and it gets a bit cooler. Plenty of animals where we're going."

She had no idea if he'd just called her a rude name or told her to wait. Both men had such heavy accents, it was hard to understand them when they deigned to speak. Scary, but she was starting to get used to the way these guys communicated in a sort of verbal short-hand, as if they were too busy to bother with complete sentences.

"About sixty miles from here we'll pass close by a waterhole. By the time we reach it, the animals will be coming down to drink. Here's our turn," Coetzee said, turning the wheel off the tarred road and into the long grass. The vehicle shuddered as he put it into four-wheel drive.

Here's our turn? There wasn't a signpost or even a rock indicating any sort of road or trail. Taylor glanced back to see the other vehicles following in precision formation. Her teeth snapped together as the jeep bounced and thumped along over hill and dale. She missed that nice comfy road.

The incongruous sound of a fax machine hummed. She wasn't surprised. These guys had lots of interesting toys.

"Aerial photos," Viljoen muttered, hand hovering over the paper coming out of a fax machine cleverly built into the console between the seats. He passed the first sheet back to Hunt.

"Aerials confirm village head count, one hundred and sixty," Hunt said into the mic, then proceeded to read off a string of numbers to his men as Viljoen passed him the fax pages.

Taylor craned her neck and strained her eyes, looking for wildlife. "What's that?" she asked, pointing to one of the enormous conical mounds of dirt as they passed. There were hundreds of them, all over the place.

"Termite mound," Viljoen offered, in a vaguely British accent as he opened his window and lit a cigarette. "See how smooth is the sides? Elephants use them as scratching posts."

"*Ag,* man," Coetzee groaned. "Don't get him started—"

"I don't think we're looking at the same thing." Taylor peered back over her shoulder as they passed a mini mountain. "That thing is all of thirty feet tall." And there were a *lot* of them.

"Termites." Viljoen, elbow on his open window, blew out a plume of pungent smoke. "We's call them *rysmeer*—rice ants—around here, you know? But they're *termites.* Very interesting. Inside is a hella complicated series of tunnels that—"

Coetzee knocked Viljoen's hat off into his lap. "Nobody cares, *oke.*"

"I'm interested," Taylor assured him as he grumbled and returned the felt hat to his head. But apparently Viljoen's loquacious moment had been quelled. When he didn't expound on the subject of termites any further, she went back to trying to spot wildlife in the long grass, or perhaps lurking in the shade of the wide, spreading thornbushes dotting the veldt.

They passed through the tiny, dusty town of Blikiesfontein. Population twenty-seven. The road they were on was Main Street, and actually ran through the middle of town. It was no more than two rows of houses, a volunteer fire department, medical clinic, a bar, and a little grocery store. The only sign of life was a dusty red pickup truck parked in front of one of the houses, a big ginger and black cat sleeping bonelessly on the sidewalk in front of the grocery store, and a large black bird perched in a Stephen King–like way on the railing nearby. The brilliant sunshine wasn't flattering to the little ghost town.

"Used to be miner's housing way back, you know?" Viljoen told Taylor as they drove through. "The Blikiesfontein mine played out back in '74. Morales bought it from DeBeers in '98 through a dummy company, which was incorporated through a succession of other dummy companies. Guy's as slippery as shit."

Tension knotted the muscles in Taylor's neck. A nice lion attack would get her mind off worrying that maybe she'd bitten off more than she could chew. What if she *couldn't* get into this frigging mine of Morales's? What then?

She'd be responsible for killing everyone for miles around. Not to mention over a million innocent people in Las Vegas.

"How many vehicles?" Hunt asked into the lip mic.

Coetzee said, "Four, not counting the red *bakkie*. You?"

"I only made three," Viljoen said, clearly put out.

Since all Taylor had seen—and she'd *looked*—was the red truck, she had no idea which town these guys had passed through.

Hunt listened for a few moments. "I counted six, seven with the pickup. Not a surprise that he's here. He'll keep a low profile. For now."

Oh, great! No pressure here.

Hunt gave her a reassuring smile. Her eyes were intensely blue, and filled with so much fear, Hunt felt it echo in his own gut. "You're going to gnaw a hole in your lip if you keep doing that," he said quietly.

"What if I can't do it?" she asked quietly. "What if we get there and I haven't a clue?"

I'll breathe for a change, and happily put your sweet ass on a flight to Paradise, Hunt thought. Instead of voicing the concerns gnawing at him, he said calmly, "Then we'll be no worse off than if you hadn't come."

She swallowed, then resumed chewing her lower lip. "No offense, but we both know Francis doesn't have the experience to do it."

Francis? Who the hell—ah, Frank Fisk. "My money's on you. You're the best, aren't you?"

"I'm the best," Taylor told him fiercely, "because retrieving stolen articles for Consolidated Underwriters is a *game*. Nobody's ever gotten hurt. It was *fun*. But this . . ." She waved at the bushveld as they passed. "People will *die*—millions of people will die if I don't—if I can't—"

"Maybe you're right," Hunt cut her off. "Maybe you *won't* be able to open whatever the hell it is we find when we get there. But you know what? No one on our team has a *tenth* of your skill. So at least with you here we have a shot, don't we? A chance that you'll know exactly how to do it, and because of that, perhaps *nobody* will have to die."

People *would* die. That was a given. Who, and how many, that was the question.

Taylor gave him a steady look. "Do you really believe that?"

Please God, Hunt prayed, *keep Taylor safe.* Because the answer wasn't just no, but *hell* no. "Yes. I do."

She leaned over and brushed a kiss to his jaw. "I don't either," she whispered.

The sun streamed into his side of the vehicle. Even with the air conditioner blasting, it was too hot to be this close. But Taylor turned Hunt's face toward her with her cupped palm and softly kissed the grim set of his mouth.

"I'm going to ace this one," she told him firmly. "We're going to find that thing in time, and the good guys *will* win."

He shifted to wrap an arm about her shoulders, then pulled her tightly into his side. It was like cozying up to a blast furnace. She rested her head on his shoulder. He nuzzled the crown of her head with his chin.

Taylor stared out of the window, listening to the steady beat of his heart beneath her ear. He was deep in thought, and clearly those thoughts weren't good. She wished she hadn't had to worry him further by telling him of her concerns. But better he be prepared now. Just in case.

Please, God, she prayed. *Don't let him get hurt.*

For the next hour, she alternately dozed against Hunt's shoulder in the soporific heat or watched the countryside speed by beyond the windows. She was entranced by the grace and beauty of a small herd of deer—*springbok*, Viljoen told her—as they ran and jumped through the grass as if they had springs on their hooves.

She thought she spotted an elephant in the distance, but it could've been one of the soft, fluffy wisps of gray clouds on the horizon. Knee-high grasses on gently undulating hills went on for mile after mile as far as the eye could see, the line of sight only broken by the amazing termite mounds and a few sparse trees.

"There's your lion," Coetzee said, pointing to the right through his window.

She looked, saw a tree . . . "Oh. *Oh!*" A pride of lions lay in the shade under one of the thorn trees. Three females with half a dozen adorable cubs, and a male, young one in his prime. As the vehicles passed within a hundred feet of them, the big animal rose, all coiled strength and rippling gold muscles, to guard his harem. The ruff of his tawny mane framed cunning yellow eyes, narrowed to slits as he watched their caravan. He opened his mouth—*Lord, it was big*—and roared.

"He's telling us to bugger off and leave his ladies alone," Hunt interpreted.

She put a hand on Coetzee's shoulder. "Slow down. Please?"

Then, riveted and craning her neck as they passed slowly, Taylor whispered, "My God, look at him. He's absolutely magnificent. He must be at least eight or nine feet long. I had no idea . . ."

She actually felt a weird little clutch in her heart, seeing the animals. Not just because they were almost close enough to touch and were without the confidence-inspiring safety of zoo bars between them, but because of the incredible beauty of observing them here in their native habitat.

No need for a camera to remember this moment. Without thinking, she reached out her hand to take Hunt's, wanting to share the moment with him. His fingers curled around hers. Strong. Sure. Safe.

Taylor's heart skipped a hard beat. Then another. And another as their eyes met.

Taylor didn't know how to interpret the sensation that suddenly arced between them. It was wholly unfamiliar. Oh, God. She was in trouble here.

Big, big trouble.

The sensation was a heart-pounding mixture of delight and horror. The *very* last thing she wanted, damn it, or *expected,* was to fall in love. *Especially* with a man like Huntington St. John.

Emotional attachments didn't last; she knew that on the most basic level. She'd never been foolish enough to let a man get *that* close. Not Jörn, not even Daniel.

She broke eye contact with difficulty, half terrified, half exhilarated. Her heart beat fast and her vision blurred as she turned to look blindly out of her window. How had this happened? When? Was it his swift action in ensuring Mandy's safety, no questions asked? Oh, God. Perhaps it had been before that. When he'd held her head as she'd thrown up after the bad guys had gassed them? Hardly a romantic moment, and yet . . .

Oh, God. Oh, God. She couldn't be in love with this man. It was completely . . . improbable. Impossible. Insane.

She vaguely heard the *shsss* of a can being opened. "Here." Hunt thrust a cold soda into her hand. "What the hell happened? Suddenly you look pale as hell."

"Low blood sugar. Thanks." She took a gulp, then held the cool metal to her forehead. Maybe she was misinterpreting the feeling? she thought a little hysterically. Maybe it was something as simple and uncomplicated as *lust.* Lust was okay. Lust was manageable. Lust did not rip out one's heart.

She glanced at him under her lashes. It was lust, all right, lust deluxe. He was everything she'd never known she wanted in a man. Everything she'd never allowed herself to dream about on those long lonely nights alone in her bed when half-formed thoughts had been pushed ruthlessly back into her subconscious.

The swaying grasses outside Taylor's window blurred like a muted watercolor. She felt raw inside, stripped of her customary protective layers, which left her vulnerable to this avalanche of unfamiliar feelings.

Hunt squeezed her hand, and she turned like a sleepwalker. "Do you want to stop the car? Are you sick?"

She shook her head.

Fortunately, another long fax came through just then. The next hour was spent discussing thermal satellite imaging of the mine and what that might mean in geometry terms, something little more than a vague school memory for Taylor. She didn't want to start something with the manly men, but *her* way of doing a job required that she see the target for herself. They could technobabble themselves into a coma, she'd still do it her way.

As the sun slid with reluctance toward the horizon, they crossed a river over a wooden bridge so rickety, Taylor was amazed it could bear the weight of the cars. Fortunately, it was a short span. It was a long, *long* way down into the gorge.

"The wall's unusual," Hunt said into the lip mic as they approached the village Taylor had seen on the satellite pictures. The seven-sided wall built around the round huts blocked most of their view, but Hunt assured her that their approach had been noted and prepared for when the convoy was a good twenty miles away.

"Stop here," he instructed. "Fisk, Savage, Viljoen, Burton, and Gardner, with me. The rest of you, stand by."

Hunt opened his door, then glanced at Taylor. "Stay in the car."

"Not a prob," she said, happy to obey her first order. The grasses were thigh high, and insects buzzed and crawled everywhere. "I think there be snakes in them thar grasses."

"Don't look now, darling," Hunt said mildly, his attention concentrated over her shoulder. "But I think snakes are the least of our problems."

Taylor swung around to see what he was talking about.

Circling the vehicles were at least a hundred native warriors in full war paint, and nothing else. They all carried skin shields, long, metal-tipped spears, and looked extremely annoyed.

Thirty-seven

TAYLOR FOUND IT IMPOSSIBLE *NOT* TO LOOK AT THE HUNDRED or so gleaming, healthy, *naked* male bodies surrounding their vehicles. Most of the men didn't have on so much as a loincloth, and their dark skin gleamed in the fading light as if oiled.

Of far more concern, Hunt's group were ridiculously outnumbered by at least three to one. He was the only one outside the vehicle, and her heart was pounding so hard, she couldn't hear anything else.

Each vehicle was surrounded, and the occupants were being impatiently motioned to leave their jeeps. The gesture was done with wild movements of the long spears. They didn't appear to speak English. She hoped one of the South Africans, Daan or Piet or one of their team, could interpret.

"Keep your hands where they can see them," Hunt told them calmly. "And get out of the car."

With the sun setting, the temperature had dropped. It was not

cold, but Taylor shivered as she swung her legs out and paused, looking to Hunt for direction. Vaguely, she heard other doors in their convoy open and shut.

Hunt took her hand, pulling her to her feet in the dry thigh-high
golden grass. The air smelled hot and arid, stinging her nostrils every
time Taylor inhaled. Insects buzzed and hummed and droned as they
darted and swarmed around the newcomers.

As the two men emerged from the front seats, Hunt indicated that
they should talk to the natives closest to them. Daan Viljoen sprouted
a string of words filled with strange rhythms and many clinks of the
tongue. The locals looked at him, puzzled. He tried another language.
That one didn't seem to work either, as the men looked at one another
and then back.

"You give it a try," he told Piet Coetzee.

None of Coetzee's attempts brought understanding either, and the
native men whispered among themselves.

Other than the noise of the insects, an occasional screech from a
bird, or a cry of an animal, the entire situation was eerily silent. Three
men approached Hunt. They used the spears to point. He shifted her
behind him, then held up his hands, showing they were empty.

Taylor frowned. *Why* wasn't Hunt carrying a gun? Why weren't
any of the T-FLAC people carrying a weapon of some sort? They'd
known these people were here before they'd arrived.

Clearly, Hunt knew something he hadn't shared with her, because
no one in his right mind would walk into a situation like this unpre-
pared.

A flying insect feasted on her sweaty neck. Taylor was scared that
if she moved, one of these guys would . . . Do what? Throw a spear?
Stab her with a spear? She presumed one could die from a spear
wound, but it seemed pretty damn primitive. In fact, this whole situation seemed pretty damn primitive.

At least these guys didn't look as aggressive as she'd first thought,
although they didn't look superfriendly either. The fact that nobody
was saying anything added to the creep factor.

Down the length of their convoy, everyone was being asked for weapons. Boxes and crates were removed from the vehicles and piled together in the middle of . . . nowhere.

Talk about a bloodless coup, she thought. Not that she wanted bloodshed, but for God's sake—this didn't make *any* sense at all. They were motioned to walk ahead of the men and into the village. Hunt walked next to her, and she darted a glance at his profile. He didn't look worried. Fine. She was worried enough for both of them.

"You *knew* these people were here," she whispered as they trudged through the hot, smelly grass, their feet kicking up puffs of dust and more bugs. She'd seen the infrared pictures, had listened to the discussion.

"No questions, remember?"

Right. She remembered.

They were escorted through an opening in the six-foot-high mud wall surrounding the village. Taylor glanced about curiously. She could see no women, no children, no livestock or food crops. She frowned. It was almost dinnertime. But there was no sign of food being prepared. It was as though they'd walked onto a film set.

There were half a dozen T-FLAC guys ahead of them as they were corralled into a large round hut with a thatched roof. The others followed, shifting around when they got inside and moving away from the arched doorway.

The hut was called a *rondaval,* Viljoen had said when they passed a small village of huts that morning. The enormous house was one large room, and all thirty-plus of them fit inside with plenty of room to spare. It was hard to make out anything in the semidarkness, just a dirt floor, dirt walls, and no door or windows. What was left of dusk came only as far as a few feet inside the arched doorway. The whole place smelled of musty soil and dried grass.

Taylor glanced around at the T-FLAC guys, some of whom she'd seen briefly when they hooked up at the airport. They all appeared focused and intent, but none of them looked any more worried than Hunt. Were these guys communicating telepathically or something?

Everyone migrated to the center, and she joined them there.

"They'll wait," Hunt said. For what? Taylor wanted to ask, wondering how he managed to speak so softly and still be heard. It was a gift. He touched the face of his watch and it glowed a muted green. "Let's give them five hours; 2300." He scanned the men. They nodded.

"This *kraal* is clearly the first level," Hunt continued. "The seven sides of the outside wall, the rolling meadows, and so on, would represent Dante's Limbo."

Taylor stepped up beside him, but he kept talking. "Navarro, description on Level Two?"

" 'Mute of light. Wind. Hurricanes,' " the other man said, teeth gleaming in the semidarkness. "It's the 'smite the lustful' part of the program."

"No hurricanes in this part of the world," Savage pointed out. "And hello? No hurricanes anywhere *inside*. So what does it mean?"

"It means Morales will find a way to produce one," Hunt answered. "Need something?" he asked Taylor softly.

She was surprised he was aware of her standing beside him. "Actually, I have a quick question for Viljoen." She turned to find him in the darkness, and trying to speak as softly as the men, she said, "What language were those guys speaking?"

"You know, I'm not sure. Nothing I'm familiar with, anyhow," Viljoen said meditatively. "But there are over forty African languages—"

"But they barely said a *word*," Taylor pressed. "Not even to each other, really. Did you notice? They must have a language. How would they communicate?"

"How many words do they *need* for, 'Should we boil them or fry them?' " one of the men joked.

"What's your theory?" Hunt murmured.

"Is there anything in their vocabulary that sounds recognizable to *any* of you?" Taylor asked the group.

"You know, not really," Viljoen replied. "But like I said, there're so many languages—"

"This isn't a language," Taylor stated with conviction. "They look like they jumped out of a *National Geographic* photo spread. And did you notice? No *women*. No evening fires. This is weird. Something isn't quite right."

"No, it isn't," Hunt agreed. "They walk the walk and talk the talk, but those men out there wearing beads and paint and toting *assegais* and oxhide shields are Latin."

"My thought exactly," Daklin agreed. "We knew *Mano del Dios* would be waiting."

"Morales has a bizarre flair for the dramatic," Hunt said, keeping his voice low.

"San Cristóbal inflection?" Taylor asked quietly beside him.

He nodded. "They've done an amazingly good job of coming up with gobbledygook that *could* be authentic. But they haven't quite perfected the knack of sustaining an entire conversation. Hence the abbreviated noble savage dialogue. It's to our advantage to play along.

"Farrel, get us some light in here. Viljoen, go with him to 'interpret.' Daklin, Bishop, watch their backs."

THE "NATIVES" SUPPLIED THEM WITH FOOD AND WATER, AND GAVE them free rein of the entire village. Of course they did, Hunt thought, amused. They wanted Taylor, and T-FLAC, to access the mine as quickly as possible.

Over a wooden trencher of ostrich meat, Hunt assured the "chief" that they were merely here to see the country and they meant him and the village no harm. It was a lovely little play, one that both sides enjoyed. No harm, and so far, no foul.

The fact that their weapons had been confiscated bothered only Taylor. Hunt's people were trained in hand-to-hand combat and were as lethal without a gun as with one. And God only knew, if a weapon was wanted, they'd procure whatever they needed when the time came.

It was a given that the moment the final level was breached, these guys wouldn't be lobbing those theatrical-looking spears at them. Morales's people had access to the best weaponry in the business. Hunt had already dispatched several men to ascertain exactly where that cache of weapons was and what kind of firepower they had.

What *Mano del Dios* had, T-FLAC would take. Simple.

So far, everything was running smoothly. Too smoothly.

Hunt had had a persistent itch on the back of his neck since leaving Zurich. It was an itch he never ignored, and it concerned the hell out of him. His instincts when it came to tangos had been infallible so far. The itch was telling him that the smooth sailing they'd experienced to this point was about to come to a god-awful, and unholy, end.

Soon.

He had never felt this gut-deep fear before an op.

He wasn't afraid of death, in fact rarely gave it a thought. It was part of the life he'd chosen. He knew he sure as hell wasn't going to die of old age. What he did while he was alive though, made a difference, but his own mortality didn't concern him one way or the other. In this business, death would come sooner rather than later. The people he dealt with on a daily basis lived violent lives. One of these days his good fortune would run out and he'd die a violent death. That was a given.

But having Taylor here—bloody hell. *That* fucking scared the piss out of him. He hated like hell playing Russian roulette with *her* life. Yet here she was.

Thirty-eight

A KNOCK AT THE CHAPEL DOOR BROUGHT MORALES BACK TO awareness.

The stone floor felt chill beneath his cheek. He blinked back the darkness. He must rise. Finish what he had begun. His back burned like the fires of hell as he pushed to his knees. The sticky cloth across his back pulled and tore away from the dried and still weeping wounds from his shoulders to his thighs, but he did not make a sound.

He reached for the whip beside him.

Thou shalt surely smite the inhabitants of that city with the edge of the sword, destroying it utterly, and all that is therein, and the cattle thereof, with the edge of the sword.

The knocking turned to pounding. "Señor, señor. It is time, señor." His first lieutenant pushed open the heavy steel and came hesitantly into the chapel. Aarón bowed his head as he shuffled forward. "It is time, señor."

"Turn your back! You are not worthy of seeing God's glory!"

Morales shouted. He did not permit anyone to witness his vulnerability to God's instructions.

"My apologies, señor," Aarón replied deferentially, his voice echoing off the stone walls. "But you instructed that I tell you—T-FLAC has the girl. They are guests in the village. Señor, it has begun."

"*Bueno.* Leave me." Morales knew he had work to do. Time ran on God's clock, not his, and it slowly ticked away.

"But, *Jefe*—"

"*Enough.* Send my beloved Maria to me, and go."

The end of all things is near, therefore, be serious and discipline yourselves for the sake of your prayers.

New beginnings awaited the faithful.

José wiped his blood-wet hand down his thigh, then lifted the whip and began again.

Thirty-nine

LISA MAKI SAT ON THE TOP STEP OF SOMEBODY'S BROKEN-DOWN porch on the back of their decrepit house, smoking a cigarette and drinking a warm beer. It wasn't late, but she'd sent her people to bed. She didn't know them, and she didn't fucking want to bond with them. They had their instructions. They could keep the hell out of her way until she needed them tomorrow.

She'd just spoken to the head of Black Rose herself on a disposable cell phone. Was *she* out there somewhere, *watching*? Lisa wondered, glancing around the moonlit backyard consisting of dry, patchy grass and engine parts. The Black Rose herself seemed to have eyes in the back of her head.

Lisa shook off the sensation of being watched. Her leader had sounded good. Upbeat. Pleased.

And if her boss was pleased, Lisa knew she was in good favor.

So. The girl and T-FLAC were in the village near the mouth of the mine. Tomorrow they should reach the missile. She'd let them do all the scud work. Then it would be a simple matter for her to take in her team, kill them all, and assume ownership of the *Mano del Dios* stash of goodies. The missile. The diamonds. The cash. The biochemicals, and whatever the fuck else the asshole had buried down there.

In a few hours it would *all* belong to the Black Rose.

Thanks, of course, to Lisa Maki.

Forty

TAYLOR SAT CROSS-LEGGED BESIDE HUNT, PUSHING THE FOOD around on the wooden trencher. She'd barely tasted the stringy ostrich meat.

"Force yourself to eat a little of the protein," he told her. "You'll need your strength later." They'd all depend on her strength later.

She shot him a look and picked up a hunk of meat, stuffing it into her mouth. "Mfappy now?" she said with her mouth full.

"Delirious. Chew."

She chewed with clear reluctance, but he waited for her to swallow, then picked up an apple wedge and placed it in her hand.

"Thank you, Mommy." She bit down with sharp white teeth and chewed with a little more enthusiasm.

Hunt said an unfamiliar prayer to a god who, after many years of absence, had been hearing from him a lot lately: *God, don't let a damn thing hurt this woman. You hear me?*

Because their hosts ate with them, the conversation was general and vague. *Don't speak English, my ass.* When Hunt rose, his people did too. They were led outside and directed to several smaller *rondavals* for the night. He'd have kept everyone together where he could see them. But hell, he wasn't going to look a gift horse in the mouth. He'd already designated assignments, and he let everyone decide where they wanted to sack out.

Bidding his team a casual good-night—they'd be together at 2300—he ushered Taylor toward the hut farthest from the others.

He didn't need his Maglite to see the way. The sky was a clear, black bowl dotted with the sparkle of a million brilliant white stars and a picture-perfect sliver of a moon. With the sun down, it was chilly, the air crisp and scented with the fragrance of wood fires and the unfamiliar smell of the surrounding vegetation. Insects buzzed and whirred, and in the distance a lion roared, calling its mate, reminding him that while their "native" hosts were faux, this really was the wild.

And there were things far more dangerous nearby than wild animals. Somewhere beneath their feet lay a missile that, if it were a nuke, could take out a good chunk of the continent.

"Is it safe for us to be separated?" Taylor asked, her voice pitched low.

Hunt looked over his shoulder at the rest of his team slipping into the other huts. "Not much we can do about it at the moment."

"Thanks. That makes me feel better."

He dropped one arm around her shoulders and pulled her close. "You're doing great, love. Just hang on a few more days."

"Don't worry." She slipped her arms about his waist as they walked. "I'm fine. And although I hate to say this, realizing the seriousness of what we're doing, I have to tell you, I'm also pretty damn *excited* to be involved."

Her eyes sparkled up at him in the moonlight. "This rush I get when I'm being challenged is *precisely* why I do what I do, remember? The excitement. The thrill. The danger." Her pretty mouth curved into a rueful smile that he desperately wanted to taste.

"Not that I'm comparing being blown to smithereens by a nuclear missile to being caught robbing a safe, mind you. But I *am* excited, nevertheless."

He understood perfectly. He was worried enough for both of them. For *all* of them. "I can live with that."

"How much longer?"

He knew she meant before they headed for the mine. "Three and a half hours."

Her arm tightened around his waist as she looked up at him. "Then we should enjoy those three and a half hours together, shouldn't we?"

"Yes," he agreed. "We sure as hell should."

Her smile widened. "Listen . . ."

"Yeah. Lion. Welcome to Africa."

"You okay?" she asked, looking at him with a frown.

"Not even close," he muttered, need clawing at his throat. Taking her arm, he steered her into the dirt hut.

The *rondaval* was considerably smaller than the others, but it had a heavy blanket over the door opening, giving them some privacy. Pushing it aside, Hunt had to practically bend double to get through the doorway, but once inside he could stand comfortably.

He switched on the torch and scanned the room. It consisted of the same circular design, with a thatched roof and a dirt floor. A pile of folded blankets and an earthenware pitcher of water had been set near the door.

"All the comforts of home," he said dryly, setting down the Maglite so he could spread a layer of blankets on the ground.

He lowered himself to the bed he'd made and started unlacing his boots. "Take off your boots and come and lie down. We can get in a couple of hours ourselves before we get started."

"Believe me, I am *so* not tired," Taylor said, starting to pace. "Besides, it's only about eight o'clock. Way too early."

Hunt reached up and took her hand as she passed, tugging her down beside him. "You need to turn your brain off," he told her, keeping his tone soothing. She was wound tighter than a cheap watch. He removed his own boots and put them beside their makeshift bed. "Worrying isn't going to speed this up. You'll need all your concentration when we *do* go in."

She reluctantly unlaced and removed her boots and tossed them beside his. "I wish I *could* turn my brain off. What if—"

He leaned forward, threading his fingers through her hair at the temples, and lifted her face. "Relax," he told her softly.

Her lips curved in a small smile, but her eyes, those incredible hot-ice eyes, were haunted. "Can you squeeze the worry out of my brain?"

Hunt tangled his fingers deeper into the cool silk of her hair, drawing her closer. "Let's see, shall we?"

He touched his mouth to hers—cool satin—then cradled her head in his hands, supporting her as he lowered her to her back on the blanket. He followed her down, pressing tender kisses to her neck and jaw, then covered her face with soft kisses. He brushed his mouth over hers, gently, teasing, light. Sweet, so sweetly responsive.

He reveled in the texture of her lips and the small breathy sounds she made as she opened her mouth to welcome him inside. He deepened the kiss. He wanted to absorb her, to draw her so deeply inside himself that she wouldn't know where she began and he ended. He loved the feel of her tongue moving languidly inside his mouth, and the brush of her hands as she stroked his face with cool fingers.

He felt an indescribable, overwhelming combination of lust and tenderness as they kissed. He wanted her, had wanted her from day one, with a blistering intensity that shocked him. No woman had ever had this effect on him. Part of him wanted to take her hard and fast and satisfy this insatiable craving he had for her. The other part of him wanted it like this—slow and lazy. Time to discover how many ways he could make her come apart in his arms.

Still kissing her, he started undoing the buttons of her shirt, spreading the cotton open as he went. Her skin warmed under his light touch and her legs moved restlessly against his.

He lifted his head to look at her. Her eyes were heavy-lidded and sultry, her mouth swollen and damp from his. She pulled his head down, but he resisted, making her frown with impatience.

"Don't rush it." Hunt smoothed his finger along the little frown lines between her brows. "We have a couple of hours."

He rolled to his side next to her, supporting himself on his elbow as he continued unbuttoning her shirt, fascinated as more creamy skin was revealed. Her bra, what little there was of it, was flesh-colored lace, and even so it was shades darker than the plump swell of her breasts. He ran his finger across the soft mounds, delighted that he could see the rosy peaks of her nipples through the semisheer fabric.

Keeping the fingers of one hand buried in his hair, Taylor curved her other arm over her head, watching his face. "You're driving me insane, you know."

He reached over and picked up the flashlight, moving it to a better position so the golden light bathed her body, then continued slipping each small button from its hole and folding back the edges of her shirt until he reached the waistband of her jeans, all the while allowing his fingers only the most gentle of touches, skimming over the smooth silk of her skin.

With every brush of his fingers, Taylor's skin warmed to a soft creamy blush. Her fingers tightened in his hair as he popped the top button and eased down the zipper, taking his time to reveal her waist, the small dimple of her navel, her flat stomach. She reached down to flatten a hand over his, pressing his palm harder against her mound.

Hunt slipped his hand from beneath hers. He chuckled as she gave a huff of impatience, which quickly turned to a feline-sounding purr of pleasure as he recaptured her mouth, at the same time clicking the front opening of her bra to free her breasts.

Taylor whimpered with pleasure as Hunt cupped her breast in his warm palm with unhurried leisure, then brushed his thumb across her nipple until she moaned with need. Only one side of his face was lit, giving him an almost sinister appearance. At this point she didn't give a damn if he was the devil himself. She wanted him more than she wanted her next breath.

When Taylor thought she couldn't stand another second of "slow," he lowered his head and took the hard bud into the hot, wet cavern of his mouth. She could barely control her sharp intake of breath as, using tongue and teeth on her nipple, he seemed bound and determined to drive her over the edge.

"Hunt!" she cried softly as pleasure, sharp and sweet, radiated from the tip of her breast to her womb.

"Right here, darling."

She felt as though she were hanging from a ten-story building without a harness. "This is . . . ah . . . extremely one . . . sided."

He raised his head. "You're not enjoying it?" he asked, his eyes devilish as they met hers.

"If . . . I were enjoying th-this any more, I'd be arrested. I meant I want to . . . to . . ." She forgot what she'd been about to say as he used both hands to skim her jeans down her legs, while his mouth did delicious things against her stomach.

She helped him get her pants off, God she helped him. Kicking and wiggling to get the fabric down her legs and over her feet in record time.

Her six-hundred-dollar La Perla thong disappeared as if by magic as Hunt cupped her derriere in his large, elegant hands, bringing her mound to meet his greedy mouth. "Wait . . ." She needed a moment. A second to catch her breath.

He didn't stop, clearly determined to steal her breath altogether. He used his mouth, tongue, lips, and teeth to stake his claim. She whimpered, her body moving of its own volition as his tongue thrust deep inside her, his fingers dug into her hips, his shoulders kept her body open to him. Panting, she flung her arm over her eyes and gritted her teeth. Hanging there above the earth as the intimacy of his kiss seared her flesh made her temperature rise to boiling and caused her hips to arch off the blankets, thrusting her body against his mouth.

"Come inside me," she begged as his tongue brought her closer and closer to the precipice.

His penis was velvety hard as he pressed against her, sliding in easily because she was so wet, so ready for him, that she pressed a hand against his chest as she waited for wave after wave of sensation to subside before she could let him slide in to the hilt.

She was lost.

And there was no way back.

Forty-one

W AKE UP, LOVE. TIME TO GET CRACKING."

Taylor blinked open gritty eyes to see Hunt crouched beside her, illuminated by the glow from his flashlight. Dressed completely in black, he was all but invisible, except for his hands and face. He smelled of fresh air, some kind of medicinal soap, and coffee. She wanted to drag him back into the warm, rumpled nest of blankets.

Instead she rubbed her eyes and sat up. The blanket covering her slipped to her lap and chilled air caressed her sleep-warmed body. *"Brr."*

"I've brought hot water, clothes, and coffee."

"Coffee first?" she asked hopefully, and was rewarded by his chuckle as he placed a wooden bowl of steaming, eucalyptus-scented water beside her. Kneeling, he slid the strap of a black duffel off his shoulder, deposited the bag onto the floor, then handed her a metal mug.

"Careful. It's hot." He pulled up one of the blankets, wrapping it around her bare shoulders.

She lifted her head, then used both hands to cup the warm metal container and bring it to her mouth. "Elixir of the gods. Those guys brought Juan Valdez with them." She looked at him through the rising steam and took a sip. "You said something about bringing me something to wear? I brought my work clothes."

"Nothing like this, you didn't." He held up what appeared to be a *shadow* in one large hand.

Taylor squinted, trying to figure out what the thin black . . . thing could possibly be. "What *is* that?" She reached out to finger the fabric. Thin. But not silk. Considerably heavier and more dense. Almost rubbery.

"A LockOut suit."

Taylor set the mug aside. The scalding hot coffee had warmed her insides up nicely. Wide-awake and intrigued, she said, "Okay. I'll bite. What does a LockOut suit lock out? And why am I going to wear it?"

"Think of it as a wet suit. Only better. It's like a second skin, maintaining a constant body temperature of sixty-seven degrees. Also acts as a shield."

"A shield? Against what?"

"Water and fire, for starters. It's self-healing, and almost impervious to nicks and cuts. More important, it's practically bulletproof."

Taylor rubbed the thin fabric between her fingers again. Thin. Rubbery. Weird. It felt insubstantial in her hands, and she wondered if this was like the emperor's new clothes. "You're kidding me, right? This stuff can't be bulletproof."

"Practically."

"Practically isn't bad," she said, taking it from him. It was lightweight and infinitely more practical, she decided, than Lycra leggings and ballet slippers. Cool. A new uniform. It was always gratifying to wear the right outfit for the occasion. She scrunched it in her hand. It would take up no room at all. Could, in fact, be stuffed into a pocket, once she'd finished a job. "How practical is practically?"

"Better than a bulletproof vest."

"Sold. I'll order a dozen right now."

"I thought you might feel that way," Hunt told her dryly. "Here." He nudged the lightly steaming wooden bowl closer to her knee. "Want me to wash you?"

Yes, please. "Didn't you mention you wanted to leave *soon*?"

The thought of Hunt bathing her intimately brought a flush of heat to her skin. All over. If he touched her right now, she'd go off like a rocket. "I'd better do it myself," she told him regretfully.

What she wanted to do was— *Never mind.* She reached into the bowl and wrung out the cloth floating in the water. "Thanks."

She lay back on the blankets and ran the warm, soapy cloth down her belly, her eyes fixed on Hunt's face. "The magic suit?" she prompted, not feeling cold at all. Hunt's eyes glittered feverishly as he watched, mesmerized, while she spread her knees to bathe herself. The coolness of the night air kissed her skin. The heat of his gaze spiked her body temperature.

Their eyes locked. An entire thesaurus of desire arced between them. Mouth dry, Taylor licked her upper lip. "Nudge the bowl a little closer, would you?"

He snatched the cloth from her hand. "Bloody hell. I'll do it." He plunged the fabric into the water and wrung it out with enough force that warm water sprinkled her skin. Yet when he touched the damp material between her legs, his touch was gentle.

Her nipples peaked as Hunt washed her carefully and skillfully. Sparks of electricity zinged through her body and her hips arched off their bed. She reached out a hand to grab his shoulder. "Hunt, please—"

With a snarl, he tossed the cloth back into the water and leaned over to crush his mouth to hers. Taylor wrapped her arms about his neck, and he pulled her to a sitting position as he ravished her mouth with teeth and tongue. After several moments he put her aside, resting his forehead on hers.

"No more. As much as I want to make love to you again, there's no time. Help me here, darling."

Taylor closed her eyes as the sharp anticipation of her body simmered. She cupped the back of his head, tangling her fingers in his hair. They stayed that way, foreheads touching, until her parts got the message that they weren't about to party and her breathing was back to normal. Almost.

With a final stroke to his hair, Taylor raised her face and gave him a quick kiss on the mouth. "Okay. Up. Dress. Out."

He rose and held out his hand. "Stand. I'll help you into the suit. Put this on." He dangled her thong on one finger.

Taking his hand, she let him pull her to her feet. Her knees were weak, but she locked them until she felt a little steadier. With a smile, she took her underwear from him and shot him a mock-suspicious glance. "I don't have to wear high-heeled boots and carry a whip, do I?"

"Not this time." He waited as she drew on the thong, then held out the bottom half of the suit. "One leg at a time."

"No kidding!" Taylor rested one hand on his broad shoulder— covered in the same fabric—and got her legs into the legs of the suit, pushing her feet through and wiggling her toes. The fabric felt odd, firmly hugging each part of her sensitized body as Hunt tugged it up and over her hips.

It was styled like the footies she'd worn as a kid, and he drew the top part up and over her naked shoulders. "Arm . . . other arm. Jesus," his voice was thick, "you have beautiful breasts." He drew up the zipper from her waist, slowly, his knuckles brushing the centerline of her body all the way up until he reached her chin, then he brushed her lower lip with his thumb. "Done."

Taylor lifted her arms up and down as though she were flying. "This is amazing! I feel . . . naked."

"Don't I wish."

She grinned, starting to feel the usual before-a-big-job rush of an- ticipatory adrenaline surge through her system. "Do I need my boots?"

"No. You don't need anything. I have your tools," Hunt told her, his normal taciturn self again as he swung the duffel back to his shoulder. "Let's go. The others are waiting."

THERE WASN'T MUCH OF A CLIMB TO REACH THE MOUTH OF THE mine. The bright moon hung in the black sky, illuminating the shrubs and vegetation. Hunt wasn't being particularly stealthy, but it didn't matter, since the "natives" knew what was going on as they pretended to sleep. Taylor walked lightly beside him.

The dark shapes of his team came into view as they crested a small berm and Viljoen joined them. Because it was so bright, the team had positioned themselves to be completely hidden by the dense shadows from an enormous outcropping of rock and shrubs nearby.

"Okay," Viljoen said quietly, in his element because he was the mining expert on the team. He acknowledged Hunt with a brief glance before continuing. "What we have here appears to be room-and-pillar mining, you know? Unusual, 'cause mostly here in S.A. they have open-pit mines, not— *Ag,* never mind the lesson." He quickly reined himself in.

"So, what we're gonna find in there will be the typical low-angle adits connecting to some sort of horizontal access level," he finished.

The entrance was an unimpressive wooden structure. Only close inspection showed it was new construction, with heavy-duty metal bracing painted to blend in. From as close as twenty feet away the wood appeared to be part of the original 1970s mine.

"You didn't tell me I could've worn cool makeup," Taylor whispered to Hunt as they approached the rest of the team. They all wore cammy paint on their hands and faces.

"Only the people who'll be staying out here are wearing it," he said softly.

The smell of her, standing so close beside him, filled his senses. It was no longer novel to him, so he should be immune by now. Yet the very familiarity of it distracted him. Dangerously so. He took several steps forward and motioned her to wait.

"Who's inside?" he asked softly.

"Bishop, Savage, Navarro, and Fisk," Daklin told him. Hunt gave him points for not staring and salivating at Taylor in the skintight LockOut suit.

They'd retrieved their weapons hidden beneath the floorboards of the vehicles, and everyone else wore heavy artillery in cleverly crafted holsters—guns, knives, and ammo. But on Taylor there was nothing but the unbroken line of matte black material hugging every curve and hollow of her body. She might as well be naked and wearing a thin coat of black paint.

"I'm off with my team," Daklin said, sounding as though he were smiling, but no emotion showing on his face. "Anything you need before we split?"

Most of the team would remain aboveground, while Hunt, Taylor, Fisk, Viljoen, Coetzee, Tate, and Bishop went through the levels inside. "Keep alert for anything," he told the first away team led by Daklin. "If a snake of any sort so much as yawns—shoot it."

He was talking to thin air.

He looked up as four shadows blended from the pitch-black interior to the deep black of the shadows outside. "Fisk. What have we got?"

He was looking at Fisk, but preternaturally aware of the woman beside him. Hunt kept Taylor in his peripheral vision at all times, as though she might suddenly disappear.

Jesus bloody Christ, he did *not* want to take her in there. *All right, God. Here's the deal. Make this simple and quick. Make Taylor completely redundant on this op, so I can have her taken the fuck out of here, and I'll swear to kill Morales more quickly and humanely than he could ever deserve. Out. I mean . . . Amen."*

"Any chance you can open whatever it is on your own?" Hunt asked Fisk.

"He just tried," Savage told him. "He's never seen such a complex—"

"I can represent myself, thank you," Frank Fisk told her, then turned to Hunt. "We need Taylor."

"Savage?" Navarro called so softly, his words seemed like part of the barely there breeze.

The man was a woman whisperer, Hunt thought as Savage reluctantly turned. "Let Bishop—"

"You're my sharpshooter," Hunt told her. "I want you with them. Go."

She opened her mouth. Hunt waited. Her shoulders straightened and she raised her voice slightly so it would carry to her team. "On my way."

"Step lively then, beautiful," Daklin told her, melting into the shrubbery with the others.

Were you listening, God?

"Ready to rock?" Bishop pulled his hood over his hair and neck, leaving only his features visible, more for warmth than as a disguise.

"Let's do it," Hunt said grimly, taking Taylor's hand in his and walking with purpose.

He wasn't capricious, never had been. He didn't have premonitions, or psychic dreams, or extrasensory perception, but he trusted his gut instincts implicitly. They'd never failed him.

In all his years as a T-FLAC operative, Hunt had experienced everything from motivational hatred for the scum he dealt with to anticipation and interest when he was on an op. But now, as he walked toward the rickety-looking entrance to the Blikiesfontein mine, Taylor at his side, he felt intense fear. In his thoughts, in his gut, in his impervious heart.

Suddenly, he wished he'd never met Taylor.

He cursed himself for his dogged persistence in tracking her down.

And he felt profound guilt that he'd caved and permitted her to accompany T-FLAC, *him,* to Africa.

Because his gut was telling him what he knew in his bones.

Quite simply, Hunt knew, he was going to be the death of her.

Forty-two

THE PASSAGEWAY SLOPED GRADUALLY, AND THE DEEPER THEY walked, the narrower it became. Surprisingly, there was no musty smell inside the mine. In fact it smelled of dirt, and was not unpleasant. The area immediately surrounding them was illuminated by the powerful flashlights each of the men carried. They were also all armed to the teeth.

It was pitch-dark. Fortunately, she had no fear of either darkness or confined spaces. But she was having a hard time adjusting to the outfit she wore. It was so insubstantial that she felt naked, and had to run her hand down her hip or touch her sleeve to be sure she was wearing anything at all.

She and Frank Fisk walked side by side as they followed Bishop and Viljoen. Hunt, Coetzee, and Tate brought up the rear. The situation was a little surreal. Her heartbeat was delightfully fast, as it always was preceding a job. Clearing her mind so she could focus was *de rigueur* at this point, as well.

Focus.

"Here's what we've got," Fisk told her as they walked briskly through the tunnel. "No safe, per se, simply the door and the mechanism embedded in solid rock. No markings to ID it, but it's an Allied 763."

"The big guns right off the bat," Taylor said, her pulse racing pleasurably at the anticipation of the challenge. She all but rubbed her hands together in expectation. "1998 DV model, do you think?" The year that particular model had been perfected. "When did you say Morales bought this place, Daan?"

" 'Ninety-eight," Viljoen said over his shoulder. "Watch your step. There's a big dip right here, you know?"

"It's possible he had the latest, greatest installed right away," Taylor said, "but not probable." She turned to Fisk. "What month was the new DV763 model released? June of that year, right?"

"Yeah," Fisk agreed. "So it's likely the '96 model. Ever cracked one of those?"

"Actually, I managed to get into the '98 model last year." She smiled when Fisk gave her a goggle-eyed stare of admiration. "Morales had it installed in one of his Spanish warehouses. It was a bitch. And worth every penny of its hefty asking price."

"Impressive," Fisk murmured.

"Fortunately for me, because of its remote location I had an entire weekend to fool with it. And trust me, it took that long."

Too bad Morales had moved the Blue Star diamonds somewhere else that very week—a little detail that had stolen some of the thrill when she opened the safe, only to find the treasure gone. But she'd at least had the professional thrill of having defeated a safe that "couldn't be cracked." Anything could be cracked if one had the time and patience.

"Did you do an ultraviolet scan, or dust it for prints?" Taylor asked as they walked. Sometimes it was almost too easy if there was a keypad. The owner's fingerprints gave away the combination. After that, figuring out the order was pretty much child's play.

"Clean." Fisk grabbed her elbow as she took a misstep. "The '96?"

"Thanks." The tunnel curved slightly and dropped at least another six or seven feet in a sharp declining slope. She was grateful for his quick save. "Twice," she told him, mentally bringing up the schematics for Allied. "The first time I did a '96 it took me about four hours. I sweated bullets for every one of those 240 minutes."

The Petersons had been asleep upstairs. She'd been accompanied in the study by the family's two Doberman pinschers, who'd watched her every second and then followed her to the French doors, stubby tails wagging, as she walked out with the Fabergé eggs that had been stolen from a British royal three weeks before.

Dogs always liked her.

"The next time it took a smidgen under three." Not great, but not bad either. The Burmese sapphires.

"Kurt Peterson then Lorenzo Jordan," Hunt said grimly behind her. "Two more of the terrorists you're so fond of pissing off. You certainly like to live dangerously. Know what either of those two would have had done to you if they'd even *suspected* you'd robbed them?"

"Well, they *didn't* know it was me," she told him cheerfully. "And even if they did, who could they tell? They'd both acquired their treasures illegally in the first place."

"Here we are," Viljoen said, stepping aside for Fisk and Taylor, but keeping the high beam of his flashlight on the seven-foot-high titanium door embedded in the solid-rock walls. Fisk's small computer sat on the floor at the base of the door.

"It *is* a '98 DV763," Taylor confirmed the second she saw the handle on the locking mechanism. She indicated the computer. "That didn't work, did it?"

She assumed Fisk had used software to run a sequence of numbers until it hit the right combination. Unfortunately, on this particular model they'd taken high-tech theft into account and programmed in a firewall to block access.

"I do love a challenge." Grinning at the big silver beauty, Taylor reached for her tools. "Okay, people, back up and give me some room."

Hunt knew that every safe had a fundamental weakness. It had to be accessible to a locksmith or to those authorized to open it. In this case, Morales had been his normal paranoid, wily self. He'd chosen the best safe on the market, then efficiently dispatched everyone who had anything to do with its invention, sale, and installation.

"Drill through the face?" Fisk asked Taylor as they both stood there looking at the door.

"Nope. I brought my diamond-bit punch rod—but it's not going to fly. They've got a heavy-duty cobalt plate back there. Doing it that way would take forever and a day, and more drill bits than we have access to."

"There's no side access, so no drilling that way either," Fisk told her, covetously eyeing the tools she was laying out on the ground. "How about the plasma cutters—or that thermic lance over there?"

"No, no, and nope." A wide smile lit her face. "We're going to have to do it the old-fashioned way."

"Walk me through what you'll be doing," he instructed calmly.

"First we determine the contact points," she told him, oblivious to everything else as she gently ran her fingers over and around the dial face in a loverlike caress. "The drive cam has a notch in it like the wheels in the wheel pack." She crouched down to look at it from a different angle, talking almost to herself.

"Notch is sloped down to allow the lever and fence to pass through . . . Want this, Francis?" she asked, handing Fisk her own earpiece so he could listen with her.

"When the nose of the level makes contact with the slope—left and right—we'll hear a small click."

She kept quiet as Fisk listened, face set, eyes closed. "Seven left."

Taylor wrote it down.

"Two right."

"Each of the numbers has a corresponding wheel," Taylor whispered. "When Francis is done, we'll figure out how many wheels are in the wheel pack. Then— Sorry. Was I talking too loudly?"

"No," Fisk muttered impatiently. "But I can't hear a fu—damn thing." He rose and handed her the stethoscope. "You try."

Hunt and the rest of his team stood back. There was nothing they could do to help. Fisk and Taylor were on their own. Right now, the only job the five men could perform was keeping the lights focused and handing the two safecrackers what they asked for as they guarded their backs.

Hunt felt like an E.R. nurse.

Taylor and Fisk worked hard for the better part of five hours. If they hadn't all been wearing the LockOut suits, they'd be sweating profusely. It was hard work. Yet Taylor showed no indication of exhaustion or impatience at the tedium of what she was doing. Instead, her lovely features were lit with an inner light and her eyes sparkled like brilliant blue-white diamonds.

She might not feel the urgency, Hunt thought—he and his people made sure she didn't—but he sure as bloody hell did. Even the most sophisticated and complex locking mechanisms had six or less numbers in a wheel pack. They'd penetrated seven of them already.

Taylor told them she suspected there might be as many as eleven. "Eight," she whispered triumphantly as she penetrated another. Fisk sat on the floor beside her, graphing each new discovery on a special wristwatch computer. They'd taken turns, but it was clear Taylor had more experience, and considerably more manual dexterity, so Fisk had volunteered to graph and learn.

After this many hours at close quarters, Hunt knew every inch of the surrounding area. The banded ironstone of the walls overlaid dolomites and limestone with weathered yellow kimberlite streaked with unweathered blue, indicating what had previously been a classic diamondiferous kimberlite pipe.

A track inlaid in the center of the hard-packed floor indicated a mechanized vehicle of some sort used to bring the diamonds to the surface in the heyday of the mine.

"Nine," Taylor said triumphantly, her voice less than a whisper.

"Water. Drink." Hunt handed her a canteen. As she took it from him without looking up, he noticed the fine tremor in her hands. Not exhaustion, although God only knew she must be. No, there was a feverish energy that pulsed around her as she slugged the water, then absently set the container down beside her as she went back to work.

She had a remarkable ear and infinite patience. It was a pleasure watching her work. No wonder she'd been so successful at what she did. Fisk, now standing beside her, was spellbound by her expertise.

"Ten." Her shoulders slumped and she rested her head against the metal door. "We have the contact area." She glanced up at Fisk, her partner in crime.

"That's it?" Viljoen asked.

Fisk snorted. "Hardly. Now she dials the number on the lock that's in an opposite position from the numbers on the contact area."

"Want to park the wheels?" Taylor asked Fisk.

"Nah. You earned it. Nobody move until she gets it," Fisk warned.

"No. Give me a sec. I need a break. I want to walk around a bit." Taylor straightened and rotated her head on her neck. A faint dew of perspiration gleamed on her skin, making it look like alabaster.

"Want to get some fresh air?" Hunt asked, moving behind her to rest his hands on her narrow shoulders. He started to knead the tense muscles in her neck.

"No. I want to— God that feels good. Thank you. I want to get this sucker open before I'm too old to care. I'll take another slug of water—thanks, Daan ..." She gulped from the container, then handed it back, ". . . then get back to it."

"What does 'parking the wheel' mean?" Bishop demanded. Hunt knew the other man meant, What did it mean in *time*?

"*Reader's Digest* version? This is a three-hundred-number dial. Big by any standards. The contact area is forty, so I'll park the dial at . . . What do you think, Francis? Ninety?" He nodded. "Yeah. That's what I thought too. When I turn the dial to the right, the drive cam will reengage to begin spinning the wheels from that position. So every time the dial passes ninety, the drive pin will click as each wheel in the wheel pack—Your eyes are glazing. Never mind. I have to count clicks now, so no noise."

Another hour and seventeen minutes passed before Taylor straightened and stepped away from the door. "We're in."

"Good job," Hunt told her.

"*Good job?*" She raised her eyebrows. "That wasn't a good job.

That was a masterful job. It was brilliant job." She grinned, pleased with herself. As well she should be.

"Am I the best, or am I the best? I'm taking a well-deserved rest. You guys pull this puppy open, I'm too weak and feeble."

There was nothing weak or feeble about her, he thought. Jesus. She was magnificent. "You are, without a shadow of a doubt, *the* best," Hunt assured her as Tate and Bishop pulled the heavy door open.

The second the thirty-six-inch-thick titanium door broke away from the seal of the doorframe, a deafening, thunderous roar filled the tunnel. The force of the noise yanked the five-ton door out of their hands. It slammed open against the rock hard enough to dislodge enormous chunks of limestone from the walls and ceiling.

Hunt threw himself at Taylor, taking her down to the ground. The safe door trembled like tinfoil as the noise blasted through the opening. He covered Taylor's head with his arms, and buried his face in her hair, as the *sturm und drang* continued unabated.

Level Two.

Dante's Unforgiving Winds.

Forty-three

Hunt quickly gave Taylor a set of earplugs from his belt pack, installed his own earplugs, then shone his Maglite into the cavern through the open door. Even with the heavy-density earplugs, the sound of the four-turbo diesel engine in the floor was still unbearably loud. He glanced at Tate for a reading of the noise level. The other man held up his wrist PDA for Hunt and the others to see: 162dBA.

Logarithmic scales. The dBA of a *jet* taking off was 140. Bloody hell.

Hunt shone his light around the walls. There were no acoustic materials in the approximately 300-by-300-foot cavern. Morales had indeed produced his own infernal hurricane.

Taylor stepped back behind them so that he and his team would have room to ascertain what they were dealing with. Fortunately, T-FLAC had a simple and expedient nonverbal form of communication. With hand gestures, the conversation was fast and furious.

The only way to go was across.

But across to *what?*

Six flashlights strobed the circumference of the cavern. Small apertures in the walls appeared black. Some looked to be as small as a foot in circumference, others some six or eight feet in diameter. One of them would lead to where they wanted to go. The others . . .

Hunt picked up an oil-stained chammy from Taylor's bag of tricks, still spread at his feet, and tossed it through the doorway into the vertical air tunnel as a wind-drift indicator.

Sucked in, it swirled upward in a dizzying spiral of blurred motion, then flattened against the ceiling some hundred feet above their heads. And stayed there.

Jesus bloody Christ.

He did a quick calculation on his own PDA, gave a low, soundless whistle, then turned it to the others. The propeller was spinning at a hair over 250 mph.

They'd all had flight training, all done thousands of hours of parachuting and freestyle and 3-D dives, so they knew the correct body positions to navigate. But those drops had been done at a minimum height of four thousand feet, giving them time to control the fall rate; 7,200 was safer. This was only three *hundred* feet. Far too low to maneuver. Safely or otherwise.

And those jumps had been with proper equipment. All right, with damn *im*proper equipment, depending where they were—but this— fuck it to hell—this was suicide. Terminal velocity alone would kill them before they had a chance to go belly-down. Hunt felt a clutch of sheer undulated fear as he watched the speed and ferocity of those five spinning blades.

First they had to establish which of the openings they wanted. With sign language, they eliminated a dozen. Fisk did a quick, rough schematic on his wrist PDA as they worked, eliminating then adding back in when Hunt thought a particular hole large enough for a man to get through.

Then, how in the bloody hell to cross the uncovered prop blades without getting sucked in and chopped to pieces before they were swept upward on the airstream?

Only one way to find out . . .

Coetzee indicated that he'd go first for recon. Hunt nodded.

The smaller man flung himself from the door opening and was immediately caught by the blast of air and swept upward in a dizzying spin. He managed to spread his arms and legs wide. But it was impossible for him to control his movements enough to stabilize himself. He tumbled and spun, slamming into the walls again and again with bruising force.

Taylor came alongside Hunt, slipping her arm about his waist as she too watched. Hunt would've given his left nut to have her back in Zurich right now.

Hell, both nuts.

High above them, Coetzee's face was bleeding. He'd gone nose-first into a jagged outcropping of limestone and couldn't even wipe the blood from his eyes because the wind wouldn't allow that kind of finite movement. He tried to indicate which way he was going, but then the wind would spin him off in another direction.

He braced, then hit the opposite wall with both feet, clinging to a projection of rocks, and pulled himself inside a small cave. He flung himself back into the wind tunnel moments later.

No go.

He managed a pretty decent controlled loop, followed by a roll. And gave a thumbs-up as he angled toward one of the larger openings.

Hunt knew they had to speed things up or they'd be here for a month. The whole team should be up there inspecting those holes to see which was viable. The only problem was, the wind didn't show any sign of slowing down. Once in there, it would be practically impossible—no, not practically, plain *impossible*—to get back down to this doorway. And he was damned if Taylor would be a guinea pig.

Hunt indicated he'd go next. Jesus. He didn't want to leave her, but if he could find the way through this nightmare, he could make her safer. And speed this along. Because he knew in his gut that she wouldn't be safe until they had finished the op—and preferably Morales—and were out of Africa.

Tate grabbed his arm and shook his head. He'd try. Not waiting for an answer, he launched himself after Coetzee. The two men spun and circled, carried by the capricious wind, but eventually found some sort of rhythm and managed to inspect a dozen wall openings between them.

Fisk kept track of their painful communications on his PDA. Every time one of the men was flung against the walls in an ungainly heap, Taylor's fingers tightened against Hunt's side.

It took over an hour, but eventually Tate managed to crawl into one of the last four unexplored holes about twenty feet above the spinning blades. He disappeared.

They watched as Coetzee made it to yet another opening, then launched himself off the rim of the hole when he couldn't penetrate it more than a couple of feet.

Two to go.

Tate was still not back. A good sign? Hunt hoped to hell.

Coetzee tumbled and spun, then belly flying, aimed for a large opening above where Tate had disappeared ten minutes before. He'd figured out how to grab the edge of an opening, and used sheer brute force and determination to pull himself into it, or at least close enough to—

The deafening silence was profound as the engine shut off without warning.

The quiet throbbed in Hunt's ears as he watched helplessly as Coetzee, arms and legs flailing uselessly, dropped. He tried—the poor bastard—to straighten himself out, but it was such a short drop, he wasn't able to control the terminal velocity of the fall. He plummeted a hundred plus feet straight down, like a rock through the still air at 120 mph.

Viljoen started forward. Hunt slammed his arm across the man's chest without looking at him. "No." There was nothing they could do.

The diesel engine started up again with a deep-throated, full-throttled roar.

Hunt grabbed Taylor around the neck and yanked her head against his chest, turning her away a second before Coetzee was sucked into the fast-moving propeller. The whole thing took seconds.

But just before Taylor's nose was pressed against Hunt's chest, she caught the flash of red and squeezed her eyes shut. It didn't matter that she'd seen nothing. It didn't matter that all she'd heard was the earsplitting shriek of those engines. Behind her closed lids she *saw* Coetzee being minced and diced and flung—everywhere. And God. She imagined the sounds. Screams. Bones grinding. She swallowed bile and wrapped both arms around Hunt, burying her face against his chest, sick to her stomach.

She stayed that way, too appalled to lift her face, for a good five minutes. Until, in fact, there was once again a deep, throbbing silence. Then she lifted her head and took a step back, averting her gaze from beyond the doorway.

"I think I've figured—" there wasn't a drop of spit in her mouth. She tried again. "Ah . . . figured out how the timing works." Her voice was a hoarse croak as out of the corner of her eye she saw a slow movement . . . something . . .

Sliding down the blood-splattered titanium door was a—a gory lump of— Oh, God. Hunt had a speck of what she presumed was Coetzee's blood on his forehead. She couldn't stand seeing blood on him. Even if it wasn't his own. She reached up and wiped it off, then scrubbed her hand down the slick material covering her leg.

The engine started again. She checked her stopwatch, heart pounding. *Yes!*

Hunt communicated with his men. They all looked grim. Tate wasn't back yet, Coetzee was dead. The damn engine was going a mile a minute, determined to break their eardrums. But she had an idea.

The next time the engine stopped as abruptly as it had started, Taylor was ninety-nine percent sure.

A man yelled.

They all looked up.

Tate.

"This is the one," he yelled from three stories above them.

Hunt talked into his lip mic. "How far in does it—"

Taylor looked at her wrist, put her hand out to stop him from talking. She put up three fingers.

Two . . .

One . . .

Now. The engine started up again. The noise, in spite of the earplugs, was bone-rattling.

Fisk started forward, ready to launch himself inside. Taylor grabbed his arm, shook her head. Held up her palm. *Wait.*

He glanced from her to Hunt.

Hunt indicated he should do as Taylor said.

She kept her attention on her stopwatch, counting off the minutes.

And waited. And waited. Heart pounding with anticipation . . .

And waited . . .

Off. Yes! Fisk gave her a high five and she grinned.

"Tell me that wasn't a wild guess," Hunt demanded into the throbbing silence as he turned to look at her. "Or have you really figured out this son of a bitch?"

"I think it's a simple math equation," she told him excitedly. "The first time the engine was on for about ten minutes. I wasn't timing it, but I'm guessing. Let's say it *was* ten minutes. Subtract three—on for seven seconds, then add one—on for eight minutes, then subtract one—off for a second. Alternating seconds and minutes. I think it represents Morales's birth date: 1/31/1942."

"And you know Morales birth date . . . why?"

"It's my *job* to know things about the people I'm going to rob," she told him impatiently. "They use that sort of information for safe combinations. Never mind *that.* What do you think?"

The demon engine fired up again. She looked at her stopwatch again, then held up five fingers. Four. Three. Two. One.

Go.

Fisk launched himself through the door and into the vertical wind tunnel. He was immediately sucked up to slam into the ceiling with bone-jangling force. Taylor watched him flail, holding her breath. If the damn thing stopped again . . . But no.

Thank God. Fisk made it over to Tate, who grabbed his wrist and pulled him inside the opening with more speed than finesse.

Viljoen took a running start and powered off next.

Hunt tapped Bishop on the shoulder to get his attention, then signed for him to take Taylor and go back to the surface.

Teeth aching from the incredible noise, she brushed her fingers across Hunt's tense jaw until he turned his head to glare at her. Knowing he could read her lips, she said, *she* thought quite reasonably, "Morales needs me to get in. He'll only bring me right back."

Without expression, Hunt motioned Bishop through the door after the others.

And then there were two.

Their eyes locked. Hunt took her arm and folded back the thin black fabric covering her wrist. Taylor realized that while the fabric was matte, it had ingeniously been manufactured to deter anyone grabbing hold of the wearer.

Hunt clamped his fingers tightly over her wrist. Using her other hand, she turned back the hem of his sleeve, then curved her hand, holding on to his much thicker wrist in return. Her fingers turned white from the pressure.

She held her breath. Listening. Was the engine slowing? Did it sound any different now than it had a second ago? Five minutes ago? A lifetime and Coetzee ago?

Did she have the wrong birth date for Morales? Were her calculations off? Would worrying about *her* endanger Hunt?

"Together," they mouthed at the same time, then jumped into the wind.

Forty-four

THE FORCE OF THE WIND JERKED TAYLOR ASS OVER TEAKETTLE in the opposite direction, almost wrenching Hunt's arm from the socket. He held on. Nothing was going to make him release her.

Having watched the others and done thousands of hours of flat-flying and 3-D training in similar environments himself, the sheer ferocity of the wind tunnel didn't surprise him. The force of the wind shot them up to the ceiling in seconds with stunning, breath-stealing force.

Hunt did his best to cushion her strike. But it was impossible to position himself. His shoulder hit the ceiling first, then his arm. He made a grab for her, managed to catch her elbow, but she still hit the solid rock hard with wide eyes and a loud oomph. *Ah, hell . . .*

He managed to haul her closer to his own body and get her attention, indicating how to do a standard "box man" position—belly down. The more surface they presented to the updraft, the better chance they had of maneuverability. She got it right away. Thank God she was fit and athletic. It was hard even for him to sustain the belly-down position consistently because of the extremely strong wind currents buffeting their bodies.

He glanced down and saw both Tate and Bishop leaning out of the cave to catch them on the fly. He angled his body, head down now, using every means in his power to navigate the current across the vast open space and reach his men.

As soon as Taylor saw how he angled his body, she tried to follow suit. It wasn't easy. He swung her by her wrist, using all his strength to at least get her flying in the right direction. Her momentum pulled him along after her.

Far beneath them, the propeller blades rotated in a deadly silver blur. *How soon . . . ?*

He managed to get them closer to the cave. There was no ledge, nothing to grab hold of as they passed. Tate lunged halfway out of the cave, the idiot, and made a futile grab for Taylor's other arm. He missed.

Bloody hell.

The force of the wind took them up. Twisting in the wind. Up. And up. They needed to go down and sideways about nine feet. Hunt hit again, this time protecting Taylor by using his forearm to prevent them from smacking into the ceiling. He pushed off with his shoulder. They went careening into the side wall. Taylor stuck out her foot, which saved her from the body slam, but sent them in the wrong direction immediately.

Wrong direction and upside down.

How long did they have? Hunt wondered. How fucking bloody long? He straightened them out, maneuvered in the right direction. Slow. Systematic. Patient.

Had the tone of the blades changed?

No, bloody hell, they had not.

A few more feet. *There!* He grabbed Tate's forearm, then pulled Taylor with him as they docked with Tate and Fisk's assistance.

"Oh, Lord. That was amazing," Taylor shouted with sheer unadulterated glee in her voice as she lay flat on her back, panting. She sat

up smiling, then grimaced, putting a hand to her forehead and closing her eyes. "*Ew.* Vertigo."

"Fix on a point until it settles," Hunt told her, knowing the feeling. He rose to his feet, and his head brushed the roof of the tube they
were in. "What do we have?" he asked Tate, glancing down to make
sure Taylor was coping with the dizziness. She looked okay, and he
held out his hand to pull her to her feet.

"The codes to Level Three," Tate reminded him. "And I can't *tell*
you how happy that makes us."

Whatever the good news was, Hunt welcomed it. It meant they'd
get through faster. "Walk and talk," he told the others. "Distance?"

"Two point six miles," Fisk offered.

" 'Eternal rain and putrid waters,' I believe," Hunt mused. "The
gluttons will be punished by Cerebus."

"Who, or what, is Cerebus?" Taylor demanded beside him.

"A canine monster with three heads and red eyes who tears at the
damned."

She shuddered, "Geez, *that's* creepy. I'm guessing we're the damned,
huh?"

"Not this time," Viljoen told her. "We can circumvent this level.
But you can get a look at a damned effective three-pronged laser that
could slice right through you in about thirty seconds flat. Brace yourselves for the smell. It's rank. I'm afraid we'll have to endure the 'putrid, stinking mud' for the duration."

"While the entertainment level is high," Taylor said somewhat
ironically "there's no way Morales flies up here like a bat. How does
he get in?"

"I suspect he has some sort of remote-control device to turn off
the toys once the codes get him through each level," Hunt said almost
absently.

It wasn't just a case of a single man getting past that turbojet prop.
How had Morales gotten *things* inside the mine? Hunt wondered.
Where was there a tunnel wide enough, high enough, to transport all
the things Morales had been stockpiling? He knew Morales hadn't
personally *carried* any of the crates down here.

They were missing a detail, because somewhere down here there was a form of transportation. An elevator. A narrow-gauge railway track. *Something* they were missing.

Dante's unforgiving winds weren't high-tech. That wasn't the way Morales thought. He was a literal man. He'd been typically literal when he'd bombed the *Ithembalabantu* AIDS clinic in Durban two years ago, killing 509 men, women, and children. To Morales, AIDS and homosexuality were synonymous. The reality, and the actual facts and details, were irrelevant in the strength of his beliefs.

Hunt kept a sharp eye out for any side caves, anything that might indicate another route. He glanced back to check on Taylor.

She was running her fingers along the rock wall as they walked. "Look how smooth the walls and floor are." She spoke as softly as the men had. "I can't begin to imagine how Morales got people down here to do all this stuff. And how *many* people, I wonder? It must've been an incredible feat of engineering just to dig tunnels this large, let alone hauling all the Dante's Inferno deterrents down to each level."

Taylor was a woman of unpredictable interests, fascinated by everything she encountered. No one else would realize it, but Hunt knew she was scared. Her speech was a little too fast, and she was trying too hard to be cheerful.

Still, he'd bet his last paycheck that coupled with her fear was the exhilaration he knew she enjoyed when she was pulling a heist. The woman loved to live dangerously.

The damn air ride would have scared the piss out of anyone. To Taylor it had been yet another adventure. Another learning curve. Something else to include in her bag of skill acquisitions.

He moved her in front of him to protect her back as the tunnel narrowed and they had to walk single file. "There's something decidedly cocked-up with this place," he said.

Her ponytail was crooked, and the loose shiny strands brushing her shoulders drifted as she walked. Oblivious that she had the disheveled look of a woman fresh out of a man's bed, she turned to frown at him over her shoulder. "What is cocked-up, and how and why does it sound so ominous?"

"Let's say Morales had all five disks. He comes up here, he opens the safe door into Level Two using the correct codes. He wouldn't have had that turbo going full blast. Ergo, there was a way to turn the bloody thing off."

He almost walked into her when she stopped and turned around fully to face him. Her eyes glittered with amusement in the torchlight. *"Ergo?"*

"Therefore."

"I know. I've just never heard anyone say it before."

He made a "turn around" gesture with his fingers. "Walk."

The tunnel widened and the four men paused up ahead. Hunt and Taylor joined them. Viljoen rubbed the side of his nose. "So we missed an off switch somewhere inside the door?"

"I doubt it was anything as simple as a switch," Hunt answered dryly. "The information would have been on the disk with the combination for the lock." He removed the canteen strapped to his thigh, uncapped it, and handed it to Taylor as he talked. "My guess is there's another way in."

"I don't think he could have walked across where that propeller was," Bishop pointed out. "That thing was at least twelve feet below floor level."

"Ja, I agree, man. Not walk across those props, and surely not climb up a hundred feet to here?" Viljoen said.

"And how," Taylor said, handing Hunt back the water, "would he bring *things* in and take them out? You're right. It doesn't make sense." Something glittered in the wall, and she crouched down to look at it. "Hand me your flashlight, would you?"

Hunt unsnapped the light from his thigh, handed it to her, then turned back to listen to his men.

Taylor had never seen a diamond in the rough. She ran her fingers over what could be, might be ... *Was* it? There were seven, small, shiny, translucent, metallic-looking ... She scratched her thumbnail over one of the forty-point stones as the men, oblivious, walked ahead, Hunt bringing up the rear.

She'd bet that without turning, he knew to the *inch* precisely where she was crouched and what she was thinking. It was as disconcerting as it was fascinating.

"Unless there's a shortcut or another route somewhere," Fisk suggested.

She ran her finger over the small ridge of stones. There was a slight oily film, which a raw diamond should have—*maybe*. As interesting as her discovery was, there were far more important things happening up ahead. She hurried to catch up.

"There's a shortcut for sure," Viljoen was saying. Taylor listened carefully. He was their mine expert, after all. "It would run above and parallel to Level Three. Like a catwalk, you know?"

They got a hint of the stench of Level Three before they saw it. "Just the smell would prevent gluttony." Taylor's voice was muffled by the hand she'd slapped over her nose and face. It didn't help one bit. She needed a hazmat suit. Lord. What could *possibly* smell that gross? And did she really want to know? Not really.

"This is only the teaser," Tate warned.

"Jesus. It gets *worse* than this?" Hunt asked Viljoen.

"*Ja.* According to the disk, 'fraid so."

Here we go again. Taylor waited a beat for Hunt to start turning in her direction, then said a firm, if muffled, "*Forget it.* I am *not* standing here in this cold, drafty, *stinky* place waiting for you guys to trot off and find a shorter shortcut."

"Are you done?" He paused. "I was about to suggest you forge ahead with Fisk and take a look at the next 'door.' "

Her heart did a ridiculous hop, skip, and jump as he looked at her with those deep, smoky eyes that even in the dust-moted golden gleam of the flashlight, saw exactly who she was. "Liar," she said softly over the lump of emotion in her throat.

He stepped back against the wall, flattening his body so she could pass him in the narrow space. "Go with him anyway." He pointed the flashlight after the guys.

"Okay." She started to squeeze past him, doing a slow, full-body glide against his. Cruel, but it felt so good she wanted to do it again.

She pushed his hair off his face, then cupped his cheek in her palm as a hot wash of lust suffused her body. "Does this adrenaline rush make you horny too?" She'd only noticed how hot it made her since she'd met *him*.

Hunt briefly shut his eyes. "Jesus, Taylor . . ." The flashlight in his hand pointed to the floor as he drew her against him. "St. John?" One of the men's voices echoed from farther down the tunnel.

Hunt's mouth broke from hers. "Got to go."

"Hmm." She stood up on her toes and pressed a kiss to his mouth, then moved away. "*That* didn't help me much."

He took her hand and started after his men. "Help you with what?"

Taylor reminded herself why they were both here in the first place. *Saving the world, check.* "My adrenaline lust," she told him, covering her nose as the smell once again intruded. "Hey. Do you realize that when you were kissing me, I totally couldn't *smell* this?"

"Funny you should mention that, neither did I. However, *now* I do. Let's speed this up. I think that's our three-headed dog barking up ahead."

DANTE'S INFERNO
LEVEL THREE

LEVEL THREE WAS INCREDIBLY CREATIVE. HUNT GAVE MORALES credit as he looked down at the canine monster wallowing in black odoriferous mud. Morales was taking Dante not only seriously, but quite literally. Cerebus was a twenty-foot-high robotic masterpiece, and clearly manufactured by special-effects people. Either theme park or film company expertise. It was an incredible feat of engineering, and a realistic-looking three-headed dog. Hair and all. Six red laser beams arced and slashed the air in constant motion.

Its growls and snarls sounded like the genuine article—times three. A foamy-mouthed, rabid guard dog protecting the next level.

From their vantage point on the catwalk twenty-five feet above, they could observe a narrow tunnel leading, presumably, to Level Four. If they'd been down there in the putrid muck, it might well have taken them hours to figure out which mouth to enter. If they hadn't been ripped to pieces first by the beast's "teeth" or drowned in the five-foot-deep foul-smelling mud.

The catwalk had a five-foot cantilevered wall constructed to look identical to the surrounding rock. From below, the walk would have been all but undetectable. Did Morales stand up here and imagine his enemies drowning in that pool of bubbling, disgusting-smelling slop? Hunt figured he must have. He could see no other reason for all these theatrics.

Theatrical they might be, but it was only with the help of disk three that Fisk had been able to open the safe door leading him to the mud cavern earlier.

And it was only because Tate had backtracked after recon that *he'd* discovered a narrow opening in a side wall, visible only when traveling north. The narrow tunnel had switched back on itself several times, but eventually led Tate and Fisk back to the wind tunnel. Every instinct in Hunt's body warned that Morales did *nothing* without good reason. While it might amuse him to use the elaborate deterrents, there was usually method—twisted to hell and gone—in the tango's madness.

He'd killed a thousand people on a cruise ship, by remote detonation of a small bomb, because it was a cheese- and wine-tasting trip. Gluttony. Hunt had long since given up trying to figure out the twisted patterns of a tango's logic.

"This place sure is noisy!" Taylor shouted as they rounded a corner and backtracked before turning south again. The sound of rocks striking each other, *hard,* was intermittent, violent, and loud.

"What do we get in the fourth level of hell?" Taylor turned in front of him to yell. Her hand covered her nose and mouth, but her eyes were crinkled pools of light, dappled blue.

"Avarice," he told her. Bloody hell. He wished he felt half that sanguine. But the reality was, he'd had a spider of fear crawling up his ass for days. Something was going to go bad. As sure as he was smelling shit and decay, something was going to go very, very bad.

At any other time that would not be a problem. He and his men were well trained and could handle anything anyone sent their way. But the more the itch intensified, the more concerned he became.

They were trapped down here. Had been beneath the earth for— he checked the lighted dial on his watch—over seven hours, and they were only on Level Four out of seven. And that was with exact and explicit instructions on how to enter Level Three. They also, thank God, had the codes to Level Five. But there were still three levels they had no way of entering without spending a considerable amount of time. And somewhere deep in the earth right beneath them, a missile waited for the launch signal.

Forty-five

Just before the River Styx is the Fourth Level of Hell. Here, the prodigal and the avaricious suffer their punishment, as they roll weights back and forth against one another. You will share eternal damnation with others who either wasted and lived greedily and insatiably, or who stockpiled their fortunes, hoarding everything and sharing nothing. Plutus, the wolflike demon of wealth, dwells here.

THE CRASHING, THUMPING RACKET THEY'D HEARD WHEN THEY started south on the catwalk became fainter instead of louder. Either the noise had echoed from Level Four back into Three or they were now going in the completely wrong direction. And since, apparently, they had only two choices, forward or back the way they'd come, that was problematic.

The catwalk sloped down, then melted into a tunnel again. Not a good sign, Taylor figured. And of course it wasn't. But thank God the smell also got fainter the farther away they walked from Level Three.

Despite carefully searching the walls for one of those secret backward entrances to a side branch as they walked, Hunt and his guys hadn't found one, and once again they ended up at a dead end.

When Taylor saw yet another titanium door, she thought Hunt and the others would curse. They didn't, even though it must have been incredibly frustrating for them.

The floor flattened out, and there was enough room for all six of them to gather around the door. This time there was a keypad. It was a pain in the butt that all her tools had to be left behind in the wind tunnel. Especially since she'd made most of them herself. Well, she'd made them once, she could make them again. Or pick them up on the way out.

"This won't take long," she assured Hunt. The 1991 Hamilton 200CF had been one of the best in its day, but great strides had been made in the industry since then. "Morales was pretty complacent by the time he outfitted this level."

Dante's Level Four, Hunt had told them, was for the avaricious. They should expect some sort of weights swinging or something heavy rolling back and forth. Which fit with the rocks-rolling-around sounds they'd heard earlier.

They should also expect another demon. This time a wolf named Plutus.

Morales could make a fortune opening up this place to suicidal tourists, Taylor decided. She knelt down in front of the door and gave the keypad a little pat.

"How long?" Hunt asked.

"Sixteen minutes tops." She flexed her fingers like a piano player. Tate, standing beside her, smiled.

"Tate. Bishop. Backtrack," Hunt instructed. "We missed one of those reverse tunnels. Find it. Viljoen, go with them. Come and fetch us when you find it."

Taylor waited until the sound of the men's footfalls faded, then rested her cheek on the cool metal door and placed her fingers lightly on the keypad. She closed her eyes and imagined herself inside the electronics as her fingers danced across the keys.

After the final, satisfying click, she rose and glanced at Hunt. "How'd I do?"

"Fourteen minutes eighteen," he said dryly. "Not bad."

"Not bad!" Fisk said, outraged. He gave Taylor a slap on the back that made her stagger. "That was fu-shitting *amazing*. Take me on as your fu-damn apprentice. Honest to fucking—sorry, ma'am—God. I'll *pay* you."

Taylor grinned, feeling like one of the boys.

"Earplugs, then open the door, Fisk," Hunt told him, lips quirking.

"T-FLAC should hire her on the fu—*friggin'* spot," Fisk told Hunt seriously, inserting his earplugs as he spoke. "Do you have any *idea* what we could do with skills like this? I mean seriously, we should call—"

"*Mmmm . . .*" Taylor mused aloud, glancing from Fisk to Hunt and back again.

"Thank you for the infomercial, Mr. Fisk." Hunt glanced over to make sure Taylor was set. She gave him a thumbs-up, and he turned back to Fisk. "Now open the bloody door."

Morales liked noise and big . . . *gestures,* Taylor thought in awe, standing in the open doorway with the others. This cavern was about sixty feet across, the floor curved like the inside of a bowl. Fisk and Hunt shone their flashlights ahead, and they all took an instinctive step back. Hunt with his arm protectively across Taylor's midriff.

It took her a few moments to process exactly what she was seeing, as a blur of motion only two feet in front of her made it hard to focus. The obstruction moved to the left. Rapidly. Rolling. Thunderous. Behind it, another appeared, rolling in the opposite direction. *Wow!*

Five or six, it was hard to tell from here, enormous round stones rolled in a seemingly random sequence. The boulders were perfect spheres, about fifteen feet in diameter, and looked heavy enough to flatten a car, let alone a puny human.

And all Taylor could think was, *How the hell had Morales gotten them in there?*

They rolled up the wall on the left, down and up the wall on the right. When two were in different positions up on the left, another was rolling across the floor in the middle and the others were in various stages of climbing the right wall.

It was an amazingly well-choreographed ballet, Taylor thought, boggled by the ingenuity of the precision timing. The balls were in constant motion, leaving little or no space between them as they rolled past one another.

Hunt turned his light to the wall beside the inside of the door, reaching out to run his hand across the surface. Looking for some sort of off switch. His shoulders were too broad. Every time the stone rolled past him, his hair blew in the wake, giving Taylor cold chills.

Since he wouldn't hear her, even if she'd bothered to speak, she kicked his thigh to get his attention. Which it did. He spun around so fast, he was a blur of motion, dropping into an instinctive crouch, immediately relaxing when he realized it was only her.

She motioned for him to hand her the flashlight. *She'd* slide into the two-foot space between the wall and the closest moving ball.

Without expression, Hunt pulled her farther out of the doorway, back into the tunnel. With swift economical movements, he pulled up the hood of the LockOut suit, tucking her hair carefully inside.

He cupped her face in both hands. "Be careful," he mouthed. Taylor waited for him to kiss her, but he didn't, and it was too dark to read his expression. It was enough for the moment that he trusted her to let her do this. He unclamped the heavy flashlight and handed it to her.

Flashlight in hand, she turned back to the doorway and waited for the closest sphere to roll aside. As soon as it rolled up to the right, she stepped into the chamber, immediately flattening herself against the wall. She'd have to run her hand up and down the wall to find some sort of control, and knowing Morales, it would be hidden or disguised. And she had only a minute, maybe less, at a time before the ball rolled back down, giving her perhaps eighteen inches of space.

When that rock came rolling past her, she'd better not have any body parts in its way or she'd be flatter than a fritter.

God, she thought, running her fingers over the rough wall. This was as exciting as retrieving a ten-million-dollar diamond necklace from a terrorist's personal safe.

DANTE'S INFERNO
LEVEL FIVE

JESUS BLOODY CHRIST. WHERE WAS SHE? HUNT CHECKED HIS WATCH, although he sure as hell didn't need to. He'd counted off the 302 seconds. Over five bloody minutes. If she hadn't found some sort of control near the door, it either wasn't there or was on the side Fisk had tried to search.

He couldn't even see the glow of the flashlight anymore. Worse, there was no way he could follow her. She'd been like an eel, sliding between the rock wall and the pendulum of the boulder with only inches to spare. Fisk had offered to try, but he was too big as well.

Hunt wondered absently if God was puzzled by his frequent requests of late. They hadn't exactly had a close relationship over the years. He shot off another prayer at the same time he and Fisk tried to make sense of the boulder's movements, timing one and then the next in the hope of finding a pattern, as Taylor had done for the wind tunnel. And while he did this, he kept his peripheral vision attuned to any break in the darkness on his left, indicating Taylor's return.

Where in the bloody hell *was* she? He had to constantly remind himself that she was smart and resourceful. Not to mention double jointed. She'd eluded the authorities on seven continents. She could get into and out of the smallest, most impossible spaces—she was fine. Just fine. *Please, God . . .*

The three men he'd sent off to look for a side tunnel hadn't returned yet either. Another cause for concern. One way or another, he and Fisk had to go forward. As soon as they figured out how in the hell to cross between, under, or over these bloody boulders to the other side—

Wait a second—The noise *changed,* the balls started slowing down. Slower. And slower. And slower. Having lost their momentum, they eventually all came to rest in the center of the floor, rocking slowly in their tracks as gravity pulled them down to teeter back and forth in ever-decreasing rolls.

Fisk shone his light down the length of the tunnel, where, now that the balls were at rest, they could see the deep channels, like ribs, up the curve of the walls.

A beam of light strobed high above their heads. "*Hey!* Romeo! Up here!"

His relief at hearing Taylor's voice was profound. A sensation Hunt had never felt before filled him. He was confused as hell by it, but this wasn't the time for self-analysis. "How did you get up there?" he yelled. He still couldn't see her.

"Go the way I did. Follow the wall. There are steps—"

"Stay right where you are." He'd already motioned to Fisk, and they jogged down a narrow strip of rock floor between the wall and the first track for a hundred yards before they found the stairs. The others, when they came to look for them, would have to follow.

The steps, carved out of the solid rock, zigged and zagged steeply. The low ceiling made it hard for them to move quickly, since they couldn't quite walk upright. If one were expecting an enemy to follow, the design was ingenious.

Taylor waited in the tunnel at the top, her flashlight pointing to the floor. "Amazing, isn't it?"

"Amazing," Hunt agreed, suddenly angry. Angry with that madman Morales for concocting this ridiculous spectacle. Angry at his men for not finding the catwalk in the first place, and angry as hell at Taylor for scaring the crap out of him, disappearing like that without a word.

"I haven't seen the others," she told him soberly. "Should we wait?"

"No. They'll catch up. Or they won't. Here, give me that." He took the flashlight from her. "You did good. Now, walk between us."

Without waiting, he strode off, his light leading the way.

He'd been worried about her, Taylor decided. That's why he was cranky. Knowing that made her feel all warm and fuzzy inside.

Level Five was a breeze since they had the code, although she wouldn't have needed it to open the door anyway. The locking mechanism was an XLR92, a safe she was familiar with. Still, without those codes, it would have taken her at least three to four hours to get through.

Hunt had told them that Level Five was supposed to be the River Styx. Punishment for the wrathful. She wondered if she should sweetly suggest he stick his wrathful head in the fast-flowing, black, muddy river down below and get over his snit. It had been sweet and touching an hour ago. Now it was getting on her last nerve.

She knew she wasn't being fair. Hunt was quiet. Focused. He'd hardly so much as looked at her in the last hour. But then, he had a lot to worry about. She understood that. And the annoying, voiceless . . . *dirge* coming through hidden loudspeakers wasn't helping any. The combination hymn/chant wasn't particularly *loud,* just incredibly *annoying.*

And that rushing water wasn't helping her disposition any either. She'd had to say no when Hunt handed her the water bottle earlier.

She stopped bothering to stand on tiptoe to look over the wall. River. Black mud. Been there. Done that. "What's next?" she asked Hunt's back. They were walking fast—practically jogging.

"Heretics," Hunt said shortly. "Iron walls. Burning tombs. Blood. The three infernal Furies with limbs of women and hair of snakes."

Allrighty, then. Another fun ride. She wondered if she should mention she'd never met a snake she liked. No point, she decided. Either they'd bypass this level or she'd have to suck it up and brave the slithery, slimy, little critters. She hoped they'd be able to bypass—

Hunt reached back and thrust an arm across her chest. She was going to have to speak to him about that. She peered around him, trying to see what had stopped him, just as he turned off his flashlight.

A thin beam of dusty light angled upward like a sword out of the solid rock wall on their left.

Forty-six

O H, JOSÉ. *NOVIO!* YOUR POOR BACK!" MARIA HURRIED DOWN the nave toward him.

José turned his head to watch her. His Maria wasn't as thin as the girl he'd married thirty-eight years ago. Her hair was graying instead of the glossy black of her youth, and her smooth pink cheeks had become lined with the years. But to him she was as beautiful today as the day she'd walked down the aisle of the cathedral in San Cristóbal all those years ago.

His love for this woman was only second to his love for God.

"My love." José reached out his hand to take hers, and with some difficulty his Maria knelt beside him. Her lovely eyes were dark with concern, her powdered brow furrowed as she touched his face. Her skin smelled of cooking and the perfume he had custom-made exclusively for her every year for her birthday. The fabulously expensive Jasmin Absolute oil took over three million flower heads to produce one kilo. Ounce for ounce, the cost approached the price of pure gold. And she was worth every penny, his Maria.

"Come up to the house," she begged. "Allow me to put salve on your wounds."

"My wounds cannot be healed by salve, *mi querido.*" He placed his hand over hers where she had it pressed against his cheek and brought her fingers to his mouth. He kissed each one.

"Constantine and your men are soiling all my good carpets with their big dirty feet," Maria told him, eyes filled with tears. Not for her carpets, José knew, but for his pain. "Come and talk to them."

He used her hand to stroke his face. Her skin was so soft. "We will be gone soon."

Tears rolled down her cheeks and she closed her eyes. "God cannot want this, José," she said passionately, then looked at him again, her voice soft, pleading, as she whispered, "God is not this vengeful."

His heart was heavy. *Ah, my Maria. So foolish.* "You have spoken with God today?"

"No." There was a hitch in her voice.

Of course, God had not spoken to Maria. José hated to see her so torn. He stroked her soft hair. "It will be over soon, *novia,* over very soon."

"I beg you again, José. Do not do this terrible thing. Consider that there are hundreds of churches in Las Vegas. Churches filled with believers . . ." Her eyes widened. "What is it? Why do you look at me so?"

"Who did you tell about my disks to the mine, Maria *mi querida?* Only two people in all the world knew the codes even existed, and that I had them in our safe in San Cristóbal. Me. And you, my most beloved wife."

She didn't deny it. "*I* could not stop you, though I begged many times. I hoped—"

"No one can stop God's will, my love," he told her softly, his heart filled with love and overwhelming pain for this woman who had betrayed him.

He still held the thin, blood-soaked whip in his other hand. José coiled it around his beloved's throat, where it left an obscene red stain on her white skin.

Maria's eyes went wide. "José, *Madre de Dios!*" She brought her hands up to grasp the braised leather as her flesh bulged around it.

He'd spent many years with this whip. He knew its strengths and its weaknesses. He tightened it inexorably around his wife's throat. Her eyes went wild and her body started to thrash. He pulled tighter, cutting off her air. "Nobody betrays José Adalbaro Pabil Morales. No one. Not even you, beloved wife."

When he was sure there was no breath left in his Maria's lifeless body, José gathered her close and sobbed his despair and pain against her soft, jasmine-scented hair.

Forty-seven

THE SPEAR OF LIGHT MOVED UP AND DOWN THROUGH THE chink in the solid rock wall. "St. John? Come through," a disembodied voice said.

"Who is that?" Taylor asked, crowding behind Hunt.

Her hair tickled his neck. "Daklin." He glanced over his shoulder. "Fisk. Check it out."

Fisk slid sideways through the incredibly narrow opening in the rock and disappeared.

Bloody hell. He should have gone through first. But he wasn't leaving Taylor behind alone, and he sure as hell wasn't going to send her through without him.

"Just the entrance is tight, St. John," Fisk yelled, his voice faint. The man hadn't been gone long enough for him to be any distance. Hunt frowned. "—ost . . . team . . . here . . . side."

"What are we waiting for?" Taylor demanded from inches away.

"A trap?"

"That's *Francis!*"

With everything else they'd encountered since arriving in Morales's bizarre Dantesque tribute, this fissure in the rock could lead them straight down to hell. "Here. Take my hand. And don't let go unless I tell you to."

"Ditto," Taylor told him, taking his right hand with her left in a viselike grip. "Want me to go first?"

"No." He exhaled, going in sideways. Jesus, it was a tight fit. But for the protection of his suit, he'd be ripped to pieces by the rough stone.

"Holding up?"

"Of course," she said, a lilt of her typical good humor in her voice. Her hand felt small in his. Small, but incredibly competent.

"Fisk?" he shouted.

No answer.

"Fisk? Tate?"

Nothing.

"Bloody hell."

"Why don't you save your breath until we get to where we— *Ow!* Damn! *That's* going to leave a mark."

His fingers tightened around hers. "What happened?"

"Knee. Keep moving, would you? I'm not claustrophobic, but I could start to be any minute now." Even though she was an arm's length away, the rock absorbed the sound of her voice. He gripped her hand even tighter.

"Think there are snakes in here?"

He had no fucking idea. "For all I know, pterodactyls could morph out of this wall. Morales seems to have thought of everything else."

"*Hmm. That* could be interesting . . ." Her voice trailed off. Then, "Don't you think?"

"Scared, love?"

"Well . . . yeah," she said with disarming honesty. "We are kind of a human-sandwich filling with this wall, and there doesn't seem to be an end. Makes me think of all those creepy black-and-white movies they show late at night. Maybe we'll be absorbed into the walls, and years from now people will excavate and find our images embedded—"

"You have a very active imagination," he said dryly, amused, but also impressed that she was going to such lengths to focus herself on the task at hand. That natural ability was one of the traits screened for by T-FLAC.

Whoa! Hang on! his brain screamed. Had he really listened to Fisk's inane suggestion that she was T-FLAC material? Not possible. Not her. Not when he— "I see a light at the end."

"Either the Angel of Death," she said gloomily, "or a high-speed train."

Hunt chuckled. He was still smiling as he pulled her out of the crevasse on the other side. *This* tunnel was considerably larger, better ventilated, and reasonably well lit. His team looked at him with varying expressions of amazement.

"What was in there?" Navarro asked Fisk. "Laughing gas?"

"Wasn't funny for me," Fisk assured them. "Check out what it did to my suit." He paused and looked around. "*All* our suits," he corrected.

"We've been grated," Taylor decided, looking down at the front of her suit. While it hadn't torn, even over her left knee, which had taken the brunt of a scrape, it was . . . ruffled, as though it had been rubbed against a cheese grater. This was some miracle fabric. If none of them had been wearing it, the rock would have sliced their skin to pieces.

"Thanks." Hunt accepted a weapon from Daklin. "What do we have?"

"For one thing," Daklin told him, pointing to the hard-packed dirt of the floor, "serious tracks."

"I see that." Hunt scanned the tunnel on either side of them. Thirty feet wide and at least fifteen feet high, the tunnel had a double track running down the center and was well lit. The track was in excellent condition and looked well used.

"How did you guys get in?" Hunt asked, glancing from man to man. "Which way? This?"

"*Ja.*" Viljoen walked beside Hunt. "Once you go through those passageways, you can't get back into the Dante areas, you know?" Viljoen told him. "No loss to my mind, mind you."

"We went through," Tate added. "Couldn't get back to you, and decided to split up. I followed this and ended up on the other side of the village about three miles."

"It certainly appears to speed things along," Hunt agreed as they walked. The smiling man was gone. "Anyone go on ahead?"

"Just got here ourselves," Savage said, joining them.

"Are you telling me," Hunt said tightly to Navarro, Daklin, and the others, "we went through all those fucking gyrations for nothing? That you simply *walked* in?"

"Now wouldn't that've been nice?" Daklin said darkly. "We did a little flying, a little wading, a little zigging and fucking zagging. There's no damn way Morales uses that same route."

"We suspect he has some sort of remote-control device," Hunt told him. "Do we have him yet?" They were expecting Morales's people to be right on their tails, and had left access for just that reason. The thought didn't faze Hunt one iota. He looked forward to it.

More important than getting the *Mano del Dios* people, Hunt wanted *Morales* on-site. Not off somewhere watching the liftoff from a control room.

If T-FLAC inadvertently screwed up and didn't deactivate the missile in time, then José Morales could damn well die down here like the rest of them.

Maybe Morales wouldn't be quite so eager to put his own ass on the line.

"No Morales at the moment, and apparently no City of Dis," Hunt stated flatly.

"*City of Dis?*" Savage said over Taylor's left shoulder.

Navarro answered by rote. "Level Six, 'You approach Satan's wretched city where you behold a wide plain surrounded by iron walls. Before you are fields full of distress and torment terrible. Burning tombs are littered about the landscape. Inside these flaming sepulchers suffer the heretics, failing to believe in God and the afterlife, who make themselves audible by doleful sighs. You will join the wicked that lie here, and will be offered no respite. The three infernal Furies stained with blood, with limbs of women and hair of serpents, dwell in this circle of hell.' Pretty much snakes, blood, and burning," he summarized with a faint smile. "No," he answered Hunt, "this track bypasses all that. It should be a straight shot to hell."

Yay, Taylor thought. She had absolutely no desire to see snakes, blood, or burning. She glanced at Hunt. "This must be saving us hours. Will we make it in time?"

"Depends on how much time Daklin and Navarro need."

Taylor glanced from one man to the other. "How much—"

"It'll take as long as it takes, ma'am," Daklin told her politely.

Hunt paused, listening to someone on his earpiece. "Good man." He looked at his group. "The 'natives' are in custody, and en route to Jo'burg for extradition. Let's do it, people. En masse, they sped up, jogging down the tunnel, eerily silent in their black LockOut suits, weapons drawn.

Taylor found herself—she wasn't sure how—maneuvered right into the middle of the group. Protected on all sides by Hunt's guys. It was no problem for her to keep up with them. They weren't running flat out, just moving at a steady jog that didn't utilize too much energy before they'd need it. She was grateful that she kept herself in peak physical fitness for her job, because they didn't stop or slow down for more than ninety minutes.

Only to come to a solid wall of rock.

The narrow-gauge track they'd been following ran straight into the wall.

They spent precious minutes stroking the surface, looking for a way through to the other side.

"Here," Taylor called softly, finding an opening near the floor and going down on her stomach. She could see clear to the other side, some thirty feet away. She gulped at the sheer magnitude of where they were. That was a lot of rock.

"Stop right there," Hunt told her. She wiggled backward, looking at him over her shoulder.

"I think you'd better all follow me," she said, but she waited for him to give her the okay.

"Let Fisk reconnoiter first," Hunt told her gruffly.

She sat up, letting Fisk take the lead. When Fisk yelled, she slithered after him as quickly as a greased eel.

By the time the tunnel opened up into the vast cavern of Level Seven, she was slightly out of breath, and more than happy to stop. They all stopped at the entrance. It was a hell of a sight.

The vast cavern seemed to go on endlessly. A warehouse for Morales's madness. The space was piled high with wooden crates. Ceiling to floor. Row upon row. All neatly labeled and stacked in precise rows. Thousands of them.

Weapons. Ammunition. Explosives. Chemicals.

Both Morales's and Dante's Level Seven were reserved for assassins, tyrants, and warmongers.

And in the center of the man-made cavern, rising from an opening in the floor and continuing through the ceiling high above their heads, the *Mano del Dios pièce de résistance.*

The missile.

Taylor had known it was there. Hell, she knew what a missile looked like. She'd seen the old Cape Canaveral launches on TV dozens of times. She'd never imagined she'd have the opportunity to stand less than a hundred feet from one.

Her eyes followed the sides of the gleaming red and white cylinder as it soared high above their heads and disappeared into a hole in the rock ceiling. This . . . thing was *enormous.*

"Phallic-looking, isn't it?" Savage asked, coming to stand beside her.

Completely bereft of speech, Taylor could only nod. Fear, vast and immediate, had grabbed her by the throat the second she'd seen it. She wanted to dash over to Hunt, grab his wrist, activate whatever it was, and see how many more minutes they had before this monster blasted out of the mine and left them all behind as bits of charcoal dust.

"Snap out of it, cupcake," Savage said.

Mouth dry, Taylor licked her lips. "How—" *Did they get that thing in here?*

Savage smiled. "Long to liftoff?" Another excellent question. The operative tilted her wrist, activated the watch, then looked at the missile. "Three hours, six minutes."

That didn't seem long enough to Taylor. She looked for Hunt. He was talking intently to a group of men, all of whom looked dead serious.

"You do realize," Savage said conversationally, jerking her chin toward the warehouse of boxes, "that just that shit over there could feasibly blow the African continent out of existence? The rocket is pretty much overkill."

Taylor shook her head. "TMI!" Too much information.

Savage patted her shoulder. "Keep out of the way, cupcake. I see a nice vantage point up there with my name on it. Feel free to join me."

The woman was way too chipper for Taylor right now. She looked where the T-FLAC operative was pointing. "Up there" was the first row of wooden crates with a direct visual line to the entrance to the cavern. Hunt had told her that Catherine Seymour, Savage, was one of the T-FLAC's top sharpshooters. She was going to climb twenty feet above the floor and sit and wait to pick off the bad guys as they came in.

Taylor knew she wasn't going to be anywhere near flying bullets if she could possibly help it. "Thanks, but I think I'll pass."

"Suit yourself, but keep an eye out for the bad guys." Savage jogged off.

"I'll do that," Taylor told empty air. "I most certainly will do that." She wondered where the safest place to do that might *be*.

Argentina?

Forty-eight

WE'RE GOING TO NEED AT LEAST A HUNDRED MORE MEN IN here to transpo this topside," Hunt told Viljoen. Daklin and Navarro had each taken their teams and gone to see what they could do about disabling the missile. They'd send one of their people back to him with exactly what they were dealing with—as soon as they knew themselves.

"*Ja,*" Viljoen told Hunt. "I thought so. I have them on standby. ETA thirty minutes by chopper. Having them flown in, so we can start getting this shit moved outside. By then, the lorries will be here."

"Good. Let's see what we have to deal with here." Aware of exactly where Taylor stood, Hunt mobilized his team. Nobody needed instruction. And though he'd not worked with many of them, T-FLAC operatives were well trained and resourceful. They knew their business and immediately got to work in pairs, IDing contents of crates and sorting them for transportation to the surface.

"Anything I can do to help?" Taylor asked, coming up beside him.

Yes, he thought. *Go outside and wait for those choppers.* Hunt desper-

ately needed to touch her, to run his lips over the worry lines between her lovely eyes, to feel the beat of her heart beneath his fingers,
to assure her that everything was going to turn out all right. He did
none of those things.

"If I asked that you go back topside accompanied by some of my
people, would you do it?"

"Yes," she said without hesitation, her gaze steady, "I would. If you
asked me to. But I'd rather stay here until you leave."

Jesus.

It had made him nervous as hell watching her wiggling into that
small hole. And he'd been frankly floored when she'd done as he'd ordered.

Taylor Kincaid was a woman who kept her promises.

He resisted touching her. "I'm not leaving until this is done."

She gave him a small smile. "I know."

His people were crawling all over the place, their black-clad figures melding into the darkness between the crates. High above the
cement floor, Savage had taken up point. Beside her, three shadowy
figures were setting up automatic weapons. Weapons that could not
be used down here on the main floor because of the ammunition and
chemicals contained in the crates.

When it came down to it, they would have to fight hand-to-hand.
Unless Morales was even crazier than Hunt thought, and didn't give
a damn if he blew himself and his people up.

He tried again. Wanting Taylor to make the decision on her own,
but acknowledging she'd worked just as hard on this as his other team
members. She deserved to be in on the payoff. But, Jesus bloody
Christ. He didn't want her anywhere near Morales and his insanity.

"It's crazy to stay down here. You know that. Morales will be here
any minute. We're counting hours, not days, for this all to turn to
shit."

"Then tell me how I can be the most useful, and go and do whatever it is you plan to do." She reached up and pressed two fingers
against his mouth. "I'm not stupid. In fact, I'm sensibly scared of this
whole situation. I won't be doing anything either foolish or heroic. I
promise."

He brushed a kiss to her fingertips, wanting to hold her in his arms and beg her to leave. "Why don't you go over there and work with Tate. I need to look around. Something still doesn't feel right to me."

Taylor cocked her head. Most of her hair had come loose from the band around her ponytail and was now wild and every which way after being tugged at by the rocks as they'd come through the wall. She looked so sexy, Hunt wanted to swoop her up in his arms and— Bloody hell.

"Yeah, yeah," she said, smiling. "You have to go to work. Go." She waved him off with the back of her hand, but when he turned to leave, she grabbed his arm. "Hunt?" Her voice was suddenly dead serious. "Don't do anything overly heroic yourself, okay? Promise me."

He touched her cheek with the tips of his fingers. More would be dangerous. Everything about her begged to be touched. This was neither the time, nor the place. "Stay out of trouble," he told her without answering. Then walked away.

"No, you big moron. *You* stay out of trouble!" Taylor said to his retreating back. Of course he didn't hear her, and if he had, he was ignoring her warning.

Half an hour later Taylor was clambering up and around the crates with Tate, calling out the information stenciled on the boxes as he inputted them into his wrist PDA when Hunt called her down.

"I have something that will interest you far more. Come down and I'll show you."

"You okay for a bit?" Taylor asked Tate.

"Sure. Go. He's the boss." He laughed when she made a face and started to protest. "No, really. Go. We have enough people. We're covered."

Released from duty, she climbed down the mountain of wooden crates. She decided she'd rather not know the contents of some of them. There was an area that Hunt, Daklin, and Tate had decided should not be touched until another hazmat team arrived with more suits and equipment, and she was fine and dandy with that.

Hunt reached up and took her hand to help her down off the last crate.

"What do you want to show me?"

"You'll have to wait and see."

Curiosity sparked, Taylor followed him across the cement floor. Morales had constructed a warehouse in the middle of nowhere. No one could get in or out without those codes. It was diabolical and brilliant. But now she'd seen it, experienced it, lived it. She'd like to see sky and smell fresh air pretty soon.

"Oh. My. God!"

Hunt had pushed open a tall mahogany door, ushered her inside, and closed the door behind them. Taylor did a slow turn, trying to take everything in.

"I found the lights and fired up the music. Wanted you to get the full effect."

Taylor turned around slowly. "The effect is pretty freaking incredible."

The room was large, beautifully lit, and filled with paintings hanging against a backdrop of rich, red, African Padauk, a rare wood. One of the homes she'd robbed had reported to their insurance company, and hence the newspaper reports that the thief had destroyed the walls of their study, paneled in this rare and expensive wood. Not true. And bad press.

"This is hideous enough to be a Picasso." Taylor approached the butt-ugly painting.

"Stolen from the McGills the day after they brought it home from Sotheby's in '89. Valued at forty-three million."

She whistled as she moved down to the next painting bathed by special lighting. "Van Gogh's *Irises*. Forty-nine million. That Renoir over there? Seventy-eight."

There were sculptures from sculptors she'd never heard of. Hunt was familiar with many of them. Once she heard the names, Taylor could fill in the blanks. Many of the pieces in Morales's fantastic collection were on Consolidated Underwriters' lists of retrievable objects.

A Serra worth five million. A Bonheur worth eight. There were two of Emperor Qin Shihuang's life-size terra-cotta soldiers, and a small bust of a sweet-faced young girl. There was a full-size bronze horse, and a collection of Fabergé eggs, millions of dollars worth, scattered on a velvet cloth on a side table.

"No wonder he went to such lengths to keep people out," Taylor whispered in awe as she walked around the room. There must be well over a billion dollars worth of stolen artwork and precious jewels here.

And her fingers itched to touch it all. "I can't believe anyone would go to such elaborate lengths to accumulate all this . . . magnificence, only to turn around and blow it all to hell and go, Oh! Oh! Oh!" she whispered, sinking to the floor in a boneless puddle beside a beautiful little glass-fronted display case.

She spread her hand on the glass like a pink starfish against the black velvet-lined shelves inside. Shelves filled with bling. Shiny, brilliant, priceless, perfect diamonds in every shape and color. Set in gold. In platinum. In silver. Artistically sprinkled like stars around and between the jewelry were hundreds of loose stones, tossed like glitter against the midnight dark velvet.

Taylor thought she'd have a heart attack right then and there.

All those lovely diamonds blurred into one as her eyes feasted on the set right in front, dead center. The earrings. The bracelet. The—oh, Lord—the necklace.

The czar's Blue Star diamonds.

Her Blue Star diamonds.

"Come to mama."

She tugged at the fist-sized, flame-red silk tassel attached to the intricate inlaid gold and ivory door handle. The door swung open on well-oiled hinges.

Reaching in, she reverently slipped her very dirty fingers around the necklace and took it out of the cabinet without taking a breath. She draped the ornate platinum setting across her palm so she could admire the necklace close up.

"My God," she whispered. "Even though I've followed her all over the world, I was never really sure she was *real*. Her existence reached mystical proportions over the years."

"Her?"

"Yes. *Her.*" Taylor ran a finger gently over the face of the center stone. *Lord.* "Beautiful. Filled with fire. Strong. Beyond price. Have you ever *seen* anything this exquisite in your life?"

"Yes." Hunt's voice was husky. She thought she felt the brush of his hand, moving lightly over her hair. "As a matter of fact, I have."

She moved her wrist so the light could play across the surface of the necklace. She didn't need her loupe. The center stone was a 51.84 carat Fancy Deep Blue round brilliant. Another sixty carats of smaller but equally exquisite blue diamonds ran up each side, all surrounded by ninety carats of F's. Pure, white, absolutely flawless, colorless stones.

The diamonds contained fire like Taylor had never seen before. Not only were the stones huge and flawless, they represented the finest Antwerp cuts in the history of gems. Exactly and lovingly chiseled so that hundreds of tiny prisms refracted light in a way that nearly made the stones seem to radiate all on their own.

The stones were cool to the touch, yet the luminosity of each perfect stone shone like distant stars against her filthy palm.

"Take a couple of deep breaths," Hunt said dryly as he stood over her. "Want to put it on?"

"Oh yeah," she murmured reverently.

"Those stones are the exact color of your eyes. Only your eyes are brighter and much prettier." He reached for the necklace, and Taylor's fingers automatically closed over it. "You're going to have to let go if you want to wear it, darling."

For the first time, Taylor was more interested in the anticipation of his touch than the feel of the gems in her hand. She opened her fist, and he plucked the priceless work of art out of her hand.

How had this happened? When had his touch—even the promise of it—become paramount to her year's long search for this necklace?

Warm fingers brushed aside her hair, then she felt the heat of his mouth against her nape. Taylor closed her eyes, dizzy with sensation. Senses overloaded by it all. The place. The gems. *Hunt.*

She sucked in a breath.

Most of all—Hunt.

She loved him.

Simple.

Pure.

He fastened the ornate clasp, then lifted her to her feet, turning her in his arms as he did so. The necklace was heavy against her pounding heart as Hunt cupped her face between his palms. His gaze searched her face, then he pressed his mouth to hers in a gentle kiss. Taylor wrapped her arms about his neck as his tongue sought hers.

Lord, yes.

What could be more perfect—

Something crashed loudly beyond the door.

They broke apart.

By the sound of it, all hell was breaking loose outside.

Men shouted.

Shots sounded.

Hunt moved in a flash of sleek, black-covered muscles, weapon in hand even before he straightened. He removed the gun the shaggy guy had given him and handed it to her. "Stay in here. Lock the door if you can. And please. Stay here." There was a brief flash of— *something* in his eyes. "I'll be back for you."

"Yeah. Sure," Taylor said to empty air as the door slammed behind him, leaving her with a big black gun in one hand, and a $75 million necklace in the other.

Forty-nine

HUNT SLAMMED THE DOOR BEHIND HIM, SIZING UP THE CHAOS before he stepped into the melee.

Morales's people had arrived in full force. There was no sign of the man himself—yet—but Hunt recognized several others, including that malevolent Greek, Andreas Constantine, currently trying to fend off Bishop.

With a feral smile, he stuck the H&K back into the holster strapped to his thigh. Any fool who used their weapon in here would pay dearly. T-FLAC agents got that—Morales's men did not. A couple of Morales's imbeciles got off a few shots. His own people had their weapons safetied for the duration.

Should a bullet strike any one of the thousands of stacked crates, they'd all go up in a blaze of glory. Well ahead of Morales's scheduled launch. A few stray rounds pinged into the walls, sending large chunks of rock into the fray. But the weapons fire soon stopped as word was quickly passed and reality took precedence over the firepower.

Now, the fight was quieter, but just as deadly. Bone hitting bone.

The thump and thud and scrape of bodies tumbling on the cement as the men moved in for violent hand-to-hand combat.

"Incoming!" one of Viljoen's men shouted, lunging as a *Mano* guy raised a small launcher to his shoulder. The terrorist got off a shot seconds before the T-FLAC agent tackled him to the floor in a flurry of arms and legs.

Jesus bloody Christ. They were six thousand feet underground, and Morales's people had brought in *rocket launchers*?

Insane! But of course they didn't care. They were so dedicated to their cause they were prepared to die down here.

It would be bad enough if a stray bullet hit the crated ammunition. But thousands of those crates also contained biochemicals. And if that wasn't bad enough, in the middle of it all, the missile.

Two thousand feet away, the small rocket slammed into a neat stack of crates containing ammo. The resulting explosion was deafening and instantaneous; the detonation punched Hunt's eardrums. The contents and the heavy wooden containers exploded, debris shooting high into the air. Chunks of metal and wood rained fire on the combatants below.

For several minutes pandemonium ensued as men ran for their lives, pelted from above with flaming projectiles and jagged shrapnel. Acrid smoke filled the air, and the floor became littered with huge chunks of burning debris.

But no sooner had the wreckage landed than the men were back beating the shit out of one another. Hunt let them have at it.

T-FLAC's job was to find the bad guys, break their toys, and kill them, not necessarily in that order. His people would deal with the former. He kept his eye searching for the prize. The person he wanted was Morales.

T-FLAC intel indicated that Morales would want to be close to the action. Not close enough to die for his cause, but close enough to observe the minutiae of the culmination of his lifelong dream. Morales had planned this for years. Hunt knew he wouldn't be satisfied sitting safely in San Cristóbal awaiting news. He'd be right here in the thick of things.

He'd want to do the countdown personally. And press the launch button himself. Which is why Hunt had dispatched a group to find and bring Morales to him. Here. If the head of *Mano del Dios* wanted to witness his creation, then he could bloody well do it up close and personal with everyone else.

There were more bad guys than T-FLAC operatives. Just the way they liked it. Hunt ran like hell, zigging and zagging across the warehouse. Just because guns were verboten didn't mean knives were too. Ka-bar in hand, he kept his eye out for his prey as he moved through the flaming bonfires and bodies. Both dead and alive.

His headset clicked. "St. John." It was one of Viljoen's men who'd been sent to search for Morales. "Find him?"

"Yeah, he has a house on the other side of Blikiesfontein. He was all spiffed up and ready to detonate. Oh, yeah, and by the way? The sick fuck killed his wife."

"He killed his wife?" Hunt repeated, startled.

"I shit you not. Strangled her. We found her in the chapel behind the house."

"Grab a chopper and bring him to the circus," Hunt told him. "I'd hate him to miss the show."

Fifty

L ISA MAKI HAD BEEN INSTRUCTED BY THE BLACK ROSE HERSELF to hold her people back, and to wait in Blikiesfontein for her signal. Although it made sense for T-FLAC to do Black Rose's grunt work for them, she hadn't enjoyed the wait. They'd observed the vehicles and choppers converging on the African village a few miles away, and her heart had pounded with anticipation.

She and her group were eager to go in, kick some butt, and stake Black Rose's claim to the power and glory of *Mano del Dios*.

Finally it was time.

By the time Lisa and her group arrived down on the lower level of the mine, it was almost impossible to see anything. The cavern was filled with choking smoke. Small fires burned, then jumped and spread among the wooden crates, and men lay dead or dying across the floor. Through the veils of thick, gray smoke, the sight of the missile—enormous and eerily white—made Lisa's breath catch.

No guns, the Black Rose had warned. Made sense with the missile, the Black Rose's ultimate prize, projecting through the floor like a giant white penis. Besides, Lisa much preferred hand-to-hand with her Nepalese-commando, Khukri, crescent-shaped combat knife. She preferred the intimacy of knife fighting. It was fast, fluid, and lethal.

The curved amari hilt fit comfortably in her hand as she fondled it, looking into the mass of humanity before her. The gleaming, well-honed, nine-and-a-half-inch steel blade was like an old friend. They'd done some fine work together. Lisa smiled. Slashing and stabbing were made simple with a good knife, but the Khukri also did a *fine* job of decapitation.

T-FLAC or the *Mano*. Both enemies would feel the slice of her blade. She couldn't wait.

She motioned her people into place. The men and woman she'd been given awaited her signal. Lisa felt a surge of power so profound it was almost sexual. She smiled. "Let's show *Mano del Dios* and T-FLAC who just joined the party."

Fifty-one

"ST. JOHN?" ONE OF DAKLIN'S MEN, HUNT THOUGHT, AS THE KID came running full-tilt toward him.

Hunt swiped a hand across his smoke-streaked face as he pulled the guy aside behind the temporary shelter of a crate of AK-47s. "Talk." Jesus, they were hiring them young. The operative, redheaded and freckle-faced, looked about twelve. A scared twelve at that. He was probably twenty, Hunt thought, and an MIT protégé.

"We went down the assembly launch tower. The warhead weighs in excess of twenty-three percent of the missile's weight . . ."

As he listened, Hunt scanned the scene before him. Fires had sprung up everywhere. His people were attempting to put them out as fast as possible using the fire hoses they'd found somewhere. Putting out fires and fighting off *Mano del Dios*. Both formidable tasks.

The lights flickered off, on, off, then on again.

Jesus. The kid had run hell-bent for leather across the combat zone to bring him a message, and now was having trouble getting to the point. "Where's your headset?" he asked, interrupting.

"Daklin made us . . . It was distracting—"

"Message? What's the bottom line?" Hunt demanded, watching the action behind Daklin's guy.

"We've crossed it, sir. *We've fucking crossed it.* With that weight—ah, geez—it gives it an effective large kill envelope, and the highest lethality against soft-skin targets. Oh, fuck. Oh, God. Oh, shit. Las Vegas is screwed real bad. Sir."

Soft-skin targets. So, it wasn't a nuke that would have taken out buildings as well as people. The payload was chemical. Fuck. "How long will it take your team to destroy the guidance chips and deactivate the bloody thing?" Hunt asked calmly.

The kid was still hyperventilating. "Four hours, Daklin said."

"Remind him he has seventy-six minutes. *Move.*"

The kid's eyes widened, his Adam's apple bobbed, then he turned and hauled ass, weaving and dodging through the mayhem. He disappeared into the smoke and flames.

"Morales," a voice said through his earpiece. "ETA fourteen minutes."

"Good man," Hunt murmured into the voice-activated mic. "South entrance Level Seven."

"Affirmative."

Hunt quickly transmitted the information to his team leaders.

Through ribbons of drifting gray smoke, he scanned the vast area. It was a beautiful sight, watching the black-clad T-FLAC operatives whip Morales's goons . . .

But *that* wasn't one of Morales's people.

Hunt's eyes narrowed as he recognized two more faces. Both ID'd by T-FLAC as Black Rose terrorists.

Excellent, he thought with satisfaction, spotting several more Black Rose members. Two tangos for the price of one. That expedited things. The two groups were hard to ID as separate groups. Not that it mattered now.

Dead, they'd be easy to identify. Sometimes they had to see their bodies to be sure. The Black Rose members all wore the tattooed rose on their backs.

Things were shaking down nicely. He passed Savage, her red hair streaming loose and wild around her shoulders. A small, vengeful smile curved her mouth as she crouched, throwing her knife from hand to hand as she and one of Morales's men circled each other. She'd unzipped her suit down to her waist, and her bare breasts threatened to spill out. A calculated distraction she enjoyed. Savage was very good with misdirection, and even better with that Ka-bar. He knew the guy didn't stand a chance.

Three men rushed Hunt simultaneously. One of the aspects Hunt enjoyed most about his job was hand-to-hand combat. Usually, he didn't get many opportunities. A fast bullet was far more expedient. But presented with this opportunity, he took it.

As the man closest to him came in, Hunt, keeping his arms tight to his body, extended his leg with a smooth snapping motion, connecting squarely in the center of his opponent's chest. The man went flying into the guy directly behind him, and they both went balls-up, skating along the cement floor.

The third man came with fists raised. Using the momentum from the last kick, Hunt rotated at the hip, kicking the inside of his opponent's leg, at the same time grabbing the front of the man's shirt, taking him down to the floor in a quick, smooth sweep.

Controlling his opponent by the arm, Hunt did a front kick to the man's knee, preventing him from rolling out of the way. The crack of the bone was almost lost in the noise around them. The man shrieked, trying to rise. Hunt stomped his head. He lay still.

He quickly stripped the fallen man of his weapons, then tossed the gun and knife to a T-FLAC man who'd just neutralized his own opponent. Just in time, Hunt saw, as he half turned, a blonde woman coming at him at a run.

She advanced, wielding a Gurkha Khukri fighting knife with skill and speed. He could see she knew her way around a knife, but then, so did he.

Not one of Morales's, he thought, crouching, Ka-bar dancing from hand to hand as she came closer. Morales had no women in any of his cells. So the Black Rose had sent in their own people to try and take the *Mano del Dios* ordnance and missile before Morales blew everything to hell and gone.

When he'd first started working for T-FLAC, Hunt had loathed taking on a woman, especially in hand-to-hand combat. It went against everything in him to hurt a woman. He'd gotten over that aversion pretty damn fast when a female terrorist attempted to cut off his balls ten years ago.

A terrorist was a terrorist was a terrorist. No matter if they had the face of a pug dog or, like this woman, looked as sweet and angelic as the girl next door. Sunny ponytail bouncing innocently, she came at him with that lethal knife, knowing, as he did, *exactly* where to cut to kill.

The stomach was where most people aimed. It was usually unprotected and the biggest meaningful target. Not to mention that the thought of receiving a gut wound terrified people. Hunt preferred the carotid. He didn't toy with his opponents. If he had a weapon in his hand, his intention was a quick kill.

They danced around each other, knives flashing and slashing. She was small and light. He was more experienced and a hell of a lot faster.

He arced his arm high and brought it down in a blur of silver. She glided around his hip and lunged. The sharp blade of the Khukri curved up, slicing painlessly into his side. He chopped at her wrist with the side of his hand. Her fingers loosened on the hilt but she managed to catch the knife in her other hand.

Hunt tossed his blade to his left hand as well. She backed up. He advanced. They circled each other, orange flames dancing along their blades, smoke billowing and eddying in their wake as they moved.

She stumbled up against a stack of crates and her eyes went wide. "Please don't hurt me," she begged, knife hand dropping to her side. Blood from her slashed arm dripped on the floor beside her Nikes as she stood panting, fear stark on her face.

Face. Not eyes.

Hunt anticipated the move a split second before she lunged. He shifted, letting her momentum carry her. He spun and cut down fast and sure. She grunted as the blade sliced deep into her knife arm. She feinted left. Unlike the blonde, Hunt wasn't utilizing only his knife. His entire body was involved as he twisted away from her lunge, brought his left leg up, over her knife hand, and connected his booted foot to her temple.

She dropped like a stone. He bent to relieve her of the Khukri, then slipped it into the sheath strapped to his right thigh.

He heard a faint voice, and realizing that his earpiece had slipped, reinserted it. "Talk."

"Morales awaits your pleasure."

"On my way." He turned to see Savage, who'd dispatched her own opponent. "Take care of this, would you?" he said, nudging the blond with his booted foot.

"I live to do garbage detail," she grumbled, but grabbed the other woman by the shoulders and started dragging her to a tightly guarded holding area several hundred yards off to the side.

"Daklin?" Navarro's voice sounded in Hunt's ear.

Radio silence. Then an unfamiliar voice. "He says don't talk to him, for fuck sake. He's busy!" Then Daklin's mic was disconnected.

Fair enough. Hunt didn't want anyone distracting Daklin either.

He glanced at his watch. Forty-seven minutes to detonation.

Fifty-two

TAYLOR SAT ON THE PLUSH BURGUNDY VELVET SOFA, HOLDING the gun with both hands. It was a lot heavier than she'd expected. She'd never fired one, but figured if someone came through that door, she'd aim and pull the trigger. At this distance, she couldn't miss.

The problem with guns and knives was, if you didn't have a *clue* what you were doing, and someone else *did,* they could take the weapon away and use it on *you.* She made a mental note to find a shooting range when she got home. A skill she hadn't found necessary before now seemed of incredible importance. Not just for her, but because she knew one thing with absolute certainty—any bad guy she killed couldn't kill Hunt.

She had no intention of leaving this room. And she wouldn't open the door for anyone other than the good guys. She knew she'd be useless out there anyway. She couldn't fire the gun with any accuracy, and she wasn't handy with her fists. In her line of work, she hadn't had to be proficient at either.

She'd had some experience with hitting and punching as a kid. But she hadn't enjoyed it when people hit her back, and had avoided physical confrontation ever since.

No, she'd stay put. Hunt had told her he'd be back, and she believed him, as much as she feared for him. The seconds ticked in slow motion as she listened to the violent sounds on the other side of the door.

Please be okay.

The door didn't *have* a lock, but she considered having a door to close a plus. Who did Morales shut out when he was down here in his lair? She figured he didn't get many visitors. Not unless they had a good seven or eight hours to run the gauntlet of sick, Dante-inspired levels.

She'd dragged a heavy marble-topped table in front of the door. It was the best she could do. So far nobody had tried to get in.

She'd spent her time inspecting everything in the room. It almost took her mind off what was directly beneath her feet. And the activity gave her something to do other than wonder where Hunt was and what he was doing. Well, she had a pretty good idea of what he was doing—she just didn't want to think about it. Not when it caused her chest to tighten and a lump to clog her dry throat.

There were some *very* fine baubles in here. Many of which were, or had been, on the lists of Consolidated Underwriters. Taylor looked around for something to carry some of them in and found a handy black alligator briefcase. It wasn't big, but she knew how to pack.

The selfish bastard had all this incredible, priceless artwork down here for his eyes only. She tried to decide between the ruby Fabergé and the twin, smaller, more delicate diamond and translucent emerald enamel pair on plinths of rock crystal. Exquisite. All three, she decided. The little ones would tuck into corners. Two were from the same Russian museum. The third—she couldn't recall where *that* had been stolen from. She remembered seeing the photograph in the book of stolen items.

She hoped Hunt and T-FLAC returned everything to their rightful owners, and shoved Morales in that stinky river of *whatever* for the rest of his natural life. No, on second thought, she wanted Morales to die—slowly and painfully. Maybe in the propeller blades like poor Piet Coetzee.

She couldn't believe the son of a bitch didn't give a damn about destroying all of this beauty when his missile took off. He must have been hiding the things he had stolen down here for years. Not only was he an evil, deranged terrorist, but he was a selfish bastard for hiding these treasures away and keeping them to himself.

She patted her chest where the Blue Star diamonds nicely warmed her skin under her LockOut suit. She'd report in to Consolidated when she could. But for now, the Blue Stars were hers.

From the sounds of it, the raging battle out there seemed to be winding down. Just knowing that men were beyond that door killing one another, however, freaked her out. She knew Hunt and his men were professionals, that they dealt with stuff like this every day. But, damn it, she'd heard that enormous percussion bang minutes after he'd left. Forgetting that she'd promised to stay put, she'd flown out of that door so fast she was a blur.

A fire raged in one of the stacks. She had a moment of concern as the flames and smoke made visibility difficult and she heard men coughing and gagging. She reminded herself, as she scanned and tried to identify the men, that she'd paid attention earlier as Hunt and his guys had discussed the incredible ventilation and air-conditioning system Morales had installed in the mine to keep the temperature so moderate and the air fresh.

Where was Hunt?

She'd narrowed her eyes against the smoke, tracking from left to right, eliminating this figure then that, until she recognized his broad back. As soon as she saw him, alive and well and sprinting across the warehouse, she'd returned to the room, shut the door, and leaned against it for several seconds, breathing a prayer of thanks.

But that had been a while ago, and her concern was building to yet another heart-tugging crescendo as she paced the floor, no longer seeing the priceless artifacts.

How odd. The only person she'd ever worried about before was

Mandy. Now her stomach was in a knot of anxiety over Hunt. As good as he was, as professional as he was, he was still flesh and blood. He *could* be killed.

The thought scared her. Terrified her.

She couldn't begin to imagine a world without him in it.

She knew they had no future. People like them *didn't*. That was a given. Neither of them was a picket-fence, two-point-whatever-children kind of person. She wasn't going to be a Brownie mom and bake cookies, and she couldn't imagine Hunt spending a Sunday afternoon mowing the lawn.

She adored kids. *Other* people's. But she didn't have a burning urge to produce any of her own. She was only twenty-seven. There was no rush. When or *if* the time came, she'd do something about it. If the time never came, she was fine with that too.

What she wanted was more time with Hunt.

She was in love with the maddening man.

How could she be so in love with him when their entire "relationship" had been no relationship at all? Actually, she was stunned to find herself thinking the *L* word at all. She'd never even considered the possibility for herself.

She wasn't a quiet-walks, learning-about-each-other-over-leisurely-meals kinda girl. She'd never expected to feel this all-encompassing sensation of needing him more than she needed breath. It was too fast.

But maybe that was good, she thought now. Maybe she was destined to fall in love the same way she lived her life—risky. All or nothing.

Still, she wanted time for slow lovemaking in a big bed. Hell, she'd like fast sex on the floor, for that matter. And she wanted to hear him laugh again. How could a man laugh so seldom?

She could make him laugh.

Something—some*one* crashed into the door, startling the hell out of her. Heart in her throat, Taylor jumped to her feet, leveling the nose of the gun at the middle of the door.

"Taylor? It's Savage—*Catherine*—open the fucking door! Hurry!"

Taylor raced to drag the heavy table out of the way so Savage could slip inside. "What the hell took you so long?" Savage snapped, dragging another woman through the door behind her.

Taylor glanced at the angel-faced blonde who looked as though she'd gone ten rounds with a prizefighter. "Who's your friend?"

"This," Savage said savagely, shoving the woman in front of her, "is the head of Black Rose."

From the look of Savage's knuckles, *she* hadn't been reticent about hitting someone. But Taylor didn't feel any sympathy for the woman whose nose Savage had broken. She was a bleeding mess and clearly less than half conscious as Savage kicked her to the floor. The woman's eyes rolled as she slumped to the museum-quality Chinese silk area rug and lay still at Savage's feet.

"What are we supposed to *do* with— Shit, watch out!"

The younger woman suddenly sprang to her feet as if catapulted from a cannon. Taylor took an instinctive step back out of the way, but the woman wasn't going for Savage—she was coming at *her*. With a feral shriek, the blonde powered into Taylor, knocking her off her feet.

Holy crap!

The gun went flying as they thudded to the floor in a tangle of arms and legs. Taylor didn't enjoy fighting, but she didn't intend to let some strange woman beat up on her without getting in a few punches of her own.

She pulled back her arm, brought up her elbow, and smashed it into the woman's broken nose. The blonde bucked, gurgling on her own blood.

Sick to her stomach, Taylor shoved at her. "Are you just going to stand there?" she yelled at Savage. "This is your job, not mine!"

The blonde still had a lot of fight in her. She raked her nails down Taylor's throat above the necklace. Taylor kneed her in the side, and they both rolled, smashing into the marble-topped table that had been barricading the door. Taylor's head hit the wooden leg and she saw stars. "Savage, damn it! Get over here and help—"

Savage lunged as the terrorist staggered to her knees and lunged for the discarded gun on the floor near the door. Savage tried to reach the weapon first, but the blonde got hold of the gun. She smiled then, a grotesque bloody mask, as she leveled the gun squarely at the center of Taylor's chest from three feet away.

She was not going to miss.

Fifty-three

José Morales stood calmly amidst the chaos, waiting for Hunt. Dressed in a natty black suit, crisp white shirt, and old school tie, the terrorist looked like a gentleman on his way to the office. Except for having his hands secured behind him, his ankles hobbled, and a phalanx of heavily armed T-FLAC operatives surrounding him.

Hunt was twenty feet away when his earpiece activated. Double click. Daklin himself transmitting. An excellent sign. "We're clear," Daklin told him.

Jesus—Hunt glanced at his watch—two minutes shy of 1500 hours. "With time to spare. Good job," he said with classic understatement.

A local T-FLAC operative jogged to meet Hunt halfway. The man handed him a small black handheld device with a small screen on it.

Hunt paused to glance at it. Bloody hell. Here it was. Here was the real secret to Morales's stronghold. This, coupled with the disks holding the combinations, was what made it possible for the terrorist to enter the secret passages. "Where did you find it?"

"On the wife's body. We checked it out. Too powerful for any household electronics. Hell, too powerful for just about anything."

"Does he know we have this?"

The man shook his head.

Hunt suspected that *Maria Morales* had been the woman feeding them information over the last few months. He stuck the device in his weapons belt and strode forward to face Morales.

"Your launch has been deactivated," Hunt said by way of greeting.

Morales smiled. "Do you think so?"

Hunt knew so; Daklin was *the* best. "You think not? We'll all wait together. See what happens in the next thirty-six minutes. In the meantime, you can have a ringside seat as we dismantle your life's work. *Mano del Dios* is no more, Morales."

" '*Then I saw an angel coming down from heaven, holding in his hand the key to the bottomless pit and a great chain,*' " Morales quoted. "*Revelation 20:1.*"

Right, Hunt thought with an inward chuckle. *Your angel is defiantly holding the key.* "See those men loading the crates into the railcars behind you?" Hunt motioned over Morales's shoulder. The tango didn't turn to look. But the sound of boxes being loaded was unmistakable. They were making good headway. Better yet, if this device they'd found on Mrs. Morales helped them navigate through sheer rock face.

"The carts," Hunt pointed out unnecessarily, "are almost full." Dressed in Level Four hazmat gear, Navarro's team were loading the biochemicals and toxins first.

"The train, as *you* might observe," Morales pointed out genially, "is facing a rock wall thirty feet thick."

"There you go, underestimating T-FLAC again." Hunt pointed the remote-control device, depressed several buttons until he found the right one, and smiled as the entire wall slowly, inexorably, slid aside to reveal the tracks down the tunnel.

Morales spun to look at Hunt, a mask of horror on his face. "How is this possible? From where did you obtain that device?"

Hunt held it up. "This? Your lovely wife Maria had it in her pocket when they found her." He jerked his head. "And take a gander to your right—those are your people being led away in the custody of *my* people. Check and mate. Game over."

There was a double beep in his ear. "A second countdown has just been activated. Same time," Daklin snarled, "different tune." The line went dead.

Well, fuck.

Without warning, the floor started shaking. A few seconds later a mechanical, grinding sound joined the hellacious noise of thousands of neatly piled wooden crates crashing to the cement floor. The shattered crates spewed their contents: weapons, ammunition, and machine parts, all of which rolled beneath the feet of the men still fighting.

Morales's smile widened.

"What have you done, you sick fuck?" Hunt snarled over the noise, wrapping his hand around Morales's throat.

"The top of my little mountain is opening for the launch." Morales's eyes gleamed brilliantly as his excitement and anticipation rose feverishly. He was oblivious to the manic activity around him. To the smoke. To the small fires burning about his warehouse. To the men piling his crates near the railcars. To dozens of men still locked in mortal combat.

"Here is a call for the endurance of the saints, those who keep the commandments of God and hold fast to the faith of Jesus," Morales shouted over the din. *"And I heard a voice from heaven saying, 'Write this: Blessed are the dead who from now on die in the—' "*

Hunt grabbed Morales by his hair and jerked his head back. Light glinted on the blade of the Ka-bar as he pressed it to Morales's carotid. "How do we deactivate the second launch sequence?" He sliced a little deeper. Blood stained Morales's shirt collar. *"Now."*

"It cannot be turned off," the head of *Mano del Dios* said complacently. Pleased with himself, and unfazed by the cold steel at his throat, he smiled again. "There is a fail-safe system in place. Nothing can stop the launch. God's command shall prevail. *'For this slight momentary affliction is preparing us for an eternal weight of glory beyond all measure, because we look not at what can be seen but at what cannot be*

seen; for what can be seen is temporary, but what cannot be seen is eternal.'
2 *Corinthians 4:17-18."*

A double beep in Hunt's ear. "Daklin?"

"Need Taylor ASAP," Asher Daklin said tightly. "There's another fucking keypad behind the control panel."

Hunt released Morales. His heart thudded with dread. Jesus. So close. "Bring Taylor ASAP to the south entrance. She's in the room on the northeast quadrant," he snapped into the lip mic, talking directly to his team. "All of you. Stay with her. Haul ass. *Now.* Go, go, go."

He gave José Morales a cold look. "Will you tell us how to deactivate the missile?"

" *'Discipline yourself, keep alert. Like a roaring lion your adversary the devil growls around, looking for someone to devour.' 1 Peter 5—"*

Hunt pulled out his H&K and pushed it under the man's chin. "What is the deactivation code?"

"I am not afraid to die."

"Too bad." Hunt pulled the trigger. As Morales slumped to the floor, Hunt glanced at Viljoen, standing nearby, his own weapon drawn. "I just hate fucking unresolved issues, don't you?"

Fifty-four

TAYLOR CROUCHED IN FRONT OF THE MISSILE.

Behind her, Hunt, Asher Daklin, Bishop, and Francis Fisk waited. Her heart pounded like a drum inside her chest. She shook out her hands to get rid of some of the nerves and drew in a slow, deep breath.

Some of the guys had come to get her in Morales's secret room. She'd been hit on the head and had just regained consciousness a few minutes before they burst in and practically dragged her here.

She was damn sure, pretty sure, almost certain, that Savage had been the one to hit her. It didn't make sense, and she didn't have time to try to figure it out. Savage had saved her from being shot by the Black Rose terrorist . . . hadn't she?

Her head throbbed where she'd been struck. When she'd come to, the blonde terrorist was dead. Savage was unconscious and bleeding beside her, a big knot on the back of her head . . . *and somebody's* blood on her.

None of which mattered right at this moment.

Concentrate, she told herself firmly.

By some miracle, someone had brought her tools from where she'd left them so many hours ago outside the wind tunnel. That was the only good thing about this situation. Everything else pretty much sucked.

The area surrounding the base of the missile was a tight fit, a circular cavern carved out specifically for the base and armature of the metal monstrosity. With five of them in there, it was hot, it was crowded, it was tense.

Taylor could block out all *that.* It was the other occupants of the claustrophobic space that made the hair on the back of her neck prickle and her mouth go bone dry.

The rough rock floor was awash with snakes.

They were *small* snakes, Daklin had pointed out mildly when she first saw them and shrieked like a girl. Yeah, sure they were little. But there were *thousands* of them. Black snakes, green snakes, and yellow snakes.

Live, venomous, creepy-crawly *snakes.*

One slithered over her instep. She shuddered, then froze. "Ah, geez—"

"Got it." Bishop reached between her knees from behind, plucking the yellow serpent off her foot. He tossed it aside. "I told you I'd keep them off of you. And," he muttered under his breath, "I'm hoping St. John didn't see where I just had my arm."

Hunt had assured her that the flicking tongues couldn't pass through the LockOut fabric. She almost believed him.

"Focus, people," Daklin said softly directly behind her. "I changed the trajectory in accordance with coded RF pulses." He was talking to Hunt, who was behind her. "We bypassed two out of the four circuits, receiving and decoding, steering control. I didn't give a shit about the transmitting, command, and fail-safe detonation controls—"

"North Atlantic?"

More soft murmuring and mumbo jumbo behind her.

"It's a CDL2009," Taylor said, more to herself than the men

watching her. There was only enough room for one person to be directly in front of the panel. She was point man, or rather, woman.

She tried to forget that three feet away from her nose was the slick white metal skin of the missile. She tried hard to forget that if she didn't open this keypad and get to whatever Daklin needed inside—

Seventeen minutes. That's all she—they—had.

Seventeen minutes.

Now it was up to her.

The keypad was six by eight inches and centered in a dark gray titanium door approximately one foot square in a shallow indentation in the side of the missle. Bits of what Daklin had defused and discarded were scattered on the floor with the snakes.

"Give me your earpiece," she said to anyone. "Hurry."

"Don't freak," Fisk said softly, laying his headset on her left shoulder. "This is the *cord,* not a you-know-what."

Taylor was grateful for the heads-up. She quickly twisted the tiny earpiece open, then used the amp inside to press directly against the keypad, sticking the other end into her ear. "With me, Francis?"

He'd enter the numbers into his wrist PDA as she heard them and called them out. "There's nobody I trust more to do this than you, Taylor. I have your back."

She went to work, listening for the sound of the tumblers falling into place as she danced her fingers across the pad.

At this point she didn't even notice how fast the men around her were plucking the snakes off her. She was a hundred percent focused. She frowned. This wasn't that hard. The tumblers clicked away. She listened, rearranged the order, and was done.

"How much time do we have left?" she asked, memorizing the last number.

"Don't worry about it," Hunt said, directly behind her.

"Are we in?" Daklin demanded, incredulous, as she tossed the earpiece aside.

"Surprisingly, it wasn't that hard." Taylor shifted, ready to move aside so Daklin could take her place. She punched in the numbers in the correct sequence, then waited for the door to pop.

It didn't pop—it *exploded* open, releasing a spray of fine white powder directly into her face.

Blinded by whatever had hit her, Taylor screamed as somebody grabbed her from behind, pulling her back onto the floor.

"Keep your mouth and eyes *shut!*" Hunt shouted. "*Shut, goddamn it.* Get me something to irrigate with . . ." His voice faded as he spoke—yelled—at someone. Then it grew loud again as he crouched over her. "Keep everything closed." He blew across her face. Blew again. And again.

"Anth—" Somebody started to say and was cut off.

"Here's a rag, use it to—"

"No. I don't want to risk rubbing it into her skin. Good girl, keep your pretty eyes and mouth closed for a bit, all right, darling?"

Me, floor—snakes! she wanted to point out. The puff in the face had startled her, but it had been more air than substance, and it smelled a lot like baby talcum powder. She tried to sit up, to figure out what she was doing lying down, but her muscles wouldn't cooperate. Hunt seemed very tall as he loomed over her. One minute he was standing, the next, without appearing to have moved, he was crouched down beside her. She liked that about him. He moved so— She frowned.

Hunt said, "Lie still," in a commanding voice.

She lay still. The LockOut was skintight. Hunt wouldn't allow a snake to get inside her clothing.

"Navarro?" Hunt said, and then, "Jesus, fuck, then where the bloody hell *is* he? Tell him to rendezvous, south entrance . . . *Now,* goddamn it! Taylor's been hit with . . . I don't know. Yeah. Fine. Less than minutes."

Hunt picked her up, which was a big relief, because she itched all over just thinking about all those snakes.

"Nothing to worry about, love," Hunt told her calmly as he walked. "Just keep everything closed until Navarro checks you out. I don't think it's hers."

She guessed he meant the blood. "Sava—"

"Shut up," he said, sounding annoyed.

She shut up.

"Navarro? Talk to me."

She frowned, trying to concentrate on Hunt's voice. She could feel it resonate against her chest.

She liked it . . .

She loved him . . .

She felt dizzy and sick to her stomach. Hot. Cold. One minute she'd been fine— She shuddered. My God . . . Had Savage shot her? Frowning hurt, she discovered. The thought slipped away in a whirling mist. She'd never been sick a day in her life. Never.

She didn't like it.

She blinked her eyes open. They stung a little, as though she'd been crying—had Hunt made her cry? She didn't remember.

If not now, then later, she thought as a man swam into her vision.

Devil eyes came toward her, his hair mussed up. He had lovely hair. She tried to smile. Tried to tell him . . . *something.* "Hi, Daklin."

He scowled at her, but his voice was soft, "Hi, honey, howzit going?"

Her vision dimmed. "Not so hot."

"Put her down over here. I want that washed off ASAP."

ASAP was a great word. "A sap."

Hunt laid her down on something hard. She whimpered, and he pulled her back against his chest, then sat down with her in his arms. Much better.

"Think I want *two* fucking patients," Daklin demanded, spritzing something cool on her face. It felt good. "What happened?"

Good question. Her lips felt thick. Unresponsive. And it was getting harder to breathe. She had to get help. "H-Hunt . . ." She needed Hunt now. Right now. Something was horribly wrong.

She whimpered. Horrified at how pathetic she sounded. She tried to shake him off. He held her tighter.

Someone held her face still. Cold water poured over her head and chest. "Hang on, honey, let me get this crap off you, okay?"

She tried to frown. Why was it that none of her muscles worked? "Not—" She couldn't remember what she was going to say.

Her head flopped against Hunt's chest and she heard the rapid *pat-thud-thud* of his heart under her ear.

"Was she hit? Keep spraying her with that," Daklin instructed someone.

"The blood's not hers," Hunt said, sounding grim. "She does have cuts and abrasions . . ." He faded out.

". . . have to tell you the severity . . . cutaneous *and* inhalation—anything up to . . . anthrax . . . sake!"

Her tongue felt fuzzy, her brain muddled. Suddenly Hunt was moving at superhuman speed and everything blurred and blended sickeningly.

She blinked to clear her vision, frowning as she attempted to wrap her mind around the fact that she must be underwater, as everything undulated in a wavy back-and-forth motion that made her sick to her stomach.

"Tell me where you hurt, darling."

She gritted her teeth. She'd tell him if she knew, but then maybe not. The task of speech was so overwhelming, and the pain so vast . . .

"I hate to point out the obvious, pal. But you're bleeding like a stuffed pig yourself."

"A scratch. Stay with me. Damn it . . . hell. Stay . . . chopper . . . ASAP . . ." His voice sounded terrified. "Bloody hell, open your eyes!"

Hunt. Hunt. Hunt. She wanted to comfort him, opened her mouth. Nothing came out but a whimper. Oh, God, that couldn't be good, could it? She tried again, forgot what she'd been trying to do as her brain went cottony. But she felt so far away. Spinning into a huge echoing void. Falling through the earth at a million miles an hour. She felt so small. So lost.

Seven levels of hell. Hot.

Violent tremors coursed through her body, shaking her muscles and hurting her bones. The three-headed dog blew fire on her, singeing her skin with the heat of its breath.

Other hands on her. Helping Hunt turn her over. A laughing voice. Not Hunt's, for sure. "She's very well accessorized, I see . . . out of the LockOut?"

Every touch hurt her skin.

"Jesus, don't cry," Hunt said raggedly, and Taylor felt the warmth of his fingers brush the acidic tears off her cheek. "Hell, yes. Let's strip her. That shit's all over her. See what we're dealing with here. Navarro, find something to keep her warm, she's going into shock."

Rough hands yanked down the zipper on the front of her cool spy suit. *Don't,* she wanted to say, but nothing came out except deep, bone-jarring shudders that shook her body and made her teeth chatter. She tried again. Important. "Brief . . . case. Don't leave—"

"Christ! She's going into convulsions!"

Fifty-five

I T WAS AN OPERATION OF MONUMENTAL PROPORTIONS. THE RAIL-
cars being loaded were hastily uncoupled, leaving just the engine.
Hunt was carrying an unconscious Taylor. There were a dozen
men being triaged before going topside. Savage was one of them.
She'd been shot in the shoulder and was unconscious.

Hunt barely spared her a glance as she too was loaded into the
railcar. He fixed his gaze on Taylor's colorless face, her blue-tinged
lips . . . Jesus bloody Christ. It could be anything. *Anything!*

Double click on his headset. "Give me some fucking *good* news,"
Hunt snapped.

"Thanks to Taylor, we're clear," Daklin told him jubilantly. "The
missile has been neutralized and formally put out of business."

Hunt closed his eyes for a second as relief swamped him. "Daklin
did it," he told the others.

A cheer went up. A brief show of relief before everyone got back
to work.

Navarro started up the electric engine. "Good news indeed. And thank God Morales at least had the foresight to make his own access and egress swift. It's a hell of a lot faster getting out than it was getting in."

While they traveled through the tunnels in the railcar, Hunt kept her on his lap, her head against his chest, her breathing shallow. Daklin messed with Hunt's bleeding side until he told him, in no uncertain terms, to leave him the fuck alone. The only person he wanted to be receiving medical attention was Taylor.

Her confused state, the heat of her skin, and the convulsions scared the hell out of him. Scared Daklin too. And, if anyone, Daklin would know just how scared to be. There were so many biotoxins. So many *lethal* biotoxins in that hellhole.

The possibilities were infinite, for Christ's sake! Hunt went over every single possibility. None of them were good.

Twenty minutes later they were at the surface level.

It was dark, cold, and clear. The first chopper, which delivered Morales, had landed close to the entrance of the mine. The *whop-whop-whop* of the chopper blades thundered through the air, its lights a bubble in the darkness.

Hunt, Taylor in his arms, ran. He ignored the fire in his side and bolted like a sprinter trying to break the three-minute mile.

Navarro yanked open the door, climbed in, and reached for her. Hunt didn't want to hand her up, but he had no choice. Navarro took Taylor in his arms while Hunt climbed in. Daklin handed Savage up, then followed her in, yanking the door shut behind him.

"Go, go, go," Hunt yelled at the pilot, and the chopper took off in a smooth, vertical lift.

The medic clambered around the others. He looked from the blanket-wrapped but clearly naked Taylor, to Savage sprawled on the floor, to Hunt's side. "Which patient should I take first?" he asked.

"Navarro, see what you can do to contain Savage's bleeding," Hunt replied. "Here's your priority, Doc," he said, nodding at Taylor. He felt irrational. Insane. Out of his mind with worry.

"Let's have a look then, all right?" The doctor's Afrikaans accent was thick and hard to understand. Hunt needed every nuance to be crystal clear. The doctor peeled off the blanket, leaving Taylor pale and bare against the gray wool blanket. The Blue Star diamonds winked like white fire around her slender neck.

She looked vulnerable, defenseless, lying there. Hunt wanted to punch something. Someone. "What can I do?" he demanded, feeling helpless as he kneeled on the other side of her.

"Take the necklace off, okay? I'll check her out."

Hunt fumbled with the clasp, then drew off the heavy jeweled collar and stuffed it into his pocket. He kept his attention on the man's hands as they traveled competently over Taylor's still body. Her pale skin looked translucent. Fragile. Her eyes sunken and shadowed, her lips white. She appeared as if every vestige of her life force had been sucked out of her. *Ah, Jesus!*

"Tell me her symptoms from the very beginning, will you?" the doctor said, then continued examining every inch of Taylor's skin as Hunt rattled off everything he'd observed.

The symptoms *sounded* almost as bad as watching her experience them. The doctor merely made a sound in response and continued checking her. Hunt's heart was firmly in his throat as he watched the man's every move.

Panic, an unknown emotion, swamped him. He reached over and took Taylor's limp hand, then noticed that his own hand shook. Bloody hell. His hands *never* shook. "Navarro, find out our ETA . . . Well?" he demanded, as the doctor took his sweet time.

"No lesions—not yet, at any rate. Can somebody hold a light? *Ja,* like that. *Danke,*" he told Daklin as Daklin trained his searchlight near his hands. "Let's turn her over."

Hunt's jaw clenched as he eased Taylor over onto her stomach, turning her head gently to face him as the doctor ran his fingers over her back and down her hips and legs all the way to her slender feet.

"There are a couple of good hospitals closer," the doctor told him. "But I want to take her to Jo'burg General. They have an excellent poison control unit. Without knowing what the substance is, I can't risk giving her anything until the lab identifies it."

"You can't just do *nothing,*" Hunt insisted, feeling his own heartbeat escalate as his fear grew.

The doctor raised his eyebrows. "The wrong antidote could kill her faster than the poison. Without proper lab work, I can't even risk giving her fluids. They might speed the absorption rate of whatever is in her system. Do you understand?"

Yes. Hunt understood. He understood that his heart was being ripped out, as every second Taylor slipped further and further away from him.

"ETA, thirty-eight minutes," Daklin yelled over the sound of the blades.

Too long. Too goddamned long.

"Taylor will make it," Hunt said as he met the doctor's eyes. "She *will* make it."

But the expression on the doctor's face told him that was highly unlikely.

Fifty-six

JOHANNESBURG

DAKLIN SLUNG AN ARM OVER THE CHAIR BACK NEXT TO HIM AS Hunt walked around his outstretched legs. "If you continue pacing like a caged tiger," he told Hunt. "That ferret-faced little nurse will come back in here and ream you. Again. You just had sixty-some stitches taken in your hide, pal. Maybe you should do what they told you to do. Take a load off. Relax. You've scared the shit out of enough people that they'll hotfoot it in here to tell you the second there's news."

Hunt had to step over Daklin's feet again since the other man's long legs were stretched directly in his path. "Why the hell is this taking so long?" he demanded, ignoring his de facto babysitter's editorial comments. He rubbed a hand across his unshaven jaw. Christ, he hated the stink of hospitals. They all smelled the same. Antiseptic. Fear. Death. He turned around when he got to the far wall—eighteen paces—then went back the other way.

His skin felt clammy and his heart raced uncomfortably. *Admit it,* he taunted himself. *You are one shit-scared bastard.*

He hadn't had this fixation, and felt such a bone-deep fear about anyone's mortality, in twenty years. This kind of nerve-grinding fear was like riding a goddamned bicycle. The feeling was coming back to him in a sickening rush.

He closed his eyes briefly and prayed. He couldn't lose her.

This was taking too long . . .

". . . before they stuff *you* in a bed and strap you down," Daklin was saying.

Hunt merely grunted. It seemed that every muscle in his body was rigid with unleashed tension. They refused to let him see Taylor in the isolation ward. Not until they knew precisely what she'd been sprayed with. Jesus bloody Christ. Like he gave a continental fuck about his own health. If she was contagious, he might as well be too.

Christ, she'd been so pale on board the chopper en route to Jo'burg, her eyes sunken, her lips tinged blue. He'd crouched there, holding her, praying, trying to breathe for her. Only when the doctor on board kindly pointed out that he might break every bone in Taylor's body holding her that tightly had he loosened his grip on her. A little.

He was scared. Deep down-to-the-bone fucking *terrified* that the doctors would come in here and tell him she was dead.

He pressed a fist to the monstrous ache compressing his chest as he again strode back the way he'd come. Over Daklin's feet, past the coffeepot, to the far wall, back again. The soreness in his chest felt similar to the dull pain he'd experienced the few times he'd been shot.

Hunt thought savagely that this ache—in his chest, in his gut, in his heart—wasn't going anywhere. Not until he'd seen for himself that Taylor was in full recovery. That she was back to her sweet, sassy, brave self again. He needed to see the clear blue of her eyes, needed to hear her laughter, needed to run his hands over that pale creamy skin to assure himself that every inch of the woman he loved was whole and healthy.

He wanted to press his lips to her throat and feel her lifeblood pulsing through her veins.

Oblivious to his surrounds, he absently stepped over Daklin's feet on every circuit. He had to see her. Touch her. Make sure . . . Hell.

Will her to live, if that's what it took. This was one of those situations that he couldn't control, couldn't manipulate. He couldn't shoot his way out of this, or use any of T-FLAC's considerable resources. There was no gadget, no muscle, no *anything* within his power that could change the outcome of what would happen to her.

And his highly prized, much vaulted patience and control had gone down the chute—the longer the doctors worked on her. Nine hours was a lifetime.

He hadn't had enough time with her. Hell, they'd barely scratched the surface. He was being cheated here, goddamn it. He wanted to tell her that he loved her. He suspected even when he did, she wouldn't believe him. Everyone Taylor had ever cared about had left her. Her mother, when the going got tough, and her father, by being irresponsible enough to pull an armed robbery with two young daughters dependent on him.

There were millions of things he didn't know about her. Jesus. He didn't even know her favorite color, or her favorite books, or movies, or . . . a million other things, large and small.

Yet he knew the velvety feel of her skin. He knew she loved drinking champagne and eating chocolates before she went to bed at night. He knew she wasn't afraid of heights and that she favored very brief, very expensive lingerie.

How had this happened? he wondered. How had this woman crept into his heart where no one had trespassed before? How was it that she was everything he wanted and needed, when he hadn't known about those wants or needs until meeting her?

They'd had completely different childhoods, but they both lost their mothers too young. And they both had chosen work that kept them at an emotional distance from those around them. But he was fortunate in that he had friends. Taylor didn't have any close friends because of what she did.

She was bright. Self-reliant. And funny as hell. She should be surrounded by people who adored her.

Instead, she was alone.

Unacceptable. *He* could give her companionship, share with her his hard-won friendships with several T-FLAC operatives. He could give her . . . anything she wanted. Everything she wanted and needed. If he was given the opportunity.

What he found unconscionable—and terrified him the most—was that Taylor didn't expect things to be any different. She accepted the isolation of what she did. She didn't realize that she could have the thrill of her job, take care of her sister, and still have a life of her own. She didn't believe that she could have it all.

If . . . *When* she survived, he'd make her understand what he had to offer. He loved her enough to make up for the losses and the loneliness. He needed her. Needed her lush, pale body. Needed her warm arms wrapped about him. Needed her laughter to warm this crushing chill consuming him.

The pressure in his chest increased. He raked his fingers through his hair in frustration and clenched his teeth against the turbulent emotions ripping through him.

Please God, he pleaded. *A soul is a soul. If you need one, take mine. A straight-across swap. Because I don't hold with that crap about the good dying young . . .* He'd repent for the guilt of taking Taylor into such a dangerous situation later. Right now he could think of nothing other than bargaining, pleading, or bullying God into keeping her alive.

He'd never get over the responsibility of involving her so deeply with Morales. But without her, they would never have been able to defeat two of the deadliest terrorist cells in the world. Thanks to Taylor, Daklin had deactivated the missile, and Las Vegas was free to continue sinning to its heart's content, never knowing how close it had been to total annihilation.

Damn it to hell, they'd been in there working on her for bloody *hours.* He did a U-turn and started back across the room just as a familiar figure appeared in the doorway.

"What's new?" Max Aries asked, strolling in.

Hunt frowned as though coming up from the pitiless blackness beneath the ocean. "Why aren't you in Poland?"

"Brought you this." Aries handed him a padded envelope. "And got the S.O.S you needed backup. Man, you look like hell." Max gave him a concerned look. "The situation there wasn't nearly as exciting as we were led to believe."

"Backup?" Hunt took the envelope, folded it a couple of times, then casually stuffed it into his back pocket. He gave his friend a puzzled glance. "We don't need backup. Op's over, pal. *Mano del Dios* is out of biz. Morales neutralized. Missile defused. We saved the world." He rubbed a hand across his jaw and got to the most important fact. "Taylor's down the hall in ICU." He shot Daklin a look. "Get your size thirteens the hell out of my way, I'm too bloody tired to have to take that extra step."

Daklin shot him a half smile and withdrew his legs.

"The doctors figured right away the substance Taylor inhaled wasn't anthrax," Asher Daklin informed Max.

Hunt tuned them out as best he could.

"Even the heroin-cornstarch mix was everyday fare around here," Daklin continued. "It's the ricin that they discovered in the mix that's the concern right now. We're waiting for the lab results."

Hunt went to the window and stared out at the parking lot. Cars came and went. People in the hospitals lived or died.

"Do they think Morales tampered with or altered the genetics of the ricin to include a virus of some kind?" Max asked behind him.

Hunt's fist clenched against the window frame. The ricin could be made even more deadly if someone had screwed with the genetics. If it was mutated, not only could Taylor die, but they could well be faced with a situation that would kill who knew how many people before it could be contained. There were a hell of a lot of fucking *ifs*. Even in death, José Morales was wreaking havoc. Hunt turned away from the window and resumed pacing. He'd seen a polar bear in a zoo in Russia many years ago. The memory had stayed with him to this day of that too-small cage and that large beast, frustrated and frantic to move. It had gone around and around in circles until it went mad.

He knew just how it felt.

"She makes him *laugh*," Daklin told Max as Max went over to the half-filled coffeepot.

"No way," Hunt's friend mocked. "Thought that was just a rumor."

"I shit you not," Daklin drawled. "Witnessed the impossible myself. Several times. He's got it bad."

Hunt glanced at his watch. Nine hours eight minutes seven seconds. He wanted to punch something. He needed to run ten miles or swim a hundred laps.

"Before you ask," Max said, drinking from his cardboard cup, "I put in a call to Paradise; Amanda Kincaid is fine, she and Kim are having a blast, and apparently Marnie showed up with A.J. for some R&R as well."

It took Hunt a couple of seconds for the words to be heard and computed. "Thanks for that. Taylor will want that news the second she opens her eyes." *Please God.*

"From what I heard, she saved your ass." Max handed Hunt a paper cup.

Hunt took the coffee, although he knew he wouldn't drink it. His lips curved into a stiff smile as he started another lap. "Taylor was, in a word, amazing."

Max took his own coffee and settled into the chair next to Daklin like he had all the time in the world. "Why don't you come sit down and tell me all about it?"

Hunt's laugh was hollow as he massaged the stiffness that had settled at the nape of his neck. "What? Now you're my *therapist*? No thanks. Swear to God, if I don't keep moving I'll detonate."

He vaguely noticed the inquiring glance Max shot Asher Daklin as he resumed his manic marathon. "Sixty-two stitches for a knife wound," Daklin filled Max in unnecessarily. "Four cracked ribs. The usual dings and dents. He'll live."

Max settled back in his chair. "Pretty much a hangnail for us tough guys. Of course, at this rate, he may walk himself to death."

Fifty-seven

THE GREEN-PAINTED HOSPITAL ROOM SMELLED LIKE SPRING. A dozen vases held huge bunches of brilliantly colored blooms, many of which Taylor didn't recognize. Since the only people she knew in South Africa were the T-FLAC team, she presumed the flowers were from them.

She knew there were several men in the waiting room. The doctor had told her so. She hadn't asked if one of them was Hunt because logic dictated that he'd be long gone, on to his next assignment. And since she knew him to be a decent and honorable man, he'd left a couple of his buddies here to keep an eye on her.

The thought made her want to cry.

Focus, she told herself sternly. *Focus, get better, get out of here.* She'd known the separation would hurt like hell. This wasn't a surprise. She wasn't sad, she told herself. She was ticked off that Hunt hadn't at least had the decency to tell her good-bye face-to-face.

The door swung open then, and she almost got whiplash turning to see who had come in. Hunt. Carrying a brown paper bag. Her difficulty breathing had nothing to do with what she'd inhaled in the mine and everything to do with the sheer, unadulterated *joy* she experienced seeing him.

"You look worse than I feel," she told him. Oh, Lord. He had come in person. Her hungry gaze took in his lean, far from elegantly dressed body, his disheveled hair, jeans, and too-small T-shirt. He was not his usual sartorially splendid self, but seeing him brought a lump to her throat. The sight of the bandage beneath his obviously borrowed shirt made her frown, and she pushed herself up off the pillow to sit upright. "You're hurt!"

"It's nothing." He came toward the bed. "The doctor gave you a green light." His British accent was back in spades. "The muscle weakness was expected, but they say you insisted on walking a few steps anyway. To stay on the safe side, they want to keep you here a couple of days for observation."

You don't want to be here, do you? Taylor thought, the pressure in her chest unbearable as she sensed him distancing himself. "I know. The doctor told me. Thanks for stopping by." She thought she was doing a credible job of sounding sophisticated and casual. Unfortunately, she felt the pressure of tears behind her eyelids, and the steel band around her chest hurt like hell. "I guess you're on your way to somewhere exciting—"

"How are you feeling?"

Ridiculously disadvantaged, sitting here in bed with an extremely unattractive, threadbare surgical gown exposing my behind. "Okay," she told him brightly.

Apparently he was displeased with that response because he scowled down at her.

"Fine," she assured him. *"Better."* A heart was merely a muscle, she assured herself for about the billionth time in the last few hours. Muscles did not break. People left people all the time. Nobody had ever died of a broken heart. She didn't think . . .

Hunt placed the large brown paper bag in her lap, then stepped back and shoved his hands into his front pockets. A very un-Hunt-like thing to do. *Oh God. Here comes the kiss-off.* She braced herself. It wasn't as though she hadn't expected the "great-knowing-you-but-we-were-just-ships-that-pass-in-the-night" speech. But she had the childish urge to put her fingers in her ears and sing loudly so she couldn't hear it.

"You brought me a present?" *Oh shit. Proof he felt guilty that he was going to give her the brush-off.* That made it worse, and made her appear pathetic. She looked down until her vision cleared and she was positive that when she spoke her voice would be steady. "Thank you." She shot him what she hoped to God was a remote, easy smile. "I do love presents." Ironically, she couldn't remember when last she'd received one.

She reached inside as he lingered near the foot of her bed. *Great. Not exactly subtle.* "A teddy bear?" A huge white bear wearing a pink tutu and the glittering spill of the Blue Star diamonds around its fuzzy neck.

"The necklace, I'm afraid, has to be returned," he told her. "But you have permission to hold on to it until then. And the bear—well, I was limited to the hospital's gift shop. It was either ballerina bear or doctor donkey, and I didn't think your prize belonged on an ass." He smiled. "Hospital patients should have something to hold on to during their incarceration."

I want to hold on to you. She tucked the bear wearing a $75 million necklace beneath the covers next to her and spent a few moments arranging its arms to her satisfaction. All the while feeling Hunt's X-ray eyes boring into her brain. *I'm fine that you're leaving,* she tried hard to project. But she didn't feel fine at all. She felt as though Godzilla was ripping a hole in her chest while eating her brain.

Far from feeling joyous and happy as portrayed on sappy Valentine cards, she felt like crap. One-sided love was the pits. She decided from now on she'd enjoy a nice long stretch of celibacy. For, oh, ten or twenty years. Because, damn him, he'd ruined her for any other man.

She stuck her hand back in the bag, pulled out a can of 7-Up, and gave him an inquiring glance. "From a czar's diamonds to 7-Up? You're a very eclectic guy."

"The diamonds weren't mine to give," he pointed out. "The soda is, in case you're still nauseous."

Having him holding her head while she threw up was a once-in-a-lifetime experience she didn't care to repeat. "I'm not." She noticed that he was gripping the footboard with both hands. His knuckles were white. *It did not bode well.* "But just in case I am later," she assured him cheerfully, "I'll put it right here." She set the can on the bedside table and stuck her hand back inside the bag.

Honest to God. The man was going to present her to death. And she wasn't sure how much longer she could sit here with him so close and not want to grab him and hold him tight, or ask him coolly to please be humane and leave while she still had a shred of dignity left.

She wished to hell he'd just kiss her good-bye and *go!* He must realize just how damn cruel, not to mention rude, it was to drag this out for so damn long. Fine. Good. Great. The man didn't owe her anything. They'd been lovers for a while. Great lovers. Stupendous lovers. But there'd been no promises made. She hadn't *expected* any promises to *be* made. Then again, she hadn't expected to fall in love with him either. So much for expectations.

She frowned down at the weird feel of something inside the paper sack, and pulled out a blue freezer bag. Interesting. Confusing, but interesting. Inside were half a dozen not-quite-frozen orange Popsicles.

What on earth . . . Holy crap! These were some of the things he'd given his mother before she—"Oh. My. God." She shot Hunt a look of horror. "I'm *dying*?"

"Jesus, no! Of course not."

Good to know, but somehow dying seemed easier than watching him awkwardly lead up to the kiss-off moment. "Well, that's certainly a relief. Did you guys figure out what Morales had in all those crates?" she asked a little desperately, inserting the one Popsicle she'd taken out back in the freezer bag, then setting it on the bedside table.

"It'll take months of painstaking work to process the contents," Hunt told her, stroking his palm along the curved edge of the footboard. "Just because a crate is stamped 'Crayons' doesn't mean it came from Crayola."

He'd stroked her body like that. The memory made her nipples tighten beneath the thin cotton of the hospital gown. "What about everything in his secret room?"

"Loaded and en route to Consolidated Underwriters. They can

figure out who gets what. They said your commission check would be suitably impressive."

She wasn't particularly interested in what was sure to be a seven-figure check. She was now taking very shallow breaths just to partic-ipate in this sham of a casual conversation. Perhaps he'd leave when he noticed she was turning blue? "Vegas still standing?"

"Missile defused and out of commission, thanks to you." Hunt started to pace. Another very un-Hunt-like thing for him to do. If she had an ounce of compassion to spare, she thought, she'd put him out of his misery and spare him the awkward good-bye.

Unfortunately—for him—she needed these last few minutes to look her fill. She had to store up memories for when she lay on her stupid, four-hundred-thread-count sheets beneath the cashmere blan-kets. Alone.

She felt the cool air of the room caress her bare back. And wanted his hands there to keep her warm. She wanted to put her hands on him. All over him. "Were you shot?"

"Knife wound," Hunt said dismissively. "I'm not nearly as inter-ested in my condition as I am in yours, love."

Was that the British condescending "love"? The casual love, or a term of endearment love? Or—God this was brutal. It was like going bald, one plucked hair at a time. Why couldn't the damned man just shoot her?

Okay, be a big girl, she told herself. A big girl clinging to a teddy bear. *Damn! I can do this. Stay casual, stay aloof.*

"Thanks for stopping by," she said with forced cheer through the clog in her throat. "My days as a spy were an eye-opener, and I—"

"Shut up."

He came around the end of the bed, sat down beside her on the narrow mattress, gathered her in his arms, and a moment later had pressed his lips to hers. The gentle pressure of his thumb on her chin caused her to open her mouth to him. But she kept her tongue to herself. Really. This was incredibly unfair.

Hunt lifted his head, his eyes hot as hammered silver. "Stubborn. Kiss me back," he murmured fiercely.

So he wanted to play with fire, did he? She wound her arms about his neck and felt a thrill of triumph as he groaned deep in his throat as she kissed him back. Slowly, delicately, she slid her tongue into his mouth, gently exploring. Loving the taste and texture of him. Memorizing each texture, each subtle flavor. Her fingers threaded through his hair, holding his head exactly where she wanted him as his tongue played with his in choreographed perfection.

A sigh left his body, as if he'd been holding his breath, and he kissed her back, pressing her onto her back against the thin hospital pillow. "I missed you," he murmured against her mouth. "Missed you abominably."

Her lips curved. "Like the snowman?"

"I certainly felt that cold without you."

Taylor wanted him so badly, she ached with it. She allowed herself a few seconds of prolonged contact that her heart and soul cried out for before she managed to pull away and said with commendable steadiness, "I don't think you should kiss me anymore."

His eyes narrowed. How could gray look so hot? "Really? And why is that?" Because it had taken just one look at him, one touch of his hands on her bare skin, and she knew that she'd never forget him. That she'd stay in love with Huntington St. John for the rest of her natural life.

That was a very long time to miss someone. The thought depressed her. He waited with an uncanny stillness as she fumbled for an answer. She had a million and none. "Because . . . just because."

"God, you're a stubborn woman."

"You say that like it's a bad thing."

With a small shake of his head, he pulled her into his arms again, his mouth coming down on hers this time with hungry possession that brooked no argument. She whimpered softly as his tongue came out aggressively to meet hers, demanding a response that was there for his taking. Was his heart pounding as fast as hers? She couldn't tell where she stopped and he started.

After several heavy heartbeats, she wrapped her arms about his waist, not too tightly, not as tightly as she would have liked, pressing her face to his shoulder.

"Please don't," she whispered, her voice a raw, broken thread. "You have to—" *Go. Please,* she begged silently, *make it quick. Like ripping off a Band-Aid. Go. Leave.* Instead she whispered, "Stop."

"Open your eyes, Taylor," he said, pulling back, his voice soft but inexorable. "Open your eyes and look at me."

She could deny him nothing, and blinked away the tears clinging to her lashes, knowing he'd see that her eyes were awash in pathetic tears.

"What is it, darling?" he whispered, his beautiful, elegant hands framing her face, pushing her hair away from her tear-dampened cheeks with a tenderness that made her heart ache unbearably. "What brought this on?"

"I just want to get out of here," she said desperately. "And don't you have to get back to—wherever?"

"I have to get back to *whomever,*" he murmured, his mouth close to hers.

"Look," she told him. "Much as I'd love to have sex with you once more before you move on to greener pastures, this is neither the time nor the place." She couldn't take much more of this. She really couldn't.

"You're right, it isn't the time, or the place. But don't mistake sex for making love."

The sharp blade of his words was so finely honed that it took several seconds for Taylor to feel them pierce directly into her heart. *Well, that was plain enough.* She tried to summon a smile to send him on his way with no regrets, but it was a dismal failure.

She met his gaze, making no move to break free of his hands, still cradling her face. "Let go of me," she begged. Having this last taste was almost more than she could bear.

"Oh, sweetheart," he murmured, "I can't do that." He eased her into a sitting position, pulled the thin cotton gown back over her shoulder where it had slipped, then used his thumb to wipe away the moisture on her cheek. "Is this the same woman who bashed me over the head and handcuffed me to a bed?" he asked ruefully, his gray eyes hot and filled with . . . Taylor had no idea what.

She was more confused than she'd ever been in her life. She'd been so braced for the thanks-but-no-thanks speech that she wasn't prepared for this different script.

He continued to brush her cheek with his thumb. "The same woman who tried to knee me in the balls the first time I touched her breast?"

"You deserved it at the time. What's your point?"

He chuckled as he pulled her into his arms. "The point is," he said against her hair, "stop fighting it. Stop fighting me." His warm hands slid possessively up the cool skin of her bare back beneath the skimpy hospital gown before he slanted his mouth down on hers. His tongue teased her lips open in an almost desperate, searching kiss.

Still confused, she held herself stiffly, willing herself to think of other things.

He lifted his head a fraction, his eyes blazing with banked passion and a hint of laughter. "You're supposed to kiss me back, love."

Without giving her time to answer, his mouth caught hers again. She lost what little reasoning abilities she thought she still possessed as his kiss melted both her brain and her resolve. She tightened her arms about his waist and met the thrusts of his tongue with moves of her own. She couldn't think, and she couldn't fight it anymore.

This last kiss would have to sustain her for a long, long time. With a low moan she sought his tongue with hers, losing herself in the heady thrusts and parries. Her fingers fisted in the back of his shirt, feeling the play of his muscles beneath the fabric. They kissed until she was giddy and breathless.

Too soon, he lifted his head. It took every scrap of Taylor's willpower not to whimper and drag his mouth back to hers.

"You told me once that you had no defenses against me," he told her softly. "Well, the feeling is mutual. I have no defenses against you either. I've fallen in love with you, Taylor. Jesus," he laughed ruefully, "I can't believe I'm actually quoting a song here, but you light up my life in ways I could never have imagined." His smooth, firm lips brushed hers as he tightened his strong arms around her.

He stroked a large hand over her hair, then cupped the back of her head. "Crazy in love," he whispered hoarsely. He put her away from him and gave her a rueful, amused look. "That look of pained disbelief is hardly encouraging, darling. Maybe this will convince you." He lifted himself off the bed and retrieved a folded envelope out of his back pocket.

Taylor tucked her hair behind her ears with shaking hands and watched him curiously as he tore open the flap. "What is it? A letter of reference?"

"As a matter of fact—yes." He picked up her left hand. "Marry me, my love," he said softly, opening a velvet jeweler's box, then sliding a ring onto her finger.

Taylor glanced down at her hand. The subtle gleam of the diamond looked softly romantic even in the harsh lighting. It was the most beautiful ring she'd ever laid eyes on, four-prong, old-fashioned cushion-cut. Simple, old-fashioned elegance.

Without drawing a breath, incapable of drawing a breath, her eyes flew to his.

"It was my mother's." His expression was very still as he watched her intently, and Taylor realized that the cool, sophisticated man she knew was nervous. "If you hate it," he began gruffly, "we'll get something that suits you better—"

Her throat got tight, and she squeezed her eyes shut for a minute. Her fingers fisted defensively. "This suits me *perfectly*! I love it."

He was sitting still, an intense look of shuttered hope in his gray eyes. As if waiting . . .

Taylor lifted her hand and traced his stern mouth with a fingertip that trembled with the depth of her emotions. "I love *you*."

He grabbed her, holding her tightly against him. She could hear the rapid pounding of his heart. Racing urgently, as if something had frightened him. But nothing could ever frighten a man like Hunt. "Thank God," he said gutturally against her hair. "Thank God."

He held her away from him, his fingers cupping her shoulders. He smiled, and Taylor's heart soared with the joy of it. "As soon as possible," he told her gruffly, "I'm getting you out of here."

"So you can have your wicked way with me?" Taylor asked, stroking his arm.

"That too. We're going to Paradise."

She loosely curled her arms over his broad shoulders and smiled at him. Because she could. "Anywhere with you will be Paradise."

"Paradise Island? The place your sister is frolicking in the surf right now?"

They'd talk about Mandy, Taylor knew, soon. But right now was just for the two of them. "Ah, hot sunshine. Cool water. And you." Her smile widened. "Paradise indeed."

"The island is one of T-FLAC's training facilities," he told her officiously. As all business as a man could be when his eyes were molten and his hands were stroking her naked bottom. "If you're going to insist on working with me, you have to be suitably trained to go into the field."

Her eyes widened. "Into the field? *Really?* Oh, Lord. That is *so*—"

"Not really true," he interrupted. "You've been offered a job training our operatives in all things nefarious as far as B&E, and safe-cracking goes."

"Ah, man!" Taylor pulled him closer and leaned her forehead against his while she shifted her hips closer to him. "That is so tame, so lame, so . . ." She shrugged off the thin hospital gown. Thanks to him untying it in back, it fell around her waist, leaving her quite naked in the afternoon sunlight streaming through the windows.

"Unfair," Hunt murmured, pushing her naked body back onto the pillows.

Taylor wound her arms about his neck, laughing up at him. God, she loved this man. "What if someone comes in?" she whispered against his mouth as he bent to kiss her.

"Stuck one of your lock picks in the keyhole." He nibbled her jaw.

Her heart smiled. "As long as you used the right tool for the job."

He wrapped his strong arms around her, stretched out beside her on the narrow bed, then pulled her against his body. "You'll have to teach me." The only thing that would've made it better was if he was under the covers with her.

"We'll teach each other," Taylor told him, her tongue tracing the contour of his lips. "I'll teach you to smile more often, and how to open safes."

"And I, my love, will teach you that there are far more exciting things to do than scaling buildings and leaping across rooftops."

Taylor nuzzled her nose against his neck. She loved the smell of him. She sighed with sheer, unadulterated joy. "I know," she said happily. "Like learning how to shoot a gun, and how to defuse a bomb. Hey! How about teaching me to fly a helicopter?"

Taylor loved Hunt's smile, and she found that she loved his laughter even more. Even better, she knew she'd hear it for years and years and years to come.

About the Type

This book was set in Bembo, a typeface based an on old-style Roman face that was used for Cardinal Bembo's tract *De Aetna* in 1495. Bembo was cut by Francisco Griffo in the early sixteenth century. The Lanston Monotype Company of Philadelphia brought the well-proportioned letterforms of Bembo to the United States in the 1930s.